POCAHONTAS

POCAHONTAS

JOHN CLARKE BOWMAN

NEW ENGLISH LIBRARY
TIMES MIRROR

First published in Great Britain by W. H. Allen & Co Ltd, 1974
© 1973 by John Clarke Bowman

*

FIRST NEL PAPERBACK EDITION JULY 1975

*

NEL Books are published by
New English Library Limited from Barnard's Inn, Holborn, London, E.C.1.
Made and printed in Great Britain by Hunt Barnard Printing Ltd., Aylesbury, Bucks.

45002242 0

For Lynn

My own particular star
still shining bright

ACKNOWLEDGMENT

There are many to whom I am grateful, especially those contemporary writers who serve to corroborate and bring to life the legend that Pocahontas has become in our folklore.

But my everlasting debt is to Captain John Smith, that most derogated of American heroes. In his *General History of Virginia*, he describes so much more than the saving of his life (in fact, he makes very little of it); he shows us the child: 'Bid Pocahontas bring hither two little baskets, and I will give her white beads to make her a chain', which he includes in his wonderful glossary of the Powhatan language; and he gives us the woman, when he quotes her words at the time she sees him again, in England: 'They told us always you were dead, and I knew no other till I came to Plymouth. Yet Powhatan commanded Tomakkin to seek you and know the truth, because your countrymen will lie much!'

Yet, it is not only for the immortalizing of Pocahontas that we should be grateful. He wrote a history which has been quoted by every Virginia historian from Beverly to Dabney, a description of the aborigines, or Savages, as he calls them, hardly to be surpassed by anyone from Marco Polo to Margaret Mead. He assayed the characters of Powhatan and Openchancano, showing their villainies and generosities; and he wrote an account of the flora and fauna of Virginia which was used by Thomas Jefferson in his *Notes on Virginia*. And aside from being a man of great curiosity and action, he was, as he called Pocahontas, the Nonpareil among the colonists and explorers of his century. Virginia was only one of his ventures. He explored New England, which he named, mapped its coastline, named the landmarks around Cape Cod, including Plymouth Rock, told how a colony could survive. It was this account which the Pilgrims, then living in Holland, purchased. They negotiated with him to command their colony, but his price was thought to be too high, and they engaged Miles Standish, an able, but by no means *so* able, leader.

For over two centuries, Smith stood as a founding father and a hero in American history, and the events of his adventures went unchallenged. Then, in the latter half of the nineteeth century, detractors appeared to explode cherished myths, and though they were contradicted by such eminent historians as Fiske and Arber, who called on his contemporaries to corroborate Smith's facts, it was not until the middle of this century that history began to vindicate him, and his great contribution to our history was acknowledged. Certainly, *I* must be grateful, for did he not give me Pocahontas, Powhatan, Nantequos, Opechancano – and Johnsmith?

There was nothing but the fog. Not even the sea where the ship rode motionless was visible. Then a sudden gust whipped the sails, the halyards whined, joints creaked, and with a lurch that made her catch the rail the prow bit into wave. The mist swirled and eddied.

'Land ho!' she heard from the crow's nest, and her straining eyes perceived a dim coastline for an instant only, tantalizing after seven weeks of a sea voyage that seemingly had no end. Even when he had described it, she had not visioned a world that was nothing but water, or that she would be borne by this fragile craft to an alien land.

She was aware of Argall before he spoke.

'The wind at last. Today you'll be in England.'

'It is cold – like a land of death,' she said. 'It is strange the white men love it so.'

He laid his arm on her shoulder as though to give her warmth.

'It is home,' he said. 'It is your home now, Rebecca.' She did not respond, either to his touch or his words.

'Are you thinking it is *his* home?' He wanted to hurt her. 'Are you hoping to see *him* when you look out there like that?'

They turned at the sound of footsteps. Rolfe stared at them suspiciously.

'I came to wish your lady joy on her safe arrival, John,' Argall said easily.

'Must you embrace her to do that?'

She hardly listened, nor did she turn when Argall said good-by.

Rolfe came close to her. 'What did *he* want?'

She looked at him attentively a moment.

'To make love to me,' she said without inflection.

'Well, keep him away from you!'

'That is for you to do.'

Rolfe stopped short at her words and tone. He paced the deck, re-creating his wrath. 'The cuckolding bastard! He'll not put horns on me, y' hear?' He turned and glared at her, irritated by the calm he could never hope to pierce. 'Wanton! It's the name your own people call you. Wanton! And they are right.'

She gazed into the vapor. The chill was such that she set her jaw to keep it from chattering. 'It does not mean the same,' she said, her voice distant.

It had not meant the same:

The scene before her was engulfed in the glare of blinding sunlight. She closed and then opened her eyes to accustom them. A fall of water shimmered and sparkled, splashing into a cool green pool. Overhead, bright parrots beat the air with their wings, their beady eyes searching for the late insects, uttering raucous cries through red beaks. The trees loved by the Winter God were dark and spirit-laden, while through the forest the trees of the God of Summer were brilliant in war paint, prepared for the hopeless battle against their ermine-clad enemy.

She was lost and torn with weeping. She remembered it so vividly because it was the last time ever she shed tears. She sat and dangled her tired feet in the cold water, then pulled at the sere grass and discovered a beetle which scurried away from her. The parrots saw it and swooped, lifting it and fighting over it in mid-air. She watched them tear it apart. Then she searched in the red and golden and black forest, trying to believe with every turn of her head that her mother or stepfather would appear.

They had left her but yesterday, and she had been full of their love and their desire for her happiness, knowing that since she had passed her eighth summer she must go to dwell with her father, who was the Powhatan. Her mother had told her of her father, how he had loved her mother and she him, but that when a child was born the Powhatan no longer kept his wife: he sent her away with gifts and the right to remarry if she would; only the child, when he had passed his eighth year, must return to be the child of the Powhatan. She had accepted this as a law that could not be changed, but she had not known her father was a stone-cold man and she would be a stranger in his city. She had felt empty as if they had torn her vitals from her, and she had not believed her mother ever loved this man.

Now she had left the city of her father to find again the home that she loved and the parents who loved her. But as she looked at the ominous forest she was obsessed with the knowledge that it could not be, that they were far and she could not find them nor they her. Forlornly she raised her skirt to her eyes, then buried her head in her arms.

She heard a shout and looked up, terrified, to the head of the falls. At first it seemed the Spirit of the Water or the God of Winter himself was upon her, for stretched out like a giant bird about to take wing was a being who looked enormous, his naked body painted red, a snow-white wolf's pelt over his head and shoulders, the open fangs glaring down above his face.

'Ho! What are you here for, Matoaka? And do you cry like a soft Matatiske?'

She stared up furious with resentment. Matatiske was her mother whom she loved. And the god-seeming one was only her brother, the Powhatan's child like herself, who had but this morning returned from battle.

'Quiet!' a voice said sternly, and her father appeared. He pushed her brother aside and slid down the rocks, his great body catapulting toward her. She shrank back slightly, expecting a blow from his hand or perhaps from his tomahawk, but instead he caught her up and held her close against him. She could feel the heavy throb of his heart.

'Why did you go?' he demanded. 'From me? Have I not been kind to you, Matoaka?' She could not answer because there was still an evil one caught in her throat, which had been choked back when her brother spoke so suddenly to her. 'She cries,' her father said to her brother and to others who had gathered around, 'because she is a child and she is frightened. What of me?' he asked, looking down at her. 'I was frightened – yet I do not weep.'

Her arms crept up and around him. 'I want to go home,' she said and fought back the tears.

'Ho! You are pocahontas! Willful one! Wanton one! I am your home now.'

And she knew it was. She would never go back to her mother and her stepfather. She was the great Powhatan's daughter, and she was at home in his arms.

Home and Father! The meaning was the same, since the dwelling place was of little significance. Father meant so many things in Powhatan's language: God and King, friend and lord. John-smith had called Powhatan father, and she had called John-smith . . .

BOOK ONE
THE NONPAREIL

Virginia
December 1607 – June 1610

Powhatan . . . sent his Daughter . . .
which not only for feature,
countenance and proportion much
exceedeth the rest of the people
but for wit and spirit the only
nonpareil of his Country.

— JOHN SMITH,
Newes from Virginia, 1608

Some propheticall spirit calculated
hee had the Salvages in such
subjection, he would have made
himselfe a king, by marrying
Pocahontas, Powhatans daughter. It
is true she was the very Nonparell
of his kingdome, and at most not
past 13 or 14 yeares of age.

— WILLIAM PHETTIPLACE and
RICHARD POTS, *A Map of Virginia*, 1612

CHAPTER ONE

Her body was painted crimson with puccoon juice. She wore pearls in her ears, and a necklace of pearls wrapped three times around her neck hung down between her developing breasts. Four years she had lived with Powhatan, and he had delighted in her mischievous spirit. He kept her ever beside him, Pocahontas.

She hid behind him now as he sat on his bed at the end of the Great Wigwam, close against his mantle of raccoon fur dyed in stripes of red and purple. She hid because she did not like Opechancano, who was her father's brother. Opechancano did not like her either; he said she was too wild, not fit to be a wife to Werowance or brave, and that Powhatan spoiled and favored her.

She stayed in the Great Wigwam not to greet Opechancano but to see his captive, the golden warrior, who some said was a god and others that he was possessed of mighty magic. She did not believe these things, or he would not have let Opechancano's men take him, though it was said he fought bravely, one man against many. It was like the stories they told of her father when he was the young Wahunsonacock, before he bound the tribes together with a band of copper, how he had come from a land far to the south and proclaimed himself Powhatan, how the people came to him, believing him to be a god, and how he had made the Powhatan the strongest of all the tribes on the Chesapeake and defeated the kings of those tribes till there was peace on all the rivers.

In the wigwam they heard the shouting, and they waited. Her eyes darted to her father's wives, who sat at either end of Powhatan's bed of piled-up mats. Owerowok sat as a wife should, placidly stringing shells into a necklace, but Ponoiske, Pocahontas noticed jealously, could not take her eyes from Powhatan's graven profile. Her he had taken to his bed for the first time last night, and she was little older than Pocahontas herself. Willfully she drew Ponoiske's eyes and then let her arms tighten about her

15

father. He covered her hand with his, and she laid her head against the crisp fur of his mantle, aware of Ponoiske's wistful gaze. He loved her, his daughter, more than any wife, she thought triumphantly.

The clamor outside the wigwam was louder, and all looked to the entrance. Through the flanks of braves that guarded Powhatan, past his Cockarouses, the wise men of his Council, and his chieftains, the Werowances, past the crested Priests and Conjurors with their rattles and sacks of magic, his brother Opechancano strode the long distance from the tunneled entrance. He was painted fearsomely, and over his shoulder, so that he looked two-headed, glowered a panther's head, the mouth open, the teeth white and gleaming. Behind him ranged his warriors, and though Pocahontas could not see him, she knew they held the prisoner. She buried herself deep in the raccoon fur when Opechancano stood in front of Powhatan. Even so she felt his reluctance to prostrate himself, though when he spoke she realized with satisfaction that his voice came from the ground.

'Mighty Powhatan!'

Powhatan arose, leaving her unguarded. He lifted Opechancano and embraced him.

'We rejoice that you have come, Brother.'

Opechancano told of the battle and the magic of the warrior, but Pocahontas did not heed him for watching the captive. His face was covered with hair and whiskered like the northern cat. She wondered if his body were hairy, too, but she could not tell because he was clothed to his neck; even his legs were hidden voluminously, a skirt for each leg. The parts of his skin that were visible, his nose and cheeks, were golden under gold-flecked brows, and his eyes were startling, large and strangely light – not bright as turquoise, but nearly so.

Opechancano's warriors leaned on him to make him kneel, but he resisted till their weight forced him to the ground. Still he seemed not to kneel, for he held his head high, staring at Powhatan who stood over him.

'Are you the great Powhatan?' Apparently he needed no assurance, for Powhatan was mighty to look upon. 'Why does Powhatan use his friends this way?' he demanded.

The words sounded uncouth on his foreign tongue, but his voice possessed a quality that made Pocahontas's shoulders arch, as when the Conjuror recited the glories of Powhatan when he was Wahunsonacock come from the southern land. It was a hero's voice.

Now, remembering, she knew how wonderful it was he spoke

her tongue so well after those few months on an alien shore – she recalled her own arduous efforts to learn English – but then, listening, she was aware only of the voice and its power.

Powhatan seated himself, and she clung fast to his mantle, but she no longer feared Opechancano's notice; her face peered over her father's shoulder at the strange warrior.

'Why have you brought your people to our land?'

The stranger moved his legs so that he sat on the ground, facing Powhatan, and she was fascinated by the strength and hardness of the blue eyes. She had seen no one, not even Opechancano, who could meet Powhatan's gaze unfaltering.

'In a storm our ships – the great canoes – put to this shore. When we landed at Chesapeake the people shot at us, but at Kekoutan they welcomed us. We asked by signs for fresh water, and they told us up the river there was fresh water. Our ship was leaky, and we were forced to stay and tend her, till Captain Newport, who is the Weroames, King of all the waters, comes to take us away.'

There was no sound as all strained to hear his labored speech. When he had finished, Openchancano spoke softly and rapidly to Powhatan.

'He lies! They have built a city of wood, and they have come to take your land.'

The stranger watched Opechancano, trying to tell what he was saying, but the words were too rapid for him to understand.

'Why did you go farther – up the water of the Chickahominy?'

'I search for the salt water to the west – the great sea that stretches till it meets the Sea of the East . . . ' He made a circle with his arms.

Pocahontas wondered if he were mad, since he could believe the salt water reached under the earth, which she knew was flat and round as the leaves that float on the still ponds.

Powhatan made no sign of surprise. He spoke to Owerowok, who arose and left the wigwam. Opussokonuske, who ruled the Appomattucks, very tall and graceful, came forward with a bowl of water which she proffered the stranger to wash his hands. Her copper crown and bracelets and earrings gleamed with flashes of light from the fire against her scarlet-painted body as she bent to him.

He greeted her, for she had been among the first to entertain the white men when they had come to the Chesapeake.

'Fair Queen, this is not how *you* used me when I came to your country. Can you not tell Powhatan that I come as a friend to his people?'

She did not answer directly, but looked into the bowl she held for him. 'Powhatan will know – the truth, Johnsmith.'

Owerowok returned and brought feathers to dry his hands, and then her women came with bowls of food, venison and beaver tail, hominy, and matoume bread buttered with deer suet. They set the food before the captive warrior.

Johnsmith looked at it, and Pocahontas could see he did not want to eat, but he knew that all were watching him. He ducked his head at Powhatan.

'I thank you,' he said, and hacked at the venison with his knife.

Opechancano sat on the ground close to Powhatan.

'It is true he is a Conjuror, but if you take his magic from him he is helpless.'

'What magic?'

'His sticks which spit out lightning and thunder.' Opechancano grinned slyly. 'But I have secured a sack of the black seed that feeds these sticks, seed which he calls gunpowder, and in the spring it will be planted, and then we, too, will have a crop. . . . '

'What other magic?' Powhatan demanded.

'He has what he calls a tablet, and he makes signs on a leaf which he tears from it, and he can send long messages to his friends at a great distance. I know, for I sent two messengers with this leaf to his city, and his people did what Johnsmith said they would do. And he has a strange jewel that points always to the north, wherever it is held. . . . '

'I would see this jewel,' Powhatan said.

Opechancano pushed Johnsmith's shoulder. 'Show Powhatan your jewel.'

Johnsmith left off his eating gladly enough. From the strange sacks he wore about his legs he took an object and handed it to Powhatan.

Powhatan held in his palm a round ball that seemed like bone, but wonderfully polished. Those in the room crowded around and marveled as Powhatan examined it. Within the ball a strange sign was drawn, and from its constant movement there was what looked like an insect stuck on a thorn, yet it was surely metal that moved and breathed. But most unbelievable of all, you could not touch it, for over it the air had frozen hard as rock, but not cold like ice.

'Tell me of this magic,' Powhatan commanded.

Johnsmith took the jewel and held it out so those around him could see.

'When the skies are hidden,' he said, 'when there is no sun nor moon nor stars, when there is no moss upon the trees, nor any sign, this needle will point ever north.' He turned slowly, pausing as he turned, and with each movement they could see the strange metal jerk swiftly so that it pointed always in one direction.

He gave the jewel again to Powhatan, who turned it in his fingers suspiciously. He shook it and then cupped it in his palms and peered at it through a crack in his fingers.

'You cannot fool it,' Johnsmith said. 'It is like Powhatan. It knows the truth.' The hardness had left him, Pocahontas thought, but not the power. He was eager, and he enjoyed showing them his marvel.

'You did not believe me, Powhatan, when I said the Sea of the West would join with the Sea of the East, but that is truth, too, for the world is round as that globelike jewel.' He pointed straight above his head. 'From the highest point in the heavens, where the sun crosses at midday, there is a line that passes to the true center of the ball we call the earth, and it controls this needle, and this could not be true if the earth and skies themselves were not balls as the sun and moon and stars are also. For you have seen the sun chase the night from east to west, and so he does around the earth, where at the other side it is day when Powhatan sleeps, and night when he awakes. And there are nations, as here, with people as strange as the white man is to you, and I have seen many of those people, some of them with skins that are black and some with yellow skins, as yours are red and ours are white. Even now, in England, my people rise, for it is day.' He took the jewel and held it between his thumb and finger. 'For we are to you the Antipodes.'

They listened awestruck. Whether they believed his words or not, he spoke like a god, and Pocahonta's heart beat so fast she could not breathe and felt that she must surely smother.

Opechancano reached out and grasped the jewel from Johnsmith's hand.

'*Now* you cannot tell north without sun or moon or stars or moss on trees,' he said gruffly.

Johnsmith looked at him, and the light went from his face, which set in its hard, grave mold.

'No,' he said, 'I cannot.' He took back his jewel.

'He lies!' Opechancano turned to Powhatan. 'He has come to take our land and kill our people. It is why he rode up the Chickahominy – already he has killed many of my men.'

'I came up the Chickahominy in a canoe with three white men and two Savage guides. Would it be likely that I came to kill with a force as small as that? It is your men who murdered – my

19

three Englishmen. I killed only when you came on me alone with two hundred braves.'

'He must die, Powhatan. It is my right for my men he killed.'

Terror was a fever that fired her veins. Pocahontas sank back against the matted wall in anguish. When she could raise her eyes to the captive's face, he stood white, but hard and seemingly unafraid.

Opechancano's men brought in the great death stones and put them before Powhatan. There was no sound save the movement of their bodies. She gripped her father's shoulders, and he bowed his head slightly. It was a second before she realized that she had asked a question and he had answered.

Opechancano's men surrounded Johnsmith. He saw their intention, and for a moment he thought of resisting, but the room was crowded with braves.

'My father, Captain Newport, will take many lives for this day's work,' he said.

They dragged him down and onto the stones and held him while the clubs were raised.

Pocahontas slid between their legs and threw herself on top of him, her head on his.

Opechancano let out a bellow of incredulous bafflement. He grasped her shoulder to tear her aside.

'She claims his life,' Powhatan said gravely. 'That is *her* right, Brother.'

Opechancano stood silent, mastering his wrath.

'You have grown old and soft,' he said in a toneless voice. 'And as you have made your kingdom, you will destroy it. For I tell you, his people' – he touched Johnsmith with his foot – 'will drive our people from the land. They will come in twenties and fifties and in hundreds. I tell you!'

'Perhaps he has been spared to be our friend and brother,' Powhatan said in a low voice.

Opechancano's face was twisted in disbelief and contempt.

'Your love for her has ruined you,' he said and stalked from the wigwam, his men following.

She arose, and Johnsmith got to his feet. He stared at her, and his mouth moved to speak, though no sound came, for he was parched from fear. He bent and drained off the water from the bowl the Wironausqua of the Appomattucks had brought him. Pocahontas fled to her place of protection behind Powhatan's red and purple cloak. Johnsmith wiped the water from his mouth with the back of his hand and faced them, his legs forked.

20

'Your daughter is brave as Powhatan,' he said. 'I had not thought to owe my life to a child.'

'By our law she has claimed you,' Powhatan said.

They took Johnsmith from the wigwam, and the others followed in whispering excitement. Pocahontas heard Powhatan tell Owerowok and Ponoiske to seek their own beds, and she moved carefully to leave unnoticed. She knew that her father must be very angry because of what Opechancano had said to him. Perhaps he would have Opechancano taken while he and his braves slept in the forest. Opechancano deserved to die, she thought indignantly.

'Matoaka.'

'Yes, Powhatan.'

'Sleep here, Pocahontas.'

It had been some moons since he had told her she must not sleep beside any man, not even her young brothers. She looked at him in surprise, then stretched lengthwise on the great bed. Powhatan threw off his robe and removed the cord and patch of soft hide from between his legs. He stood straddled to empty himself into a bowl half-filled with water. She marveled at him as she had since she was a child, his long, strong body, more powerful than her brothers or any of her uncles, and taller than any man she knew. He had heard the call of the geese many times, the wild shrill cohonk that marked the bright time of the Fall of the Leaf. Fifty-eight, he said, had passed since he was born, but his hair was black, only slightly streaked with gray, and his face was as it had ever been. She felt his magnificence with a familiar pride and surprised herself by wondering about the captive warrior. Was his body golden like his cheeks and brow, or was it covered with the tawny, curly hair?

Powhatan gently wrapped her in furs against the moment when the heat from the fire would leave the wigwam. He slapped a sack of squirrel skins sewed fur side in on the bed and climbed into it. He lay quietly, and she lay beside him, watching the flames send out short and long gleams onto the roof of laced boughs. The smoke and the heaviness of the air from the bodies and tobacco bore upon her so that she closed her eyes in spite of herself and longed to curl into a small egg and sink back into the waters of the womb.

'Opechancano is right,' Powhatan said.

No. No! She forced herself to wakefulness.

'No wind blew them to our land, and they will not go away when Johnsmith's father, whom he calls the Weroames, returns.

They have built their city to last many cohonks.'

'But is it so great a lie, or so terrible a thing for them to have come, if they are here as friends?'

'The weapons they call cannon are turned to the forests, not toward the river mouth. . . . '

This she could not answer. She thought of Opechancano's words: 'Your love for her has ruined you,' and a great bitterness against him rose in her heart. Powhatan reached out a hand and softly smoothed her hair.

'I do wrong to worry you with this.'

She caught his hand, thinking of the blue eyes that had stared back in pride and in defiance. 'Once Wahunsonacock came a stranger to these shores. . . . '

He held her hand in perfect quiet. They listened to the 'Ho' and answering 'Ho' of the four sentinels who guarded Powhatan's wigwam.

'It is *that* Opechancano remembers,' he said. 'How we battled together against the Werowances and the braves of the former Powhatan, until at last *I* was proclaimed Powhatan over all the nations. Opechancano is thinking that I am old and it is to him my robe should fall. . . . '

Her heart leaped like the stag at the impact of Powhatan's arrow, for he had never spoken of the succession.

'Opechancano is your enemy after today, Pocahontas,' he added gently.

'He has always hated me.'

'Aye, for he has read my heart. . . . '

She knew it was the law that Powhatan's robe must descend to his brothers or his sisters' sons, and that Powhatan had offered her to Opechancano as his consort, not a wife to be put aside after the birth of a child as her own mother had been, or as Owerowok and Ponoiske would be, but as Wironausqua of the Powhatans in her own right, like the Wironasqua of the Appomattucks. But Opechancano had laughed at the idea, and it was then he had said she would make no fit wife for any brave.

'We will learn more of this Werowance, Johnsmith,' Powhatan promised her and buried his face in the squirrel skins.

She closed her eyes and lived again the scene in the wigwam, the stranger's talk of the sun and moon and the earth, all round like melons. And of the different-colored people who lived at the bottom of the earth, upside-down people – no wonder their skins had turned to yellow and black. She wondered if they were whiskered as he, and then she wondered if he wore his strange clothing to hide the fact that he was hair all over. Where had he said he came from – the An-ti-po-des?

She awoke, instantly aware. She shivered, and at first she thought it was the cold that had waked her, but then, as the empty wigwam came to life, the colors smudged by the smoke becoming definite to her clear-eyed perspective, she thought what she had done.

She had defied Opechancano. *She* had claimed the White Warrior, and he was hers. Powhatan had not struck her down, but had proclaimed that it was her right. And Opechancano had retreated. Powhatan had said that her uncle would be her enemy now, but with an exultant life she realized that she had no fear. She stretched and breathed deep till the icy air filled her lungs. She was alive as she had never been. She was Pocahontas.

It was the cohonk of the Great Frost, colder than even Powhatan could remember; but the snow that had fallen was soft as feathers. Pocahontas sped so that the moisture could not penetrate her moccasins. She entered the cookhouse and was surprised to find the women feeding the children and themselves. She went quickly to Owerowok.

'Where are the braves? Have they eaten already?'

'They are in the House of the Oke.' Owerowok handed her a loaf of acorn bread.

Pocahontas took it and went to sit beside her younger brother, Tahacope, who had recently been sent by his mother to live with his father, the Powhatan. She felt Ponoiske's resentful gaze and tossed her head pertly. Could *she* help it if Powhatan had not sent for his new wife the second night?

'What do the braves do in the House of the Gods so early?' she whispered to Tahacope.

'Opechancano returned before the Sun's Rising. He has demanded of the priests that they secure an answer from the Great Oke as to the life of the White Werowance.'

'Ho!' Pocahontas said. 'What can the Great Oke answer with Powhatan there? I claimed him by the laws of Oke himself. Did you hear what I did, Tahacope?'

He nodded gravely. 'What is he like, Pocahontas?'

'He is mighty and terrible, with eyes like blue stone,' she said in a tone awesome enough to frighten Tahacope. 'And hair sticks out from his face like an unplucked priest.' She giggled suddenly. 'Come,' she said, grasping his hand. He scrambled to his feet. At the door of the cookhouse, she put her arm around him and whispered, 'I will show you what he is like.' The child hung back. 'You need not be afraid,' she said. 'He cannot bite you with his whiskers. And I want to see if he is hair all over like a shaggy bear.'

They approached the wigwam where Johnsmith was kept. A tall brave, his face painted with red and black and white, was on guard. Holding his spear he trotted methodically in one spot to keep himself warm.

'Ho, Amokis,' Pocahontas said and offered him the uneaten portion of her acorn loaf.

'Ho, Pocahontas,' Amokis said and stopped prancing. Because he felt he should, Tahacope handed the guard the crumbled portion clutched in his hand. Amokis took it. 'Ho, Tahacope,' he said. He stuffed both portions into his mouth at once and went on bobbing up and down, masticating in rhythm.

Taking her brother's hand, Pocahontas peered into the dark interior, then moved silently in. The gray ashes from the fire were sodden where the snow had drifted from the smokehole. By its filtered light the figure of the captive could be dimly distinguished. He slept, though he stirred restlessly from the dank and chill.

Pocahontas took an armful of sticks from the pile that lay at hand, and, squatting, she dug into the pit of ashes till she uncovered live embers. Carefully she built the fire until the vaulted roof was aglow and dancing with the flames. Then she and Tahacope sat in a shadowed corner to wait and watch.

As the warmth penetrated to his body through his damp clothes, Johnsmith turned toward the fire, and his eyes blinked open. Then he sat up so suddenly that Tahacope started and would have scurried off had not Pocahontas held him rigid, her arm on his shoulder. Johnsmith looked around, trying to orient himself, and gradually his face came alive, and his lips curved until he spouted out a deep laugh.

'It an't hell, after all, Johnnie lad!'

He got up, flailing himself with his arms. Then, searching through the folds of his strange garments, he spread his legs and sent a stream of water sizzling onto the fire, which hissed and steamed. When he was done, he turned to examine the room, and the children held their breath as his eyes skirted the edge of gloom which concealed them. A bark platter with venison and bread and a bowl of water were set near the pallet on which he had slept. He picked up the water and gingerly prodded at its coating of ice.

His features were so mobile under his whiskers, the spectacle so

24

droll, that Pocahontas and Tahacope gripped each other to contain a spasm of laughter.

The mighty warrior tasted the water, drank a deep draught, and then suddenly splashed the rest of the bowl into his face.

'Brr!' he shouted and shook his head so violently that icy drops shot from his beard in all directions.

Tahacope exploded, and Pocahontas gasped. There was no pause in their reactions. Like startled squirrels they leaped for the opening. But the cold water had made the White Werowance alert. He jumped for them, and reaching out two arms which seemed to uncoil to any needed length, he grasped their long hair, and jerked them back, knocking their heads together.

As he felt the lightness of their weight, he dropped them in surprise, and they lay trembling at his feet. The fierceness left him; his hands relaxed and found a resting place on his padded hips.

'What devil's spawn are you?'

Pocahontas rose slowly to her feet, trying to muster her dignity, but Tahacope ignominiously crawled on his belly toward the opening. Johnsmith reached down and gathered him under one arm, and at the boy's involuntary squawk gave him a hot swipe across the buttocks, then turned to face Pocahontas's indignant stare. He almost dropped Tahacope.

'It's the Princess!' he gasped.

'Release my brother!'

He looked down at the squirming backside, then wiped his forehead.

'Is it the whole royal family?'

He spoke in a language she did not understand, but his predicament and his mock despair were so obvious that she had difficulty hiding her amusement. He set Tahacope gently on his feet, but did not release him until Pocahontas's arm firmly encircled him.

Johnsmith addressed her in Powhatan. 'If Pocahontas will keep the Prince till I have made my peace with him, my life will belong to her twofold, for if he goes squalling to the guards . . . '

'Tahacope is no longer a child. He does not cry. Do you, Tahacope?' She looked down severely into her brother's face. He was blinking back his tears, his mouth set; he shook his head resolutely.

'Look,' the warrior said anxiously. He searched in his clothing and pulled out the magic jewel. He tried to take Tahacope's hand to draw him nearer to the light, but the boy would not willingly be touched by him. Johnsmith spread his hand and let the ivory and crystal ball roll gently on his palm.

'Take it, Tahacope,' Pocahontas commanded. 'See how it points to the north and tells how the earth and moon and sun are round as melons. I already know all about it.'

It was a challenge Tahacope could not resist. He took it to the fire and examined the needle and the dial, and when he looked up he was filled with many questions, but neither Pocahontas nor the Werowance paid him any heed.

'I would have welcomed you differently, Pocahontas. I did not see you come in.'

'We came in while you slept,' she said. 'We waited till you . . .'

'No!' He was so aghast, for the first time so truly horrified, she found herself utterly at a loss. Sensing her innocence, he smiled.

'I am honored,' he said in Powhatan's language. 'Did you come – to light the fire?'

'No,' she said. 'We came to see if you are hair all over.'

He stared at her, and then the laugh that started so mysteriously at the base of his belly engulfed the wigwam till Amokis poked his head through the opening to see if Powhatan's offspring were being devoured by the White Werowance.

'Of course you want to see.' He knelt in front of the fire and untied his doublet and his shirt. Tahacope had lost all interest in the jewel, which was doubtless full of magic but which told *him* nothing of the sun and moon or earth either. Now he was to see something *he* could tell about.

The hairs on Johnsmith's chest caught the firelight like the golden ripples on a ruffled pond. They were not thick like the hairs on his face, but lightly dusted his flesh, which was white as doe's milk. Tahacope reached out a hand, and, Pocahontas knocked it aside.

'Let him,' Johnsmith said.

Pocahontas laid the tips of her fingers on his skin. Amokis came to stare over her shoulder. Tahacope tried to pull down Johnsmith's belt, and the White Werowance quickly got to his feet.

'It is enough,' Johnsmith said, tying his points. 'I am the same all over, except that I am not plucked as your braves are.' He touched with some vanity his carefully trained mustachios. 'In England this is a fine thing to possess.'

And it seemed to the three of them that under eyes so brightly agleam his curly whiskers indeed made a fine show.

Opechancano and his braves left before the midday meal, stomping off in a silence that left Powhatan's city of Werowocomoco steeped in a disturbed hush. Pocahontas sought her father, but he gave her scant attention, and finally when she pressed her questions he ordered her to go and look after the younger children. Still she had to know at once what had passed between Openchancano and Powhatan. If it was war she felt she could almost be glad, for deeper than Opechancano's dislike for her she sensed his bitter envy of Powhatan.

Her uncles had been in the House of the Oke, but they would tell her nothing, sliding as they did on the thin ice between their two powerful brothers.

She saw Nantequos at the door of his wigwam. He passed his bowl to his bride and spoke to her, and she retired to return with his fishing rod and lines. He took them without speaking and started off through the woods. Pocahontas followed him.

Nantequos was the comeliest of Powhatan's sons and most like Powhatan. Since Pocahontas had come, they two, most loved by their father, had been closest – until the time of Huskanan, when Nantequos and other youths went to undergo the ceremonial bestowing of manhood. In the Full of the Moon the youths were herded for Werowocomoco to the beat of drums, the trill of flutes, and not until the third Full Moon did they return, at which time it was the law that they should have forgotten all their past life, their boyhood, and their softness, for they were now braves and members of the tribe.

There were strange stories of what happened: the dosing with the wysoccan herb until oblivion was complete, strange rites that made the man glad to forget the boy; but for most it was only a perfunctory forgetting – youths who had pulled her hair or doused her in the falls, or tried to impress her with their incipient manhood, tried it still after Huskanan. Of them all only Nantesquos seemed truly to forget. He who had soothed her aches avoided her now; he who had dragged her at the heels of the hunt, who had taught her to wheel round the great fire or to dance in joyous abandon for Powhatan's pleasure, sat now a silent onlooker. Powhatan had given him the maid that he had loved, and already his bride was bursting with child; had offered him a nation of his own; but it was as if he still tasted the wysoccan with which they dosed him. Not wife, nor coming child, nor wanton sister, nor even Powhatan could rouse him.

From the bare-branched trees Pocahontas watched him wade out into the icy stream, impervious to cold as he was to love. He threw the line, and as it trickled downstream toward him, she moved quietly and sat upon the rock where he had left his basket of bait. He untangled his line from the rocks, examined his empty hook, and moved toward her. He saw her, and she stayed motionless, waiting for him to speak. He baited his hook and returned to the center of the stream. Again he lost his bait and returned. This time he took his basket and started off downstream. Still she did not stir. He paused halfway. 'Pocahontas!' he said harshly.

It could be a reproach as well as a pet name. She sat, head between her knees, staring down at the flecked stone, wondering why the brother whom she loved should refer to her other than lovingly. She sensed that he came back and that he sat on the small rocks below her, fumbling with his line, that his glance stole upward, but she no longer wished to question him. She drove her hands into her braids and loosened them till her hair fell about her like a curtain.

'Pocahontas!' The inflection was different, and then, sweet as melody, 'Sister!' and the voice was no longer strange but that of the youth of a year ago.

Inside her curtain of hair she waited as one waits behind a cloak of leaves for the hummingbird's swoop to its nest.

There was a grating sound, and she sensed that he was sharpening the points of his bone hooks. At last he left them and climbed upon the rock. He pushed aside her hair.

'Opechancano threatened Powhatan – with war even – unless Powhatan would give you to him, as his wife.'

Her eyes shot wide and she found herself staring into her brother's face. 'Why? What would he do with *me*?'

'That is what Powhatan asked. But *I* know. He would get you with child and then be done with you.'

'How would he get *me* with child?' she asked scornfully. 'The branches where I would climb would break and crash him to the ground.'

'That is what I told him,' her brother said.

'You did?' she asked, and then, 'What did Powhatan tell him?'

'He told Opechancano that he had conquered the nations and ruled them against all the laws of succession, and if he willed it, he would name his successor against the same laws, and he would be obeyed.'

Her blood flamed. 'You and me, Nantequos!'

He shook his head and turned to untangle his wet line. 'I have no desire . . . '

The sentence was incomplete, and yet an ache in her heart told her that he had said everything. She reached out and pulled him to her awkwardly but with such strength that he could not deny her without being cruel.

'Brother! Does the wysoccan make you forget even your sister . . . ?'

He pulled away from her and gazed wildly for refuge. 'Yes,' he said, 'even you. Only Opechancano and Katoka I remember. . . . '

Katoka was Nantequos's wife, a maid who had been close to Pocahontas, but who, like her lord, had withdrawn from everyone since their marriage.

'Katoka and Opechancano!'

He turned to her and held her hands tightly. 'You will keep what I tell you, Pocahontas?'

'If they flay me!'

'You believe, as Powhatan and all our peoples, that I had Katoka before Huskanan and that she carries my child.'

What she had to realize was too terrible. So often she had seen Katoka slip from her playmates underneath the falls and dart among the rocks and into the trees and Nantequos followed her. The child that was due too soon had seemed the result of those antics, known to all who watched them, and it had seemed that Powhatan had known of them, too, and married his favorite son to the maid of his choice because of his love for both the maid and the youth.

'I never lay with Katoka before – or after – we were wed,' Nantequos said in a rasped voice. 'When I came to her after our marriage, she told me – she wept and told me. Opechancano took her against her will while I was in the Huskanan pen, and she was already with child. . . . '

'His child!'

'He knew I was to wed her, and where would Powhatan's law of succession be then – his child in my wife's belly. . . !'

'And you have not taken her – you have not loved her since. . . ?'

'He had her not once but two times, three times . . . he had to be sure, and she – she did not climb a tree!'

Pocahontas reached for him and he went into her arms, sobs tearing at him till it seemed he was a part of herself and her own vitals were being torn out of her. Her sympathy for Katoka was buried in her anger for the brother who seemed now younger than herself.

She shook him. 'If Powhatan knew . . . Opechancano would be staked!'

He sat up and wiped the tears from his eyes with the heels of his hands.

'Pocahontas, none knows of this but you. Think what would happen to Katoka if Powhatan knew.'

She tried to shut out the image of the flayed flesh, the bright screams of the maid who had been her playmate.

'You love her?'

'No!' he said decidedly. 'But I no longer hate her. She was only weak. It is Opechancano I hate. And you he shall not have!'

'Ho! You shall tell Powhatan,' she said, transferring her own power to him, 'that Johnsmith is mine according to the law of Oke, that I will not wed Openchancano though he kill me. . . .'

'And me!'

'. . . though he kill *us*!'

Nantequos looked at her with pride and pity.

'You are the tree in the forest, straight, with arms widespreading, and it is you, out of all the rest, the lightning will strike.'

She shivered. 'You will be there, Brother, when the lightning strikes.'

'I will be there, Pocahontas, if I live.'

She leaped to her feet. 'Let us go back, and you will tell Powhatan what we will not do.'

A messenger met them before they reached the palisades of Powhatan's city.

'Opechancano has come back, and Powhatan wants you both to come to the Great Wigwam.'

Pocahontas looked at Nantequos. 'We will be there. Hurry,' she told her brother. 'I will wait for you. We will go in together.'

The started off at once, swiftly, for their wigwams.

The air in the Great Wigwam was oppressive, for the fire had burned since before dawn. The braves who had sat in Council were stooped and wearied, their bodies glistening with sweat. Only Powhatan and Opechancano sat unbent, carved in red granite. Silence possessed the room, for every argument had crashed against the rocks of their resolves.

There was a movement at the entrance, and all heads turned, relieved at the distraction. Pocahontas stood a moment, accustoming her eyes to the murk. Her body was painted with the bright juice of the puccoon, her hair was oiled and shiny, crowned with a coronet of peak – white gleaming shells, woven in a band six inches high. It was weighted by strings of copper disks. In her ears and about her neck were pearls, and over one shoulder was slung her puttawus, a cape of bright blue feathers so closely worked that it appeared a fabulously wrought fabric. Tall and fearsome behind her was Nantequos, his face painted in blue and yellow, the spread wings of a bluejay caught in the crest of his hair. Through three holes in his ear a small green and yellow snake was caught; it crawled and lapped itself about his neck and familiarly sought his lips.

Powhatan stared at them and the granite of his face seemed

suddenly translucent from the brilliance of his eyes. It had been long since Nantequos had stood, arrogant and impudent son of the Powhatan, flaunting his manhood.

Ignoring Opechancano, they came quickly and bent, their brows touching Powhatan's feet.

'Ho, Pocahontas . . . Nantequos!'

'Ho, Powhatan . . . Father!'

Powhatan drew Pocahontas to sit beside him on his couch. Nantequos sat near them, facing Opechancano. Their eyes met and locked, nephew and uncle; no muscle quivered; only the weaving snake stirred in its sinuous dance, making it difficult for Opechancano to maintain his stony stare.

Powhatan spoke: 'Our love brother, Opechancano, Werowance of the Pamaunkeys, has brought a request which because of our closeness to him, bound in blood and love, we would regard favorably if we could. What he has come to ask concerns you closely, Matoaka.'

'Let him speak then,' Pocahontas said coldly. It was the first time she had even sat not afraid in the presence of her uncle.

Opechancano's voice seemed to rise from the ground, so deep and measured were his tones.

'I ask, Pocahontas, that you forego your right to the prisoner you have claimed.' Before she could speak he went on quickly, as though he would placate her. 'It is your right to claim his life, that is not to be disputed, for the Great Oke said that it was so. But in your youth and eagerness you have done something which can bring great harm to our nation, for he is not like a captive from another tribe who can be made a blood brother of the Powhatans, but a stranger, foreign to our race and to our land, who has slain my braves, and whose tribe will go forever farther. . . .'

Pocahontas moved to speak, but Nantequos stopped her.

'Let us hear all that Opechancano would ask.'

Openchancano stared at him glumly. 'Nantequos has recovered from the wysoccan, apparently.'

'And has learned much that is strange and new and bitter since the Huskanan,' Nantequos said stridently. 'What else has Opechancano come to ask?'

'That your sister, Pocahontas, be given to him as wife,' Opechancano said ponderously.

'As Wironausqua?'

'As wife.'

'You have little use for the children of Powhatan, Opechancano, knowing well the law of succession of our race, which precludes

31

them, but you should know that Powhatan has reserved for Pocahontas a native of her own, even as he has given the Appomattucks to Opussokonuske, or the Tappahannas of Oholasc.'

'If she is to have a nation of her own, I do not object,' Opechancano said.

'Yet when she was offered to you by Powhatan, who would then have made her Wironausqua of the Powhatans, you said she was not fit to be a wife.'

'Maids so young can be taught,' Opechancano said, suddenly angry, 'and you speak too much for one who has so recently come from the Huskanan pen, not yet a Werowance. . . .'

'I speak as one who knows well how you would pollute the blood of Powhatan.' Nantequos bent to glare into his uncle's face, and the snake spiraled, waving in front of their eyes. Opechancano brushed it away roughly, and it hissed in disturbed modulation.

Then to the amazement of all and to Nantequo's exultation Opechancano's eyes dropped. There was a strained silence. 'Let Pocahontas speak for herself,' Opechancano said at last.

'I do not wish to be the wife of Opechancano,' Pocahontas said strongly, 'nor do I relinquish Johnsmith to him. He can become a member of our nation, for I do not believe the white man's blood flows less red than ours.'

There was a long silence. Powhatan spoke: 'The Oke has granted her this right. And Nantequos speaks the truth; Pocahontas can be a Wironausqua without a husband if she chooses. You have heard all, Brother!'

Opechancano did not move. 'Bring the Calumet,' Powhatan said in a low voice. Owerowok got up quietly and returned with the great pipe of peace, decorated with its wings and woman's hair and beads. She held it to Powhatan, who filled it before the eyes of all. She lighted it for him. He smoked silently and slowly, then passed it solemnly to Opechancano.

Opechancano regarded it, looked up at his own braves, standing ready and fierce, and then at the braves of his brother, who blocked the entrance far into the wigwam. Grudgingly he took it and inhaled deeply.

'Ho!' Powhatan said with satisfaction.

'Ho!' Opechancano said.

CHAPTER TWO

Opechancano told Powhatan his need to be in Pamaunkey, his own nation, and left stiffly, his braves following him from either side.

Pocahontas watched them go, and the exultation of this morning possessed her. Once more she had triumphed over Opechancano and had saved the life of the White Werowance with the milky, gold-dusted skin. She repressed a smile of excitement.

Tired braves and Cockarouses rose from their heels, bowed, and left till only the guards and the two children of Powhatan remained Nantequos stood and stretched elaborately. The green and yellow snake still sought his lips, and for the first time he brushed it away. It sibilated and retreated.

'I would have Opuiske for my bedfellow,' Nantequos said.

Powhatan's eyes shot to his son's face, but there was no change of expression, so that only because Pocahontas loved them both did she understand how Nantequos had startled his father: to see his son once more strong and positive! And now that he had heaped upon him all that a father's heart could devise, a kingdom and the maid he had wanted, to hear him thus off-handedly ask for a maid he had scarcely glanced at!

'Take her then,' Powhatan said.

Pocahontas climbed into Powhatan's knee, and her arms crept under his fur cloak.

'Powhatan has won a mighty battle – and not a brave has fallen.'

He arose, letting her slip off his knee, but holding her so that she would not fall.

'Powhatan is too old – as Opechancano thinks him.' He loosened her arms and turned, glaring down at her.

'Tomorrow, we will take this mighty White Werowance of yours to be one of us. Until that has been done, you are to stay

3

away from him, according to the laws of Oke. Do you understand that, Pocahontas?'

She knew Amokis had talked, and for that she vowed revenge, but she was too frightened to say anything in her own defense.

Outside the Great Wigwam she held her brother's arm. The difference was great between him and the near boy she had held so closely by the stream. Glad though she was, she loved him less somehow, this brave who stood deliberately scrutinizing the maids till his eyes lightened and fastened on the virgin, Opuiske. She thought of the night, of Katoka, her onetime friend, lying mute and tragic in a corner. . . . To be great one must be cruel, she thought. Better she should grieve with Opechancano's child in her belly, than that he . . .

Pocahontas turned to go, but he caught her back.

'We told Opechancano! You and I!'

'We told him. But you must know this White Werowance, Nantequos. Before tomorrow, I want you to know him.'

'They will take him tonight into the wigwam in the forest. Before dawn I will go.'

He pressed her hand briefly and left her. She watched him stride purposefully toward the group of maids.

Nantequos pulled his mantle, fur side in, closely around him and moved silently through his wigwam so as not to awaken his women. Outside, the great cold was static since no wind blew, and the stars were numerous and frosty. He bent to fasten the thongs of his mocassins and then moved stealthily past the outer ring of wigwams. His own wigwam was outside the walls, or else he could not have hoped to escape the guards. They would not have stopped him, but they would have had to report his absence. It was the hour when vigilance flagged, when darkness blurred and grayed, the hour for attack. Silent as the shadow of a hawk he ran crouched across the clearing between the city and the forest. Once within the shelter of the trees, he straightened and ran, his mantle caught up about his middle, his naked legs carrying him in swift, paced rhythm.

After the Huskanan, he had run like this for hours into the night, until he had flung himself at last at the foot of some great tree. Then he had been running away, to forget and to seek sleep at last from sheer physical weariness. But tonight no raven's wings of despair fluttered behind him. He ran, head up, breathing deep of the cold which made his heart as buoyant as a bubble. He was free from the agony and lethargy of his own inadequacy.

34

He had met his enemy, face to face, as an equal. He had dissipated the stigma against his manhood in the warm womb of Opuiske. She would bear him a son who would be his own. And some time – soon, he prayed – he would meet his enemy again. After that there would be no shame or blame. The dead belong to Mahomny who dwells beyond the sun.

Smith sat with his back to the fire, his eyes on the low tunnel of laced saplings, the only egress from the wigwam. Since they had taken him from the town into the forest his doubts had been renewed. Tomakkin, the brave who was in charge of his guards, had told him that Opechancano had returned, and it was hard to believe that the little Princess would prevail against his malignancy.

Low voices outside alerted him, and he quickly huddled his cloak about him and lay back, feigning sleep. If someone came at this hour, he must not think Captain Smith sat, sleepless with fear.

Stooping, Nantequos emerged from the tunnel, his eyes on the fire. Beside it, almost in it, the White Warrior slept on a bed of skins, his great robe wrapped around him in bunched folds. Nantequos stood, regarding him.

He had a wide face, even without his ugly standout whiskers. It was chapped and roughed by cold and sun, but still his paleness made him look unreal in the flickering light. There were creases that rayed out from his eyes which told of good laughter as the deeper furrows in his brow told of determination and concentration. His mouth, set in his whiskers like a crayfish in a bed of moss, was softly moulded like a woman's. *Was he afraid?* Nantequos wondered, and did not doubt he was. He had heard from all of this man's courage, and Nantequos knew well what it meant to stand undaunted when one quaked with fear inside. He touched Johnsmith's shoulder.

Instantly Johnsmith started up, his hands groping for his absent weapons. 'What do you want?'

Nantequos stepped into the light, revealing himself, weaponless and naked except for the patch over his groin.

'Speak softly,' he warned.

'Who are you?'

'I am Nantequos, son of Powhatan.'

Johnsmith got to his feet. 'What have you come for?'

'To know you.'

Johnsmith studied him. They stood, looking without speaking.

35

At last Nantequos said, 'I come in friendship.'

Johnsmith's face relaxed. 'In that case, you are welcome.' He grinned suddenly, his whiskers parting to show white, strong teeth. He sat down on his bed and indicated a place beside him. Nantequos sat. They still stared at each other.

'I have no Calumet,' Johnsmith said, 'but I can offer the peace sign of the English.'

'Offer it.'

Johnsmith held out his right hand, palm outstretched. Nantequos looked at it, then extended his own. The other put his hand inside Nantequos's and clasped it. Both men grinned.

'Since we are friends, perhaps you can tell me what your father means to do with me.'

'He will offer you a country and my sister, Pocahontas, to be your Wironausqua.'

Johnsmith's smile faded, and he sagged suddenly as though Nantequos had struck him with his tomahawk.

'I thought he meant to kill me. I heard that Opechancano . . . '

Nantequos smiled broadly, happily. 'Opechancano would have you killed,' he agreed, 'but I stared him down. He smoked the Calumet and left. I, and Pocahontas,' he added as an afterthought.

'*Quels enfants!*'

'What?'

'I thank you – and the Princess Pocahontas.'

'You will live with us. You will be our blood brother.' Nantequos had no idea what Powhatan intended for Johnsmith, other than to spare his life in the custody of Pocahontas, but now Nantequos had made up his mind.

'But my own people . . . '

'You will take ours.'

'They depend on me as yours depend on Powhatan – *will* depend on you.'

'Not on me,' Nantequos said, suddenly morose. 'It is not the children of Powhatan who inherit – it is his brother, Opechancano! You will be our ally against Opechancano,' he said, bright again.

'Willingly. And I will be your blood brother, if you will have me, with all my heart. But I must return to Jamestown – to my people. And – I cannot marry the Princess Pocahontas.'

So he does not want Pocahontas, Nantequos thought. *Undoubtedly he has many squaws more beautiful than she.*

'You must help me persuade your father to let me return to my people.' Nantequos looked suddenly so bleak that Johnsmith's whiskers twitched in a suppressed smile even while he touched Nantequos's hand. 'You will visit us and I will show you the wonders of the white men and teach you their magic.'

There was a hissing sound and both men turned. Tomakkin stood in the entrance. 'It is the change of the guard,' he whispered.

Nantequos gripped Johnsmith's hand in the English assurance of friendship.

'Trust me. I will persuade Powhatan.'

As he raced through the forest he thought, *I will keep my promise, but I will also make Powhatan offer all that I said, for if he stays with us he will forget his people. Also, it is what Pocahontas would like.*

With the rhythm of his running feet, his heart and mind caught up the song that he had breathed into the cold night: *I have met my enemy face to face. Opuiske shall bear me a son who will be my own.* And in the bleak, yellow dawn, he added a new refrain: *I have found a friend, a great Werowance, who will be my blood brother.*

CHAPTER THREE

Nantequos did not attempt to conceal his return to Werowoco-moco. As he came to the clearing he slowed his pace to a proud, rapid walk and strode past the surprised sentinels without greeting them.

Pocahontas was waiting at the opening to her wigwam. She ran forward to greet him.

'You have seen him?' He nodded. 'What . . .'

He caught her hand, pulling her after him. 'Come, we will talk to Powhatan together.'

They found their father among the elders, chipping arrow-heads, for he worked at the chores his braves worked at. His robe of weasel, fringed with tails, surrounded him like a wigwam, with his head emerging as if from the smokehole. They knew he was aware of them, though he did not recognize their presence. The arrowhead he worked on, they noticed, was not for fowl or smaller animal but was large and of the finest flint. A war arrow! Against Openchancano? Or against the strangers?

They squatted unceremoniously beside him. He turned to look at them, and moved his eyes slowly from Nantequos to Pocahontas. Then he returned to his delicate work.

'Powhatan,' Nantequo said, 'what do you intend to offer John-smith?'

Powhatan's hands stopped working and dropped between his knees. He lifted his head and gazed steadily at Nantequos, who looked intense and serious, in spite of the fact that his eyes glittered and his skin was burnished from his lope through the forest.

'Offer him?' Powhatan said at last. 'Is not his life enough?'

'No, it is not! He is a mighty warrior, and my friend. . . .'

'*Your* friend?'

'We pledged friendship this morning in the wigwam in the forest. . . .'

38

Powhatan pushed the arrowhead and his tools onto the ground and rose, his robe swinging around him. He looked down on Nantequos, his eyes sockets of fury over his beaklike nose. Pocahontas quailed.

'I told you he was not to be approached!'

'You told my sister!'

'And you did not think I meant you, too! *Even* you!'

Nantequos rose and faced his father. The lift of his head was prideful, not supplicating.

'I knew you meant me, too,' he said. 'I had to go.'

The anger left Powhatan so swiftly that he felt empty and weary. For many moons he had longed to shake this cub until he showed some spark. And now in two days he had defied both Opechancano and himself, old panthers who had ruled too long. A warm feeling replaced the emptiness.

'Come and tell me what you *had* to do,' he said, his expression sour as though he had bitten into an unripe persimmon. Pocahontas scrambled to her feet. 'Not you,' he said gruffly, and then, 'Oh, well, you, too,' and he stalked ahead of them into the Great Wigwam.

'What magic has he got – greater than firesticks and stupid jewels – to bewitch you both?' Powhatan cried out after an hour of their cajoling.

Nantequos shook his head. 'I saw no magic.'

'*Your* magic,' Pocahontas said.

Powhatan's eyes nailed her as if they had been arrows. Her eyes met his, and the arrows plunged into limpid depths.

'He is Wahunsonacock – come from afar.'

'And like Wanhunsonacock he is to conquer the old Powhatan?'

'No!'

'A stranger to rule your people?'

'Wahunsonacock was no stranger – yet he came from a distant land. He married Powhatan women. . . .'

'He has no wish to be Powhatan,' Nantequos said triumphantly. 'He has many squaws in his own land, young and fair. He refused Pocahontas when I offered her to him.'

Pocahontas gasped. Powhatan looked from Nantequos to her stricken, shamed face. For the first time he felt amusement at these strange antics.

'*You* offered him your sister? Was this *your* doing, *pocahantas?*' There was no doubt from his inflection how he used the word. She could not answer, but there was no need. Powhatan smothered his grin in his fur robe. The first words he spoke were impossible to understand. ' . . . nobody wants Pocahontas.'

'Oh, *someone* will,' Nantequos said reassuringly.

He was amazed to be whirled around by a wild creature which sought to tear out his eyes. Her nails ripped his cheeks as she endeavored to climb him.

Powhatan controlled his laughter with difficulty. He reached out and gathered in his arms and sat holding her close and rocking her. At last she ceased struggling and turned her face to the warmth and haven of his shoulder.

'Nantequos,' Powhatan said over her head, 'you should make a great warrior, you are so stupid about women.'

'I did not mean . . . '

'Go,' Powhatan said. 'She is well here.'

Nantequos cast a distracted glance at his sister and fled.

Powhatan looked after him amused, then, his smile fading, he bent his head and laid it on hers, loving the live oiled blackness.

'The white men have not a woman in their city. Johnsmith has no squaws or even *a* squaw. He refused you because you are my daughter, and he has sense, which Nantequos has not.'

Pocahontas pulled away from him. Her eyes were dry and bright. 'I do not care for *that*,' she said, 'or if he has squaws or not. But if he has not even *will* . . . '

'To be Powhatan?'

She did not stir, but he knew. He knew *her* will.

'Nantequos is like a moonstruck, one-forked buck who has mounted his first doe,' he said with more meaning that he knew. 'He does not care if *he* is Powhatan,' he added belatedly and with regret. 'But till yesterday I thought he cared about nothing.'

The child in his arms should have been a man, then it would have been worthwhile to fight. What was to come for her? A squaw for whom? He thought of the White Werowance. *She* believed in him. But Powhatan recognized a greatness. 'If he has not even will,' she had said. Will for what? For power? There was a will in Johnsmith which Wahunsonacock would not have recognized. But *Powhatan* – fifty-seven cohonks – fifty-eight, for the geese had passed again and their resonant call had left its melancholy mark – *Powhatan* knew that there was a power in Johnsmith – and Opechancano knew it. He *had* a will. But it was the will of a Powhatan, not of a Wahunsonacock or a Pocahontas. Johnsmith cared about many things, but none of them was himself.

She lay back, heavy against his arm, looking up at him. 'Are you thinking: how wicked Nantequos has been, how willful

40

Pocahontas, we shall stake Johnsmith tomorrow?'

'Some of those things,' he said.

'That's what I would, too. All of them.'

'It is well you are not Powhatan.'

Her arms crept up. 'After Sun's Power you go to him?'

'Yes.'

'What are you going to do?'

'Give him his freedom – send him home. Give him land here if he wants it – and all with it. They can stay – for now. I am as confused as you and Nantequos. *They* may be evil, but *he* is a mighty man.'

Her eyes closed, her arms tightened around him, and he rocked her back and forth, thinking of Opechancano. . . .

CHAPTER FOUR

Smith sat for a long time after Nantequos left him, thinking of the strange interview. It could not be likely that the boy, so eager, so like the hero-worshiping youth of his own country, could wield the influence he claimed, or could prove an effective protector for Smith. However, it had been an exciting meeting. It was a handsome stable the old man sired, Smith told himself: Pocahontas, Tahacope, and Nantequos!

'He will offer you a nation and my sister Pocahontas. . . .' Smith laughed quietly. In his twenty-eight years he had been many things: farm boy, mercenary, Turkish slave, pirate, colonist. What he wanted most was to be *colonist*, to lead this band of unruly gentlemen and wastrels so that they should make of this fair, virgin land a second England – a better England! Now he thought of himself, crowned with peak, naked save for the patch over his privities, the mantle of a Werowance across his shoulders, making his choice from a score of beauties, their bodies pounced with colored markings – Pocahontas's skin has not yet known the needle, he thought unexpectedly – stained scarlet and oiled till the odor overcame all else. He thought of them, slippery and agile, escaping from his hands, and it reminded him of the game of greased pig at home, so that his laugh grew deeper. 'And my sister Pocahontas to be your Wironausqua!' The child, half-formed – too slight for his clumsy body. But Nantequos had dreamed. What Powhatan had decided on for Smith was something other than a kingdom and his daughter.

He built up the fire and lay down in front of it, trying to lose the hours in sleep. But as soon as he started to doze his mind pictured the death stones of Powhatan, the clubs about to pound his skull to a pulp, he thought of the death of Cassen, the stupid Englishman whose folly had betrayed them to Opechancano's braves. They had bound him to a tree, and severed his joints singly, while they scraped his skin from his face and hands with sharpened shells; having done this they ripped his belly and then burned him, tree and all. He thought of his enemies in Jamestown and how they might hope this was his last day, as it quite probably was. If he did return, how would he be greeted? He remembered the gallows they had raised for his coming once before. His loyalty was not toward these, but toward his own, the soldiers, the workers, and toward the sweet land, Virginia! Yet his enemies would not put it past him to accept a kingdom from Powhatan and marry a heathen princess.

He wondered, between sleeping and waking, why that was a fate so difficult to accept. He wondered why he had deserted the beauty and the relish of the Lady Tragabigzanda in Turkey, where he could have been a prince. He had made love and proved himself with some gallantry, but he had had no love – had never thought of marriage – with pagan or Christian. A man whose life is always at his sword's point has no business to think of marriage. . . . The girls in Lincolnshire . . . Molly Ware had been the first to pull down his breeks. . . . She had been a big wench six years older than he, and he had lived in terror for weeks lest she come with child and his father learn. He laughed now, doubting that he had come near getting her with child, eager little rabbit. But that experience had kept him continent for four years.

Someday, he told himself, I'll go back and find me a maid . . . she'll have flaxen hair and English skin and blue eyes, and she'll not be forward, but she'll yield to me because my hands are gentle and my heart loving . . . and she'll be willing to come to the new world and bear my children. . . . He thought of children: Tahacope blinking back his tears; Pocahontas like a fairy sprite, her head on his to save his life, and then her coming to see if he was hair all over; and Nantequos – a man would be proud to have a son like Nantequos.

Someday, he thought, I will go back and find me a maid with flaxen hair, and she will come. . . . The thought, *today I may be killed,* crossed currents, and at the same instant he fell asleep.

When he awoke he felt curiously alone and yet not alone, oppressed. The room, many ells long, was now divided by a grass curtain that had not been there when he went to sleep. He sat up, rubbing his joints, and looked about suspiciously.

Slowly, in a rising crescendo that made his hackles rise with it, a doleful sound issued from behind the curtain. It was not singing, or instruments, or anything he could identify. It was like the combined voices of lost souls, and it was something they were using to scare him to death, he thought between fear and amuse-

43

ment. He gathered his robe around him and sat Turkoman-fashion on his mat, glaring ahead of him, as he had seen Powhatan glare.

The curtain lifted and a series of black devils issued into his portion of the room, painted all over with coal and oil, their faces striped with red and white, surrounding him, chanting a weird monotone in tune with a flageolet which issued a single note.

This is my final judgment, or this is something I do not understand, he thought, and emitted a mighty yawn.

The chief of the black devils stopped, staring, and the others came, perforce, to a halt behind him.

'Ho, Powhatan!' Smith said.

There was a hush, a sense of confusion, as though each devil said: *How mighty is this Werowance, to recognize Powhatan among all the black devils!* Powhatan weaved slowly toward him, in one hand a rattle, in the other a club which could easily have brained an ox. His head was decorated with dead weasels and snakes stuffed with moss, which formed a circlet around his half-shaven pate. He raised his club and rattle and launched into a passionate invocation. Smith heard his own name – 'Johnsmith' – among the gibberish. Gradually he found some meaning in the jumbled words: he was a captive deserving death, but he had been saved by the King's daughter – he was to be initiated into the tribe of the Powhatan. . . .

'Willingly,' Smith said. 'I am a friend to Powhatan and all who are his allies. But to prove *his* friendship, Powhatan must set me free so that I can return to my people in Jamestown.'

One of the devils, fiercer than the others, came from the circle and brandished a knife before Smith's face. He tried not to flinch. He caught the word 'brother' and he nodded. A devil came from the ranks and knelt beside him, holding out his arm. Smith sensed, rather than recognized, that it was Nantequos. Then Nantequos pulled up Smith's sleeve so that his pale arm was bare.

The devil with the knife slashed Nantequos's arm neatly so that blood ran, coagulating against the coal dust and the oil. Then he slashed Smith's arm, and pressed the two together, binding them with a sinew of deer gut. The devils danced around them shaking their rattles; the flageolet struck an impossible note that echoed and made Smith's eardrums ache. He turned and looked into Nantequos's eyes, and they were warm with brotherhood. Smith's senses reeled; he felt himself, against his will, grow pale and start to swoon. A tourniquet was tied about his upper arm, and he found himself alert again.

44

When his eyes focused, Powhatan was sitting beside him look-ing anxiously into his face. They were the eyes of Nantequos, but they were old and consciously fierce.

'You are now our blood brother, blood of my blood,' he said. 'Tell the truth. Why did you go so far up the Chickahominy?'

'I seek the back sea, the other side of the main, where there is salt water.' It seemed to him a stupid reason to give. What did these heathen care about a second sea?

Powhatan took the arm that had been slashed by the Con-juror's knife.

'You are now a brother to Nantequos — you are of our nation.'

Smith pulled away, distrusting him, but not wanting to be untrustworthy himself.

'My nation is in Jamestown — and across the sea.'

'You are brother by blood to Nantequos. . . . '

'Yes. . . . ' Smith said. For if the lad were English would one not be proud to be his brother — or father?

'We will send you corn and venison, or whatever you need, and you will make us hatchets and bring us copper.'

'I'll do all that.'

'And you shall send me two great guns — cannon — and a grindstone, for I have been told you have these stones to sharpen knives and axes so that they will cut a single hair at one swift stroke — and then we shall know you trust us.'

'From Jamestown?' Smith asked, for the last thing he would ever do would be to give cannon to these heathen.

Powhatan said, 'With four men I will send you to James-town. They will protect you and guard you and bring back the cannon.' Smith thought of the great weight of the cannon and the grindstone. 'When this is done I will be your father and love you even as my son Nantequos.'

Smith tried to smile, but he was tired — he was so tired. 'I'm a blood brother, and I haven't had a single thing to eat.'

Powhatan called out, and into the wigwam came a file of women bearing dishes. Smith looked looked at them and feared he could not eat.

CHAPTER FIVE

Rawhunt took Johnsmith to Jamestown and returned with his braves, but he did not bring the cannon or the grindstone. Pocahontas met him first in the forest, and she questioned him, but he seemed to have little to tell her.

'I go to Powhatan,' he said briefly.

'But, Rawhunt . . . ' Pocahontas said. This gnarled, deformed intimate of Powhatan had been her teacher, and she was not as free with him as she was with other braves aware of her position and charmed by her willfulness.

'If he wants you to know, you will know,' Rawhunt said.

Once again Pocahontas hated him. It seemed, as she thought of it, that most of her life she had hated him, for he never softened.

'I but wondered . . .'

'Wonder then!'

Nantequos emerged from the forest, and Pocahontas brightened. Rawhunt would not treat him as though he had not learned his lesson, could not count to ten turkeys on a tree, and tell how many were still there when two of them had flown.

'Ho, Rawhunt!'

'Ho, Nantequos!'

'How fares the White Werowance?'

'He fares.'

'I know he fares – unless you slew him, which would have been against Powhatan's orders. *How* fares he?'

'As you, or I . . . ' Rawhunt wriggled his crooked shoulder, 'or anyone who fares.'

'He lives and walks and breathes – he fares!' Rawhunt grunted agreement. Nantequos looked at the free-handed braves. 'You bring no cannons and no grindstone?'

'No.'

'Perhaps they were too burdensome.'

'Perhaps.'

'Rawhunt, we have a cruel punishment for squaws who talk too much. Have you ever thought that Powhatan might consider you an old woman with a wagging tongue?'

Rawhunt looked at him in amazement.

'Without speaking,' Nantequos said, 'tell us *all* that has happened.'

'You are a silly youth,' Rawhunt said brusquely. 'He sent you gifts,' he said to Pocahontas.

'What?'

'And me?' Nantequos demanded.

'No gifts – but a message.'

'Then tell it!' Nantequos said impatiently, pushing Rawhunt's crooked shoulder.

Rawhunt stumbled and resumed his pace. 'I will tell Powhatan. You will be there,' he added disapprovingly.

Gifts! Pocahontas thought, and then wondered if she would not rather have a *message*.

In the Great Wigwam Powhatan felt himself surrounded. Pocahontas crouched on his bed behind him, her arm laid upon his shoulder. Nantequos squatted at his feet, but his eyes turned from Rawhunt to his father, as though Powhatan were incapable of evaluating Rawhunt's news.

'Where are the cannons and the grindstone?'

'He offered them to us,' Rawhunt said. 'But not twenty men could lift one of them. We could not even shift them.'

Powhatan wondered. 'So mighty!'

'He had the cannons loaded with stones. And then he had them fired. They shattered the forest a hundred paces off. A noise more terrible than the God of Storms. And from the trees snow and ice fell with a crash that frightened us. . . . '

'You ran?' Rawhunt nodded. 'He meant you should. I would give half my lands for a gun like that.'

'We could not have carried it, Powhatan,' Rawhunt said guiltily.

'He knew you could not. He never meant you should.'

'He gave us gifts,' Rawhunt said. He uncovered copper, beads, and two hatchets. 'The beads are for Pocahontas.'

'And the message for me?' demanded Nantequos.

Rawhunt turned. 'That you are brothers. That his gift for you is great and one he cannot send.'

'I will go to him,' Nantequos said eagerly.

'And hope it is not rooted in the earth like my cannon. His

own braves?' Powhatan asked Rawhunt. 'How did they receive him? Are *they* bewitched – like my children?'

'There was a cry from the walls – they had believed him dead. But he has enemies. . . .'

'Ayiiii!'

'His people were so few – while we held him here, Powhatan. They were so few – we could have wiped them out with less than fifty braves.'

'Less than fifty?' Powhatan marveled. 'Why not now?'

'He has mighty magic. Remember, Powhatan, how he said the ship of his father Newport would come in two days. It came as he said, with ten times as many men, and the English are strong again.'

'Tell me of this Weroames Newport.'

'He has but one arm. He has lived about forty cohonks. His face is bitten. His eyes are keen and crinkled like Johnsmith's. His voice is like the crash of the falls over the rocks, and his laugh is too loud. He is not so great a Werowance as Johnsmith.'

'He rules Johnsmith!'

'I doubt he does.'

'I would know him,' Prowhatan said slowly, 'this father of Johnsmith, his Weroames. . . .'

'Can I not. . . ?'

'May I. . . ?'

'No!' he thundered. 'Do I want those whom he has bewitched to go? But *you go*!' he said to Rawhunt. 'I will have a trail of scouts to tell me the news day by day. Less than fifty braves,' he said bitterly, 'could have killed them all!'

Rawhunt's scouts brought back word that Newport's ship carried many men but few supplies and that Father Newport and the sailors from the canoes with wings traded much more liberally with the Powhatans than Johnsmith had been willing to do, that as much copper as you could comfortably tuck into an arm now bought corn and squirrel meat which the niggard Johnsmith had paid for with barely enough to make the palm of your hand tighten.

Powhatan's lip twisted sardonically as he visualized the generous Newport.

'He must come soon to visit me, for *I* would trade with Father Newport.'

Then the birds of the forest chattered the news so that it was rumored even before it became known. The city of the English had burned. Jamestown had burned to the ground! In the greatest frost in over fifty cohonks the English were driven from their homes to seek shelter in the trees, on the icy ground, not knowing, as Powhatan's people knew, that they could build their homes in a day from the laced boughs of saplings. And they died – of cold, of hunger, of sheer weariness.

Powhatan listened quietly, wonderingly. One did not die of cold when there was wood for fires – of hunger when the forest was full, for the cold had driven all the animals from the north – of weariness, what was that?

'We will go – we will take them food,' Nantequos said.

Powhatan glared at him. 'Let their Oke provide for them. If he chooses that they shall perish!'

But he was troubled. There was much they owned that he would possess, much knowledge they had he, too, would learn. For him the story was but half told. He had not seen the Weroames, nor fully penetrated the Conjuror, Johnsmith.

'You and Pocahontas will go to Paspahegh – to Jamestown. . . . ' He twisted the odd name on his tongue. They were silent instantly. 'And you will take food and gifts to Johnsmith and his people. You will tell them that we will help them to build their city, to keep them warm – every four or five Suns we will send food. But you will tell them, too, that Powhatan, who is mightier than the King of England, who is mightier than the Weroames Newport, and whose Oke is mightier than their God, would have this Father Newport come.'

'Even Rawhunt says he is not greater than Johnsmith,' Nantequos said defensively.

'Perhaps not,' Powhatan said. 'But he is more generous. And if I am to save your precious blood brother and his people *I must have copper!*'

CHAPTER SIX

Jamestown was a charred triangle. It might have been inhabited by the dead, for no voice rose, no being stirred.

Pocahontas and Nantequos left their train and stepped out from the forest into the clearing. She was afraid, but she was not afraid when she thought of Nantequos. *The mighty cannon that could sweep the trees at one hundred paces would not lay low a blood brother of Johnsmith.* They walked side by side toward the burned palisade.

'Do they not have guards?' Pocahontas asked uneasily.

'Johnsmith will sense us with his magic,' Nantequos answered stiffly, moving without grace because he was alert.

There was a shout, and they stood, frozen. *Now*, the crash of thunder, the rake of stone?

And then, suddenly, Johnsmith, the points of his doublet unfastened, running to them across the frozen field, running and calling. Pocahontas and Nantequos stood, feeling his warmth engulf them.

'The Princess Pocahontas – and Nantequos!' He embraced Nantequos, but he did not embrace her. Instead, he took her hand and touched it with his lips. She watched his head, his hand and hers, then as he drew away she watched still her hand, which tingled and was warm as her cheeks. She put her hand suddenly in the folds of her robe.

'Powhatan has sent you food,' Nantequos said. 'And we have come to help you rebuild your city.'

Johnsmith paled and closed his eyes, as though he could not bear what he had heard. He rubbed his hand across his face and shouted, and white men came scurrying out like strange animals to gawk and stammer words she knew meant 'thanks'. She stared at the dirty, ragged, starved men and looked again at Johnsmith, who moved with authority among them, with catlike grace. She had thought of the great cats when she had seen him first, with his whiskers and his tawny coloring. He seemed as foreign to these, his people, as he did to the race of Powhatan – more, for Johnsmith and Powhatan were alike, though Powhatan was tall and Johnsmith not, though Johnsmith's body was white and gold, like sunlit cloud. . . .

Nantequos had called their train from the forest, and they came bearing venison and squirrels, raccoons and bread, and many baskets of corn. The eyes of the English gleamed so that it was unpleasant to look at them; she knew if it were not for their Captain they would have fallen on food and devoured it raw.

Her people would not take their gifts inside the charred walls, but laid them there in the center of the clearing, and then retreated to the safety of the trees.

'And you,' Johnsmith said to her, 'are you, too, afraid?'

'No,' she said, gazing at him straight.

'You must not think that for such a great gift as this my people would be so base as to betray you. Our Father Newport, the Weroames, would thank you himself.'

He ordered men with guns to guard the food while it was carried inside the walls, and she thought: *How perfidious are these people that their own Werowance cannot trust them!*

But the English were not all as base as the hungry men without. There was President Ratcliff, a man of great self-pride and blustery manner, Master Scrivener, whose hair was so light it was almost white, falling to his shoulders in thin wispy curls. He frightened her at first because he seemed to wear eyes over his eyes, set in square boxes, but later she was amazed to learn that, like Johnsmith's magic jewel, they were covered by frozen air which the white men called 'glass'. And Master George Percy, a handsome brave who peered down at her over a lifted nose. He wore a long knife at his side, and he kept his hand on the butt, bright with metal. But most she liked 'Master Hunt, our Preacher,' who was alive and taut like a stretched sapling, whose eyes were bright and probing, and whose smile was gentle. 'What does he say?' she asked Johnsmith. 'He says he likes you.' And she nodded, satisfied.

Johnsmith took her hand and led her and Nantequos down to the shore where a canoe with a hacked-off tail was being pulled onto the sand.

A man in clothes that seemed very fine after the others' – all but George Percy's – climbed out and came quickly toward them.

'It is our Weroames, Captain Newport,' Johnsmith said.

His face was furrowed and nearly as dark as Powhatan's, like old deer leather. His hair was gray, though he was not old. Before he reached them he spoke out in a booming voice that startled them.

'The great White Chief bids you forever welcome in his city, and he thanks you now for coming with many gifts,' Johnsmith translated.

'Powhatan urges that you send a canoe up the river, so that he can load it with corn. He desires that Captain Newport comes, so that they can know each other.'

Captain Newport ordered boxes brought from the clumsy canoe, and he opened them upon the beach.

'He brings you gifts from our great King in England showing his love for Powhatan and you,' Johnsmith said.

Captain Newport presented them with a long knife such as George Percy carried, its handle ornamented with yellow metal. With a flourish Johnsmith drew it from its case, and its blade quivered and shimmered in the sun.

There were bracelets of copper for Nantequos and Pocahontas and Powhatan. There was an earthen jug that Johnsmith handled gently.

'It is firewater,' he said. 'I would like to be there when Powhatan drinks this.'

'Fire! Water! It has fire in it?' Nantequos hesitated to touch it.

'No! It looks like water and it tastes like fire. If Powhatan does not like it, tell him to take another drink. But tell him, not too many at one time. It has the quality of bestowing great happiness in the night – and great sadness in the morning.'

Captain Newport was speaking. 'He asks,' Johnsmith said, 'if you will stay and share the feast for which you have provided the food.'

'No,' Nantequos said. 'We must go.'

'But we will come again,' Pocahontas promised, 'in three Suns – with more food. And we will bring braves to help you cut the trees. . . . ' Her eyes swept the burned fort.

Johnsmith ordered men to carry their gifts to the gates. Then he walked with them out of the walls and across the clearing. He had not spoken of his gift to Nantequos, and she knew her brother wondered.

As though he read her thoughts, Johnsmith stopped and caught Nantequos by the shoulder. 'Alas, my great gift for you went with all else, in the fire. I must wait until our ship has gone again and then returned from England. Now, to show my love, I have only this.'

From the depths of his great leg coverings he drew something and held it out on his open palm. It was a stone and a small piece of metal. He bent and gathered the dry grass and twigs and made a little pile. They watched him as they watched their Priests at home, but they were more sure of Johnsmith's magic.

He struck the stone and steel sharply together once and twice, and nothing happened, but the third time a little spark flew out, and the fourth time the grass caught fire. They exclaimed in awe, for fire, which was so carefully cherished, had never been produced like this nor so quickly – from a stone and a tiny piece of metal. Johnsmith put the two pieces into Nantequos's hand. He looked at them; then, as Johnsmith had done, he gathered grass and twigs. He struck the stone rapidly, once, twice, three times, four – and no fire came – five and six – Johnsmith took hold of Nantequos's hands from behind and struck the metal, just so, against the stone – a spark came out – and the grass burned.

Nantequos handed back the gift to Johnsmith. 'Without you, I cannot work your magic,' he said sadly.

'You can work it. Try once more – not too fast – not too slow.'

Once again Nantequos gathered the grass and twigs as though he followed a ritual of the priest – and then, just so, he struck the stone with the metal, a spark flew out, and the grass burned. Nantequos jumped backward to view his handiwork in fascination and fear.

'All the world will call me Firemaker,' he said.

Johnsmith laughed heartily and happily, and then they three laughed. Nantequos embraced Johnsmith.

'What gift could I give you to equal this?'

Johnsmith smiled at Pocahontas. 'And what gift can I give you to equal yours to me?' She looked into his eyes that crinkled though they showed regret.

'I need no gift.'

He drew out a little bag and opened it, and taking her hand he slipped a band of bright metal on her finger.

'My blood, which I did not shed because of you, is yours. And since you do not ask my life, I give you a drop of my heart's blood so you will think of me and know – if one is needed to shed his blood for you, *I* am that one!'

She listened so intently to his words she did not look down till he raised her hand and slowly turned the ring. A bright red stone shone as she had never seen a jewel give light. She gasped and covered it quickly with her other hand. His blood and Nantequos's had mingled, but for *her* he had taken his *heart's* blood.

He lifted her hand to his face and brushed it with his lips, which fluttered with the lightness of a moth's wings.

Her heart constricted so that she could not speak. She turned away toward the forest, her hands still locked.

'Show me, Pocahontas,' Nantequos said.

She started to run, not answering.

CHAPTER SEVEN

She was no stranger to Jamestown. She knew them all, the braves and the starvelings. And all honored her, for she fed them. Each six or seven Suns she came with her maidens, who now entered the fort fearlessly and talked with their hands to the Englishmen or bartered with them. Nantequos came, too, but his braves worked in the forest or showed the English how to make their wigwams – better, Johnsmith told her, than any they had had before. 'But in the spring, when the ground has thawed, we will build true palisadoes and a fort. . . .'

'Against whom?'

He looked at her. 'All your father's nations are not our friends.'

Opechancano, she thought. And she accepted that.

She knew them all: the mighty Weroames, who seemed not so mighty, in spite of his great voice and unreal laugh, as Powhatan or Johnsmith, no mightier than her uncles Opitchapan and Kekatok, who were Werowances but by no means Weroames; and Master Hunt, whom Johnsmith called the good, who talked to her excitedly and ardently of God, his hands sweeping the heavens. Is their God, too, beyond the sun?

She knew Johnsmith's enemies and friends, knew them better than Johnsmith, she felt, though she did not speak their language nor they hers, but with her they were not guarded. She knew, too, much of the magic of the white man, had learned it was *not* magic, but part of the wonder of knowledge that they possessed. She longed, more than their magic, to possess their knowledge, for the humblest of them accepted naturally secrets which were to her unfathomable.

Johnsmith's books had burned, and he grieved for them, more than for anything else. And what were books? He showed her one, and she traced her fingers over the strange signs, so tiny that one marveled they were ever painted, without beauty, without color or pattern. He told her knowledge was within these books, and she wanted to take this poor burned thing and sleep with it between her breasts, so that she would learn all the things these English knew.

But Johnsmith took it from her gently. 'Don't make an idol of it. I will teach you to read, and then you will learn – with *such* speed. For *your* magic is in here,' and he bent and kissed her brow.

Each time he touched her with his lips, she felt strange, as though she must go away and be alone, so that her skin would not lose the permeating sensation.

Johnsmith *wrote* books, and that meant his knowledge must be greater than theirs, for he put the knowledge into them for others to take out.

She loved to watch him write, to sit without stirring, while he made the strange patterns on the white substance he called paper, to watch him making knowledge. He asked her questions some-times, as he wrote, for he was making knowledge about the land of Powhatan.

'And when you have passed ten, how many?'

'Ninghsapooeksku.'

'How many is that?'

She spread her hands twice.

'How do you say . . . ' He held up his hands once, and then one finger.

'Kaskeke necut.'

'Ten-one,' he said, and wrote.

'Now again . . . ' He held up his hands twice.

'Ninghsapooeksku.'

'Ve-ry slow-ly.'

'Ningh-sa-poo-ek-sku.'

'Impossible. He rubbed his head. 'The sounds . . . '

'*You* say them,' she said, surprised.

'I parrot them. But – Do you have an alphabet, Pocahontas?' He tried in the sounds of her words. 'Ah-beh-chuh-del – But no, you don't have a "d",' he said, in English. "Say deh" – "deh." '

'Teh teh!'

'And you don't have an "f". Say 'eff"!'

'Ev!'

He wrote, his brow creased in concentration. What he had asked her had seemed so strange, she got up to peer over his shoulder as he wrote, though she had no hope of finding meaning in the black symbols.

'What do you write?' she asked at last, wonderingly.

He showed her. 'Only numbers. This means' he bent to study his own letters – ' "Ninghsapooeksku." '

Suddenly he held up his hand. 'Wait!' For a long moment he bent over the paper, mumbling sounds as he wrote. At last he pointed to it with pride. It meant no more than anything else.

'What does it say?'

'Here in English . . . ' He read: 'Bid Pochaontas bring hither two little baskets, and I will give her white beads to make her a chain.' And in Powhatan he translated: 'Kekaten pokahontas patiaguaugh niugh tanks monotyens neer mowchick rawenock autowgh.'

Her eyes were wide. 'Does it say *that*?' she gasped. '*My* name? Have you made knowledge with *my* name?'

His eyes glowed as he looked at her. 'Yes,' he said gently. 'I have made knowledge with *your* name – Pocahontas.'

CHAPTER EIGHT

They set out up the rivers, and Werowocomoco waited to receive them.

'Tell me again of this Weroames,' Powhatan demanded.

'He is a man of great friendship,' Pocahontas said. 'But it is here,' she touched her teeth, then her heart, 'not here.'

'Yet why does he pay so great an amount in copper, when Johnsmith will not pay?'

'He does not barter. He says, 'What do you want?' and that is what he pays.'

'And if I say, "I want your guns, your land – I want *all* your copper" – will he pay then?'

'No, he will not do that. He is a clever man, but he is not such a man as you or Johnsmith.'

'He sounds like a fool.'

'He is not a fool, but you will bargain with him well. Tell him to put all he wants to trade upon the ground, and *you* will say what it is worth.'

He stared at her incredulously.

She told Powhatan what would help, for was he not her lord and father? Told him all except that the English were weak and owned no magic. She told him to still the ache in her chest which was the wound of her self-doubt.

'And Johnsmith?' Powhatan asked.

'As Rawhunt said, a great length of copper buys the corn Johnsmith would have given you a wrap-around-your-finger for.'

Powhatan studied her, and she knew he was wondering, because of what she told him, if she was free from the bewitchment.

'They are different from Johnsmith,' she said simply, wanting him to know.

He understood. 'He would not leave them?'

'No.'

'When he comes, we will treat him as our Werowance. He can

58

have what he wills from us – what *women* . . . ' He looked at her questioningly, but he made a statement. 'That will not change him.'

'No.'

They sat, unstirring, and neither cared to probe the other's thoughts.

The great canoe rode the river, but Captain Newport did not come ashore; Johnsmith with twenty men moved across the floods toward Werowocomoco, and Johnsmith was suspicious. Though it was Nantequos who greeted him, Johnsmith crossed no bridge until his men and Powhatan's were intermingled, Powhatan's son always in the middle.

'*Why* is he suspicious? *Why* is he afraid?' Powhatan demanded.

'Johnsmith is like Wahunsonacock,' Pocahontas said softly. 'He will make no mistakes.'

He considered that. 'But how do I know they will not seize me – in my own wigwam – with their guns and magic?'

'Captain Newport bears an order from their King James that the Savages – which they call us – must never be offended, that they must move among us in friendship and not arouse our anger.'

Powhatan stared at her in amazement, for Rawhunt had told him nothing of this. But if it were true, then why did Johnsmith come armed and alert?

Forty platters of bread were stretched to make a path for the guests. The sound of pipes pierced the air, and rattles shook in rhythm. Powhatan sat on his leather cushion decked with pearls and shells, his robe broidered in designs of peak, on either side a stag, and on the back a man. Around him were grouped his wives, those who were fair and young. His braves and Cockarouses flanked him in rows.

'Ho, Johnsmith, Werowance of Powhatan!'

'Ho, Father!'

It was the first time he had said it, and it stirred her as the firewater Nantequos had brought and which she had sipped. Powhatan had said: *You are a chief and welcome to sit in our councils.* And Johnsmith had said: *You are my father, and I will obey your will.* But she doubted he knew what he had said, for he called Captain Newport father, yet he obeyed no will but his own.

Powhatan's eyes glowed with pleasure, and he ordered Owerowok to make a place, so that Johnsmith could sit beside him. The

Wironausqua of the Appomattucks brought the Calumet, and it was passed, Johnsmith drawing deep to the satisfaction of all.

He called and ordered that the gifts he had brought be placed before Powhatan. Powhatan's eyes fastened on the entrance, and he said, without turning, 'Captain Newport has not come.'

Johnsmith said nothing. When a large box was set before him and opened, he took out first a coverlet stuffed with the down of fowls, light but warm as bear fur. And then a headdress, a rich affair with a high crown and narrow brim to which was fastened a red feather, curled and thick, such as she had never seen. He set it on his own head, and it was prouder than the bluejay Nantequos wore. Then he set it on the head of Powhatan, and he looked fierce and magnificent.

When he was done and Powhatan's eyes had accepted in pleasure, and Kekatok and Tomakkin and Rawhunt would have spoken to tell the love of Powhatan for the White Werowance, Johnsmith held up his hand for silence, and an Englishman was pulled into the room by a white creature with dun spots such as could not be dreamed of: like a rabbit, save with four long legs, a pointed nose like a weasel, but large – to meet your knee – panting and straining at the rope that held it. It leaped upon Johnsmith and licked his hand, while all the Court of Powhatan gaped.

'It is an animal from England,' Johnsmith said, lifting and fondling it. 'A dog – not like the creatures here – it is the truest friend to its master.' He bent and let it lap his lips with its pink tongue. 'It is swifter than Powhatan's swiftest braves. And when the arrow has found its mark and though Powhatan's eye has lost the quarry, *he* will find it.'

He released the animal and pushed it toward Powhatan, and quickly it was standing upright, its paws on Powhatan's knees, its tongue seeking Powhatan's face.

'It is a great and faithful friend to man, so loved in England that our people have named a star for it – the Dog Star.'

Powhatan pushed it away as though he was not sure he cared to hold an animal for whom a star was named, but Pocahontas gathered the beast in her arms and felt his love and desire to be loved.

'We will call him Pummahump,' she said.

'The Star,' Johnsmith translated into English.

Powhatan spoke, and almost instantly there was food at his side. He selected a morsel and held it out to the dog, and thus he weaned him from Pocahontas.

'These are precious jewels,' he said. And instantly Kekatok and Tomakkin and Rawhunt started their orations.

They spoke long. Sweat rolled from them, as each declaimed passionately of the love of Powhatan for the White Werowance who had come over the bottomless sea, from the land which was the Antipodes. Kekatok faltered, but Tomakkin caught his groan on a rising note, and told how the generosity of Johnsmith was only excelled by that of Powhatan, who was the most generous of all. And as Tomakkin's voice quavered, Rawhunt picked up the thread and told in tones which never seemed other than sarcastic of the boundless devotion of this bringer-of-gifts, whose life had been saved by the daughter of Powhatan and who was blood brother to Nantequos and therefore to the whole nation of Powhatan, and of the everlasting league of friendship which existed between the English and the Powhatans.

It seemed to Pocahontas that they would never cease, but they did, one after the other, till even Rawhunt gasped for breath and gulped eagerly the drink Owerowok held for him.

Powhatan sat back in the welcome silence, a sleepy Pummahump on his lap.

'I am very contented that you have come. But where is your father whom I much desire to see? Is he not with you?'

'He is still aboard the pinnace. Tomorrow he will come.'

Powhatan thought, stroked his chin with one hand, the dog with the other. Suddenly he looked up, smiling.

'I hold this beast, and gifts of value have been placed before me, but your first promise to me you have not kept. Where are the pieces that shoot stones and fire, and where is the grindstone?'

'I gave them to Rawhunt,' Johnsmith said innocently, 'but he refused to carry them.'

Powhatan's eyes shot to his messenger, and Johnsmith looked, too. Rawhunt's twisted face twisted into yet more awful expressions.

'Is that not true, Rawhunt?'

Rawhunt breathed deep so that his crooked shoulder spasmed and he caught it with his other hand.

'Aye!' He snarled the word.

Powhatan held his belly and laughed. 'Can you not find a small piece,' he demanded, 'that is *not* rooted to the ground?'

He sent Nantequos to lead Johnsmith and his men to a large wigwam which would lodge them. Then Powhatan invited them to come and feast, and they talked long as they filled their bellies with the deer's head soup, the roast oysters served on green leaves, venison and beavertail, roasted herons flavored with hickory ash, and bread made from chinquapon nuts.

They danced and sang before the fire, and Powhatan told ancient stories of their race. Johnsmith told of the woman who had been Queen of England for forty-five cohonks and had died but four cohonks past. He told of her red wigs and her many wigwams which were built of stone, towering into the sky itself; how she had built tall ships which had conquered the sea and sent her Werowances around the world, so that she ruled them all – the sky, the sea, the land. When Powhatan had finished speaking, or Johnsmith had, the other would pause appreciatively, for each told mighty tales.

Before Johnsmith retired to his lodging, Powhatan said to him: 'You have been received as a Werowance of Powhatan. What we have is yours. Demand what you will for your comfort and pleasure for the night.'

'Powhatan is my father,' Johnsmith said, and Pocahontas doubted that he knew what was being offered him. Powhatan waited, and she held her breath, since she knew *why* he waited. 'He is generous and has given me all that I desire.' He bent from the waist and left with his men.

He had not asked what Powhatan had been so sure he would, and Powhatan sighed, whether in relief or regret Pocahontas did not know. She only buried her head in his broidered cape till the shells hurt her.

Powhatan sent a virgin and Ponoiske, his own young wife, their bodies painted red with puccoon and oiled, to be Johnsmith's handmaidens and bedfellows.

For Johnsmith had not asked for Pocahontas, as Powhatan had been sure he would.

Ponoiske and the virgin, Antra, returned before Pocahontas had left Powhatan's wigwam. He stared at them.

'He sent us away, Lord,' Ponoiske said defensively.

'Did you not please him?'

'We tried, Lord.' Ponoiske was close to tears. 'He *said* we pleased him. He said he was hot with desire for us and longed to frølic with us both nightlong, for the English are mighty makers of papoose. But as Werowance he could not sport so in the presence of his braves, for they had none. . . .'

'Does he think I have wives and virgins for his whole nation?' Powhatan said indignantly.

'He said if he had his *own* wigwam . . .'

'And he touched you not, nor the virgin either?'

'His braves were calling out and begging us to come and lie with them, and he was angry and ordered us to return. . . .'

'Next time he shall *have* his own wigwam, and we will learn how mighty are these English. To me, it is mightier yet they are alone these moons and have no squaws,' Powhatan marveled. 'Do you think he speaks the truth about his friendship if he will not mate with our squaws?' he asked Pocahontas.

Pocahontas did not know.

Johnsmith brought his White Father to Powhatan with a brazen toot of trumpets and a show of power. Soldiers marched before, their armor glinting in the sunlight, which lit the damp world to brilliance, its light reflected in the drops that glistened on the leaves.

Powhatan received them, and the Calumet was smoked.

The English Weroames talked at length in his loud voice, which rang in their ears, and he laughed much, though when Johnsmith translated, nothing seemed amusing.

They feasted, but it was not as yesterday when the tales had savored the good food, for they were under the constraint of speaking through Johnsmith, and he was short in his words. It was plain he was not sure how his Weroames might act and hence did not himself act freely as he had before. And he did not translate all that Captain Newport said.

Instead of talk there was much dancing, and Nantequos and Pocahontas joined to stir the others. Squaw and brave, in and out, they wove the chain about the fire, to the certain rhythm of the rattles.

And then one or then another showed his feat, as rattles clattered in sudden discord to indicate applause. Nantequos leaped till it seemed his body, stretched from toes to fingers, was no thicker than an arrow's stem. Pacahontas was a deer and fled the hunter. With bounds she leaped the thickets, sought the heights, and stopped to hear and scent her fell pursuer. But his arrow found her and she, a desolate beast, sank, sick-eyed, in the firelight.

Posts painted with maidens' faces were planted in a circle, and Pocahontas locked arms with two maidens and pivoted for the wild gyrations of the braves, who, armed with whips, branches, and tomahawks, protected the maidenhood of Powhatan. In a mad whirl the braves raced, while the maidens slowly turned, their eyes watching those who came on hands and haunches to invade the sacred circle. When they tried to enter they would be beat or even hit with tomahawks, but if they gained the circle they, too, could dance, chanting, around the maids.

It was observed that Captain Newport put his hands over his

ears to protect them from the high notes of the pipes, but none remarked upon his action, which was lacking in courtesy.

Abruptly, Powhatan ended the festivities, and it was agreed that tomorrow they would bargain. The English gathered their men and returned to their boats.

Early, Powhatan awaited their coming, and they came as yesterday, wearing armor and carrying guns and hatchets atop long poles. Again they smoked the Calumet, which was not usual the second day, but Powhatan feared their suspicion.

He said nothing till they had eaten. Then he looked at Johnsmith and Captain Newport, his eyes hooded.

'Why do my friends come so?' he asked, indicating the guns and armor. 'Seeing that I am your friend and do not come with bows or arrows? What do you doubt?'

'In our land it is an honor that we accord great rulers,' Johnsmith said. 'It is not to doubt your kindness, but to appear before you in our best, as you wear paint and headdresses to impress your friends as well as your enemies.'

Powhatan grunted, satisfied, but Captain Newport demanded to know what had been said, and when Johnsmith told him, he ordered all their men to retire to the waterside some sixty paces distant, and Johnsmith seemed annoyed.

'Let us trade, Powhatan,' he said gruffly.

'We need not take so long. Let your people put all your hatchets and your copper together, and for it I will give you corn.' Pocahontas sensed the breathlessness with which her father spoke, for he did not believe the English would do these things.

Johnsmith smiled scornfully. 'The Chickhominies acquainted me with that trick. Show me what you will give for one piece, Powhatan. And we will trade.'

Powhatan's eyes studied Johnsmith's face and then Captain Newport's, who anxiously tried to understand what passed. Powhatan looked affronted.

'It is not agreeable to my greatness to trade for trifles in his peddling manner.'

'Powhatan!' Johnsmith said in disgust. 'You take us for children – and behave like a child.'

Pocahontas gasped, but she knew Johnsmith was right and that it would be told from city to city if Powhatan bettered the trades that had been made hitherto by his Werowances, but she trembled at her father' wrath, for he shook with fury at Johnsmith's words.

Captain Newport was pulling at Johnsmith's sleeve, saying a

hundred things which always ended in the high note of a question.

'You, who have trust in none,' Powhatan said loftily, 'fear to tell your Weroames what I have said.'

'I trust both him and you, but this is a trick. I know it.'

Captain Newport was not to be denied, and at last Johnsmith turned to him with a flow of angry words, and it was plain he quoted what Powhatan had said. Captain Newport seemed surprised that there had been a disagreement, and he turned beaming upon Powhatan. Pocahontas thought, not happily, how Powhatan should thank her for the advice she had given him.

Captain Newport roared an order, and Johnsmith walked away, unwilling to have anything more to do with such nonsense.

But even Powhatan gasped when Captain Newport ordered sailors to bring twelve great pieces of copper. Then, composed, Powhatan had as many baskets of corn laid before the Weroames as Pocahontas knew Johnsmith had received for only one such copper.

With signs – for Johnsmith refused to return, pretending to be busy with the barge – Powhatan and Captain Newport congratulated each other, smiled and raised their hands in friendship.

When they were done with the trading and Powhatan had invited them to feast, Johnsmith came slowly back, whistling, his eyes pensively on his hands which played with some blue beads that Pocahontas saw and coveted, hoping he had brought her a present.

Powhatan saw them, too, and his eyes were nailed.

'We must return, Powhatan, without . . . ' Johnsmith said ironically ' . . . the boatload of corn you promised me. But, perhaps, like our cannon, your corn is still rooted in the ground.'

Powhatan could not take his eyes from the beads, seeing them so few and precious and so beautifully bright. He could not conceal his disappointment that Johnsmith had not brought them to trade.

'You must stay to feast,' Powhatan said, and in the same breath, 'What are those blue trinkets?'

Johnsmith quickly hid the beads in his leg covering.

'The tide is near ebb, Powhatan.'

'May I see your blue beads?'

'These?' Johnsmith brought them out again and held them carefully before Powhatan, but he did not relinquish them from his own hands. 'They are sky-colored,' he said, giving them importance.

Powhatan nodded. 'Pretty.'

'Yes.'

'For them I will give a large basket of corn.'

Johnsmith drew them back hastily. 'Not these, Powhatan. These are King's beads, and I will take them to my King in England.'

'Two large baskets!'

'Powhatan, I told you . . .'

'I will fill your *boat* with corn!'

The beads were again almost out of sight in Johnsmith's clothes. Slowly he raised his hand, looking at them lovingly and reluctantly.

'We-ell . . .' he said.

Powhatan seized them covetously. 'Let us eat!' he shouted, but he would not pause till he had carried his treasure to his wigwam.

Pocahontas moved to Johnsmith and smiled innocently.

'What will Powhatan say when he finds that every mother's son in Jamestown has blue beads by the peck to trade?' he asked ruefully.

'He will say: 'What a mighty trader is my White Werow-ance!'' '

'Jamestown has to eat,' Johnsmith said, and they laughed.

But still she wondered.

After the English returned to Jamestown Powhatan heard from Rawhunt's scouts: the Weroames and Johnsmith were no longer friends, but quarreled much; Johnsmith wanted the great canoe to sail again to England, because Newport's sailors were devouring the food that they had purchased; but the Weroames would not leave, since he was mad to find a golden metal he was sure was in the rivers, and he kept his men digging and washing, digging and sifting, and he stored the dirt aboard his ship which now rode low in the water where before it rode high.

CHAPTER NINE

The great geese retraced their flight northward, throating their vibrant cohonks, filing out behind their leaders to form arrowheads against the sky.

The early flowers pushed through the damp mold, budded and bloomed, the reds and purples first, more leisurely the yellows and the blues, preferring a warmer welcome. Dyes boiled in the pots till the women's hands matched the flowers' bright coloring; braves daubed their faces and their bodies with paint and ran and leaped in warlike exercises, shooting low with large arrowheads. At night they danced the graceful frenzied war dance to the beat of walnut shells against taut hide stretched over bowls half filled with water, while the dog Pummahump yelped and barked in ecstasy at their antics or howled at the sustained notes from their pipes.

There was no talk of war from Powhatan or the old and wise Cockarouses and Priests, but the God of Winter had moistened the ground with fertility, and the spring was the time to think of war and love. Without conscious purpose, braves sought squaws with urgency to make a papoose who would someday fill the places of the fallen.

From Jamestown, Rawhunt brought word of the building of the English city, the felling of great trees, the repairing of the palisades, the planting of corn, and the building of a wigwam for their Oke, whom they called God. All this was at Captain Smith's command. He drove his braves till their hands were blistered, their joints sockets of pain, and they cried out words of blasphemy against the God they claimed was great. These words were counted, and each night within the walls cold water was poured down their arms inside their clothes, a pitcher for each oath, which seemed not so great a punishment. But the white men howled, the blasphemies ceased. And, in spite of all, Rawhunt reported, those who followed Johnsmith loved him.

In the building of the fort, neither Captain Newport nor his men took any part, for from Sun's Rising to Sun's Lowering they shoveled earth from the back river, sifted it, and loaded what was in their nets into the ship. Because of this there was dissension between the Weroames and Johnsmith.

'What is this gold they seek?' Powhatan demanded, and Pocahontas pushed Johnsmith's heart's blood into her palm and showed him the yellow band.

'They call it also brass,' Powhatan said. 'It is not so fair as copper.'

And then came the news that Father Newport was to sail.

At last! the colonists cried, weary of his hungry sailors.

Powhatan sent twenty turkeys aboard his ship and asked for twenty metal swords as a parting gift – and got them! Powhatan's face gleamed when he saw them brought to Werowocomoco and laid at his feet. He lifted one and handled it, tested its point. They were not so fine as that King James had sent to him, but their reach was longer than a tomahawk, their purpose more sure, if the point was thrust at the right spot. 'If only,' he said, 'I had an English grindstone to make them sharp.'

The Captain sailed. The wings of the canoe spread like the white fowl of Oke himself, and Powhatan thought: *Johnsmith is niggardly and will not want to deal with us as his White Father has dealt. And* yet, *he has his Weroames's orders:* We are not to be offended.

He sent twenty turkeys to Johnsmith and demanded twenty swords.

He waited for his messengers, and when they came there was a sheet of copper and a basket of white beads and a string of ten blue beads.

Powhatan walked away from them in fury.

'Does he value so little a gift for which his father exchanged twenty strong swords?'

'It is as much as he would have paid before Captain Newport came,' Nantequos said unhappily. 'He has always refused to trade his weapons.'

Powhatan called for Rawhunt, and they squatted together, the straight, powerful Powhatan and the shriveled, crippled leader of his scouts, and his children could not hear what was being planned.

But Nantequos learned by the orders which were passed from Rawhunt to his braves, and soon hatchets and swords, and even a gun, were brought swiftly through the forest of Rawhunt's scouts and laid at Powhatan's feet.

'They are stolen,' Pocahontas said scornfully.

'Did he not trick me with his King's beads? And why would he keep his weapons from me? His Red Father? Does he mean to use them against me?'

'When he learns what Powhatan has done, will he not feel forced to use them?' Nantequos asked.

Powhatan's eyes were triumphant. 'How will he know? If a Paspahegh who comes to bring him an opossum lifts a hatchet, or a Youghtamond who brings a basket of red dye take away a sword beneath his robe, how will he know that the hatchet and the sword rest in the house of Powhatan?'

But Nantequos and Pocahontas knew that it was not thievery alone which Powhatan plotted when he sat with Rawhunt, his eyes gleaming balefully. They could not learn the treachery, but that it was intended they were sure.

But the news that Rawhunt brought next spread confusion among the Werowances of Powhatan. Another great canoe had come to Jamestown, its wings slanted to the wind and folding as it found its harbor. It was a ship that had sailed from England with Captain Newport and had been thought sunk in the heavy sea, but the Wind Gods had borne it to the islands in the south, and at last it had arrived, laden with foods for the worried white men and with strong and healthy braves to swell their number.

' "They will come in twenties – and in fifties – and in hundreds. . . . " ' Powhatan said glumly, quoting Opechancano.

But more! Johnsmith and sixty braves drilled and practised war outside the city walls, shot their firesticks at targets he had placed many paces off. And Johnsmith taught his men to seek the shelter of the slim trees, like Powhatan's braves, to cover themselves with leaves and branches, to stalk the forest, and to know the telltale signs the wariest brave could not conceal.

Powhatan turned to Nantequos accusingly. 'Why acts he thus?'

'I know only that there are few who know how to fight, and he would teach them.'

'Why now?'

'Before there were not men to work, and all were ill and miserable.'

'But whom does he mean to fight?'

'Perhaps he brings an army to find his lost hatchets and his arms,' Nantequos said.

Powhatan glared, but Rawhunt grunted. 'Perhaps the giddy son of Powhatan speaks well.'

'You mean Johnsmith knows. . . ?'

'He knows that red men, of one nation or another, increasingly steal from his stores. And all nations are subject to Powhatan.'

Powhatan sat moodily, staring inward. 'Has he said anything?' he asked at last.

'To me? I have not seen him. But he has *done*.'

'Done what?'

'Johnsmith has himself caught several thieves and beat them on their rumps with his sword flat, and some he has put in chains, including my scout, Borras,' Rawhunt said with approval. Pocahontas knew that in spite of his suspicions, Rawhunt admired Johnsmith and did not care for Powhatan's traffic with the Weroames.

'And how do our braves behave under this?'

'Many pieces have been returned, being said that they were found. And those who brought them were rewarded.'

'But does he think where these lost arms might go?'

'He knows only that none who steal are Pumaunkeys, and so he trades more generously with the braves of Opechancano,' Rawhunt said.

Powhatan twisted his great beak violently, grimacing. It had by no means been his purpose to profit Opechancano.

'I would send you to Jamestown, and you will ask him why he does these things. . . . '

'About the thieveries?' Rawhunt inquired.

'No, them you will not mention,' Powhatan said quickly. 'Say nothing of the thieveries. Ask Johnsmith why he readies his army. Does he intend to come into my country and destroy me? Ask him that! And say that the shooting of his firesticks can be heard in my own lodging, and it frightens my women and my children – and my daughter Pocahontas,' he added as a happy afterthought.

'What if Johnsmith asks of *our* war practises?' Nantequos said.

'Of them you will say that they are games. With us, it is not to prepare for war, but to practise our braves for the hunt, since after a long winter they are sluggish and ill-fit.'

'If Captain Smith asks Rawhunt about the thieveries?'

'If he speaks to you about them' – Powhatan said, and thought a moment – 'you must say that we are grieved that the children of Powhatan . . . Tell him to give you their names and tribes and we will see that they are punished fittingly,' he added on a positive note.

CHAPTER TEN

Rawhunt returned from Jamestown to say that Johnsmith knew the truth, that he had caught many thieves and had brought them to confess by threatening them with the terrible gunpowder.

And they had told him everything – that Powhatan sought his weapons and intended to preserve him and his men till Captain Newport returned. Then there would be a feast and Powhatan would destroy them, Johnsmith and Captain Newport and the whole race, and rest happy, counting coppers, puzzling over the guns, planting gunpowder, and *who* should be so mighty? For the magic of the white man was not magic, and Powhatan, possessing their knowledge, would conquer nations that threatened his extremes.

'He knows it all!' Powhatan said. 'There is nothing left but to destroy him, or destroy ourselves, battling him.' This had been Powhatan's constant philosophy from youth.

The Cockarouses of the Council nodded, but Rawhunt's crumpled face stayed in a grimace; he *thought*, and from the look in his eyes, it could be seen he thought.

'Speak, Rawhunt!'

'He speaks of you truly as "father" and himself as your "son".'

'But he will not forgive me *this*. You have told me that he *knows*. . .'

'He knows but does not want to know,' Rawhunt said. And then reluctantly he added, 'Have you thought of the cannon of the English – the firesticks that shatter a squirrel at a hundred paces? Have you thought that Opechancano is closer to Johnsmith than he has ever been because no Pamaunkeys have been caught stealing?'

'Let Rawhunt speak,' Powhatan said carefully, 'for he has thoughts.'

71

'Powhatan has thoughts also, for he said: "and my daughter Pocahontas" . . . '

Powhatan moved stiffly, as though he were afraid he would break a shoulder or a wrist.

'Speak further.'

'For Pocahontas, Johnsmith will do strange things. Let her go to Jamestown and ask the lives of those Powhatan is bound to protect. Let her tell of Powhatan's love for Johnsmith — not for the Weroames Newport, who may be lord over the waters and over all when he is here, but who is nothing when he has gone.'

'You mean that he desires Pocahontas? He could have had her. . . . '

'I wish it were that simple,' Rawhunt said. 'But send her anyway.'

There is an instant in the Budding of the Leaf when one's eyes quicken, because, save for the bare patches of ground where the grass has not yet sprouted, it is so like the Fall, for the sap of the trees is red, and the new leaf is red, and to stand on a rise and overlook a valley it is as though it has been touched by the paintbrush. It was on such a day that Pocahontas went to Jamestown.

She strode across the clearing ahead of the stooped and crooked Rawhunt because she feared to pause and would not have them think she was afraid. She stood before the gates, and they opened, and then her heart felt a welcome-home since Johnsmith waited for her. He let her make her orations to the newly come Captain Nelson and to President Ratcliff. But her eyes sought only his.

'I have come to beg the prisoners whom Johnsmith has kept,' she said quickly so that there would be no doubt of her mission, so that *he* would know she came from Powhatan.

They honored her, and in her bleached doeskin apron and cape she sat and let them bring her gifts, but she wondered why he did not send them all away, his Captain and his President, why *he* was humblest.

'Powhatan grieves,' she said, 'that some of the captains, or others of his braves, have acted in bad faith, and he would punish them as they deserve. If you will give them to me, Powhatan will deal with them.'

He did not answer. 'Pocahontas, if you will spend the night within our fort, you shall have my wigwam, and I will sleep outside like one of your guards. It should not be strange, for I have slept within the power of Powhatan.'

It was not strange at all, save that he should sleep outside.

In the night he walked with her among the crude buildings of

72

the English, and they looked at the merry moon and at the stars.

'Pocahontas, all you ask you shall have, for I will keep no prisoners from you. You saved my life.'

She regarded him soberly, fingering his heart's blood, accepting this reason for his giving her the prisoners.

He turned to her and smiled, the quick gleam of his teeth shining in the moonlight.

'Powhatan does not love the blood brother of Nantequos as much as he used to.'

'No, not so much.'

'Is it because of the blue beads?'

'It is because Johnsmith takes the orders of Captain Newport. Before, when Johnsmith dealt alone with Powhatan or the Werowances subject to Powhatan . . . ' She hesitated to go on, but he understood.

'Powhatan does not think me so great a Werowance as he once did – or so powerful?'

'No,' she said unhappily.

His arm encircled her shoulder, pulling her against him. 'I will tell you truly, Pocahontas – in my own land I am not a great Werowance, and few listen to the voice of John Smith.'

'No!' she cried, thinking she had hurt him, and he would now make himself less than he was.

He laughed wryly. 'Truth. But *here* I am a great Werowance, for the English do not eat unless I feed them. But even in Jamestown I have enemies who would as soon see me stretched on the bilboes or dangling from a tree arm.'

She caught his hand fiercely. 'Then gather up your army and Powhatan and Nantequos will help you destroy these enemies. And you *will* be a great Werowance, for Powhatan will give you a nation of your own.' For she knew how Powhatan believed in Johnsmith, and how he would reward such a brave if he sat, trustworthy and loyal, in Powhatan's Council.

Johnsmith laughed. 'Many believe I would do just that,' he said. 'But I don't want to leave the English – only to teach them to feed and to protect themselves and to live in this rich, happy land.'

She remembered what Nantequos had said to Powhatan, and she thought with the same ache: *He has not the will!*

She lay long in Johnsmith's wigwam, silent among her sleeping maidens. What a secret he had told her! How it would affect Powhatan and Opechancano and all the Werowances of Powhatan's nations if they knew that among his own people he was accounted less than great. And Johnsmith had known what it meant when he told her. Even while she grieved that he had not the will to make himself great, she guarded a warmth against her heart because he had trusted her and her alone. *I have the will,* she thought, *the will for him.*

She rose and threaded her way among the squaws to the door, which was a patch of golden whiteness from the moonlight. She stood a second, breathing deep the fresh night air of early spring. Then she stepped outside.

Johnsmith did not lie beside the wigwam as he had said he would, and she knew an instant of disappointment. *But*, she thought, *he has gone to share the wigwam of Master Scrivener, his friend, or to sleep next his braves.* Then she saw a light, and she moved toward it.

Inside, framed by the entrance, sat Johnsmith, his head bent in a pool of light from two candles, one long, one short. He was making knowledge with his stick and his little pot of black paint, and she felt drawn as a rabbit by the snake's magic.

He was unaware of her for a long time. Then he looked, squinting, and she was there with him, included by his smile, though she had not moved closer than the door.

'My Princess,' he said. 'You, too, are sleepless.'

'Do you ever sleep who take the stars of night into your room to work by?'

The candles had been a marvelous mystery to her, and he had given her many. She had lighted them for Powhatan, who prized them for they held the light so much more steadily than the oiled torches which smoked and flared.

'This is work I have not time for in the day,' he said, rubbing his eyes. 'I wish I did, for it blurs my eyes to work so finely by candlelight.'

'It is your book?'

'No, but it must go with my book on Captain Nelson's ship when she returns, and so I need to finish it. It is a map.'

'A map?'

'A picture of the land of Powhatan – the land we call Virginia.'

It was the first time she had heard the word, and she repeated it, sounding the soft syllables.

'Named for our great Queen of whom I told you, who lived a virgin all her life.'

She moved closer, and he put his arms around her, drawing her to the table.

'Here is the Bay, and here is Powhatan's River, and here the

Pamaunkey. This is Jamestown, and over here is Werowocomoco.'

She looked at it intently. This new kind of knowledge she could
comprehend slightly, for she had seen pictures like this on pieces
of bark to show a trail with a hill, a tree, a rock, or the bend of a
river as landmarks.

'Some time I shall fill all this in' – his hand covered the eastern
shore and swept north to the land of the Susquehannocks – 'when
I have explored it all and can draw it correctly. Perhaps up here is
the passage to the great South Sea. I have drawn it thus . . . ' He
indicated a bay to the west, an extention of a river which emptied
into the Chesapeake.

'Is this not a very wonderful thing?' she asked. 'Even to the
English?'

'It is the first map ever made of Virginia, and it is a true one –
as true as I can make it.'

'And will you not be a very great Werowance when your King
sees this?'

He smiled, knowing that she was troubled by their earlier conversation.

'Sweet child, would you love me more if I were a great Werowance?'

She considered this seriously. 'No,' she said at last, definitely.
'But I think it a pity, since inside you are so great – in here!' and
she touched his brow as he had touched hers with his lips, where
he had told her that her knowledge would be stored.

He gave her a hard hug, such as a brave gives a child he loves.
And he laughed to relieve the tension.

'I agree with you,' he said. 'I certainly agree with you.'

The prisoners were turned over to Rawhunt, and they did not
like his sour welcome, although they were taken to a great feast,
no longer shackled. And while they fed, Master Scrivener, whose
four blue eyes twinkled with mischief, pressed the firewater upon
Rawhunt till Johnsmith bade him stop. But then Rawhunt did
not want to stop, and in a while he was giggling and embracing
Johnsmith and Master Scrivener, and she marveled, for Rawhunt
had always been a stern teacher and guardian. But as she saw the
fun in these two braves and that they teased Rawhunt because he
was so serious, she relaxed and thought of playful tricks to tease
them with when they came visiting. These thoughts made her
laugh within herself, and for the first time since Powhatan had
sent her she was happy.

The time of the Corn's Ripening is the pleasant time, when stalks are head-high to a maid, and she can lose herself from those who long to try their manhood, when it is still a game, and laughter rules the muscles of the lips and heart . . . pumpkins are green and orange in their wide leaves, and beans trail up the cornstalks, persimmon trees lose their leaves and show stark with the not yet ripe, puckery fruit . . . the tanglewood is heavy with the odor of honeysuckle, trees are burdened with their fruits of burnished red and yellow, and cress is light and delicate and crisp.

And it is pleasant to be a host and have the baskets filled with melons and with scuppernong grapes, with haunches of the fat bear, and always turkeys, strung out on a pole, and so a-visiting, and see the bright eyes and eager smiles of hungry men who find importance in a maid of thirteen cohonks.

So Pocahontas frequented Jamestown, and she was greeted by the highest and the lowest, and they spoke words of love to her, but they did not ask what Opechancano asked, or the driven youths among the rows of corn. To them she was a kind of Oke, and thus they reverenced her.

Johnsmith grew used to her visits and did not come out each time she came. But when she went to find him, he always smiled and sometimes took her upon his lap and showed her what he drew or what he wrote. And she thought: *How strange these English act!* Once she brought bee's honey and with her sticky fingers embraced him, leaving his whiskers smeared. And for a man who laughed so deep, his voice was soft, under his breath, though it was constant, as he washed himself in a pot of water.

Again she found him bathing in the river and she threw off her robe and leaped in, too, and though his men only stared at her and stood like wooden dolls, he swam away downstream and came up where she could not play with him.

With Nantequos he was more friendly. They swam together,

raced, and wrestled, though each had to teach the other, for their wrestling was different. Once, because it was a curious thing that Johnsmith should avoid her in this way, Nantequos said:

'My brother, Pocahontas is no longer a child, but sits with the squaws of Powhatan.'

'Truly, I know no one so young as wise as she!'

'It is past time for her to have raised on her skin the symbols of womanhood.'

'You mean the marks pounced with a needle on the brow and breast?'

'Yes.'

'Not on Pocahontas,' Johnsmith said urgently. 'She would not mark so fair a face – or body!' And so, when they came to her, she refused to permit the needle, but had them paint the signs.

She came upon him one day when everything in his wigwam was packed away. Boxes were stored in a corner. He held the book and map she had seen him make in his hand as though its value were in its weight – and then he sealed them carefully in a wrapper. She looked at the orderliness of his wigwam and asked:

'Do you go with your book? Does Johnsmith go with Captain Nelson?'

'No,' he said and pulled her down beside him on the ground so that they talked as children do. 'But when the *Phoenix* sails, I will take my men in a small sailboat, and we will cross the bay. I want to see the Savages that live there, and up the Chesapeake, and to know the great river Potomac which I have glimpsed, and the Massawomeks, whom all say are enemies to every nation, and the Susquehannocks, who are giants.'

'Why?' she asked, amazed.

He thought a second, and when he spoke it was so seriously that she was impressed. 'I want to know this land and all these waters. I would put them on my map – a better map than this. But I want to know the people, too, and how they live and what they think.'

He goes to conquer, she thought, and he *has* the will.

'The *Phoenix* sails tomorrow,' she said.

'And I sail, too, after it has left. For with Captain Nelson gone, I have no master – save President Ratcliff' – he grinned – 'who is no master.'

'What will it mean to you to conquer a nation to the north? Powhatan will give you your own nation.'

'You do not understand. I don't want a nation. I want . . . ' But she willed him to want. *Virginia*, he had called the land, and

77

it was vaster than the country of Powhatan, including as it did the Susquehannocks and the Monacans.

She left his wigwam and found the young soldiers of Jamestown, who called to her, and faster than an arrow could be whooshed she threw off her cape and put her hands to the ground and turned circles through the streets. They followed her, tumbling awkwardly, laughing and shouting, looking very comical in their cumbrous slops and heavy boots. She catwheeled down the beach straight into the water, and there they followed her, clothes and all, and would have drowned her except for Captain Smith's hoarse orders.

'Pocahontas,' he said, flushed and angry, yet gentle as he helped her from the water, 'you do not understand our men.'

'No,' she agreed, looking at him seriously.

'They ... are not used to women ... here. ...'

'What would they do, *Lord*?' She had said it, and she felt a pang, but he only looked at her because she had used a new term.

'Nothing!' he said shortly. 'Or I'd have them cut to ribbons.'

The *Phoenix* left, and Johnsmith sailed, but Pocahontas came no less often to Jamestown. She did not frolic with the young soldiers, because she remembered the fierce knit of Johnsmith's brows as he had sent them off, but still she brought them food and hoped for news, of which there was none.

Master Scrivener was her great friend. He had learned much of Powhatan's language so she could lead him to talk of the White Werowance, whom, he, too, thought was great, greater than his Captains Newport and Nelson.

'If he were in command ...' Master Scrivener said, and she agreed with all her heart. For President Ratcliff used the stores and spent the force that now remained in building what he called a palace in the forest. 'Smith is a hero of sorts,' Master Scrivener said. 'When I came I realized that, for how could any have survived without him? And his map – you have no idea how wonderful his map is, or will be. It is a thing to marvel at, to explore the land and rivers, and to see them like a bird from on high, and then to set them out so that other men can go where you have gone and find the mountain or the harbor you have named.'

Then she forgave Johnsmith for going off to the Massawomeks and the Susquehannocks. King James in England would know how mighty a Werowance made such a map.

'But his greatest art, perhaps, is languages, for he learns a tongue by only hearing it, and it gives him a power the rest of us have not.'

'You have.'

'I have studied night and day since I came here. But did you not notice how soon he spoke Powhatan's language?' She had, but had not thought it strange till she had seen how feeble were the efforts made by other Englishmen. 'He has even written it out for those in England.' She wondered if Master Scrivener had read of Pocahontas and her two little baskets. 'He speaks French and High German and Hungarian and Turkish, with various smatterings from other lands thrown in, and he has never studied them.'

Were these the tongues of the yellow and the black upside-down nations? How difficult to learn *their* languages! Had Johnsmith stood upside down when he talked to them?

One day she found Master Scrivener working, and she stood, waiting, till he looked up at her.

'May I see your other pair of eyes?' she asked humbly.

'My other . . . ? Of course you may,' he said, realizing. He removed them carefully and handed them to her. 'They are called spectacles,' he said.

She looked into them, and the world was blurred, but then Master Scrivener put her hand up close to her face, and the lines of her palm stood out clear like the rivers on Johnsmith's map. She took the spectacles off and saw in them her own reflection.

'They are like pools. I see myself.'

'Has Smith not given you a mirror?'

'No.'

He found one and held it out to her. She looked into it, and then leaped away, for another face, a face resembling her own, peered back with a terrible clarity. In the unruffled shallows of the river, in sheets of rosy copper, she had seen herself, but the image had been muted, and she had thought of herself with softly blended features, not as this startling maid with deeply glowing eyes and arched, proud nose, with lips so rounded and cheeks so high.

'You need not fear to look,' Master Scrivener said. 'It is a fair face.'

'Is it?' she asked, and took the mirror firmly, studying long, for it was a face she would know well.

'Did Smith not read you what he wrote of you in his book?' She shook her head, not looking from the mirror. 'A pity.' And he said no more till she had to look up at him, for she longed to know what Johnsmith had written. Master Scrivener was smiling at her.

'Tell me,' she said, like a child.

'He said you were as comely in your face as in your person, the fairest of your race, the very nonpareil of Virginia.'

'Nonpareil?'

'Having no equal.'

' "Nonpareil," ' she repeated the word. 'Why did Johnsmith *not* read me this?' she demanded.

'John Smith is afraid of few things and no man, but it could be he is afraid of *you*, Pocahontas.' She stared at him. 'Are your braves never afraid of women?'

'No!' she said indignantly, then added, 'Only the Wironausquas who command them – or of me because they know Powhatan loves me.'

'That is not why Smith is afraid of you.' The smile kept twinkling about his lips.

'Then why?'

'I think that I am afraid of you myself sometimes, child though you are.'

'I am a child no longer!'

He nodded agreeing, but he would not tell her why Johnsmith or he might fear her.

Smith did not come back until the Corn Gathering time. Pocahontas came to Jamestown and found him brown and bushy, his whiskers not having been trimmed. He greeted her and Nantequos and presented them robes which he had been given by the giant Susquehannocks, and a very fine one for Powhatan. He said to tell Powhatan that he would come, when he could, and relate to his Red Father all that he had found among the Massawomeks and the Susquehannocks and the Rappahanocks.

Now there was much to keep him; the English had complained to him of the extravagance of their silly President and begged Smith to take that office himself, which he at last agreed to. He stopped the building of Ratcliff's palace and instead ordered the repairing of the church and storehouse, and a new house built to store the supply which Captain Newport would bring, and the fort enlarged from three sides to five so that they could lodge the new colonists who would come. A field was prepared were he exercised his braves, and here he lined up men in files to shoot their fire sticks, with which they could batter a tree till it fell, cleft in the middle.

He told Nantequos and Pocahontas to tell Powhatan all that

he did, but to explain that he prepared his braves to march against the Monacans and the Powhatan must not fear, for John Smith called him always his Red Father.

Captain Newport came, and it seemed that the differences of last spring were forgotten. He greeted Smith with his unspontaneous joviality and said he was well content that Smith was now the President. He agreed to take the disavowed Ratcliff back to England.

He explored the fort and the storerooms and commended the assembled colonists. He continued to smile throughout the display of gunnery and during his inspection of the new glass factory and the clearing where pitch, wood-tar, and soap ashes were being produced to freight his ship when it returned to England. If his praise was niggardly, only the President noticed.

The colonists were in a reveling mood, cheered by more than the supplies he brought, for his approbation seemed to express the approval of their countrymen, their homeland, and to make their labors worthwhile.

Even Smith began to relax as they sat in his house, a bottle of the canary wine which had come in the ship between them.

'Johnnie, you've done well! *Of course* you should be President. Who can protect the Colony as you? That ass, Ratcliff – and his silly castle!'

Smith expelled a breath, then sniffed his wine. He had not expected support. Even the laugh, the teeth, the booming voice, and the arm which Newport had kept about his shoulders during the inspection, seemed at this moment pleasant. After all, in spite of disagreements, Newport was a salted seaman, had been a privateer honored by the Queen, and had commanded the voyage which had brought them to Virginia. And he was Smith's old friend.

'On the whole, the Company is pleased. But this time they are determined, Johnnie – they will accept no excuses.'

Smith tensed. 'Excuses?'

'You've got to remember what we're here for.'

Smith laid aside his cup. He wanted to get up and open the door for air – to breathe deep.

'Perhaps I need to be reminded.'

'Johnnie! But then you made your expedition after Nelson sailed. Did you find it?'

'You mean the Passage – the South Sea – or evidences of it? No! I sailed the length of the Bay. . . . '

'I'm not to return without it – or proof of gold – or one of the lost colonists of Roanoke.'

Smith arose and walked to the door; his hand was on the latch when he remembered that Newport's voice would carry into the camp. He turned and looked at his old Captain: the grizzled hair, the seamed face, nutbrown from sun and sea, the sawed-off arm.

'I can believe those in London. They look at a map, and here we are – on the other side of the world. They draw pictures of palm trees and pineapples and think of all the gold that Spain has garnered.' He came back and stared down at Newport in some sadness. 'But I can't believe you, Chris. You're here. You've sailed these shores and waters. . . . There is no gold – you proved that with your last cargo. . . . There is no Eastern Passage – not from here – maybe farther north. And Roanoke has already been searched – that land has nothing to do with Powhatan. . . .'

Newport's smile had left, a flush had spread under his dark skin, his mouth was stubborn now, no flash of teeth, and his voice held a plaintive note.

'I'm only telling you, Johnnie. My orders . . .'

Smith smiled sardonically; he raised his glass. 'Those are *your* orders, Chris. If you can accomplish one of them, I salute you. But my job is keeping this Colony alive and fed.'

'Now, Johnnie, Johnnie! We help each other. I can't do these things without you – and I have brought you what you need.'

'Food?' Smith said.

'Yes, yes! But, Johnnie, the Savages will love you as never before; you'll have no need for all these guns and marksmen. What is proposed is wonderful.' He was engendering enthusiasm, and once more the smile sparkled.

'Yes?'

'We're going to crown Powhatan!'

'What?'

'King of Virginia! I've got a crown and robes. King James himself has recognized him.'

'You're mad – or someone is!'

'Johnnie, when he senses the honor that is being bestowed . . .'

'Where?'

'Where?'

'Where are you going to crown him?'

'Why, in his city – where he dwells.'

'Do you realize that we have a month and a half to prepare for winter? We couldn't possibly send an escort there.'

'Johnnie, when he has his crown, he'll give us the world – all the corn you could ask for. Are you afraid to go – it's been said you have offended him.'

Smith dropped his eyes, then bent to pour another cup of wine. After a brief pause he reached for Newport's glass and re-filled it. Beyond a point, how could one argue?

'No, I'm not afraid to go. In fact I'll go alone, or with a few soldiers, and ask him to come here. I don't want to empty the fort now – at harvest time.'

'Johnnie, I don't think you appreciate . . .'

News of this, as much as was understood, was carried back to Powhatan. Captain Newport had brought a crown and John-smith did not wish to carry it, but wanted Powhatan to come to Jamestown. What was a crown? Pocahontas and Nantequos did not know. Johnsmith would come to invite him. Powhatan was content that Johnsmith should come begging.

He heard of the three commands which had been laid upon Captain Newport: find a passage to another sea, bring gold, bring home some survivors from Roanoke – or don't come back!

'I think King James does not like his Captain Newport, or wish to see his face again,' Powhatan said ironically.

CHAPTER TWELVE

At the Sun's Rising, on the day Johnsmith was to come, Powhatan and his Council, the Cockarouses, Werowances, and Priests, left with most of Powhatan's braves to go to Orapaks, so that they would not be in Werowocomoco when Johnsmith arrived, but would have to be sent for.

Nantequos unwillingly went with them, but Powhatan left Pocahontas and her maids to receive him.

She was not sorry to be alone with only such braves and squaws as would do her bidding. With her favorite maids she prepared for his reception. Squaws were sent along the trail to report to her each stop and stage of the journey.

The leaves and long grass wilted under the hot sun, but as the shadows lengthened, a wind cooled the sweat on the Englishmen's brows and rustled the trees, so that the reds and oranges, the crimsons and golds, mingled in a swirling cascade, and the bright leaves crackled underfoot.

President Smith led his four, newcomers all. He watched as their eyes darted from tree to tree eyes aglow with appreciation and apprehension, for among the painted leaves the painted braves would be difficult to detect.

He had overcome Newport's objections and set out, sparsely attended, to invite Powhatan to Jamestown for the childish coronation Newport planned. It would be improvident for the English to visit Werowocomoco at this time.

But it was gratifying to be in the forest, without restraint, away from the shrill voices of protest. Also, he thought, he would see Nantequos again – and Pocahontas! Nantequos had said that it was time for her to be pounced with the needle, which meant that she had reached puberty and would be mated. Smith thought of her, lithe, stretching toward a height as her father must have done, of the breasts which had burgeoned and the features which had delineated themselves in the time he had known her, strong and striking, the eyes slightly aslant, the straight lips smiling easily, the blush on her high cheekbones. Still, he could not think of her next to him, his loins on hers. Her innocence enchanted him. He could not think of her with any man.

This night, would Powhatan again offer him a wife and a virgin? And would he refuse? Could he? Lord, it had been forever since he had spent his seed! There were only four with him. Would Powhatan's wives and virgins not suffice for so small a party? But when the word went back to Jamestown to that sex-starved company, what would it do to discipline? *Contain yourself*, he commanded. *Your seed will dry.* He felt cheated by the long abstinence. *What I would do with Powhatan's maidens now*, he thought, and glanced at his companions, newbloods fresh from England's stews or hay-bounced sweethearts. *What they would do! Behave yourself, Master President!*

It was in a fair field dotted with buttercups and the bright tufts which he called paintbrushes that they came upon the Savages, a crowd of fifty, old men and squaws and children. The oldest made the sign of friendship, and he returned it. They had brought bread and fruits and fresh-water fish and offered to build a fire. Smith explained to his four that they were close to Werowocomoco, so they might partake of the Savages' hospitality.

A fire was built and racks set up on which the fish were laid as on a grill, a contrivance the Savages called a barbecue. The Englishmen settled in enjoyable languor to relax and eat, not bothered by the appraising, noncommittal eyes around them.

Suddenly, from the woods, came a hideous shrieking.

'Take your ams,' Smith ordered, and he grasped the old Savage who had invited them to feast by his long lock and held him as a target toward the noise. The English seized other Savages supposing that Powhatan with all his power had come to slay them. The Savages protested, crying their innocence, and then into the clearing came Pocahontas herself.

'Did you think that I would harm you? You can take my life, Johnsmith, as Powhatan could have taken yours. We seek only to entertain you,' and she disappeared into the deep trees.

The others, who had heard of the beneficent maiden, loosed their hostages, though they were sorry to see the Princess depart into the forest, for with her gone they felt no assurance.

'You can believe her,' Smith said. He calmly spread a fish with his knife, and holding it in two leaves, bit into the juicy flesh. But he was puzzled.

They had not relaxed before a troupe of thirty damsels came

naked out of the woods, their only covering before and behind being a few green leaves. Their bodies were painted, some red, some blue, some yellow, and some parti-colored. Pocahontas led them, a pair of antlers on her head and otters' skins dangling from her girdle and her arm. A quiver of arrows made of cat's fur was across her shoulder, and in her hand a bow. Smith looked at her with amusement and perturbation. A veritable Diana! Her maidens were horned also, and one carried a sword, another a club, another a potstick; each one with her own device.

With hellish shouts and cries, the fiends rushed among them, forming a ring about the fire, singing and dancing with great ardor, one and then another falling into a frenzy of passion, and then once again joining in the rhythm of the dance.

Smith leaned back on his hands and enjoyed himself from the beginning, and after the first shock his men found the sight fantastical and comically curious, and were able to pick out the fairest of the dancers, though if they spoke of any but the leader, Smith would shake his head and say, 'Look at the Princess. There could be none fairer than she!'

At last, with an infernal shout, the maids departed as they came. Smith rose and thanked the old braves and said they must be on their way. But before they left, Pocahontas and her damsels appeared once more, now without their horns.

'You were afraid!' she said accusingly. 'You were brave before Opechancano and Powhatan, but before a group of dancing maids you were afraid!'

'The thing we cannot fight is what we fear. And I could never fight you, Pocahontas.'

She smiled at him and took his arm. Then, six damsels to a man, they escorted the Englishmen to Werowocomoco. Smith felt that here would be some sanity, the Powhatan would hold in discipline this daughter whom Smith knew not at all, but they told him Powhatan was at Orapaks and would not return till the next Sun, though he had been sent for.

He looked at Pocahontas, but her gaze was bland and not to be construed. The maidens took them to their lodging, and no sooner were they inside than the young damsels, who had giggled and been most playful all the time, clustered about him and cried out: 'Love you not me? Love you not me?' in English.

He was shocked and embarrassed, and then angry. What was this treatment? He laughed to cover his emotions, as he tried to free himself. 'I love you all!' he shouted. 'I love you!' But they would not be put off, tormenting him, crowding, pressing, and hanging on him, crying, 'Love you not me?'

'Pocahontas!' he roared. 'Take these damned Nymphs from me!' He could see the startled faces of his men, for he never swore. 'Now, Goddamnit!'

Pocahontas ceased laughing and spoke quietly but clearly, and the ministrations ended.

Very red in the face, he turned scowling upon his men who by now were doubled with laughter.

''Od's blood, Johnnie,' Captain Waldo swore, 'I'll share your hazards any time.'

'It is only because Powhatan is away,' he said gruffly. 'It has not happened so before. . . . ' He glowered accusingly at Pocahontas who put her hands to her face in mock shame, but more certainly to hide her laughter.

They were then called to a great feast, and to the accompaniment of singing and dancing, they were fed all the dainties the heathen could devise. When they were finished and the English yawned, the damsels, still dancing and singing, returned them to their lodging, waving firebrands.

To the obvious disgust of his braves, Smith waited at the entrance till the maidens had retreated. Then he came out to Pocahontas.

They were alone as they had been that night when the moon laughed on Jamestown. But now no moon shone. Only the distant firelight was reflected on their faces.

'When does Powhatan come, tomorrow?'

'At Sun's Power.'

'I will hunt alone during the Sun's Climb. I want my braves to see that I am not afraid to wander without an army in Powhatan's country,' he added, seeming to feel an explanation was necessary. 'It is said by Captain Newport that I did not want him to come here because I had offended Powhatan and feared his wrath.'

'Captain Newport lies,' she said scornfully.

'He does not understand.'

'Powhatan is more content with Jamestown when Captain Newport stays away.'

He started into the wigwam and then turned back.

'It has been a long time, Pocahontas.'

'Yes.'

He smiled. 'It was a rare welcome you gave us.'

Her eyes glowed. 'I did not think to see the White Werowance tremble before thirty maidens. But then Master Scrivener told me that the English were afraid of women.'

'He did?'

'He said he thought you were afraid of *me*.'

'Now, why would he think that?'

'I did not understand. But in the wigwam with the thirty maidens, I thought I understood.' She smiled at him innocently.

His jaw dropped, and then though it was dark she could almost see the blood suffuse his face, his consternation was so obvious. With a small, merry laugh she disappeared into the night.

CHAPTER THIRTEEN

The sunburnt pungency of the huge blossoms was heady and a little sickening. Below her the riverbank was brilliant with late flowers and newly turned leaves. The giggling of her maids as they retreated through the wood came back to her like the lilt of a flock of swooping yellow birds. She perched herself on the branch so that she was screened by the glossy leaves and waited, hugging her body which was still wet from the river.

She heard the crash of his heavy boots. What a mighty hunter! He stopped, listened to the rustle of her maidens as though he suspected a buck had left the spot. She wanted to laugh aloud at his stupidity, but most of all she wanted to surprise him. She waited till he was beneath the tree, still listening. She slid down, over his head, through his arms, her legs tightening around him.

He was surprised, then angry at his surprise, then anxious that she should not know he was surprised. He dropped his musket and tried to shake her off, but she had the advantage. He was bare to the waist, and her legs clung easily to his body above his heavy belt.

He wrestled with her. They were laughing now, but their mouths set as they fought in earnest, he for mastery, she not to be vanquished. She caught his tawny hair and pulled his head back so that he had to come up with his arms and sweep her from him, down to the ground where he pinned her with his body. She struggled under him, her legs flailing inside his. Suddenly she felt him stiffen against her, his arms like iron, his horn hard through his leather breeks.

With a wave that was both nausea and ecstasy she threw her arms over her head. He pushed down his clothes. His flesh touched hers, and she cried out, demanding him. There was the thrust, the pain . . . her fever mounted . . . then was washed away in the blissful flood. There was the giving up, the softness, his weight suddenly great on top of her. He swung himself, her with him, so that she lay facing him in his arms.

'My love!'

She tried to translate the words into her own language, but she knew nothing to approximate them. She lay back and let the words convey the emotion she felt.

He drew away to pull out of his boots and breeks, then lifted her and carried her into the water.

Her lightness, her lithe young body, the blood, the absence of body hair, though he knew that it was plucked, moved him with a rare tenderness. It had been over a year since he had taken a woman, for he must be the enforcer of the laws and the pattern to which his men adhered. But none before had been like this sweet child.

He washed her gently, then brought her to him and kissed her lightly on the lips. He felt her nipples tense, and instantly he was rigid with desire.

He swung her down between his legs and pushed into her. She clung to him, and they were caught so, unable to move. Then he felt her contract against him, and his stored seed shot deep into her. She screamed, her fingers turned to claws, and she bit him. His knees collapsed and they sank together in the river mud, clinging to each other, he as shaken as she.

Later he lifted her again and washed both her and himself. She lay in his arms letting him do what he would.

He returned to the bank and put her down, stretching beside her. Her fingers sought over the grass and found a fallen blossom. She smelled it and then held it to his nose for him to breathe its fragrance. It was satin white save on one petal where it had turned golden brown. She laid it on his waist, matching it to the line where his clothes had hidden his body from the sun. She dried the water from him with the flower and bent to lay her lips against the spot where she had bitten him.

He reached for her, but did not draw her to him. Instead he caressed her with hands and lips till she ached to hold him. Then again the urgency. Her body rose to him, welcoming him. . . .

She held him spent and relaxed. *Soft he is to my arms, his waist and hips and thighs. Like this he is not so strong as I. My love!*

'What will your father say,' he asked, 'now I have taken your maidenhead?'

90

Father? Johnsmith is your father! Life has poured into you from your father.

She stroked his hair and throat.

'He has known from the beginning,' she said softly, 'that I am yours.'

CHAPTER FOURTEEN

Powhatan came. The feasting lasted long into the night while they told tales as they had before. But now Johnsmith talked most, for Powhatan would hear all that he had to tell of his journey to the northern reaches of the great Bay, which he said was divided into four heads, all of which he searched so far as his ship could sail them.

When it was time to seek their wigwams, Powhatan gave him a twisted smile.

'Tonight our White Werowance may pleasure himself in his own wigwam, where his braves will not disturb him, or be disturbed.'

Johnsmith looked startled. 'I . . . ' He swallowed. 'My braves might be worried, for some are new to your land. . . . '

'I doubt it.' Powhatan grinned, and Johnsmith followed his glance to where each Englishman was making signs to a maiden.

He sought Pocahontas's eyes, but she was looking into the fire.

'Powhatan feels that you will not be truly of his nation till you have mated with our squaws,' Nantequos said appealingly, for he did not understand this strange reluctance on the part of so potent a warrior.

'Yes,' Johnsmith said. 'It will give me great pleasure.'

Ponoiske and another maiden rose as Johnsmith entered. Their red bodies glistened in the firelight, and they swayed gracefully on their feet, waiting for him to come to the fire so they could undress him.

He stood, his feet planted, a puzzled look on his face.

Suddenly there was a sound behind him, and he whirled to face Pocahontas.

She spoke to Ponoiske. 'I will be Johnsmith's handmaiden.'

The two stared at her resentfully. 'But Powhatan . . . ' Ponoiske said.

'Powhatan has said that you should leave.'

They started awkwardly for the entrance.

'But he longs to frolic with *two* the night long . . . ' Ponoiske made a last attempt.

'He shall frolic with one!'

Johnsmith waited till they were gone. Then he laughed until the tears spurted from his eyes.

'Mighty maker of papoose!' Pocahontas said.

'I was a mighty maker by the river, 'he defended himself. 'Powhatan knows?'

'I told him just now that I would come to you, that you wanted me.'

'And he?'

'He wondered why you had not asked for me – and made me promise to tell him if you are as mighty as you claim.'

She came into the firelight and let her mantle fall. She was naked, and he saw that she was not oiled or painted. That morning she had regretted that he had taken her when she was not prepared for him, and he had told her how much fairer he found her body when it was fresh from the river.

He came toward her, and her hands moved to his coat.

'I would undress you, Lord.'

He caught her to him, his hands seeking all of her. At last he pulled his mouth away.

'I cannot wait!'

'Then do not wait!'

They lay, close-locked, relaxed and at peace. He looked up at the laced boughs overhead.

'I fear this is a terrible thing that I have done, Pocahontas.'

'Terrible? Oh, no!'

'I cannot take you for my wife. And I would. With my soul, I would!' She lay very still, listening to the pounding of his heart. 'It would be the end – of me – of Jamestown. They would say that I sought to make myself greater than they – that I would become a King in Virginia.'

She wondered deeply. It was what *she* could not understand.

'Though I cannot be your wife, yet you are now my lord and father. And what you wish, that will I do. I will come to you, or I will wait for you to come here.'

'That is it!' he cried unhappily. 'I would not even have them know – that tonight you sent the maids away and you lie here. Pocahontas, my fairest love! If they thought that – then you would have no peace among them. My English are not as your race,' he said bitterly. 'There is no innocence in men who know no squaws in many moons.'

It was not different, she thought, from her race – Powhatan had said as much.

'You would not have kept the others. You can send me away, Lord, and it will be as it was before.'

He bent his head and laid his lips between her breasts; his whiskers spread wings over her nipples.

'And lose this sweetness? You are a lost man, John Smith. We'll find a way, my love. For now that I have had your money, I famish till I taste again.'

She was gone when he awakened, and he dressed himself, feeling strangely forsaken. He found his comrades who walked as hollow-kneed as he, their slops appearing as empty as his felt. They grinned at each other self-consciously.

Whatever Pocahontas told Powhatan he never wanted to know, but Powhatan eyed him keenly, with a grudging respect.

After the breaking of fast, Powhatan retired to the Great Wigwam, and presently the English party entered.

'Powhatan,' Smith began, 'I come with a gracious invitation. Our glorious ruler, King James of England, who rules the world, the seas, and the skies, sends his love and pledges himself to you as an ally and a friend. And recognizing that you, too, are a King, he has sent many fine presents, such as you have not yet seen. Among them is a crown, like the one he himself wears, for he asks how you can be a King, who has not been crowned. It is his wish that you visit his city of Jamestown to receive these gifts and to be crowned by his Weroames.'

Powhatan studied him and then sat silently, looking at nothing. Once his hand reached up to twist his nose, but he withdrew it. At last he said:

'If your King has sent me presents, I also am a King, and this is my land. Eight days I will stay to receive them. Your Father is to come to me, not I to him, nor yet to your fort. Neither will I bite at such a bait.'

Nantequos followed Smith outside. 'Powhatan admires you as never before – even though he refuses the request of your Weroames.'

Smith caught Nantequos's arms.

'Brother,' he said, wanting above all to be honest with his friend, 'you know I had Pocahontas in my wigwam.'

Nantequos beamed happily. 'And you wrought mightily upon

94

her,' he said admiringly. 'Powhatan says *he* has not been thus since Matatiske left him.'

Smith sighed. Here there could be no understanding – what to him was for the shameful reaches of the night was for these pagans a proud miracle. His lustiness, which he had fought as Satan's tool, had raised him in their eyes as he had not been elevated since Newport's first coming.

'I cannot take Pocahontas with me at this time,' he said with difficulty, 'greatly as I love her. You must guard her for me, Nantequos. There will be times when I will ask you to bring her to meet me in the forest. . . .'

Nantequos tried anxiously to understand, but if Johnsmith wanted Pocahontas and she wanted him, why could he not take her? Still he said, 'I will do all you ask.'

Pocahontas was waiting for him in the wigwam. Smith shook Nantequos's hand in farewell, but still the youth lingered.

'Go! I beg you!' Smith said at last impatiently.

More puzzled than ever, Nantequos left.

Smith went to her and caught her up into his arms. She clung to him, and she felt so like a child that his own sensuality shocked him. How cruel that she would love him, who had no home or love, could have no love till he had carved his home from the wildwood. She thought him a great Werowance, but he had only to enter the palisades of Jamestown to know the truth.

'You will be back?'

'Eight days, Powhatan has said he'll wait.'

But with him would come Newport and an army, and he could not pick her from the crowd of maids and bid her follow him. *It is not winter yet*, he thought gratefully.

He related everything in Jamestown. 'Which means,' Newport said, 'that you have failed. You went to persuade the Emperor to come here to receive His Majesty's gifts, and he refused.'

'Quite rightly. His words could not have contained more dignity had he been anointed.'

'Then we must go to him.'

'I must still advise against it. With Jamestown's lack, it is not the time to go parleying. And Powhatan has showed little inclination. . . .'

'Master President, you seem to have no idea of the importance of this mission – no idea how it is regarded in England. I go – with the approval of the Company and of the Monarch – to confer a crown upon this heathen ruler. When he has realized our intention, your troubles and the troubles of the Colony will end

– for he will be enraptured by our nation's condescension. This will surely accomplish what in these years you have failed to do – to bring harmony between the Colony and these Savages.'

'And for this condescension you hope that he will freight our barges, so that we need not waste our time in harvesting, but shall put our effort to finding a nonexistent metal. You delude yourself.'

'We shall see, Master President,' Newport said smugly and went on with his plans to take the royal gifts to Powhatan at Werowocomoco, which was near a hundred miles by water since they must go into the Bay and round the point to sail up the Pamaunkey River.

On the second day after the ship had been dispatched, Newport set out himself to travel the twelve miles by land with fifty good men, for he accepted the time limit Powhatan had given and feared he would be gone.

Many of the soldiers had only recently come to these Savage shores and were fearful of the forests. These looked to their President, Captain Smith, who was a veteran and knew the dangers they might encounter; but he was sour and did not share the exuberance of Captain Newport and often would plunge ahead with a handful of his stalwarts and then return to show the trail. At last Newport's army came out of the woods to the river where their pinnace and barges floated, a cheering sight after the dark reaches of the trees.

They made camp, and at Captain Newport's orders set to work at once polishing their breastplates and helmets, while Captain Smith went ahead to the King's city to announce their coming and to provide them with food for that night's supper.

The next morning, when the air was crisp and clear and the skies of a startling blueness, they moved from the riverbank to the tootling of trumpets and tat-ta-ta-tat of tabors.

Their first view of Werowocomoco was the rows of neatly planted corn with pumpkins bright between them and the individual houses of these heathen built outside the palisades, one very long and higher than the rest, which they were told by those who knew was the house of their god or idol, called an Oke. In here lay the mummified bodies of their Kings, and the soldiers shivered, till one recalled Westminster, Canterbury, and other shrines where English Kings were buried.

Then they saw the gates of the city, open, and manned with furred and feathered Savages, their naked bodies painted garishly. The English entered in line of march, Captain Newport striding ahead, but their President remained watchfully in the back-

96

ground; it was known he disapproved of this gay doing, nor did Newport require him, for Master Scrivener accompanied him as interpreter.

The houses inside the walls were like those they had seen, but smaller, built as were the arbors at home with withes split and bent to make conical roofs. Only the Emperor's house stretched for nearly a hundred feet; but though it was at least twenty-five feet high at the peak, to enter it one was obliged to stoop and go through a low, dark passageway.

Captain Smith divided his company, leaving half outside to stare at the painted braves and the others to enter the large house in a column of twos. Since they could not do so with matches burning, there was some trepidation, especially from those in the fore, since to explore a gloomy corridor, defenseless and bent over, was a fearsome thing.

However, without mishap, they found themselves in a large hall lit by torches, smoky and mysterious and odorous, and the faces that greeted them were friendly, though behind the Emperor the wall of silent braves, lost in the murk, looked to be twice the number of the English.

Powhatan sat very straight on his couch of furs. He wore a robe of dyed raccoon fur, and red and white eagles' feathers were caught in his long lock. He was flanked by old men, hunkered down, and by a few squaws, young and old, including the Princess Pacahontas, whom it cheered the English to see.

Then from the tunnel entrance, Captain Newport rose from his stooped position with a flourish, and by the gleam of his teeth he and Powhatan expressed the same love with which they had regarded each other at their last meeting.

Under Newport's instructions, Scrivener asked Powhatan and his family to stand aside, and with a wave he ordered in soldiers who, to Powhatan's obvious amazement and uncertain pleasure, proceeded to dismantle his royal couch and to toss the pelts in a corner.

Suppressing his excitement, Newport waved again, and a large carved and gilded testered bed was brought in and assembled, then hung with brocaded tapestries. With many gesticulations, Newport indicated that this was now to be the Emperor's throne or couch.

Powhatan withdrew from his resentful silence and examined the bed, laying his fingers on the carved fruits and cherubs, picking at the gold. He was pleased, but one could see that to him it was heathenish and strange as the nakedness of the Savages was to the English.

Captain Newport motioned him to mount the stoop and seat himself. Stiffly Powhatan did so, and then his stiffness collapsed as he felt the mattress give beneath his weight. Smiles broke the faces of the English, but Captain Smith spoke sharply and with purpose, and they quickly disappeared.

Waving his hand like a magician, Newport called in two soldiers, one bearing a scarlet cloak, the other scarlet hose and shoes. They knelt and presented them, and Powhatan fondled the fine materials. But when the Captain wanted him to dress in them, Powhatan would not. It was not until Captain Newport displayed his own fine hose, fastened with a sparkling garter, and assured Powhatan that no harm could befall the wearer, that he submitted at last to allowing the hose to be fitted to his legs. They were too short, but none spoke of that, or of the shoes, which if they were too small Powhatan made no sign. Then Newport drew him up and swept the brilliant cloak about his shoulders.

It, too, was short, but the Emperor did not know it. He sat back in carmined state, surrounded by his crimson hangings, and he smiled like a child at home come Twelfth Night.

Then, with the greatest gesture of all, Captain Newport waved, and a pageboy, dressed in satin, came in bearing a silken pillow, and on it rested – and here the English, who dearly loved a crown, repressed their titters only because of President Smith's fierce visage – a copper coronet, all points. A tawdry thing, but this child-like Savage loved it. He reached out to take it. The pageboy disregarded his gesture, but knelt and presented it to Captain Newport, who lifted it ceremoniously and bade Powhatan to kneel.

And Powhatan, who had no idea of the majesty or meaning of a crown and saw but a trinket for his wearing, looked at him and waited to receive it.

'Kneel,' said Newport, and his voice was important.

Powhatan stood up.

'Tell him to kneel,' Newport ordered Master Scrivener.

He spoke, and Powhatan's eyes flashed. He answered in few words.

'He says it is you who must kneel,' Scrivener translated.

'He *has* to kneel,' Newport said loudly, 'if he wants to be crowned.'

Scrivener repeated the words. Powhatan stood straighter than ever.

'Tell him it's the way to *get* crowned!' Newport yelled in exasperation.

But Powhatan had no intention of kneeling.

'Show him how!' Newport screamed to the pageboy, who knelt stiffly, and Newport lowered the crown onto his head. 'Which should make young Watt King of Virginia,' a soldier smirked and was glared to silence by the President.

Powhatan looked at the proceeding, but it seemed with each persuasion he stood inches taller.

'Captain Smith!' Newport shouted. 'Tell him to kneel so I can give him this bloody crown.'

'He's not going to kneel.'

'What do you mean, he's not going to kneel? He *has* to kneel – else I can't crown 'im!'

The President spoke to the Prince who was Powhatan's son, and the handsome brave went to his father and spoke words into his ear.

'What's he saying?' Newport demanded. His voice was loud at any time, but now it was a shriek, and his face was purple.

'He is telling Powhatan to bend his head and receive this pretty trinket,' Smith said coldly.

'Trinket, hell! This is a *crown*! I'm *crowning him King of Virginia!*'

'He thinks he *is* King of Virginia,' Captain Smith said.

He moved forward and spoke to Powhatan, who answered him indignantly. With a gesture of camaraderie Smith threw his arm around the Emperor's shoulders, and then suddenly he pulled Powhatan's head down.

'Put on the crown!' he ordered Newport, who clapped it on.

Smith released his grip and Powhatan's head shot up.

Instantly a pistol sounded a salute outside the wigwam, and before a breath could be drawn the ship answered with a salvo that shivered the air about them.

Powhatan wheeled on Captain Smith, a sense of betrayal and fury in his eyes. The crown tumbled to the ground. Braves started up from hidden corners, tomahawks in their hands.

'Soldiers!' Newport shouted, terror in his voice.

'For the love of God!' Smith yelled. 'Countrymen, keep back your weapons! Don't move! Powhatan . . . !' He looked pained and angry, his whiskers abristle. He spoke long and forcefully in the Savage gibberish. Slowly Powhatan relaxed, and the tense arms of the braves dropped to their sides.

'What did you say to him?' Captain Newport demanded.

'I told him that you in your idocy sought to honor him. . . . ,'

'In my idiocy!'

'You've almost had the massacre you're begging for,' President Smith said. He started out.

'Where are you going?'

'To leave you to receive *his* presents. I also told him that when you had gone Jamestown would carry on,' he said tartly as he left the wigwam.

CHAPTER FIFTEEN

Smith unbent as he came out of the King's house. He saw friends, both red and white, who looked at him sympathetically, and several of his soldiers moved to follow him, but he waved them back. He left the walls and headed upriver from the pinnace. He had translated to Newport only the last of his quick words with Powhatan – only what he himself had said – and he was grateful that the words Powhatan had uttered had been too low and too swift for even Scrivener's newly educated ear.

'You have called me father,' Powhatan had said, 'and you bring these to me who are not my friends. What do you think their gifts matter to me? Let your people live as they like at Jamestown; let them sail the Bay. But do not come again to Powhatan.'

And there had been nothing for Smith to answer; he could not deny Newport or his own people. Not that that would count for him in Jamestown or in England. Newport's stupid fiasco would be placed squarely at his own door. Who in England would believe that a Savage ruler would turn down an English crown or be frightened by a salute of guns?

He came out of the thicket to the riverbank, and the free-flowing river that had given him such a kinship with this land. He pushed through the willows, wanting the river to tell him something.

Nantequos sat on a hummock, looking out with equal intensity at the tide-moved water. He did not turn until Smith exclaimed.

'What are you doing here? I left you in the wigwam.'

'I did not want to follow, so I came ahead – till you found me.'

'And Powhatan? He is still angry?'

'He has recovered his dignity. He has given Newport his old shoes and robe.'

Smith laughed. 'And that is what Newport's gifts have won. He hoped for ships of corn.'

'Powhatan will not trade with Newport, nor be his friend.'

'Nor mine.'

'He will understand – when I tell him that you are still his Werowance. . . .'

'Nantequos, will you go and say to your sister. . . ?'

Pocahontas moved listlessly, engulfed in the crossed currents of their angers, Johnsmith's and Powhatan's. For Powhatan's temper had reached its peak. He brooded malevolently. In spite of the gifts which cluttered his wigwam, he felt humiliated and resentful. To have shown fear at the firing of the cannon was a bitter remembrance.

Nantequos found her. 'The ship leaves now, and Johnsmith starts shortly with his Weroames on foot. He asks that I bring you and we follow them until they stop to eat. Then he will join us in the woods. . . .'

Her heart was glad that he had not forgotten, but she felt, too, that she was being severed by her love for him and for her father.

'Is Powhatan angry with Johnsmith?' she asked.

'I told him that the gifts and guns were not Johnsmith's doing, but he said, "He embraced me in friendship and then pulled down my head so that I bowed to his Weroames!"'

She wondered at Nantequos as at herself. *He loved Powhatan, yet was willing to do what Johnsmith asked. Do we love Johnsmith more?* she wondered, and her heart cried *No!* even as it answered *Yes!*

So fair the world when it is bright with color, and drifting leaves are brilliant winging birds! When the air and sky are vivid in their texture, and to run swiftly, not touching the crackling leaves, is like flight itself!

She and Nantequos paused in a copse of trees whose silver bark served for the temporary canoes which one could make and carry and freely leave.

They listened to the English as they built their fire, their noisy chatter, and then they heard the closer crash of Johnsmith as he entered the woods. His gun was held as though he sought game, but surely the English were no hunters, for any beast would hear and flee their noisy invasion.

Nantequos showed himself so silently that Johnsmith started and involuntarily raised his gun. Then Pocahontas. He looked at her, and his eyes were hungry, sick and hungry.

'Pocahontas!'

'Lord!'

Johnsmith turned to Nantequos. 'I thank you!' and then, 'Can we be alone' – he spanned an arc between the highest trees – 'for the time it takes the sun to move from there to there?'

Silently Nantequos departed.

Johnsmith wrapped her in his arms and held her very close. There was no tension in his clasp, but such a warmth encompassed her! Who else – who else but Powhatan – could give such tenderness?

'I am afraid,' he said against her her. 'I am afraid for us.'

She would not have him be afraid. She longed to make it so that he was not afraid. But she could not end this time when she was filled with him – not as before – he with her and she with him. She did not want to stir . . . this *now* should be forever . . . no longing, no possessing . . . *being* each other!

He lifted her face and pressed his mouth on hers, and the *now* was shattered, splintering into many-colored atomies that sparkled and exploded brilliantly inside her head.

'You have come, though Powhatan is angry.'

'You said to come. I told you . . .'

'My sweet love! And you will lie with me under the blue sky and the bright leaves?'

'Aye!' But she would rather have been held again in that sweet belonging.

Inside the curtains of her eyes it was night with golden stars glimmering a thousandfold. And then flaming arrows mounted, and she wanted to cry out, but she was mute. She opened her eyes and past his head she gazed at the sky; its color was metallic, blue seen through an almost invisible red.

'I did not pleasure you as before I did.'

'Oh, yes!' But she could not tell him of that greater ecstasy, for if he had experienced it would not have ended it.

'I have lived only for now – these seven Suns.'

Not knowing it, she thought, *he has made me not want to live unless I be wrapped again in that tranquil harmony.*

They lay, hands clasped, their bodies not together, looking upward, and talked with muted, distant voices, and she knew in their quietness somewhat of the peace and joy that he had given her before.

The sunlight lit the leaves on the second of the tall trees. Johnsmith turned and with his lips, brushed very lightly her mouth, her eyes and brow.

'Nantequos comes.' He rose, drawing her up, and then the tree's tip sliced the brilliance of the sun and Nantequos was there. Johnsmith embraced him.

'You are my true brother.'

Nantequos stood, not speaking, but her own flesh told her what he felt – as her hand had left, or brow, when Johnsmith had first caressed them with his lips.

'I will stay in Jamestown, where there is much to do to prepare Captain Newport's ship for sailing. But if you can, will you bring your sister to me sometimes – if it is not too cold?'

Pocahontas laughed. 'In Johnsmith's arms there is no cold. It is like to burning. . . . '

He flushed, that bright red of the sweet earth fruits.

'Do not bring her,' he said carefully, 'if Powhatan will be angry. . . . ' Nantequos nodded. 'Tell Powhatan – no, you can tell him nothing, for he does not know that you have come. But let him know that when Captain Newport goes . . . '

'It is Captain Newport,' Nantequos said hotly, 'who does these things. Powhatan asks, "How is Johnsmith so great a Werowance when he must take the orders of this Newport?" Why can we not kill him?'

'Kill whom?' Johnsmith asked, startled.

'This Newport! He is not so mighty. And with him dead, you would rule the English, and Powhatan would treat you as his son!'

Johnsmith blew out a gust of air as though he expelled his amazement and his disapproval, all mixed with his amusement.

'You make things too easy. Newport is a mightier Weroames than you think.'

'If an arrow found its mark, his voice would be less loud,' Nantequos said simply.

Johnsmith rocked with laughter. 'Nantequos, I love you truly and I love your sister, Pocahontas. But first and always, I am an Englishman. It is true, we do seek to found a city, perhaps a nation of our own; not to fight Powhatan but to be an ally to him. I don't love Newport, nor many others who have fought me and whom I have fought. But to this cluster of English I belong. So I cannot kill my leader, nor take your sister to be my wife, though they sound the easiest and pleasantest things to be imagined.'

He blew out a deep breath and turned to Pocahontas and cupped her chin in his hands. 'You are the flower,' he said, 'of Virginia . . . knowing no winter. The frost was joyous with the madrigals of you and your maids. If you can do so,' he said, turning to Nantequos, 'let Powhatan know that I prize his sweet maid, that I would be a true friend to you and him. . . . '

'I will,' Nantequos said. 'We will! To us, Powhatan will listen.'

CHAPTER SIXTEEN

Werowocomoco was silent; the squaws moved quietly; what braves were about were old and squatted somberly weaving their weirs.

'The Council sits in Powhatan's wigwam,' Nantequos said.

Her muscles tightened, but she did not speak. She saw Opuiske, hands folded over her enlarged belly, among other squaws.

'Ask her.'

Nantequos strode till he caught his wife's eye, beckoned, and she came to him. He asked her a question, listened, and returned to Pocahontas.

'Opechancano!'

'He is here?'

'Yes.'

'Go in quietly.' Her voice was almost a whisper as though already she feared Powhatan's glower.

The guards before the wigwam let them pass without question. They stooped their heads and, bent over, passed through the long, crooked tunnel. Nantequos tapped the shoulders of the guards inside who turned to look and then made way. He drew Pocahontas to his side, and they stood to the back, observers, wanting to absorb what had passed.

Captain Newport's bed had been taken down and Powhatan's mats piled as usual. Opechancano, crouched at his feet, talked rapidly.

'You have seen what they intend. Powhatan has weighed what Johnsmith said and what has happened. Captain Newport has come, not once, but twice, and the English have not gone with him, but rather he has left here more and more, till, where once they were thirty-eight, today they are more than two hundred. When Newport is here, he speaks tenderly to Powhatan – he gives him presents.' Opechancano waved scornfully, and all could

105

vision the elaborate bed, the robe and hose and shoes, the copper crown. 'But when he is gone, Johnsmith speaks in a different voice. He does not come begging as his *Weroames*. He comes demanding – and Powhatan feeds him and his braves. Does Powhatan remember? I said they would come in twenties and in fifties. . . . '

Powhatan held up his hand. 'I remember.'

'And they have come,' Opechancano said, evidently enjoying himself. 'And Johnsmith has sailed to the head of the Bay and made friends with the Susquehannocks, who would join with him. . . . '

Nantequos stood forward.

'Johnsmith builds homes for his braves, who will be subject to Powhatan,' he said with a magnificent desperation. 'And his braves stand ready to fight our enemies as he told you the first day. He is Powhatan's son, and when Captain Newport goes . . . '

'When Captain Newport goes,' Opechancano interrupted dourly, 'Johnsmith becomes a Werowance – if Powhatan thinks of him as such.'

'Johnsmith!' Nantequos shouted the word and then shook so that he could say no more.

Pocahontas had held her hands over her face while Nantequos talked, but now she showed herself.

'Johnsmith *becomes* not a Werowance. He has been so brave that Powhatan himself has called him Werowance of Powhatan.'

Opechancano's sneer touched her and covered her with shame where before there had been no shame.

'Let Opechancano fight him!' Nantequos said bitterly. 'Let the Pamaunkeys dare his firesticks.'

'Quiet!' Powhatan suddenly thundered. 'I want to hear no more from either of you.'

Opechancano, in some relief, settled himself to continue.

'There is no need to fight him. They are too many to fight – *now*! Let us starve them.' Pocahontas felt the words chillingly. 'They have not the sense to plant or garner, so let them come in hundreds if they depend on us to do their growing for them. You are as happy at Orapaks as here, and all of us belong to the forest and there can make our home. We will dig up our fields and disappear, and let these English starve – the more hundreds, the sooner they starve!'

Pocahontas had moved silently among the Council till she was close to Powhatan. Opechancano's gaze was on her, and she felt petrified, unable to speak, but she forced her voice. 'Johnsmith is loyal to Powhatan!'

106

'Johnsmith has lain with the daughter of Powhatan!' Opechan-cano said.

Pocahontas closed her eyes, but she must go on. 'Newport goes, and then there is only Johnsmith.'

'Beyond Johnsmith there are many – beyond Newport, many – to this King James we hear of. And if Johnsmith wants the daughter of Powhatan – has slept with her in his wigwam – why is she not in Jamestown?'

She felt helpless to negate Johnsmith's denial of her. She felt shamed before Powhatan and all his Council.

'It was you, Powhatan, who ordered that his blood and mine be made one!' Nantequos said.

'And it was you who told me to seek his wigwam,' Pocahontas cried.

Powhatan sat stiffly as though his couch were studded with thorns, but when he spoke it was with power and bitter vehemence.

'You have heard, oh Cockarouses! Our brother, Opechancano, is right. There is no truth in these English, and our land will know no peace till they have gone. Shall we do what the Wero-wance of Pamaunkey has said: Refuse to trade with them! Starve them! Till they shall all have fled. For, as my brother has said, they cannot live without us. They neither plant nor harvest. They do not hunt when the forests are full, nor place weirs when the fish smother themselves because there is no room for them all.'

A voice cried 'Aye!' and the word was caught up till it filled the wigwam.

CHAPTER SEVENTEEN

Unlike the corn of England, the fine spearing grain, the prized wheat with which they made their white bread, the Savages' corn was golden – bright gold nuggets, which, stored in great baskets, promised sustenance the winter long. But the English cared more for hard cold metal to freight the ships and make happy the Company in England.

It was gold they dug for in the rich soil of the land they named Virginia. Who would put sweating toil into planting golden kernels and fertlizing them with minnows? Let the Savages do that!

On the river bed they saw flakes that shimmered and, having no proper assayer, they let desire become belief; and while President Smith drove his colonists to make specimens of glass and to produce pitch, tar, and soap ashes, so that those in England might know what *could* be taken from these shores, Captain Newport and his crew freighted his ship with river mud.

But before they could sail with their precious cargo, they must have a quantity of the unprecious corn to sustain them on the long voyage, and Jamestown had none to spare.

So the President sailed with two barges and eighteen men, George Percy commanding the second barge, up the Chickahominy. But of the nations along the shores not one Werowance came to parley with them, and, when questioned, the Savages said only that they had no corn to trade, that it had been a lean harvest, which Smith knew to be a lie for he had seen the fields of cornstalks laden with their tasseled fruit.

When he reached Chickahominy, always an uncertain nation ruled by Priests, he abused them, saying he did not come to trade but avenge the evil they had done him when they together with Opechancano had killed his three companions and trapped him in the quagmire. This stout talk and the show of musketry frightened the Chickahomanies, and they went away to return with corn and fish and fowl.

This supply sped Captain Newport's going, and in good time, for the delay had depleted the stores which were to see the colonists through the winter. Smith ordered the former President Ratcliff to go with the ship, saying he was a troublemaker, and if he stayed Smith would erect the gallows Ratcliff had so desired should bear another burden.

On this voyage, too, would go John Smith's great new map, showing all the Bay and the reaches of the Chesapeake, together with the letter he must write telling the condition of the Colony, an answer to the carping complaints.

He started to write and then stopped. It would be so easy to go home, to let Ratcliff take over, or the lordling, George Percy. Smith didn't want it anymore, neither the good nor the bad – and it was going to be all bad from now on. Powhatan's policy – he had sensed it at every stop on the river; every negation had told him what Powhatan had ordered: *Nothing to trade and see if they survive this winter!* He thought of the Strand, of Southwark, the Mermaid Tavern. Lincolnshire! What does a cow look like? It wasn't that he had anything to gain. Even his Presidency would only last a year. . . . And who thanked him? He scowled and straightened the furrows of his face with his hand, studying the blank paper. *Virginia!* he thought. He was in the forest, and it sprang alive with the sun-drenched blades and flowers; it was summer, and life was rampant . . . he lay with Pocahontas in his arms under an electric sky. . . . The thought of leaving her numbed him with a sense of loss.

He saw the starvelings, the weaklings, flock outside the gates to gasp at the food that she had brought. . . . Each time she went away and came again, they were there – the hungry!

He thought of the great Lords and merchants in London and of their dissatisfaction. He dipped his quill and slowly began, but gradually his writing sped with nervous ferocity.

I received your Letter, wherein you write that our minds are so set upon faction and idle conceits in dividing the Country without your consent, and that we feed you but with ifs and ands, hopes and some few proofs: as if we would keep the mystery of the business in ourselves: and that we must expressly follow your instructions sent by Captain Newport: the charge of whose voyage amounts to near two thousand pounds, the which if we cannot defray by the Ship's return, we are like to remain as banished men. To these particulars I humbly entreat your Pardons if I offend with my rude Answer.

He looked at the last three words and shook his head. 'Johnnie!' he said disapprovingly. His own voice sounded like Scrivener chiding him, and he laughed.

He took out the Treasurer's letter and reviewed the items of condemnation. Suddenly, he tossed it on the table and picked up his pen. He understood *'my rude Answer'*.

He went on writing angrily and rapidly.

. . . Though I be no scholar, I am past a schoolboy. . . .

. . . For the Coronation of Powhatan, by whose advice you sent him such presents, I know not; but this gives me leave to tell you, I fear they will be the confusion of us all ere we hear from you again. . . .

. . . From your Ship we had not provision in victuals worth twenty pound, and we are more than two hundred to live upon this: the one half sick, the other little better. . . .

He wrote of his map and his discoveries and felt sorry for himself sufficiently to write of his resentment against Newport, who was well rewarded for his journeys, while for the Colony's President the Company sent nothing but censure. He paused, his anger subsiding, for he must tell of Jamestown's needs.

. . . When you send again I intreat you rather send but thirty carpenters, husbandmen, gardeners, fishermen, blacksmiths, masons, and diggers up of trees . . . than a thousand such as we have. . . .

Gentlemen and petty tradesmen, he thought. How hard to realize in London that left to their own resources they were good for nothing. The hub and axis of the city's life, and in a virgin country they could not keep tied the points that bound soul to body. He wrote:

. . . These are the causes that have kept us in Virginia from laying such a foundation that ere this might have given much better content and satisfaction; but as yet you must not look for any profitable returns: so I humbly rest.

He sprinkled sand over the page and started to read what he had written, thought that wisdom would show it to Scrivener to censor, gave a short laugh, and scrawled his name. He folded the letter, heated wax at the candle and sealed it, pressing his ring onto the wax so that his crest was definite.

Newport won't like this, he thought. And then: *Nor will any. But someone must speak for them.*

With Newport and his hungry crew at last at sea, Smith set out to test his belief that Powhatan had ordered the nations not to trade. He went first to Nansemond where they had bargained with him earlier for corn not yet ripe. The Werowance had fled, and his Cockarouses would not honor their debt until Smith's soldiers fired their muskets into the air, upon which the Savages fled into the woods. The English followed, and the first wigwam they came to they burned, with which the oldest Cockarouse came and promised that the Savages would freight the barges. And so the President returned with corn to Jamestown.

But on the next foray Smith found that from all parts the folk had fled, taking their harvest with them, till he came to the country of the Appomattucks where their tall and lusty Queen used the English kindly. She would tell them nothing of Powhatan or her neighbors, but she divided what she had and feasted them, and the President accepted her gracious invitation to stay ashore and share her bed.

Oiled and painted, she awaited him, and Smith spent himself upon her pillowy thighs and breasts. But after he had sated himself and her, he lay and thought of the green lad in Lincolnshire and his first lovemaking in the white plump arms of Mistress Molly Ware, his mind skirting the memory of the forest maid, the child.

In the morning, John Smith and the Queen gravely bade each other farewell, and he thanked her for her great courtesy.

Smith called the Council. 'It is because of Powhatan,' he told them, 'and till we have the corn from him we shall not have it from his subjects.'

The Honorable George Percy, who owned his private store and, whoever starved, always appeared sleek and groomed from the hands of his serving man, asked, 'You mean to use more force than you have used, to offend these – heathens – even more?'

Smith wheeled, his blue eyes probing. But Percy showed no reluctance to meet those eyes, and a smile broke Smith's whiskers, for Percy was a noble but no lackwit. Indeed, his courage was well proved, since he had lasted from the beginning.

'And to hell with the honorable gentlemen in London?' Smith was never sure with Percy. Did he mean to trap him? 'We are persuaded by London not to offend . . .'

'There's no persuasion will persuade *me* to starve!'

Percy raised his eyes, indolently amused.

'Agreed!' he said. 'Let us beard Powhatan.'

CHAPTER EIGHTEEN

He called for volunteers to make the journey and knew the ones who would step forward. They were those he wanted, his own, the ones these bitter times had taught him to rely on.

Captain Waldo, who had shown some force and courage, he left to come to his reinforcement if need required, for Smith expected no easy marketing.

'My very face offends Powhatan now,' he told Scrivener.

'It's a foolhardy journey, Johnnie.'

'Would you rather teach these lads to hunt and fish?' Smith asked simply. 'Your task is no less desperate, Matt, for you must act as President and keep our happy crew from testing the flavor of boiled Englishman.'

Scrivener grimaced and they both laughed ruefully.

Smith put Percy in command of the pinnace and himself went in the discovery barge with fourteen of his most trusted veterans.

A cold southeast wind retarded them on their journey down the river, and they stopped at Warraskoyack for the night. The Werowance received them hospitably and took the leaders into his wigwam where he feasted them.

In the morning they sailed out into the bay, which was like the open sea from the tearing wind and rain. They put in at Kekoutan, where they had first been welcomed by the Savages. Pochins, Powhatan's eldest son, ruled this nation, and Smith asked for lodging for his braves till the storm had spent itself.

Pochins looked as old as his father, a handsome prince. Like all of Powhatan's children, he had always showed friendship to John Smith, and he now offered kind hospitality, so that Smith was unable to divine from him what Powhatan's treachery might intend.

The rain turned to snow, which, being wind-driven, curtained all so that one could not see his hand before him. But inside the wigwams they feasted, and since it was Christmas, told the

Savages of the festival at home and sang Christian carols, their voices ringing with their homesickness, though all agreed that they had never been more merry nor fed on greater plenty of oysters, fish, flesh, and wild fowl, nor ever had better fires in England than in the dry, smoky houses of Kekoutan.

At Werowocomoco the river was frozen half a mile from the shore. Smith left the pinnace to float at anchor and had the barge driven as far as it could go to break the ice till the ebb tide left it stranded on the mud shoals.

The silence of the woods was lonely. Smith listened for the sound of friend or foe. Only the clumsy crashing of his fourteen men or the soft plop of snow as it melted from the branches disturbed the emptiness. No smoke curled into the shimmering sky above the trees; and as they reached the outlying wigwams around the wall, he knew that Powhatan and all his nation had departed.

He had come before when Powhatan was away and Pocahontas had held court; but then there had been maids and crones and old braves to guard the wigwams. Then there had not been this pall of silence.

They straggled through the gates, unbelieving. A thick carpet of snow covered everything, unbroken save where the feet of small animals had left their telltale marks. Even as the men stood, breathless, a hare hopped out from behind the King's wigwam to the center of the town where it paused to look at them without alarm. The little beast emphasized what Smith already knew. Powhatan had been gone many Suns.

A sudden shot startled him, and the hare fell, the snow around him crimsoning. Smith felt an angry twinge, but then he told himself: we have to eat.

He sent a party into the woods to see what else could be added for their supper; others he set to building fires and boiling water. They quartered that night in Powhatan's lodges, and Smith lay awake, a great emptiness in his belly, though he had fed. He had feared this journey, feared to face Powhatan in his wrath; but he had hoped that he would find the warmth of Nantequos and that tonight – though he had known that there was nothing to make him hope – all would have been right and Pocahontas would be within his arms, receiving his long-stored seed. At last he arose and sent the guard to bed, and he sat staring out into the silent village, watching the shadows and brooding over what was in Powhatan's mind.

With the dawn he sent parties abroad, leading one himself, but not a Savage did they find, nor any trace of the vanished nation of Powhatan. *It is as though the Monacans have at last descended and left no vestige,* Smith thought, and was surprised at the sadness that engulfed him.

Since it was again ebb tide, the barge was once more upon the mud. He called to the pinnace that he and his men must stay ashore till high water, which would come at midnight, and he asked for reinforcements. Percy himself came with nine men.

'What has happened?' he asked. Smith told him. 'Then you are finished here?'

'It would seem so – unless Powhatan knows of our visit and returns. But if he comes I don't know whether it will be as friend or foe. I fear he means to exterminate us in one way or another.'

They started up the hill toward the deserted city.

At nightfall the English established guards about the walls and set to making fires.

No moon lit the sky, and the company huddled about the fires, wondering what would happen now that Powhatan who ruled this land had turned against them.

Percy looked at Smith. 'You blame Newport for this, don't you?'

Smith shrugged. 'And Newport will blame me. Most will blame me. Who is to say which would succeed, I with my bluster or Newport with his gifts. Either one, perhaps, if Newport was content to pay, and keep on paying. But not both. It is when they're brewed that simple herbs make deadly poison.'

'By God, in London you would make a poet.'

'I've tried my hand at that – and other things,' Smith said, smiling.

'There's many mistake your talents,' Percy said.

'Aye, many!'

'And say you seek to achieve greatness for yourself through this Colony.'

Percy had always held aloof from him, and Smith was glad for a chance to explain to this aristocrat what he *did* seek.

'I, too, am the Colony, and I would . . . '

They were interrupted by a shout from a guard, and instantly all were on their feet, muskets cocked and ready. Smith and Percy ran to the gates.

'It's one alone – a woman or a child – running!'

And then *she* came. She sped through the gate and stopped. Her face, startled and apprehensive, was lit by the fires, but those around her were dark, the light on their backs.

'Pocahontas!'

Her eyes found him and instantly she was in his arms, her heart beating against him, her head buried in his chest.

'Father! Lord!'

'My Princess!'

'Take me somewhere – alone,' she whispered.

As he turned with her he saw the quizzical stare of Percy, keenly alert and interested, and Smith knew that that which he had guarded was a secret no longer.

'She has something to tell me privately,' Smith said. 'I will take her to one of the wigwams which has been warmed.'

He could feel Percy watching him as he led her away.

Those who were in the wigwam he sent out, and he took her to the fire. She was shivering, from cold or from agitation, and he chafed her hands. She drew them away.

'Love me with your lips – just once,' she said.

He bent and kissed her brow, her cheeks and nose and chin, and then lingeringly her mouth. She yielded herself, but only for seconds. She turned her face and caught his hands, holding him at arm's length.

'Powhatan sends you cheer – a feast,' she said. Her breath was short, and she paused.

'The white braves will be grateful.'

'My Father!' She raised her hands to cover her face. When she took them down her eyes were bright with tears, but she shook her head, refusing to shed them. My only father – for Powhatan is not!'

'Sweet love!' Smith said compassionately, sharing her sorrow. 'You must not blame him for what has been done.'

'Not for what has *been*!'

He tensed. 'Powhatan comes?' Because he was frightened his voice sounded harsh.

'Oh, go! Go back to Jamestown.'

'We cannot go till the middle of the Darkness.'

She stood looking into the fire. He knew how bitter it was to her to betray her father.

Her voice was a whisper. 'He will send braves with food, and if they cannot kill you while you feast, then Powhatan, with all his power, will come – and he will kill you.'

'How brave you are to come and tell me this.'

'I do not know,' she said. 'I do not know.'

'But never fear. We will . . . ' He stopped. He could not say that they would kill the Savages, perhaps Powhatan. 'We will be on our guard.'

'And do not go to Pamaunkey.'

116

'To Pamaunkey?' he asked, amazed.

'Opechancano sends – to invite you. It is why Powhatan seeks to come to you first.' Whenever she spoke of her father her voice lowered as though she wanted to still the thought.

'What of Nantequos?'

'He is guarded in his wigwam. But he got word to me. They did not think I knew, or that I could come – so far.' He looked at her in wonder and in pity. 'I must go. If it is found that I . . .'

'Stay with me!' Smith said suddenly and positivily. 'I will take you for my wife – and will protect you!'

She paused. standing so forlornly that he moved to draw her close to him. She was pliant but unyielding.

'I must go. There, I can – perhaps – help.'

She threw back her head to stare into his face, then pulled herself from his arms and ran from the wigwam.

Master Percy met them. 'She came to warn us?'

'Yes! And timely, too!'

'I have brought her gifts.'

'That is a kind thought,' Smith said dazedly. He told Pocahontas.

She listened and answered him, then ran away by herself, as she had come.

'What did she say?' Percy demanded.

'She thanked you, but she said she could not accept, lest she be seen with them, for if Powhatan should know, she would be surely dead.'

Percy looked at him quizically. 'You have gone far with this Princess.'

Smith sensed what he thought, that the Colony's President sought greater gain, an empire, perhaps; but he was shattered by the maid's coming, her bitter sacrifice and sundered loyalties. He could not answer Percy.

CHAPTER NINETEEN

All were alerted to expect a battle, even against those who came with gifts of food; and there was barely time, for almost as soon as the guards were called out, into the walls came braves with dishes of venison and raccoon, fish and breads.

'We are happy to bring Powhatan's bounty,' their leader said, 'but we beg you to put out your matches, for their smoke makes our braves sick. You see we come in peace.'

'The matches,' Smith said, 'shall stay lit, and before we eat you must yourself taste the food you serve.'

'But I have fed.' the startled brave explained.

Smith fingered his pistol, looking down at its embossing. 'Then feed again,' he said, suddenly pointing the muzzle, though his words and expression were mild.

The savage quaked, but he sampled the dishes. Perhaps he did not know if they were poisoned or not. However, since he did not grow blue or fall down dead, the English partook lustily, for the perils and labors of the day had brought their appetites to a peak. Only Smith ate listlessly.

'Tonight you are no trencherman,' Percy said sardonically.

'I wait the passes of the night.' Smith answered, which was not true since he felt hardly here. With her he sped the forest in this darkest night. How many miles? She would not have told him where Powhatan lay, though he only longed to travel with her in his mind. Like an animal of the forest she would creep into the camp or town, whatever it was, and into the wigwam filled with her sleeping maids. Pray God, they slept! For him she had risked this! Risked all – and fear of death had not brought the shine of tears to her dear eyes!

'We have finished. Now what do we say to these strapping naked devils?' Percy asked. Smith started, stared at Percy, then about him. '*You* speak their language so tenderly.'

Smith quickened to his sarcasm, but did not answer it. He rose and thanked the braves for coming in a speech consciously elaborate. Then tersely, he bade: 'Return to Powhatan, and tell him to make haste for we are prepared for his coming.'

One looked to the other, but none answered. The leader started out and all followed readily, because of the sickness they felt from the odor of the matchlocks.

The English were twenty-five, and each was posted on guard, gun primed and ready. There were three hours till midnight. Smith patrolled the King's city, seeing that all stayed awake and alert, but his thoughts bordered on despair.

She had said, 'They did not think I could come so far.' How far? He thought of her in the wintry forest, the utter dark . . . beset by her passion of betrayal. His arms ached, his spirit flew beside her. Why had he not insisted that she stay? What awaited her when she returned?

He had reached a wall, and nothing he knew could compass it or conquer it. He must turn back, and that decision had been certain in the wigwam with Pocahontas in his arms. He had said: 'Stay with me! I will take you for my wife!' He had been ready to defy Powhatan's power and risk God knew what with his own people. From their meeting only, Percy suspected him of – everything! And how could they survive now? He himself had said, when he argued for this trip, if Powhatan did not trade they would not find his nations. And those whom London sent so weak and helpless they could not live without the Savages' corn! Only this winter, he thought. After that it can be different. If they send farmers and laborers . . .

Percy moved from the fire to join him.

'We return,' he asked, 'with beaten tails?'

Smith straightened his shoulders. 'No, we go to trade at Pamaunkey.'

Percy stared at him. 'You are mad! Opechancano is the greatest of your enemies.'

My enemies! Smith thought. *Not* ours, *but* mine!

'He sends tomorrow to invite us.'

'Tomorrow? How do you know?'

'I know it.'

'Pocahontas told you that Opechancano will trade with us?'

Smith was silent. The wall stretched in a great half-circle around them . . . but if he could pierce it at its hardest core . . .

'We will take back Jamestown's corn – from Opechancano!'

Percy regarded him. 'You're a very vainglorious fellow,' he said.

Smith trudged on, wondering if he were.

Midnight, and none had come. Smith ordered the dousing of the fires, and by the light of firebrands the English made their way to the river where the barges floated on the tide. The men rowed to them and boarded and drove them alongside the pinnace where like mothered ducklings they clung. Smith bedded with his men on the discovery barge, only Percy and his crew going aboard the pinnace.

In the morning, there being still no sound from the land, they set sail to Pamaunkey. It was a journey of two nights, and for most it was farther than any had traveled up the river, though their Captain had been there when he was a captive of Opechancano just a year ago.

As they sailed, the river narrowed, and the banks on either side were snow-covered and barren. Then they came to rough water, and another river tumbled in to impede them, but the point they looked on, Captain Smith told them, was where Opechancano's city lay. They hove to the north shore until they were past the rapids, and then they could see Opechancano, his women, and some forty of his braves waiting to receive them on the opposite bank.

Captain Smith called to him, and he beckoned them. They anchored in a cove. The Captain gave orders that their cannon be primed, and then he, Lieutenant Percy, the young and flighty Master West, Master Russell, and others to the number of fifteen set out in the discovery barge. Smith left word that upon hearing one shot, Master Phettiplace who manned the pinnace should send reinforcements.

Opechancano greeted them with a warm welcome.

'You received my message?'

'No,' Smith said innocently, 'but we would not come to Powhatan and not seek the hospitality of Opechancano.'

He would have begun the trading the next day, but Opechancano would not hear of such mercenary dealings. He must entertain the Captain he had not seen for many moons – his dear friend.

The city of Pamaunkey sat on a rise some quarter mile from the river, and the snowy plain between was planted in the spring with beans and corn, peas, gourds, pumpkins, and other fruit unknown to the white men, Captain Smith told them.

The city itself consisted of four or five buildings, a hundred feet in length, built of split withes, but from its height Opechancano swept his arm, and a hundred wigwams could be seen, also

120

built on fertile land. He indicated that from there he must gather his provender.

Two days they feasted, and those nights they slept on the barges and pinnace, and always Captain Smith was alert, for what the Savage intended he did not know. Then on the third day he and his men climbed to Opechancano's city to trade.

Like Werowocomoco, it was abandoned, except for a lame Savage and a boy.

The English stood on guard while Smith questioned these two. But only a short time elapsed before Opechancano came with his braves armed with bows and arrows. He greeted Smith happily, then said he was prepared to trade one basket of corn for two sheets of copper.

Smith started and glared. 'What business is this?'

'Corn is scarce, and copper not so scarce.'

'Then let us take our copper and return. And why have you invited us?'

'Our love . . . ' Opechancano began.

'Opechancano! The love you profess with your tongue seems mere deceit by your actions. You know my want, and I know your plenty, of which by some means I must have part.'

Opechancano embraced him. 'Your tongue is mighty as your firesticks. Name what price you will and we will trade. And tomorrow I will bring my people better provided.'

For an instant only, Smith cocked his brow to stare at Opechancano. Then he began busily to trade.

The next day with the same fourteen Captain Smith went again to Opechancano's city where he found plenty of newly arrived corn. Opechancano received him in one of the great wigwams. He assured the Captain that in Pamaunkey he could always hope to trade, for he valued the friendship between his nation and the English.

Smith would have replied when Russell rushed in.

'We are all betrayed! Hundreds of braves surround the city!'

Smith's thoughts raced, fearsomely clear as though he drowned in icy water.

'Percy! West! Make good the house! Powell and Behethland, guard the door!' But one glance outside showed him that Pamaunkeys in numbers waited the word of their Werowance.

He reached out suddenly and caught Opechancano by his long lock, dragging his great height down until he squirmed in anguish.

Smith pulled his pistol and drove the point into Opechancano's

121

breast. His trembling was more violent than the shivering of Pocahontas, and Smith took pleasure in the thought. He shoved him past the astonished guards and out into the open where the assembled braves watched incredulously.

'Persuade your braves,' Smith said, 'that I come lovingly.'

Opechancano muttered words, and his shield and bow and arrows were brought and laid at Smith's feet. Thereupon all his braves cast down their arms.

For the first time Smith faced them. Never in all the time he had been in Virginia had he seen such an army. They were outnumbered fifty times over.

He gave a final twist to Opechancano's lock, then, raising his arm high, for Opechancano was taller that he, hauled the Werowance to his feet.

'*This* is the corn you have been gathering, Opechancano?'

Opechancano's face was purple with hate, but he dared not express it since Smith held him, and the white men's guns were on him rather than on his braves.

He rasped his orders, and his people went readily, for the sight of their Lord's humiliation was painful to them.

Since many must go some leagues distant to gather their goods, Smith, who had not slept or rested, sank down onto a load of corn. Percy sat beside him.

'Suddenly I am shaky. I don't like your hospitable Savages.'

'Keep their King at gun's point and all will be well.'

Percy nodded. There was a silence, and then he said, 'Tell me, is she greased and painted red when she comes to you?' Smith stared at him, so that in spite of himself the other colored. 'Pardon it. I did not fancy that it meant anything.'

Smith turned away. He had no right to be angered, he told himself. It was what any would have thought – a night's delirium with a Savage maid. He himself would have thought it had it been Percy.

'Did you ever think – how vulnerable?' He looked off at Opechancano, trussed and sour like an image of their Oke, under the guns of four soldiers. 'He must have seven hundred braves here, and we hold them because we hold their King. And what Powhatan could have done with his minions when we were only thirty-nine sad souls at Jamestown?'

'That we are vulnerable, I've thought of. Yes,' Percy said. 'Any man who comes to Virginia and overvalues his life . . . '

'Not my point. You spoke of Pocahontas. I am thinking of what she has done for us.'

'I've said I was sorry. . . '

122

Smith waved the apology aside. 'Some two or three hundred leagues south of us is saint Augustine, where the Spaniards are strongly established. Daily, I expect to see a galleon sail into the Chesapeake and bombard our fort. Knowing how jealous Spain is of our efforts here, how long do you think it would be before she would move in if we were exterminated, as was the colony at Roanoke. Then this vast continent would be lost to England forever.'

'You were talking of Pocahontas?'

'What you saw – the night she came – we were dead men, else. Without her, we would not be here in Virginia, precarious as it is for us at the moment. She has fed us; she has saved us at the risk of her own life.'

Percy said, 'I grant you that. I grant you what you said, she is the nonpareil of Virginia.'

Smith glanced at him. Had he at last found a friend in this haughty noble? If so, it was a friendship to be valued.

'I wonder you have not thought of marrying her.' Percy continued. 'She is a maid of spirit and beauty, and it would make you a great man here if the Colony continues.'

Smith felt stunned, to have his thoughts revealed. To hear her spoken of so and his right to her acknowledged warmed him. 'I have thought on it, indeed. She is rare – in her heart pure and loyal. Any man – but have I the right?' He paused. He was not one to unburden himself; his emotions were encased deep within him; but Percy's newly felt sympathy aroused him; and he had for so long been torn with doubts. 'If I can, I will stay here – Powhatan has offered me a nation. And I would be happy to make Pocahontas my lady.'

'You would be a king in Virginia.'

Smith smiled. 'If we live. These are dreams only. Powhatan has ceased to be our friend.'

'And Opechancano our bitter enemy!' Percy retorted. *At least it is* our *enemy now*, Smith thought. 'What do we do? How will our President find our food again?'

'We'll grow it!' Smith said forcefully. 'We've lived on their bounty enough – too much! Our dependence on these Savages is our greatest weakness.'

'Bravely spoken!' Percy said and then thought further. 'We have too many who love to idle. If they can be persuaded to work . . .'

'Too many gentlemen!' Smith said fiercely.

He felt the silent withdrawal, saw the eyes which had been friendly glaze.

'Many are brave and stalwart like yourself, but those who are afraid of roughened hands . . .'

'The orders are very strict from London as to what is to be required of a gentleman and how he is to be treated. . . .'

'But not a word as to how he is to be fed!'

They stared at each other hostilely. Then coolly Percy rose, nodded, and walked away.

Damnation! Smith thought. *Sure, I am no diplomat. I had him, and I've lost him – like that! And he was worth the keeping.*

'What in hell is so sacred about a gentleman?' he said aloud. *They starve and bleed and die and fornicate and get the clap and whine and grovel!*

At supper that night he addressed Percy in a friendly way, but from the coolness and restrained courtesy of the Earl's son he knew that what he had lost was not to be regained.

CHAPTER TWENTY

With glue made from the sinews of deer and the tops of deerhorn Pocahontas fastened rabbit skins onto the board. With a thorn she pierced the hide where it covered the hole in the wood, inserted a reed, and carefully cut a circle in the fur. This she glued around the edges so there would be no roughness.

The entrance darkened, and she looked up. Nantequos paused a second to adjust his eyes and then entered with Tomakkin.

'Have you got him?'

Pocahontas indicated their sister, Matachanna. 'He is there.'

Nantequos leaned over, and Matachanna opened her mantle to reveal the child who gulped at the air like a fish and turned back to the warmth of her body. Nantequos reached out and took him, holding him carefully aloft.

'He looks like me.'

'He looks like an opossum from the pouch,' Tomakkin said.

But Pocahontas knew it was not from doting that Nantequos had spoken. 'He is like Nantequos,' she said firmly, 'and Nantequos is no opossum.'

Both braves laughed. 'Matachanna and I will make his equal,' Tomakkin said with a sly grin at Matachanna.

Pocahontas's maidens giggled. Next Sun Matachanna would be pounced with the needle, her brow and breasts and thighs, and later would lie with Tomakkin in his wigwam.

'May he resemble Matachanna then,' Pocahontas said fervently, 'or it will be thought he is an overstuffed raccoon who seeks his long sleep with the first snow.'

'And Pocahontas's son will be born with hair on his face like the bear.' Tomakkin retorted, grinning.

'I have no papoose in my belly,' she said with dignity. She rose and took the squirming child from Nantequos. 'Now go to Opuiske,' she said to her brother.

When the two had gone, she and Matachanna oiled the baby's

125

body and then laid him upon the board, buttocks covering the hole, and fastened him by bands around his ankles, middle, and criss-crossed over his shoulders. He cried out loudly at first to be thus stretched, but Pocahontas rocked the board and infant in her arms, crooning, and the cries ceased.

'Grow straight, little bones,
  Grow strong!
To follow the stag on wingéd feet
And stretch the bowstring
Whooeesh!

'Grow straight, little bones,
  Grow strong!
To strike your enemy to the ground
And circle your love
Ayiiee!'

By a woven cord in the top of the board, Pocahontas dangled the child, swinging it to continue the rhythm. Then, cradling the board, she went out. Though the snow still lay in patches, the sun shone gaily, the air was vibrant.

Both Opuiske and Nantequos turned to her as she entered, and Opuiske held out her arms. Pocahontas gave her the baby, and Opuiske fingered the rabbit's fur, her hands hovering but not lingering as they touched the child.

'How well you have done it!' she said.

Pocahontas pulled Nantequo's mantle from a forked branch which projected beside the bed.

'Later, you can hang him here. And when he tires of that, you can lay him flat, or tilt him.' she said, as though she knew much more about it than Opuiske.

Her sister-in-law's eyes were warm and grateful and much too understanding. Pocahontas should have been full of Johnsmith's child by now – how that would have affected Powhatan she had only hoped – but though she had scattered tobacco on the water, buried the copper bracelets Johnsmith had given her in the cornfield, and offered all the prayers she knew, his seed had not taken root.

'Have you seen Powhatan?' she asked.

'No,' Nantequos said shortly.

She lifted the board with his son tentatively. 'May I?'

Neither answered, so she took the child and left.

126

Powhatan slept; a new custom to sleep when the sun was bright, but now he sat late before the fire, listening to the storytellers, or telling tales himself, as though he dreaded the solitude of the night.

Pocahontas motioned his wives to go and seated herself, gently rocking the child to keep him still. She watched her father, and such a longing, love, and pity overcame her that she thought she could not bear it.

He had never been old, but he was old now, his long locks streaked with white. He lay on his back, his mouth open, making him seem vulnerable, his beaked nose poised over it like a precarious crag. The harsh lines which seamed his cheeks had slacked, yet were no less deep; they were like the runlets of tears.

The baby squirmed and cried out, and she renewed the rocking to quiet him, but Powhatan started up suddenly.

She kept her face lowered, and at last hid it with her hand. He took her hand away, and then lifted the child, staring at it.

'Nantequos's son?' he asked. She nodded. 'And none told me? *He* did not tell me?'

Pocahontas longed to creep away on hands and knees like a sinner who has been chastised. Why had she come? She felt sure Powhatan had sensed the treachery of the two he loved the most, had known that they, either of themselves or by their connivance, had warned Johnsmith at Werowocomoco.

Very gently Powhatan laid the child upon the bed. Then he lifted Pocahontas.

'Does he think I do not love him? Do *you*?'

'Yes.' Her voice was so small, so shamed, she felt her thought had not reached her lips.

He held her close, and she swam upward in the security of his embrace. . . . '*I* am your home now!' She had sinned against him – for only a small part of her sin he would have had Werowances staked and flayed! She had betrayed him, yet still his arms were home. . . .

She could not bear the compassion. She pulled away and raised her face. 'I am sorry!'

'I have not said that you were wrong.'

He knew then – all or part of it and with the relief of his forgiveness, she was ashamed at the thought: '*I have him again! He will do what I want!*

'Bid Nantequos come,' he told her. 'We must view this marvel together.'

127

Chickahomanies brought the story first, and it was not to be believed. If they had told that the Monacans had descended and destroyed everything to the Bay, that the English had burned their fort and left, these things would have been easier to accept. But to hear that Opechancano had been grasped by the hair and made to grovel on the ground, that he had been dragged before his own people and cried mercy – and not one of his enemy fallen – Opechancano with over seven hundred braves, and Johnsmith with fourteen men!

Nantequos leaped to his feet, his eyes exulting. Sternly Powhatan motioned him to sit. What could come now but war?

Powhatan dismissed his Cockarouses and the Chickahomanies. He sat staring a long time, his face grim.

Finally Nantequos spoke, the words pouring out of him as though he could not hold them back.

'What would you have him do? Openchancano invited them only to destroy them.'

After a long time Powhatan stared at Nantequos and spoke with great feeling.

'You do not see the horror of this? That this has been done to your uncle? Might have been done to your father? Do you not see the terrible vengeance that is called for?' Nantequos stared back. 'You have not the wit of your son, so newly born. I wish you had.'

Pocahontas sensed Powhatan's thought, but Nantequos instantly was hot.

'What wit do I lack?'

'The wit to govern,' Powhatan said wearily, turning away.

'But I do not want to govern.'

'Someone has to! You are loyal! You are brave! You are eager!' Powhatan spread his hands. 'But you have no wit. I tell myself it is because you are too young – it *must* be because you are too young! A few more years . . .'

'You think I really became crazed in the Huskanan pen!' Nantequos said, hurt and accusing.

Powhatan shook his head as though to clear it.

Pocahontas ceased to listen. An awful thought had crept into her consciousness. She sat, alternating hot and cold, as though she had a sickness, and all the time she prayed to know. Hot hand – cold hand! Right hand – left hand! Good – evil! She did not notice when Nantequos left.

Powhatan looked at her. 'He does not know what I speak of – but you know.' She nodded, frightened, not of him, but of herself. 'He says I think him still possessed of the effects of the wysoccan – and perhaps I do!'

Almost in a daze, as if she were a Priest, she spoke: 'He has never been possessed of the wysoccan.'

'You remember him! Not even you!'

'When you gave him Katoka . . . '

'Aye?' Powhatan was suddenly alert. This was what he had wondered. *This!*

'You thought they had lain together – that his seed was in her – even before the Huskanan. . . . '

'Aye . . . '

'She told him – when they were wed she told him . . . ' Pocahontas could not go on. She felt strangled. Sin is not committed by acts, or deeds, or with the hands – only with words! And those who sin need not be burned. Cut out their tongues and they can sin no longer.

'She told him *what?*'

'That she was with child – by Opechancano!'

Powhatan rose as though he had been stung.

'*No!*'

Her mouth was dry; the blood had drained from her so that she could not stir. He lifted her.

'Tell me!'

She covered her face, and still she could not speak. He took her to his couch and sat her down.

'It is something in me, and I am ashamed because of it, that makes you and Nantequos fear me so.'

'No!' She looked at him. 'We are not afraid of you, Powhatan. Nantequos feared for Katoka. . . . '

'Why would Opechancano do this? Can you be sure?'

But she saw that he was sure – leaving himself, becoming Nantequos, visioning the change: first to nothingness, then to his proud stand against the uncle who had wronged him.

9

Powhatan drew himself erect as though from a stupor. 'Nantequos said: "I know how you would pollute the blood of Powhatan!"' His eyes were glazed.

She lay down crookedly; her body was as though she sat. *Oh, please,* she thought, *let this time pass! Let it be as if it never was and I not said it!*

Powhatan stormed back and forth in the wigwam, his brow heavy, his mouth fierce. He turned to her suddenly where she lay crouched.

'I am hit both back and forward. Johnsmith, whose English do not cease to come . . . ' She could say no more than she had said; she did not know what was in Johnsmith's mind. 'And Opechancano!'

One of Rawhunt's scouts brought in the message: Opechancano, Powhatan's brother, Werowance of Pamaunkey, approached.

'Does Nantequos know that you have told me this?'

She moaned. 'I would kill myself if he knew.'

'I have not even the faith of those I love. Call the Cockarouses!' he instructed the scout. He turned to Pocahontas. 'Go and prepare yourself. And Nantequos! But do not tell him that you have told me anything. My love should be a simple thing,' he added, but it was not to her, only to himself.

Opechancano was as he had never been. Inside him the four gods holding the four winds raged. He could not wait to speak.

'You have fostered them! You have nourished them! You have sent your daughter!'

'I have sent my daughter to lie with a man who is now my enemy. There are times one does not know one's enemies.'

Opechancano could not talk of what had occurred. He was changed; his color flowed as freely, but he was less brilliant. Pocahontas could imagine how the flaming of his blood had fled with fear, could vision him dragged out like an effigy before his own braves. Bitterer than death! How had his skin looked then? Suddenly she was sorry for Opechancano whose pride was greater even than Powhatan's. Fear and love drove her to look at her father whose flesh was parched, drained of moisture. Would Johnsmith have treated Powhatan so? Her jaw clenched, and she wondered how she could have betrayed her father, her people.

'So long as you keep faith, your enemy is my enemy,' Powhatan said.

130

'Then we will gather the nations, and you will lead us in a war until there is not a white man left alive.'

'No!'

The word exploded, shocking the wigwam to stillness. Heads jerked up and then away, for all feared to be absorbed in the tension that bound Powhatan and Opechancano.

'For you have not kept faith!'

'I? You are in your dotage, Powhatan! Name your heir, now, and *I* will lead the war.'

'*Nantequos is my heir!*' Powhatan's voice was like the boom of thunder but deadly as the lightning.

Opechancano rose slowly, disbelief almost softening the malevolence of his face. He wheeled suddenly, and before any could realize or stop him, he dashed to the tunnel and outside into the open.

Powhatan was on his feet. 'Arms!' he shouted, and as he spoke those inside heard Opechancano's call rallying his braves. There was pandemonium as braves scrambled to the exit. With an English hatchet, Rawhunt hacked an opening in the back of the wigwam, and Powhatan, Nantequos, and the others fled, all quieting outside to hear Powhatan's commands. Then there were the war shouts of Opechancano's braves and Powhatan's as they came together.

But even with the surprise of their attack, Opechancano's party could not stand against Powhatan's host. They fell back, forcing a retreat through the wall, and reached the forest where in the gathering darkness they were safe.

Powhatan assembled his braves and Cockarouses in the center of the town so as not to risk another ambush. He had himself raised to stand over them.

'Opechancano has made war on Powhatan, and there can be no peace till he and his rebellious braves are dead.' Powhatan addressed Rawhunt. 'Send your scouts to all the nations. Each Werowance shall send half his braves this night to Pamaunkey, for we go to conquer Opechancano. Our braves here shall stay under Nantequos, in case Opechancano tries to take this city.'

'Not under me,' Nantequos cried out. 'I go with Powhatan!'

Other braves shouted, wanting to go, but Powhatan silenced them.

'Nantequos is right. But for you others, except my own guard, you shall stay here. Before we go, Tomakkin shall take my daughter Matachanna, and he shall stay to command you, being her husband.'

In the darkness Pocahontas watched them leave, silently disappearing into the forest's depths. She turned away, frightened and sick. *This* she had done.

CHAPTER TWENTY-TWO

The Werowances of Powhatan's nations convened at Pamaunkey, Opechancano's principal city. Word had been received of their coming, but there was no resistance since Opechancano had not returned. Most of his family had fled, but those wives and children who remained were divided among Powhatan's sons and two loyal brothers, Nantequos taking his pick: three fair squaws on whom he wrought that night with bitter triumph and lusty cruelty.

Since Powhatan's words proclaiming Nantequos his heir, and Opechancano's rebellion, another great change had come upon him. He was no longer the ardent, tender youth, but like a flaming arrow shot into the night. Elation at the struggle with his enemy made his eyes sparkle, his body leap with power; all he did he did with purpose, even to the taking of his uncle's wives.

At Sun's Rising he led his braves into the cold water to bathe, and then he came alone to Powhatan.

'The Chickahomanies sent no braves.'

'No.'

'Has Opechancano sought refuge in their land?'

'Perhaps. We must wait for Rawhunt to see what answer their Priests make to my command.' Powhatan watched his son, marveling at this night's work upon him. 'You have not said anything since I named you my heir.'

Nantequos lifted his head in a proud gesture. 'May it be many cohonks that I may have time to learn and have Powhatan to be my model.'

'Yet you always said,' Powhatan probed, 'that you did not want to rule, nor to have power.'

'I will lead the nations of Powhatan.'

'In peace if possible.'

'Aye – when Opechancano is dead. For Powhatan also said, "There can be no peace till he and his braves are dead." '

'Those were violent words. I hope that he and his people travel far into strange lands so that we can both forget our enmity.'

Nantequos's face was suddenly stark. 'Powhatan, I would tell you . . . ' and he told of the defiling of Katoka. Though he had heard the story, Powhatan grew grimmer and older as he listened. 'So I can never rest till I have slain him,' Nantequos finished.

Powhatan agreed. 'You cannot rest.'

Powhatan held Council with his Werowances.

'Until we have word of him, we cannot know where he may strike if he intends to continue this rebellion, so all nations and all cities shall be readied for a war.' He paused and then went on. 'It is not well to fight the English and Opechancano at once, and if the English come to trade it may be thought we arm against them. Therefore, it will be best to resume the trade with James-town.'

'Johnsmith has said,' Nantequos declared, 'that he would be our ally against Opechancano.'

So long Nantequos has dreamed of this, Powhatan thought. Once he would have spoken curtly and quieted his son as a rash youth. The very idea of inviting the white men to destroy his brother was abhorrent.

'If the English learn that we are divided, is it possible that they will seek to conquer us in our weakness?' Nantequos moved to answer, but Powhatan went swiftly on. 'In our love for these over whom we rule we seek in all ways to protect them against any who is alien and who might be enemy.' With satisfaction Powhatan saw his son subside.

Rawhunt came into the wigwam and, advancing, laid his head at Powhatan's feet.

'Ho, Rawhunt!'

Powhatan beckoned Nantequos to sit beside him, and they two talked in low tones with Rawhunt. At last Rawhunt stepped aside, and Powhatan spoke.

'The Priests who rule the Chickahomanies have long been surly, not wishing to recognize our absolute authority. We sent to them, as to all nations, commanding that half their braves should join us here at Pamaunkey, but when their Priests received my orders, they claimed first that Rawhunt, whom they know well, did not come from me, and then that they had no cause to join a war against Opechancano. This is usurping authority which is not theirs, but mine!'

'Aye!' the wigwam echoed.

'I shall stay here at Pamaunkey, which shall be my principal city. Werowances shall return to their nations and prepare, each taking but half the braves he brought. With those who are left, and with his own braves, Nantequos, my son and my *successor*' – he said the last loudly and distinctly, pausing lest any should not have heard what he had declared before and offer here his objection; there was not a sound, and he resumed – 'shall proceed to Chickahominy where he shall demand their yearly tribute, which is past due, in corn and copper, as well as a fine of eight hundred baskets of corn and twenty chains of peak for having denied my commandment. If they have not so much at this time, he shall bring here three Priests, who will be hostages till the Chickahomanies fulfill these demands.'

His eyes circled the Werowances to see who might wish to speak, but save for a few 'Ayes!' and grunts of approval, none spoke.

Pocahontas with all Powhatan's family was removed to Pamaunkey, and it was here Nantequos came, his braves loaded down with tribute from the Chickahomanies, but since they lacked in full the payment demanded, he brought also their chief Priests.

Powhatan received Nantequos as from a great victory, lectured the Chickahomanies, and sent them home again.

'It is better that they fault somewhat in their corn, which grows and dies and grows again, than that we breed their vengeance, which will never die.'

'They claim they know nothing of Opechancano, but I am sure they do,' Nantequos said. 'With the Sun's Rising I will leave, and we will search the forests.'

'In pursuit of the stag you cannot pause and must not rest. You, as I feel impelled toward your end. I used not to flinch, for then the promise was bright.' Powhatan covered his eyes. 'Now it is dark.'

Power she had dreamed of, for herself, for Nantequos, for Johnsmith, visualizing in each the successor of the flashing Wahunsonacock. But now, as Nantequos strutted through the town, possessor of all she had willed for him, she wondered. With her he was no less loving; his braves worshiped him and would follow him to the stake; his squaws all fawned upon him as Pummahump, the dog, fawned upon Powhatan. But he was quick and brisk and *so* sure – and Powhatan was *so* weary – that she asked herself: *When Nantequos has everything will it be what he wants?*

And in her life, it seemed only that short instant in the forest, when Johnsmith had held her closely without passion in his arms and she had felt the ecstasy, had yielded full return. A moment in a life, she thought.

To the farthest reaches of the land of Powhatan, Nantequos searched for Opechancano. Word came of him where his braves had raided a storehouse, had stormed a town, leaving havoc, its people bereft of food and often squaws, who later were abandoned in his flight.

Nantequos almost came upon him once, finding his camp and women and children. These were sent to Powhatan to be distributed and Nantequos added to the wives that were already his.

For some moons they did not see him, so relentless was his pursuit. And Powhatan grew ever glummer.

By the riverbank in a bower of ferns and violets and white daisies, Pocahontas played with Nantequos's son. To the boy's delight, she wove a basket, her fingers moving so swiftly in and out that there was no fastening their play.

Here Nantequos, having come from Powhatan, found her. He stood quietly watching her and the child till she felt his presence and looked up. He took the boy and dandled him, feeling his straight body. The baby reached out for his father's long lock, and Nantequos gave it to him, laughing and making the same sounds the boy made.

Pocahontas's thoughts overwhelmed her as she watched: Powhatan would die, and Nantequos grow old and this papoose would be, perhaps, his father's favorite as Nantequos was Powhatan's, and all the laughing, vibrant youth would be burned up in grim purpose.

Nantequos put down the child. 'What of Opechancano?' she asked.

'It has been my great purpose to keep him from Chickahominy, for there he has too many friends.'

'How long will you stay?'

'I have left the braves under Kokoum, who is heir to the Werowance of Potomac.' He stretched and added, 'Powhatan is not pleased with me.'

'Powhatan is pleased with you,' she said carefully. 'He fears that you . . .'

He laughed. 'I have no wit.'

She put down the reeds. 'No. That from no desire you have too much – or only one desire.'

'Opechancano?'

'Yes.' She let her hands fall into her lap. 'And that you take his wives – so many and so fast. . . . '

He lay back luxuriously on the soft turf. 'Ho! I do not want them. He said to me, "Take what you will!" so I chose three, and it pleasured me to know the shame I put upon Opechancano for what he had done to me. And when we found the others, my braves said, "Our Werowance must take his choice," so I chose the fairest and sent word that they were mine. I would lie only with Opuiske,' he said simply. 'I dread to be Powhatan and send her away because she has borne me children.' He pulled himself up and smiled at Pocahontas. 'I am not so changed. Powhatan broke his heart because he thought me giddy and a fool. And when my enemy came and there was war between him and Powhatan, I felt that now I must be as Powhatan wanted me, for even when he did not believe in me he named me his heir.'

Pocahontas rose suddenly to her feet, pulling him with her. She caught up the baby and slung him across her back, holding him by his left hand and right leg.

'Come. This will ease Powhatan.'

Powhatan looked up when she entered, and Nantequos turned to Pocahontas. She did not hesitate. 'Nantequos has revealed to me good things: that Opechancano is his enemy whom he shall search out and slay, but it is no burning quest, for his day will surely come. And Nantequos does not take his many wives because his blood is heated to a fever, for he would keep Opuiske with him even after he is Powhatan.'

Powhatan grunted. 'Let Nantequos act so, and his people will acclaim his wisdom as they do his bravery.'

'Since you, doubting him greatly, yet showed your love for him by naming him your heir, he has hoped only to redeem your faith, and to act strongly as Powhatan would act.'

Powhatan smiled more and more broadly. He was pleased, but he was also amused.

'We need you on our Council to interpret what we think and feel, as Johnsmith translates English into Powhatan.'

'Tell him that what I have said is true,' Pocahontas commanded.

'It is true. And if it is how a Powhatan would act, I would relax from war for a small part of this fair Budding of the Leaf.'

'Yes. I have other orders. Johnsmith has taken the Werowance to Paspahegh prisoner.'

Nantequos stiffened, and Pocahontas felt her heart pause. Was it all to begin again?

'He attacked him?' Nantequos demanded, and both Pocahontas and Powhatan looked sharply, for his voice was indignant. Would he turn against his blood brother to defend a Werowance of his own people? 'Paspahegh has always been Johnsmith's host and friend.'

'That ceased. Paspahegh ambushed Johnsmith who fought him singly and dragged him into the river and unarmed him. Then Johnsmith forced him to Jamestown and has made him prisoner.'

'He is more than man!' Nantequos exclaimed.

'Aye. But now, without war, we must save our Werowance.'

'I will go,' Nantequos said promptly.

'And Pocahontas,' Powhatan said.

Her heart lifted, and her face shone joyously alive. Through the woods in the Budding of the Leaf she would go to him. When last she had gone the ground had been hard frozen, and the winds had moaned of horrors past and yet to come. The betrayal of her father had bowed her down, and the terror of that darksome night had slashed at her heels like wolves' teeth. Now her sin had been forgiven, and Powhatan sent her to her love.

Powhatan's eyes looked on her joy admonishingly. 'For what you bring, come back with Paspahegh,' he said.

Pocahontas prepared her maidens with many baskets of bread and meat and fowl for the happy journey. She wore aprons of white fringed doeskin, elaborately embroidered in shells and quills from the porcupine. With her she took her jewels of peak, her coronet, and her necklaces, as well as her blue feather mantle.

In the hush of Sun's Rising the party started out, Pocahontas and Nantequos in the lead. The river was pinkly silvered; a hollow moon hung in the west like a cast-off cicada's shell, and the birds heralded their welcome to the sun with many voices. *Tonight!* she thought, and then could not allow herself to think,

CHAPTER TWENTY-THREE

They found much changed at Jamestown. A vast tract had been cleared and plowed for planting and new houses built outside the fort as well as in. Pocahontas waited in the trees while Nantequos with fifteen braves approached the gates. He called out: 'Captain Smith!' There was movement among the guards, and then Johnsmith came onto the wall.

'Who is it?'

'Nantequos!'

'No!' He leaped from the wall inside the fort and came running through the gate. He caught Nantequos's shoulders in his hands, shook him, and took him in his arms. 'What joy!' he cried, stopping abruptly as Pocahontas revealed herself.

She was shadowed, lost in the trees; only her white apron and gleaming peak showed life. Johnsmith gasped, and he, too, stood, seeming without power. Slowly she moved toward him; suddenly he was on his knee, her hand in both of his. He raised it to his lips.

'Do not!' she whispered urgently. 'They will not understand. I should kneel to you.'

There was great merriment in Jamestown that night. Johnsmith received the gifts of Powhatan with pleasure.

'And we, too, shall send back gifts – from our plenty,' he said proudly, 'for it is not as it was. We have had workers here this year. Our land is ready for the planting. We have nets and weirs in the rivers. Our water comes from a well dug within the fort, and our animals have multiplied to sixty hogs and five hundred chickens.'

'When the snow comes, you will not need Powhatan's harvests,' Nantequos said admiringly.

'I pray we can live in respectable self-sufficiency.' Johnsmith laughed suddenly. 'Many a gentleman has calloused hands and his footman learned to dig instead of truckle.'

Master Percy came, and he, too, kissed Pocahontas's hand. He spoke many words, looking at her with admiration. When he was done, Johnsmith translated.

'He remembers always how you came in the night to save our lives at the risk of your own.'

'Ask him to forget,' Pocahontas said, her voice low.

They feasted, and Johnsmith was filled with happiness and gaiety, turning from Pocahontas to Nantequos and always back to her.

She was much content that he should love her, but she was aware always of Percy's glances. If Johnsmith wished still to hide their love, he was not doing so. At last she told him this.

He went on talking. 'You are right, and I will devote myself to Nantequos. And tonight I cannot have you wait for me by my bed, but, my Princess, I shall not live if you don't come.'

'I will come.'

His lips whitened, and then his face flooded with color so that she feared he would betray everything, but he turned and spoke to Nantequos in a low voice.

When they had finished eating, Nantequos asked as though he spoke idly and without great interest, 'You hold the Werowance of Paspahegh your prisoner?'

Johnsmith laughed. 'So that is why Powhatan has sent you? But it does not matter, I am so glad that you have come.'

'Powhatan has sent us an assurance of his love, but he asks that you cease to affront his Werowances.' Nantequos spoke carefully, but his voice was forceful and positive.

Pocahontas felt Johnsmith's start of interest, for this was not how Nantequos had ever spoken to him.

'Nantequos, I have affronted Powhatan's Werowances – Opechancano and Paspahegh – but I have tried not to affront Powhatan. Do you know what provoked me at Pamaunkey and here?'

'Yes.'

'Then know this, and tell Powhatan for me, that I will deal justly with all. He who acts treacherously, I will punish. He who comes to me in friendship, I will cherish. But if I don't track down those who wrong me I lose the respect of my own people and of Powhatan, and I am a lost man.'

'Then you will not release Paspahegh?'

Any moment now she felt she must come between them, for what Johnsmith would grant freely at Nantequos's request he would not, could not, grant as a demand.

'Whatever I have, take all. But I cannot give you Paspahegh.'

'You have killed him!'

'He has escaped.'

'Is this true?'

'Nantequos!' Johnsmith was shocked. 'Has our blood run dry? Are you my enemy?'

'No.'

'Yet you think I lie.'

'I know you speak the truth. Forgive me.'

'And you me,' Johnsmith said in a puzzled voice.

Jamestown slept under a blanched moon. Silently, like the Spirit of the Moon itself, she ran across the silver patches and sought the shadows. She rubbed lightly against his door. Instantly it opened and she was inside. He pushed the bolt and came to her. He was naked, and he held her in his arms with great urgency. She thought: *It can never be again as it was in the forest!* Then she gave herself up to him, meeting his passion, for her need, too, was great. He lifted her and carried her to the bed.

'I am like the rivers when the ice has broken and the waters flow.'

'And I am the earth long frozen, welcoming you.'

'I meant not to use you cruelly.'

'Your love has many faces, but they are all good.'

He turned her to him, holding her most tenderly. And from the stillness, not moving, she felt herself absorbed until once more they were one being, their blood answering to the single heart, and thus were swept up so that she felt light and winging, and the night was day, and suddenly they two as one were carried on a tide whose rhythm was familiar but yet different from anything she had known. 'Not just one moment in a life,' she cried aloud and was still, for this moment had its completion. But not its end, for she was bound in the sweetness of their union, and so she fell asleep, smiling against his shoulder.

When she awoke, he was squatting, his cape around him, building up the fire. She watched him sleepily, loving him thus also, his hair mussed, his whiskers not so fierce. He looked up and saw that her eyes were half open and smiled at her.

When the fire blazed, he arose, dropped his cape and climbed quickly in beside her, cuddling her for warmth. His hands moved over her, but she would stay him now, wanting to remain relaxed and loving.

'What changes you when you make love?'

141

'You mean sometimes I am a poor lover?'

'No. Different.'

'I should not have awaited you as I did.'

'I, too!' she said defensively. 'It is that sometimes you pause for nothing. . . . And sometimes – none could love like you.'

'I have held myself too long, and when it comes my time – I will be gentler with you, Pocahontas.'

But it was not what she meant.

They lay silent, and, thinking she had wounded him, she let him know her readiness, but he, too, was bothered with a question.

'If I am different – so, alas, does Nantequos change. I thought that he would quarrel with me last night.'

She smiled secretly, remembering how Powhatan had called her interpreter.

'He is grieved that he spoke as he did. He told me this. In the Sun's Climb you will find he is the same.'

'But how did I offend him?'

'You did not. His childishness has long made Powhatan unhappy.'

'Childishness! Nantequos is such a man as I could hope our son . . .'

They both were silent, and she hid her face in the hollow of his arm. *Surely, this night. . . !*

'Nantequos now commands Powhatan's army,' she said carefully, for she could not tell of Opechancano, 'and he seeks to behave as Powhatan.'

'I could have sworn it was Powhatan himself.'

'Coming with Powhatan's message, he would not have his love for you betray Powhatan's trust.'

'Tonight he was a subtle Savage.'

'And with the Sun he will be Johnsmith's blood brother.'

He rubbed the side of his head violently. 'What can I do, Pocahontas? Paspahegh has behaved treacherously to me. And it is his nation we live among. I cannot let him go unpunished. I must seek him out.'

Pocahontas thought: *It was for this Powhatan sent me.* She, also, was aware of her task.

'Powhatan would have to protect him – or avenge him.' Smith groaned. 'If you took braves and burned some wigwams – empty wigwams – captured his boats, brought home his weirs, would that not punish him?'

'Aye,' he said doubtfully.

'And if he came to you and said he had done wrong and that

142

he seeks your friendship and will pledge to live in peace forever more – would that satisfy you?'

'Yes.'

'It would satisfy Powhatan, too. And this Paspahegh shall do when you have done the rest.'

Johnsmith laughed aloud. He kissed the tip of her nose. 'You are a subtle Savage, too,' he said and covered her with his body.

CHAPTER TWENTY-FOUR

To Powhatan Smith sent a hog and chickens and other gifts. For Nantequos he drew out a leather bag. Expectantly, Nantequos opened it, and then his face contorted in a maze of disbelief and joy. Reverently, he took out a timepiece.

'I told you once I had a gift I could not send – and when you came it had been burned. I have kept this one for you since Newport's last arrival, but not till now have you come to receive it.'

Nantequos could not speak, his face set in a rigid mold. Smith went quickly on, explaining how to use the key and keep it wound.

'See that you come often so I can teach you all its uses.'

He turned to Pocahontas. With her he always felt empty-handed, she who gave to him such largesse. For a moment he was overcome with gratitude. After the unflagging toil of these long moons, the bitter self-denial and renunciation, being hated taskmaster and rough toiler all the while, to allow himself to break the strictures against her, to find release and warmth in her arms!

He gave her tawdry jewels, frowning as he did so, but she could read his thoughts and gently smiled, accepting them.

Nantequos had recovered himself and would spout out his gratitude, but Smith stopped him, fairly hurrying them from the fort. He watched them go and thought how strange it was that in all the world, they two were closest to him – a pagan lad and lass.

Because of the independence of the Colony, there was greater peace and security in Virginia than Smith had known. In this happy lull, with the crops planted, with soap ashes, tar, and clapboard being manufactured for the next ship to carry back to England, the President engaged his men in constructing a fort on top of a bluff a few miles from Jamestown to be an added defense in case, or when, trouble commenced.

This work ceased, perforce, when it was discovered that much of the corn which they had casked and stored had rotted or been devoured by rats who had come ashore from the ships and multiplied. It was a severe setback, but in the burgeoning summer, with Newport yet to come and the harvest in the ground, it was not a disaster. For these fair months the President deployed the Colony, sending some downriver to live off oysters and sturgeon, sending Master Percy with twenty to Point Comfort to fish and set out weirs, and Master West – who had better served as a scapegrace minion of King James's Court – to the Falls with twenty more to hunt and trade with the Powhatans. For the fort itself there was enough with what the Savages brought of squirrels, turkeys, deer, and that which their own nets and weirs held each morning.

But of the gentlemen with Percy, not one would cast a net. And Lord de la Warr's pretty brother, young Master West, and his company preferred to live off acorns and what they had brought with them.

'Well, let them then!' Smith said in exasperation when he heard. If they could not live in summer in this land, they were not fit to live at all. If they were not forced, *nolens volens*, to gather their victuals, they would all starve or come to eat one another.

Nantequos came much to Jamestown, usually accompanied by a large party of braves painted as for war, though they never showed hostility. Smith suspected that they scoured the country to some purpose, but what he could not guess. Or was it only, since Nantequos had been made Weroames of Powhatan's army, that he kept them trained and ready for an emergency or an attack on those who bordered Powhatan's nations?

Sometimes he brought Pocahontas. She and Smith no more made love within the fort, but met instead by arrangement in the forest, for the skies were blue and the pine needles warm and spongy. He came to understand her desire, and he schooled himself to hold her quietly, most tenderly, till he felt passion leap in her, and then in mounting fever they sought completion.

'These are the happy days. I have never known happiness before,' he told her.

'Nor I! Nor I'

You can make men dig and root and plow and harvest, but you cannot make them hunt for fish or gather fruit off trees, since on the rivers and in the woods only small groups can be sent. Those who returned empty-handed, the President decreed should not share in that which others had won, but it seemed the loiterers preferred not to eat.

Smith wondered if his own dalliance had slacked his hand in governing, but it was mostly the fault of the warm mild weather, when the winter of desperation was forgotten and a night's empty belly did not conjure up dreams of starving.

Many were sent and many fled to enjoy the hospitality of the Savages during this time till Powhatan showed himself as cruel as the English President. He decreed sardonically that those who would not work should not eat. So sadly many runnygates straggled home.

In the July heat, John Smith walked with Pocahontas in the bordering wildwood rather than by the riverbank. He had cut a willow branch and made for her a penny-whistle, and she blew it gustily like a child, and they laughed at the rasping, squeaky noise.

He had spent a bad morning till she came, assembling on paper, from the four points of the compass, all his sorry citizens. Once more they must be put to work to provide for themselves in the perilous winter. Newport had not come this spring, and God knew if he would come this autumn; and so it was 'Heave-to, lads, and store the harvest. Smoke your pork and bacon, and a prize for him who nets the largest sturgeon!'

In his mind he could already hear their busy complainings, their 'I'm poorly, Cap'n. It's my stomach . . . ' or 'my leg!' or 'my head!' 'You've got no fever, man. Brace up!' 'I know, but I *feel* poorly!'

And Percy, surrounded by his 'gents', lolling elegantly, doling out his wine to the favored few, smiling insolently at Smith. 'Do you really expect *that* of gentlemen?' 'I would think you'd had your fill of starving on the Point all summer.' 'The Company will hear of that!' 'Sink the Company!' 'You're a very vainglorious fellow!'

But the megrims had all vanished with her coming.

'Shall I go away?' She had been poised for flight, seeing him with paper, pen, and ink.

'No. No!' He had pushed aside his work and risen to welcome her. 'Where is Nantequos?' For now she never came alone. Had Powhatan some fear for her?

'He left me here. He journeys to Appomattox and will return tonight.'

'Let us, too, go away from here – get out of the fort!'

146

And now he made her penny-whistles and thought of summer days in Lincolnshire, but wished to be nowhere else than here. How bright the interludes she made! For these hours, to think not back – nor forward!

She saw it first, pointing out the white stretch of sail which seemed to skim through the trees. They ran to the riverbank. It was a frigate, none he knew.

'Ahoy there!'

'Ahoy on shore! English frigate. Captain Argall master!'

Smith raced for Jamestown harbor, Pocahontas following.

'So you're Smith?' Argall said. He looked with frank curiosity at the President.

'Yes, I'm Smith.' He returned the Captain's stare. He was as comely in his way as Nantequos, well formed as one could see through his seacloths, with a fresh clear skin in spite of salt and sun; his eyes sparkled zestfully under dark, slim brows that crooked at the peak, giving him a quizzical expression; his black hair, hacked short, was curly and fell over his forehead. He had a gold hoop in one ear.

'I have wondered about you.'

'Have you?'

'There have been – so – many – reports . . . ' His voice died out as he stared past Smith to where the trees fringed the clearing.

Smith turned to follow his gaze. Pocahontas stood, thrown in relief, her upper body warm and rosy against the green; only her short aprons covered her nakedness. Smith ignored her and Argall's interest.

'The Company has sent you?'

Argall jerked his eyes to meet Smith's, but quickly they sought Pocahontas again. 'No, I – I am sent by Master Cornelius, a London merchant, to traffic – with – the – Colony, and fish for sturgeon,' he finished quickly. 'Is she . . . ? No, of course, *she* wouldn't be here!'

'Is she *what*?' Smith demanded indignantly.

'The Princess? Powhatan's daughter.'

'Pocahontas!' he shouted. He longed to tell her to go – to take her brazenness into the forest and be gone, but all the fort was gathered, and she stood in such innocence. Gracefully she approached him.

'It is Master Argall. A ship captain,' he added as though that disposed of Argall.

The bland, unmannered sailor watched her as though his eyes were glued, as though her freshness and her beauty were to be attained. She held out her hand in the English manner, and with

147

the stupid gesture of a courtier he raised it to his lips.

Smith flared. 'It is best you wait in the fort till Nantequos comes,' he said fiercely.

She looked at him, mildly surprised, then turned and ran lightly up the bank.

'It's *said* you offend the Savages.' Argall's eyes followed her. 'Is it so?'

The other's hand went to his hip, and he appraised Smith. 'I had thought, perhaps, it was *not* so,' he said in a manner of open frankness that at any other time would have charmed Smith, 'that you were surly 'cause it was needed, and had done more than other men. I had discounted half and scored the balance in your favor. I think that I was wrong.'

The hot blood drained from Smith's face, and he stood unable to reply. What was this fever that had passed? Had he been jealous because a handsome male stared at her nakedness? All had stared, *himself* included. Argall was no West or Percy, but a man to act, forthright in his honesty.

'Perhaps you were,' he said tiredly, disgusted at himself.

'I do not think I was. You must be worn sorely with your troubles. I met your men at the Point. . . . '

Smith stared at him. Was it only youth that had this bounce? And yet there must not be many years between them. Later he was to learn that there was only one. Smith was not yet thirty.

'At Point Comfort? You met Percy then?'

'Yes.' Argall held his head as though he balanced a hat with plumes. 'A very lordly lordling. "Does London expect gentlemen to fish?" '

Smith spouted laughter, so perfect was the imitation.

'Oh, pray, let us be friends. I am more than sorry for my tone with you. I thought you were one of 'em.'

' 'S wounds, not I! And I like somewhat your fierceness.'

Smith clapped him on the shoulder, and they went up the bank together to the fort.

'You have supplies?' Smith asked.

'Yes.'

'And we have nothing to trade – some soap ash, perhaps, or tar, or clapboard.'

'Great God!' Argall said mockingly. 'You haven't gold or furs, or anyway smoked fish?'

'Your Master Cornelius has launched a bad venture,' Smith said, 'though we very much need the things you bring.'

148

'You can requisition my stores. The Company will be bound to pay.'

'They are angry enough at me. We will subsist.'

'Oh, God! Knowing you really makes it hard. But you must learn from someone. . . . '

Smith tensed. 'Learn what?' he asked, and he was glad there was no falter in his voice.

'They are sending the Great Supply – nine ships. . . .' It was tremendous news, but Smith waited, sensing trouble. 'All has been reformed – the most potent lords in England are now privy to the venture.'

'For heaven's sake, speak up! They have replaced me and I go home in chains?'

'No! But there is a Governor responsible only to the Crown: my Lord de la Warr. Sir Thomas Gates will be his deputy here – God's beard! I might as well give 'em to you – the letters!'

'God's beard! You might as well!'

'I haven't read 'em, but I know what's in 'em. They don't condemn you, but' – Argall spread his hands on the table – 'they think you could have done better.'

'And so I could,' Smith said grimly. 'Let me have the letters.'

Argall produced them, and Smith rose to leave. He stopped midway.

'Don't think that I am always thus. Today has had its own quality.'

Argall gazed at him. 'They're all dizzards. I have sense enough to know I've met a man.'

Smith's smile was bleak. He went to his own house, feeling how utterly he lacked that he had not received so warm and frank a brave with open arms. How he had longed for such!

Pochahontas and Nantequos rose as he entered. He stopped, having forgotten them.

'My braves feast with your soldiers,' Nantequos said. 'Pocahontas told me of this Captain's coming. He is an enemy?'

'No. I have not known him before this.'

They both regard him so anxiously he felt he could not bear it. He threw the envelope on the table.

'I have news from my King, and I must study it – nightlong.'

They both moved instantly to go. He felt their desire envelop him, but what could he say? He smiled at Pocahontas – and he knew it was like the smile molded in a mask.

'Good night!'

She looked at him, and there was so much he sensed she wanted to say: *Let me stay and comfort you! Do not grieve for*

149

I will come tomorrow! You are not wrong, but always right!

And Nantequos. But *he* spoke out his thoughts. 'If Johnsmith has enemies, let him name them.'

Smith shook his head, still with that fixed smile. Pocahontas took Nantequos's hand and led him out.

Smith sank down at the table and opened the envelope to read about the Great Supply.

Argall sat after Smith left. A pity, he thought. For him, it is the end. Though they don't recall him, he will not stay without authority.

But how deluded were the puffed, sleek gentlemen in England and those they had beguiled to risk everything for this paradise! Smith had been the only one to speak the truth, and they had chosen not to believe him, preferring Newport's raptures and his assurances that the next voyage – always the next – he would come back laden with cargo that would enrich them all. Those poor devils at Point Comfort! And their tales of misery and accusations against the President. He had kept them alive, hadn't he? And he said brusquely that they would subsist.

'He is a man!' Argall said aloud. 'But he is not polite. I wonder . . . '

And his thoughts flew back to Percy, sneering: 'Our President would make himself a king!'

'A king?'

'No less!'

'But how?'

'He would wed Powhatan's daughter and make himself King of Virginia.'

'Fantastical!'

'Oh? Watch how she looks at him. And if you are ashore stand outside his house when she is visiting. You will see her, secret as the night, steal within. And watch through a chink by the firelight. It will heat your blood to fever point.'

'A pretty occupation for a gentleman,' Argall muttered contemptuously. But still his own blood mounted at the thought. He leaped to his feet. Why not? If Smith should leave – and leave he surely would – and Argall should return?

'Why not all of it?' He laughed aloud at his folly. Yet one could do worse than rule this virgin land with such a Queen – no

151

virgin she, but yet . . . His flesh itched to feel her smoothness. Almost his hand could trace her body, the lifted breasts and long slope of thigh. She was like copper, like – fire! He quenched his thoughts. Dreaming is no good, he told himself.

He went outside and called his steward. 'My respects to the President, and bid him and the Lady Pocahontas dine aboard the frigate.'

'Yea, yea, sir!'

Argall stood a moment after the mate had left, then he turned and went down the bank to his boat.

Smith read rapidly, snapping the pages as he turned them. He had found no Western Passage, though all knew it was close by. . . . He had dealt harshly with the Savages, causing much unnecessary garboil. . . . He had not sent back the ships freighted, as they had bidden him. . . . The old Council had been dissolved, and they were sending out a governor with absolute authority. . . . He came prepared to accept the help of those who knew the land; particularly was he recommended to the President. . . . The Company expected still to utilize the valuable services of Captain Smith, preferably in exploring. . . .

Smith blew out his breath. Maybe with the five hundred they hoped to send – men, women, and children, the letter said – no riffraff or idle gallants . . . At least they had heeded that much of his letter. An absolute Governor! No Council! It might be for the best.

Johnnie lad, all you'll have to do is keep 'em alive till the ships come. And you've not to worry about the winter!

He thought the words first and then said them aloud. They took the weight from his heart. He stretched his neck and arms, feeling greatly relieved.

There was a knock on the door, and he shouted out to enter. Master Argall's steward came in, cap in hand.

'By your leave, Master President. Captain Argall assures you of his respect and begs that you dine aboard – with the Lady Poca – Poca . . .'

'The Princess Pocahontas,' Smith completed the name. He hesitated. There was no use in staying here to mull over the maddening letters. It would pleasure Pocahontas, and – he remembered Argall's intrigued glance – give Smith a chance to show himself a civil human being.

'We will come. And also tell your master that her brother is here, Prince Nantequos.'

The cabin was snug and candlelit. Argall was no Spartan, and his taste showed everywhere: in the napery, the polished pewter, the glass wine mugs. Sketches of the sea and the English countryside were mounted on the oak-paneled walls.

Pocahontas and Nantequos were as wonderstruck as children who had been whisked into a land of faëry. They touched everything, their faces breaking out in fresh delight at each new marvel. But most of all they loved the pictures, so lifelike you felt you could step out onto the green grass or plunge into the blue water.

'Many colors!' Pocahontas said.

'Did you draw them?' Smith asked.

'A sorry artist, but it gives me pleasure.'

'To them you are a very great artist. Their pictures are crude with raw colors. But their pouncing of the skin is intricate.'

'Hers is not pounced.'

'No,' Smith said and felt himself color. She had told him why she was not pounced.

The meal was such as Smith had not eaten in two years, and Argall's wines made his head feel empty, his body pleasantly relaxed. He had tired of translating and leaned back restfully in his chair, letting Argall woo Pocahontas as he would, and even without words he was eloquent.

See, I am not jealous! Smith thought. They made a handsome couple – handsome trio – the two comely men and the Princess like a flame between them. She wore her peak coronet, and around her neck and in her hair were woven copper chains which caught the candles' light and emphasized the ruddy incandescence of her skin.

Nantequos was painted; bright feathers dangled from his lock; a turkey's claw caught in his ear; a bizarre contrast to Argall whose cleanshaven face looked pale under his dark hair, in spite of his weeks at sea. He wore a doublet and hose of mulberry velvet slashed with white satin, and on his head a small cap of black velvet with a mulberry plume.

And I – ? Smith looked down at his ragged slops and stained doublet. *My finest!* He chuckled sleepily. Then in spite of himself his thoughts went racing off to those at the Point, at the Falls. *I must bring them back. More trees must be felled to freight so many ships. I must begin the harvest. How am I to feed them till then?*

'I *will* requisition your stores!' He said loudly, startling them all, himself as well.

He closed his door, shot the bolt, and lit a candle. Then he picked up the letter. Above the crackling of the paper, he heard a soft rubbing against the door, and his mind flew back to that other night when she had come. Quickly he blew out the light. He drew the bolt noiselessly and opened the door enough to allow her to enter, then closed and bolted it again.

'I had to come.'

'I am glad.' He was. Even with his soldiers, he was a solitary soul, battling with his wits, wrestling insuperable problems. Only with her, he lost his loneness. In her arms there would be no problems – not tonight!

'It is not good news your friend brings. All night I have thought of you.'

'Even during supper?' he parried.

'Then most of all. I know your thoughts.'

'You always do.' He knew he would tell her, but he wanted to wait. 'What do you think of him?'

She pondered this as though he had asked her a very serious question. 'He is brave and quick and very handsome – like Nantequos.'

He felt a sharp pang. 'You felt that, too?'

'He will not give up what he wants. . . . '

'He wants you.'

She smiled, not denying it. 'He wants many things, and he will not care what he does to get them. He will cease to be your friend if by cutting you down he can have his way.'

He had fenced for time, but he found her wisdom fascinating. 'Do you mean, cut *me* down, or whomever?'

'Whomever means you, too.'

He laughed and pulled her to him. 'I am glad you do not like him.'

'I feel as I do about wine. I like it, but I do not trust it.'

'Someday you will tell me what I am like. But not now. It is time for other things.'

He lifted her to him, but there was no response to his desire. She was passive, negative. He looked down at her, bafflled. Her pliancy quelled ardor as he could not have dreamed.

'This is not what you came for?'

'No.'

He laid her on the bed and sat beside her, his hands between his knees.

'This you must tell no one – not even Nántequos.' She did not speak, but he had not asked a question. 'In England there are men – very rich and powerful men – who send out ships. Although they live so far away, they rule those of us who are here and send us orders which we cannot obey. They are angry

154

with me for many things – that I send no gold, find not the Southern Sea. . . .'

She sat up indignantly. 'Would Powhatan be angry if you did not bring him the moon?'

He laughed. 'Probably, if he thought the moon was in my cornfield. But there are other things, too. They say I have treated the Savages harshly and that is why they are not our friends.'

'Yet you have Powhatan's love. And Newport, who brought silly gifts – Powhatan is not his friend.'

'Newport is there to tell them wrong is right and right is wrong. Whom would Powhatan believe, a Werowance he never saw, or Rawhunt?

'Johnsmith!' She clutched his arm. 'Newport is your enemy. You must destroy him when he comes.'

He chuckled and bent to kiss her. 'That would please the gentlemen in England. They would have a rope around my neck before you could wink this pretty eye. But – it will not be Newport now who counts. Others come, far greater than he. And they can see for themselves.' He spoke lightly, not looking at her. 'And now that I have told you what you came to hear, are you going to leave me?'

She did not speak, and he turned. She lay voluptuous as a kitten, her body as glowing crimson as though it were painted with the puccoon. Her invitation was so alluring that he exclaimed aloud, seeing the metamorphosis.

He bent to her, but she came up to him on her knees. Her hands touched lightly the points of his doublet.

'Tonight,' she said, 'it shall be my way. I am your handmaiden.'

CHAPTER TWENTY-SIX

For Smith, Argall's charm was great. His own youth seemed to have fled, unnoticed, under the weight of his responsibilities, and Adventure, which he had sought with such zest, had lost her allure. Other values, perhaps, had replaced her in his heart, but he looked back regretfully to the carefree days. For this reason Argall's youthfulness and recklessness, like Nantequos's, appealed to him. In the days of England's Navy, Argall might have been one of Elizabeth's heroes, like Drake or Raleigh. Smith sensed the quality Pocahontas's intuition had revealed – ruthlessness. But in so winning a soul it merely added color.

Argall's pursuit of Pocahontas paused not for niceties, nor was it cloaked, but she used the shield she had turned against Smith, and Argall was puzzled, intrigued, then amazed and childishly petulant when he found he could not captivate her. It was plain he had met few refusals and no rebuffs.

He would have followed her up the rivers when she and Nantequos left, but the President would not allow it. At this denial Argall cried out in rage like a schoolboy.

'You are afraid I'll win your lady love.'

'No.'

'You don't deny she is your love.'

'Would you believe me if I did deny it?'

'No, I'd not!' Smith shrugged. 'If it's not for that, then why – ?'

'If it would serve some purpose – but I am most uncertain of the Savages,' Smith said.

'Save *her*!'

'Save her and Nantequos.'

'Then you commandeer my services for the Colony?'

'I do, until the Supply arrives.'

'I'll have her, I vow it! When you leave . . .'

'I have not said that I would leave.'

And Argall sulked, but still Smith liked him.

Would he leave? Smith wondered. He would be leaving a task completed so far as he was able. He had brought Jamestown through to now, and in the year when he had been President, he had lost no man from starvation, pestilence, or cold. Someone was needed in London to tell them that. And who was there but himself? Ratcliff and his company had filled their ears. And Newport? If he stayed, what was done would not be his doing. The Company had spoken of his being employed in exploration. The Bay he had already searched. The passage all desired to madness was not there. He would like to search to the north – the bay that he had written Henry Hudson of – or around Cape Cod. Yes, he thought, I'd best go home.

And with the word he was struck with a feeling of desolation. *Home!* Was England no longer home? But here was home? This watered land he had conned like a Latin reader . . . the trees and vines and birds and fish, these had fed him, sheltered him . . . And how intimately he knew the lives and thoughts of these pagan Savages: Powhatan more than his own father, Nantequos than his brother, and Pocahontas. . . . Other women had loved him, and their kisses passed to blurred smudges on the window of his memory. There had been Hungarian Vilma whom he had thought he loved because her experience had molded his rawness and made therefrom a lover; and Turkish Tragabigzanda – love and lust! Were they not the same? Would not the beds on riverbank, of pine needles and of woven mats, pass to line themselves with Oriental couches and gilded posts hung with silver cloth? The thought of a penny-whistle brought sudden tears to his eyes.

Smith gathered the colonists; Argall lost his sulks – perhaps forgot about the exciting maid; and all settled to work and wait for the coming of the Great Supply.

A fleet of nine ships had sailed from England. When Smith's scouts brought word of four wreckages, their sails and ensigns too tattered to recognize, who sought harbor in the Bay, the President prepared defenses against possible Spaniards. It was not until the ships were in the river that Argall recognized the *Blessing, Lion, Falcon,* and *Unicorn.*

'Their flagship, the *Sea Venture,* is not with them,' Argall said.

Barges brought the officers ashore while the weary passengers stood on the decks crying out to be freed to feel the land – to send them food for they were perishing. . . .

'What happened?' Smith called to the nearest barge.

'Hurycano!'

'The five other ships sunk?'

'Lost – one sunk!'

'Where is the Governor?'

The man jumped into the water and waded ashore.

'Sir Thomas Gates was Lord de la Warr's deputy – *is*, I hope – Sir George Somers, Admiral, and Captain Newport, Vice-Admiral. None could settle which should command the flagship, bringing the commission.' He frowned at the folly. 'So all sailed in the *Sea Venture*.'

'All – three – and the commission!'

'Captain Smith – er, Master *President*!'

Smith wheeled to face Ratcliff, flanked by two of his most vicious troublemakers.

'Master Ratcliff!'

'*Captain* Ratcliff! And *Captain* Archer! And *Captain* Martin!'

Smith stared at them in such a fury he could not utter a word; these were the three who had disorganized the first venture.

'I visioned a warm welcome, but none so warm as this,' Ratcliff said insolently. He spoke to impress his comrades, Smith knew, for alone he had been a sniveling apologist.

'I am amazed you have come back.'

'Sadly, Deputy Governor Gates has not arrived. But we have been instructed that we are to form the Council.'

'Council? I have been told there is no Council.'

'A nominal affair,' Ratcliff said easily. 'And we as a majority have named Master West, Lord de la Warr's brother, President, though we have agreed to let you finish your term of office which ends next month.'

Smith regarded him, and suddenly he knew why the *Sea Venture* with the commission had not come. More devious than the workings of man – and how devious they were – were those of God!

His lips curled. 'I am President till the Governor arrives or we have word from London. And lacking the commission there is no Council, for I have no right to appoint, and those London has named are dead.' For the last, Scrivener, had died in the early spring.

They brought the colonists ashore, and they were mad things, picking up the earth and kissing it, rushing into the cornfields and stripping the green ears from the stalks, devouring them. There had been no preparation for women and children, but here they

158

were; and their demands were other than Smith had faced hitherto.

'What of your supplies?' he demanded of the masters. But their stores had been rotted by salt water. In Virginia they had been told there was food aplenty. And so, Smith thought with amazement, there almost was, with the victuals he had requisitioned from Argall, with the hogs and chickens, with what the Savages had brought, and the harvest that impended. He could provide.

But from being a president, hated by the few, loved by the many, he found himself suddenly in the midst of enemies. For those veterans, Ratcliff and his crew, had poisoned the minds of all who came, before ever they laid eyes on Smith; and he could not deal with this number, women as well as men, as he had dealt with the others. The gentlemen – so they called themselves – were not even as Percy, who was a man in the field if he was a laggard in the fort.

'Would you have me rough my hands?' one asked, and Smith sent him reeling with a blow.

And the women – goodwives and wenches – had been told that in Virginia they could play the lady, and their indignant protests were the worst to bear. *If I were Governor of Bedlam,* Smith thought, *my office would be simpler.*

One by one three others of the fleet limped in, masts swept away, their canvas in shreds. And so there were more to feed and house, more hungry, frightened souls to reconcile to this wild land. None could tell of the *Sea Venture,* which had been swept away by the storm, and though each day they waited hopefully – Smith felt that perhaps *he* hoped most of all – she did not come.

In the first arrival had been unloaded six mares and two stallions, and these, surprisingly, proved a real blessing, for the Savages reverenced them as godly animals, and certainly they did appear nobler than the human cargo.

Though they had no authority for their claims, Ratcliff and his unruly Captains pressed to change the government; and whatever company was formed to work or hunt, one of these gallants would so disrupt with strife and politicking there would be nothing accomplished, but factions blown to a frenzy.

The whipping post came into almost daily use, and Smith shamed to hear the screams, remembering the stoic Savages. It pained him sorely to resort to this. 'But I mightily fear a gallows tree will be the next,' he said to Argall.

'It would have been the first had I been President.'

Master West grew so great under Ratcliff's goading that Smith anticipated a mutiny to make Lord de la Warr's brother President. If it had been Percy he could, perhaps, have handed down the office, but that proud gentleman was so disgusted with the disorders brought by the Great Supply that he had asked for a passport to go on the first ship for England.

One morning as Smith shaved he heard hulloaing and jeering in the street and screams which made the blood drain from his face. Naked as he was, he flung wide the door to have Jack Russell run headlong into his arms. Behind him Smith was aware of a pack of the riffraff. He slammed the door and bolted it, then caught up Russell who was near swooning on the chair, blood dripping from a gash in his cheek.

Smith dipped a cloth in his shaving water and gently stanched the blood.

'What is it, Jack?' Outside he could hear the still howling mob.

'It was Ratcliff and Archer cried 'em up, driving 'em against you. I and other lads tried to quiet them, telling what leader you have been and how you'll pull us through whatever jars we face. . . .'

He paused, and Smith led him to the bed and made him lean back till the color had returned to his face.

' 'nd this Dyer, Ratcliff's lubberly servant' – he looked up, and Smith nodded that he knew the man – 'he slashed out sudden, and when the blood came the rabble went mad. . . .'

Smith dressed quickly.

'You daren't go out, Captain.'

Smith said nothing, but secured his pistols. He opened the door and stepped out into the now almost deserted street. One or two stared at him with quickly hidden smiles, perhaps having glimpsed him naked in his doorway. He strode quickly to the guardhouse, and from there with an armed escort he searched for Ratcliff and Archer. He found them in Master West's house, tippling and laughing. They fell silent as he entered, but their smiles did not leave their faces.

'Put Captains Ratcliffe and Archer in irons,' he told the guards.

Young West leaped to his feet, his petulant voice snarling. 'You can't do this. They're gentlemen!'

'They're mutineers!'

'When my brother . . .'

'I wish we would have news from your brother, my Lord the Governor, for he has mixed a witch's brew right enough.'

'You an't the strength to govern us!' West shrilled.

'Quiet, or I'll have you with 'em!' Smith indicated the two brave Captains who looked more amazed at his harshness to so

160

fine a noble than they were at their own chains. 'As it lies, I'll send you with a company back to the Falls.'

'That foul hell! I an't a-goin'!'

'You'll go. But I will come and try to make it livable – my Lord!' he said with mock deference, since West had not the title. He addressed the guards. 'Take them to the guardhouse.'

'We're commissioned by the Governor,' Ratcliff cried.

'Where is Dyer?'

Ratcliff paled but not answer. Smith moved close, his face threatening.

'Dyer will be flogged and stocked *before* his trial. Will you have the same, *Captain?*'

'He – I sent him and his cronies a half-hogshead. They're in the longhouse.'

Smith's fist came up automatically. He tensed, then contained himself.

'His reward?' he asked. 'Get them out of here.'

The effect was salutary. Dyer's flogging gathered an appreciative audience, and he made it worth their while. When he was in the bilboes, always there was a crowd of worthy dames, pelting him with nuts or fruits, or spitting on him. Dyer's sentence was longer, but in the morning Smith had him taken to the dungeon, for he could not stand the deplorable sight.

That day Master West went to the Falls with a hundred and twenty men, and Captain Martin with more than a hundred was sent to Nansemond, each company with their due proportion of all provisions according to their numbers. Suddenly there was quiet and order in the fort. Even the women ceased to chatter and harangue. *Can I keep it so,* Smith thought, *till the Sea Venture comes, or till I can send to England to right this wrong? How many months?*

He had told Pocahontas to stay away till Argall left, not from doubt of her, or jealousy, but because he had felt a sort of havoc would ensue with the new Supply – little had he dreamed! And great as was his need for her, he was glad, for though some of the Savages who came and went through Jamestown's ports spoke a smattering of English and, perhaps, understood more, he hoped that only a garbled account of the disorderliness would reach Powhatan's ears. Not that she would carry it, but when she came now it was with an ever larger train of maids and braves.

As it was, the Savages came less to trade, for the newly come English stole from them and used them ill, heavy as was the punishment for those who were discovered acting so. But now, with this many gone to other posts, and those who sowed confusion locked in jail, he had hopes of order and of peace. He must follow that minstreling fellow, West, and see that he found more than acorns to feed his host.

CHAPTER TWENTY-SEVEN

It was pleasant to leave the contentious fort and be at sail up the green river bright in the summer sun, the dipping willows reflected in their pools and the osiers stepping foot into the water like timid bathers. The barge sailed between narrowing banks which wafted late summer odors of rotting fruits and sunburnt grass.

Suddenly was cried. 'Barge ahoy!' and there was Master West, golden curls tumbled atop crinkled brow.

'It's miserable!' West said before Smith could speak.

'You've left your company?'

'Aye, I have!'

Smith wondered: Should he trounce the puppy, spank him here and take him back to share the 'awful misery'? But his brother, alas, *was* all the power there was so far as Virginia was concerned. And if they were at all alike . . . He would face that brother, here or there, and plead Jamestown's cause. And what would be the answer if this brat endured further humiliation?

'You will not attempt to free your – friends or commit any foolishness while I am here?'

'Those ratters, heh, heh, heh!'

Oddly, Smith believed him. West was the sort to love a flatterer much and forsake him when difficulties ensued.

'Go back and report to Captain Argall. I will establish your colony.'

It was a miserable affair, indeed. They had pitched their tents on the swamps where no tree could shelter them, and all were bloated with mosquito stings. *Master West*, President! John Smith thought bitterly, and then moved upriver to parley with Taux-Powhatan, Powhatan's son who was Werowance of this country.

His city was on a bluff guarding the Falls and as fair a site as

Smith could imagine in this land. It was built up with good houses and stout walls.

'Sell us this city,' he said and named a price in copper and that rarity, pork, which made the son of Powhatan's eyes glisten. 'If we are in possession of this fortress we will defend you against any Monacan invasion. For this you will send me any who steal from my people. Every house shall pay, for my thumb-joint's length and twice its breadth in copper, one basket of corn as well as a proportion of puccoon dye, which shall be the tribute to my great King James from those who dwell within sovereignty. What else we have we will barter as is our custom with your nation.'

Taux-Powhatan thought and at last sent messengers to Powhatan to learn his will. When word came it was 'Let them possess the fort.'

The exchange was made, and Smith, remembering Elizabeth's incomparable palace in Essex, named the spot Nonsuch, because on all the rivers he had not seen a site more lofty or more fertile, with a view that stretched in both directions, most pleasing to the eyes, and wonderfully defensible.

He returned to the colony West had deserted. But this bargaining for a fort, ready-built and ready-planted, had taken days, and that company were so mutinous they would have no part of anything that he initiated, denying his authority since their commander, Lieutenant West, was not there to order them. They would go up the Falls and find gold in the Monacans' country, they would return to Jamestown and feast and forget their misery, but they would not stay here or see the Nonsuch that he offered them. And with his five against their six score he was in danger.

He arrested seven of their ringleaders and retired, his prisoners in chains, to his barge with which he commandeered their ship, where were all their provisions. There, he found the mariners most content to have a captain.

Then those Savages who had been the subjects of Taux-Powhatan and now were his came to him and told him how these English stole their corn, robbed their gardens, beat them, broke into their houses; and they declared he had brought them protectors who were worse enemies than the Monacans, and begged forgiveness if they defended themselves. Since he was not, nor ever had been, as these, they said that they would join with him against the mutineers if he wished it.

At this time came two messages, one from Argall, telling that Martin had demanded thirty good shots to protect him from the Nansemonds who threatened, which Argall had speedily sent; and one from Nansemond himself who told that Martin had surprised him while he feasted, captured him, defiled his houses and his monuments, and taken possession of his isle which was the sacred burial ground of the Nansemonds. His people had risen, attacked Martin and his men, released their Werowance and taken a thousand bushels of corn which the English had stolen. Then another messenger from Argall: Martin had not tried to intercept the Savages, but returned to Jamestown, leaving most of his party, who were killed.

'It falls apart!' Smith cried, burying his head.

He set sail downriver. As the wind gathered, puffing out his canvas, the Savages attacked that brave hundred and twenty at the Falls, slaying many, affrighting the rest, gathering English arms. News of the massacre rocketed through the forest, and Smith grounded the boat till the English runners reached him. Twelve had done it all, twelve Savages, one tenth the English who defended the swampland from which they would not stir. Now, the couriers cried, the company would submit themselves to the President's will.

Slowly he moved upriver once again and put the leaders in chains. *Not Moor heads shall be my coat of arms*, he thought – for after he had killed three Turks in single combat in Hungary he had been granted this device to deck his shield – *but chains shall be my emblem.*

He supplied the mariners with guns, and under guard he marched the now tractable company to Nonsuch where he seated them, grimly amused at their surprise to find themselves with dry houses, three hundred acres of ground already tilled, and pleasant surroundings.

He sent runners to Taux-Powhatan to invite him to parley since Smith would, so far as he was able, right the wrongs this evil company had perpetrated.

But it was Nantequos who came! With an army in battle paint, his eyes flashing in anger. Unarmed, Smith went to meet him.

'I little believed that you could be here and these things done!'

'Nor I!' Smith told him. 'But those who committed them shall be punished, and all that has been taken from your people returned – and more, for what they have suffered.'

'And Nansemond?'

'That, too!'

Nantequos's face relaxed. 'Johnsmith – Johnsmith!' he said sorrowfully.

'I grieve. From my heart I grieve.'

'What devils have you spewed forth in our land?'

165

'To me, too, they are devils!'

Nantequos bade his braves wait. He took Smith's arm and led him toward the forest. Under a vast oak Nantequos paused and faced Smith.

'My brother! Strange tales come from Jamestown.'

Smith's breathing ceased and then renewed itself in a swift gulp.

'After this and Nansemond, how can I deny them?' he said simply.

'These are not *your* people, but your enemies! As they are our enemies! It is not the English Powhatan loves, but Johnsmith!'

'What do you mean, Nantequos?'

'Since you first came to us, Powhatan has offered you your own nation. Leave these' – he spurned those in the fort with a jerk of his head – 'and come to us! Take Pocahontas as your Wironausqua, and someday, when Powhatan has gone, we will rule his nation together – forever brothers! This is what Powhatan sent me to say.'

Tears rose in Smith's eyes so that he hid his face. The beauty and the love that spoke! And for the first time he longed to cry out *Yes!* In his grasp, a Kingdom and a Home, a Friendship and a Love!

He stretched himself, face downward, on the ground and motioned to Nantequos to sit beside him. He talked slowly, breaking oak leaves which he watched intently, for he could not look at Nantequos.

'My brother, could you leave this land and go to England and be an Englishman?' Nantequos started with surprise, but did not speak. 'Forsake your gods, your people – Powhatan? Not only your father, but your Lord!'

'No!'

'No more can I – foresake my God, my King, my country!'

He arose and Nantequos followed. Smith embraced him.

'Tell Powhatan – What can I say? How great my love, and gratitude, and he is forever my Red Father! And tell him, too' – Smith's voice grew hard – 'that such as this shall cease, else I will hang every Englishman in Virginia!'

CHAPTER TWENTY-EIGHT

The Company settled so far as they would allow themselves to be settled, Smith called them out and told in harsh, bitter words what they might expect if they continued their maraudings and lived not decently. 'For by the example of what befalls these scurvy knaves I take back to Jamestown you shall know what will be the reward of further mischiefs.'

Then he ordered an immediate departure, for the souls of Savages and English both cried out for vengeance against the false leaders who had betrayed them to their deaths.

In the barge he slept, secure since he had only men he knew and loved around him. The prisoners he had sent in the pinnace.

He dreamed.

He was in a tavern in Flanders spinning tales with his cronies. At a table alone was Ratcliff, a malignant sneer on his face, though Smith did not heed him. From a distance, a youth of most extraordinary beauty watched and as Smith became aware, the face in the glowing light of the fire moved slowly toward him, seemingly disembodied; in the eyes and on the lips was such an expression of love and admiration that Smith's heart constricted in tenderness. As it reached him, suddenly it was Pocahontas's face, and she was in his arms, and then they were running, running through the forest, at first with free and happy feet but as they ran his joy changed to fear, and he knew they fled a fell pursuer. With the realization, she was not by his side, and he sought her frantically. He broke through the tanglewood to a clearing; there was a fire, and she was staked. Ratcliff stood over her, kindling the blaze. 'Don't!' Smith cried, but a sheet of flame covered her face. He ran into the fire, seeking to free her, dreading to find the frightful mutilation of what had been so fair and innocent. As he moved, Ratcliff thrust a burning brand into his groin. He felt terrible pain, and then all of him caught fire.

The pain was so excruciating that he was crazed and knew not at all what had happened. His men shouted and rushed toward him, but Smith leaped from the boat into the water, where he floundered helplessly, knew not whether he suffered more from the bursting of his lungs or the agonizing fire in his loins.

They managed to haul him in, but he was so tormented that he screamed piteously for them to shoot him. His powderbag had lain across his lap, and a spark from a flint had ignited it. His breeks were shredded and scorched, and the skin under them, grimed from the gunpowder, burned and blistered. He who had struck the spark would have done away with himself if they had not held him.

They stretched the Captain out and poured spirits through his chattering teeth while others cut away his breeks. It was a painful, ghastly thing to look at, the flesh torn from his thighs for a square of nine or ten inches. They eased the wound as they could with grease and tacked with desperation to catch the breeze, for they were a hundred miles from Jamestown. But even there they had no surgeon.

For a space he lost consciousness, though he moaned and cried out, heartbreaking to those who loved him. In time he opened his eyes and spoke, asking what had happened, and when they told him he called for the one whose carelessness had caused him this agony.

'Don't let yourself be shamed or sorrier than you must, for we have shared much danger over many years. It could easily have been I who did this to you.'

The Dark Spirits had possessed Pocahontas during five Suns, and she had hidden herself to conquer her gnawing melancholy. Disaster and calamity send their brooding clouds before, but she did not know what was predestined or how to protect those whom she loved. Her ears were alerted for the messenger of evil news, so it was she who first heard the running footsteps of the brave that brought the word: *Johnsmith traveled to Jamestown, near to death.*

She did not wait, but fled to town to cross the land between the Pamaunkey River and the Powhatan, where the barge was which carried Johnsmith. Nantequos came up to her and sped past, and his braves followed. The strongest of them swooped and swung her across his back like a papoose, and so they ran. Only then did she allow herself pause to pray.

The sun had lowered before they reached the Powhatan. With borrowed canoes they sent braves down the river, while Nantequos and she and ten others paddled upstream, not knowing whether the barge had passed or not.

It loomed on them with ghostly sails out of the darkness.

'Nantequos, the son of Powhatan,' Nantequos announced himself. 'Is there one who speaks my language?'

'Aye,' a voice called out, and with a violent stricture of her organs she knew it was Johnsmith's.

'Let me come!' she cried.

'Haul her over, lads, and let the Princess and her brother aboard,' Johnsmith said in English.

They lifted her up, and Nantequos followed. She knelt to Johnsmith in a stooping gesture as a child might stretch out its hand to a fallen bird.

'You live!'

'But barely!'

'You will live! Let me tend you!'

'No!' Johnsmith said hoarsely. 'I beg you no!' He stretched out his hand to hold her.

'I can,' she said. 'I will be so gentle.'

'I would rather die than have you look. I *will* die if you look.'

'We have brought that which will ease you greatly,' Nantequos said. 'Will you let me?'

Johnsmith nodded. He reached out toward a man who held a bottle of liquor. The soldier put it to Johnsmith's lips.

During the night he raised his hand, and she bent to him.

'Sweet child, I must leave you!'

'No – no!'

'I am not dying. But if I am ever to live again, I must return to England.'

She made no sound. How desolate the land after the Dark Spirits have passed, leaving the sere and ravaged earth! But then there is no pain, only the nakedness!

'Their medicines are mighty, and I must have them.'

'Will you come back?'

'If I can.'

The water lapped. The paddles of Nantequos's braves dipped in quiet rhythm. Yet the silence in her heart was so vast these sounds jarred against her ears. At last he spoke again:

'Pocahontas, I wish I had not done what I have done.'

'Why, Lord? Have I not pleased you?'

'Yes! But I am afraid that you should love me.'

'Afraid? You are my lord and my father. I find much joy in loving you.'

'Pocahontas – my dear child – I go. . . .'

'Go! I do not hold you. You have taught me much that will make me a worthy bride.'

'*No!*'

'Will you have me wait for you?'

'No.'

'My arms are open. Go.'

'I will come back.'

'And I will wait until the sun within me sinks and no moon rises, until the circle of the skies is still and I am drained and there is a vast emptiness. . . .'

'I will come back!'

'. . . then I will know that you will not come back!'

'I will be dead.'

'That will be the emptiness, or else . . .'

'No other else. I will come back.'

She sat quietly, staring into the blackness. Her hands moved at intervals to wipe the sweat of fever from his brow. In them was her heart and will; from them poured life, for what she had she gave him freely – even the part of himself which he had rendered her, she gave back to him.

CHAPTER TWENTY-NINE

Argall's frigate lay in mid-river ready to sail. They carried Smith aboard and went to persuade Percy not to leave but to stay and be their President, since he was the only one Smith would accept. Smith's fever ran high now, and mostly he was delirious, but he had moments of sanity, and in one of these he asked that his old soldiers be assembled.

The men crowded into his cabin and out onto the deck. They stood with bowed heads, hats in hand, looking very glum and sad as though they had been called to his deathbed.

He spoke weakly but with great clarity, so that his words were heard by all the hushed men.

'Lads, I would not leave you if I had not to. Yet, perhaps, it's for the best, for my stewardship has passed beyond me.' There was a rumble of dissent. 'Aye, a good soldier does not allow these mischiefs. If I were to stay *I* would not suffer them. But I'd be small use to you like this. And without surgeon or surgery, with my commission to be suppressed I don't know why, myself and you rewarded I don't know how, and a new commission granted we don't know to whom, which, though it has not arrived, still disables the authority I had – these things point my course.

'There has been chosen for your President a strong man whom you know well, have fought with, been commanded by, a veteran. Follow him as you have followed me. I leave you content in many things. There are ships and boats for your journeys. We have commodities in trade, the harvest newly gathered, ten weeks' provision in the store. We are four hundred ninety and odd persons. . . . ' He wiped the sweat from his face, for his fever mounted again. 'Remember when we were thirty-eight?' he said with a slight smile.

'There are twenty-four pieces of ordnance, three hundred muskets, snaphances, and firelocks; shot, powder, and match sufficient; cuirasses, pikes, swords, and morions more than men.

The Savages, their language and habitations, are known to more than a hundred of us. We have nets for fishing, apparel to cover us, five mares and a horse, five or six hundred swine, as many hens and chickens, some goats, some sheep.' His voice trailed off at the end of the long inventory, and they thought: *How many times he must have conned it, watching it grow and shrink! How he has cared for us!*

He regarded their long faces. 'Cheer up, lads. Fare you well. God be with you. As the French say, *au revoir*.' He closed his eyes.

As they climbed into the barges and settled themselves, none spoke, but many wept.

In spite of Argall's outraged protests, the new Council stayed the fleet three weeks to prepare an indictment against Smith, gathering complaints where they could.

Those at the Falls complained he caused the Savages to assault them and refused to avenge their losses.

The new Council wrote that he had refused to submit to their authority, that he had threatened Powhatan unless he sent corn, that he had refused corn when Powhatan offered it and thus starved the Colony.

Others complained that he would not let them rest in the fort, but forced them to the oyster banks to live or starve.

Percy wrote that he had the Savages in subjection and would have made himself a king by marrying Pocahontas, Powhatan's daughter.

Many were permitted passage back to England who would swear these things were true.

Two of the soldiers wrote thus:

What shall I say? but thus we lost him, that in all his proceedings made Justice his first guide, and Experience his second; ever hating baseness, sloth, pride and indignity, more than any dangers; that never allowed more for himself than his soldiers with him; that upon no danger, would send them where he would not lead them himself; that would never see us want what he either had, or could by any means get us; that would rather want than borrow, or starve than not pay; that loved actions more than words, and hated falsehood and cozenage worse than death; whose adventures were our lives, and whose loss, our deaths.

Pocahontas and Nantequos followed the frigate with their braves as far as the great bay. There they stood in their canoes,

172

arms raised, and watched as long as Argall's sails were in sight. Then they rounded the point to enter the Pamaunkey.

The Dark Spirits had not departed from Pocahontas, and she sat low, brooding, her face like that of a small witch. It was not her grief that obsessed her, for that had been so devastating that only his last words, '*No other else. I will come back,*' kept alive the spark. But the Dark Spirits remained, and she stared sightlessly into the water, trying to visualize what was foreboded.

They left the canoes where they had borrowed them and started overland to Powhatan. Midway, he met them. His face was long and dour as theirs. He said no word, but he embraced Nantequos and Pocahontas and wearily returned with them to his city.

Without Johnsmith, he distrusted the English a hundred times more than ever before, and neither Nantequos nor Pocahontas tried to dissuade him, for they were bitter against these newcomers who had been Johnsmith's enemies. Rawhunt's scouts went to Jamestown and to the nations that traded with them to learn the intentions of the new government.

Having lost their Werowance, Jamestown now had twenty Werowances, fighting among themselves. Captain Martin, who had imprisoned the Werowance of Nansemond and defiled his sacred ground, strutted as before and dealt with the red men arrogantly. And Captains Ratcliff and Archer, whom Johnsmith had put in chains, were released by President Percy, and they three served on the Council, the two Captains often overruling the new President.

Master West returned to his company at the Falls, and did not meet the promises of Johnsmith, but persecuted the Powhatans to such an extent that Taux-Powhatan came, complaining bitterly. Powhatan commanded Nantequos to go with Taux-Powhatan and drive the white men from the Falls, which was done, killing half of them.

Then Powhatan held a great Council and decreed that none should trade with Jamestown.

'Now that their number is so great, let them feed themselves. Johnsmith did this with fewer braves.

His scouts reported that they gathered nothing, but daily consumed what Johnsmith had left though the frozen moons drew closer.

'They will destroy themselves. Unless we are provoked we will not strike.'

It was a winter second only to the Great Frost, and Rawhunt told that those at Jamestown died by twenties. He told also that Chickahomanies disobeyed the commands of Powhatan and traded with the English, who gave swords, arms, pieces, whatever, for corn and venison, and among them a scout had recognized a brave of Opechancano.

Then he brought more portentous news. Opechancano had shown himself and the Chickahomanies had declared themselves his ally and forsworn their allegiance to Powhatan.

Nantequos wanted to take an army to destroy Opechancano and conquer the Chickahomanies, but Powhatan said: 'Let it be! We will await the Budding of the Leaf. Winter is the ally of the besieged. Also, we must discover how these English thrive.'

When the frost was greatest, the English ate their horses, even to the hides, ate rats and dogs, their shoes; they dug up a murdered man and devoured his carcass; and one killed his wife and ate her. For this he was burned at the stake.

Captains Ratcliff and Archer came to trade, so desperate was their need. Yet they did not fail to threaten Powhatan, and he, withdrawing, sent Nantequos with his braves who killed the two leaders and the thirty who were with him, sparing only a youth for whose life Pocahontas pleaded.

'We are at war, Powhatan said.

'It will not be a long one,' Nantequos answered.

'It is time, perhaps, to wipe them out.'

'If Johnsmith returns . . . ' Nantequos said. 'Those we have killed, we have only killed in our own defense. The starving few who remain will not survive the winter.'

It was the English themselves who were their own betrayers. Master West took their pinnace and sailed up the Potomac to trade, and in his fury at finding no corn he massacred many of that ever friendly nation. He stopped at the point that they called Comfort on his return, where he was told of Jamestown's desperate need, and with that urgent news, he and his men set sail out of the Bay to England, leaving Jamestown without a pinnace.

In the Moon of the Budding of the Leaf, of the four hundred and ninety-odd that Johnsmith left, sixty remained alive, men, squaws and children, sad, crazed souls who dug for roots and herbs in the frozen ground.

Powhatan sat long in silence on hearing this.

'They are finished,' he said at last.

However, there was to be another arrival which made these people still seem to be possessed of magic. The Governor they had so long expected, whose ship had been destroyed by the Wind Gods, came not in one ship, but two, with all his company safe and well fed. They had been blown to the islands in the great sea, and there they had wintered, making of their one ship two; and now were come to swell the Colony.

But when they saw the misery and how little hope there was of sustaining life, they took those that had survived on their ships and set sail for England, abandoning Virginia.

Powhatan knew great peace.

Nantequos sped to the point that he might watch the departure of these remnants, but Pocahontas stayed, under the spell of the Dark Spirits.

She sat, staring into the fire, and as she stared she saw before her Jamestown, its streets deserted. Then Nantequos entered a gate, gazed about him with wonder and some sorrow at the empty desolation. Slowly he wandered like a newly come spirit to the Land of Death, and as she watched she felt terrible fear, she knew not why, and her hands covered her mouth, for she wanted to cry out a warning. He walked tentatively to the house that had been Johnsmith's. As he neared it, her terror mounted. He reached out and tried the door, pushed it open. There was a hideous war cry. Opechancano and his braves leaped on Nantequos and beat him to the ground with their tomahawks.

Pocahontas screamed and screamed and screamed. They came to quiet her, but she could not stop and threw herself on the ground where at long last she lay still, her shuddering subsided.

She would not tell what so terrified her. Instead she cut off her long hair and took it to the cornfield where she dug a hole with her nails and buried it, praying the mightiest prayers she knew.

They heard the wailing from a great distance. Powhatan started up, his face the color of burning embers which have been covered by their own ash. Rawhunt came. He could not speak but stood shaking like a birch in a strong wind.

Powhatan went past him and out of the city. All those who had started toward the mourners fell aside, so that Powhatan walked alone to meet what sorrow he did not know.

They bore Nantequos high above their heads, his body on a bed strung on poles, and their wailing could be heard unto the stretches of the nation.

They laid him at Powhatan's feet. Powhatan bent to him, touched his cheek. He remained so a long time. Then he arose and silenced the multitude.

'Who did this?' he demanded of Rawhunt.

'He was found at the door of Johnsmith's house at Jamestown.

He had been shot, and a musket was by his side. The white men delivered him to us, but say they did not do it.'

'The white men? They have gone.'

'Only so far as the Bay. There they met three great ships who bear their mighty Governor from England, him they call Delawarr. They returned with a larger force than ever before.'

Powhatan looked down at his son. The head that had been so fine was beaten to a pulp.

'He has been scalped. Would they do that?'

'I do not know.'

Powhatan turned and grimly led the procession back to the city.

Gone! All that he had built! All that he had planned! This, his hope, gone! Opechancano led the Chickahomanies ready to do battle. The English left and come again to drive his people farther and farther into the forests, to pour their endless hordes into his land! *It is the end!* he thought and raised his head proudly so that none should know his grief.

Pocahontas spoke not of what she had seen in the fire. She felt that now a war between the brothers would destroy them all. Inside her was the great emptiness. No sun shone. No moon would rise. And she was sure Johnsmith was dead.

BOOK TWO
POWHATAN'S DAUGHTER

England
June 1616 – March 1617

... the Kings most dear and
wel-beloved daughter ...

... she next under God was still
the instrument to preserve this
Colonie from death, famine and utter
confusion: which if in those times,
had once beene dissolved, Virginia
might have lain as it was at our
first arrivall to this day.

JOHN SMITH, A Letter
to Queene Anne, 1616

CHAPTER ONE

The fog rose from the salt marshes like vapors from a witch's cauldron, to curl over the wharves, the wet stone walls, to seep through keyhole and cranny. It pierced good solid flesh so that harbor folk huddled in their beds, though it was nearly noon. Not buyer nor seller stirred, with shop windows shuttered fast to keep out the piercing chill and doors still bolted against any but the most urgent summons. It enveloped the fishing craft whose riding lights shone dully in a jaundiced mist; it spiraled over the superstructure of a man-of-war and tore itself in fragments on the lofty rigging. It billowed out past the harbor's mouth and gave a damp unwelcome to the frigate whose pilot evidently knew well the harbor and steered her slowly and gracefully to an anchorage. She fired a salvo, steel blue and sulphur shattering the fog. The man-of-war answered, and the murk closed in.

Like a graveyard at Gabriel's trumpet Plymouthtown came to life: shutters flung back, doors banged wide, candles gleamed, and coals were heaped on fires. Men threw mariners' sheepskins over their woolen robes and issued forth to stare into the fog.

'D'you recognize the riggin', Matey?'

'It's Cap'n Argall's *Treasurer*, an' I should know it, havin' sailed wi' her.'

'From Virginny, Jem?'

'Aye, or from robbin' the French ports or the Spanish. From thereabouts, you can lay on it.'

'Then they'll be thirstin', or I don't know truth about the New World.' The innkeeper rubbed his hands and quickly ran into his alehouse to see that his barmaid and drawers were prepared.

'And buying!' The shopkeepers were already dispersing to light their goods and make them appear inviting.

'And whorin', eh Allie?' Jem asked a pretty tousled girl with thin, flushed cheeks. 'Come, I'll buy you a grog. It'll be awhile before they come ashore.'

She straightened her damp hair self-consciously, but shook her head.

'So you're savin' your prettiness for them that'll pay for it,' he said without rancor. 'Well, it's no obligation to ye, or maybe we better make it payment deferred, for I'm apt to be in a sore way by-'n'-by without a groat in my breeks.'

She gave him a smile purposely crooked to hide her broken teeth.

'Jemmy, I'll always warm your breeks, but not tonight.' She looked out at the mistily riding ship. 'I'm thinkin' there's shillin's there, in tobacco or . . . '

'Or yellow Spanish doubloons,' he said understandingly. 'Come on an' have your grog, Allie. It'll be awhile yet.'

He took her arm and she turned with him. 'I could stand somethin' to build me up to it. I'm shakin' inside like it was the ague.'

Jem was greeted as an authority in the alehouse. He had been to Virginia and could judge best the condition of those that returned from his expedition. He was not prodigal with his knowledge – not with such a present opportunity, though all had heard his tales a dozen times – and drinks were set up by Master Worsley for both Allie and himself before he would enter the discussion.

'It's a starvin' land,' he said. 'When your ship sails up the river the colonists come out to meet you, waist deep in water, callin' to you, have you got supplies? And when you sail away you feel you're leavin' the beggars at Tower Gate goin' to have their heads chopped off.'

'I wouldn't live in that there starvin' country if ye made me Queen of it,' Allie declared.

'But they always come back loaded,' a shopkeeper stated, his hopes not to be daunted.

'With tobaccy! What would *you* grow if you were starvin'?' Jem asked. 'Tobaccy? Or corn?'

They all shook their heads at the improvidence of the Virgians.

'What's the Captain like?'

'Cap'n Argall?' Jem pushed his glass and Allie's toward Master Worsley, who hesitated and then decided that Jem's preperformance audience was at least meeting the cost of fire and tapers. 'He's a darin' gent,' Jem conceded reluctantly. 'He has his way, be it with men or women either.' Allie's bosom rose and fell. 'Not with your like, sweetheart. He's the kind'd set his mind on a princess and never sleep with a woman till he'd clumb that far.

180

He's a man you don't like to serve under – not like the Cap'n – and yet . . . '

'Cap'n Smith?' several voices asked, to probe.

'Aye, Cap'n Smith. He ain't a sea captain like Argall, but even a tar like me could see he should of been. I was with Argall his first voyage and came back on the ship that brang Smith home; but Smith should of stayed, he was the one to govern 'em. You did what Argall said, all right. But Argall ordered you because of something *he* wanted. Smith made you want it yourself. And how he loved that land – or maybe that girl!'

'The Princess?' It had been told so often the response was automatic, though nonetheless eager.

'Aye, the Princess! "The numparella of Virginia", Cap'n Smith called her. Argall wanted her too. I remember when he went up the river and captured her. He ain't a man to stop short o' what he wants – not like Smith, who's beatin' his brains out tryin' t'talk the Company into sendin' him back. . . . '

They heard the crunch of feet on the wet cobbles, the clink of swords.

'It's the Governor of the Forts. They've put a longboat out!' cried Little Rob, who had been lingering at the door to catch the talk and keep an eye on the harbor.

They crowded out onto the wharf to stand behind the Governor and his guards. The fog was pierced by the flares of the torchbearers, and into the ring of light they saw the boat approach, its occupants muffled against the chill.

A line was tossed and caught, and the boat made fast. A woman, wrapped in a sable robe, was lifted into the Governor's hands.

'My Lady!'

She withdrew from his arms and let the fur drop around her shoulders.

The mist swirled and singed itself in the flares whose light picked up the sheen of the rich cloak and brought to life the blackness of her hair, which without curl or wave was vibrant and strangely stirring.

'Keep back,' the Sergeant barked.

They did not heed, but pressed close, a ring of pallid faces in the murk and torchlight.

'Is it the Princess, Jem?' The words gathering made a sibilance as though a serpent hissed.

'Aye!' Jem kept tight hold of Allie, thrusting her to the front where she could watch. 'Like I guessed, Argall's got her,' he muttered. Then added with a shadow of regret, 'An' Cap'n Smith would've cut out his heart for her.'

His words were listened to carefully and passed on till they merged in a low excited rumble.

'Order now,' the Sergeant cautioned.

She was immobile, not seeming to breathe, her dark eyes opaque. Yet she was life itself, and movement; they were intrinsic to her hair and the swift blood current which flushed her skin and left a stain that brightened or grew dark as the flares gilded the delicate, proud bones of her face.

Captain Argall leaped to the wharf. He was dark as she, save for his light eyes, and extraordinarily handsome, but he expelled the energy that she restrained. He grasped the Governor's hand.

'Sir Ferdinando Gorges,' he said, and then with something of a flourish, 'the Lady Rebecca. The Governor will accompany us to London in the name of the Virginia Company,' he told her.

'They named her that when she became a Christian,' Jem whispered to Allie.

The Governor bowed and would have kissed her hands save that she kept them clasped about her cloak. She did not move, her lips did not stir, yet from her dark eyes the veil seemed lifted, and one could say she smiled.

'And this is her husband, Rolfe.' Argall hurriedly introduced a youthful, full-fleshed man who gravely took the Governor's hand. 'You know the Marshal of Virginia, Sir Thomas Dale. And this is Lady Rebecca's brother-in-law, Prince Tomakkin.'

There was a gasp as the Prince stepped into the light, a small laugh that sought to choke itself, and then a hush, for he was not solely ludicrous, but awesome, too. He was dressed in homespun breeches and leathern doublet, his head half-shaved, the center crest and the long single braid that hung down one side ornamented with strange beads and stranger bones. In one hand he held a long stick and in the other a fearsome knife. He stared at the circled crowd as if he would commit each individual to memory, and it was some relief to see his face was round and cheerful, his expression friendly; and when one noticed these one could see his belly was round, too, and sought to separate the breeks and doublet. Urgently, he started to notch the stick with his knife.

Argall brought a Savage woman carrying a swaddled babe to the Governor. 'This is Lady Rebecca's son, Thomas Rolfe. And these are her maids.'

They clustered on the wharf, shivering in spite of their furs, their dark hair touched with trinkets of red and yellow and white, their eyes clouding before the eager stares. Their features were clear-cut and their tawny skin possessed a semblance of the lambent blush of their mistress.

'If there's one for every mariner, you might as well take me home,' Allie said to Jem.

'But there ain't, and from the way those lads' – pointing to the rowers – 'are ogling you I think they're hungry for their own sort.'

Allie turned to them quickly and smiled her crooked smile.

'We have a litter for Your Ladyship,' the Governor said.

She looked at her husband, and he explained. She laughed, and her face that had been so still and regal, almost sullen, suddenly was vivid.

'I am not sick,' she said, 'to be borne. Nor dying, save from this cage John Rolfe has corseted me in.'

'If it is your pleasure, my Lady . . . ' The Governor would have taken her arm, but when she sensed the direction she started off at a pace which he had difficulty in meeting.

'Wait!' Tomakkin called. She turned to him. 'I have not yet counted them all.'

Lady Rebecca's eyes swept the crowd indifferently and went on. He hurried to catch up. He showed the stick on which he had been making notches furiously. 'Powhatan bade me make a mark for every Englishman I see, so he will know the number of the white men. Will there be many more?'

The Governor smothered his laugh. Those who were near in the crowd were not so polite; they guffawed and repeated what Tomakkin had said.

'Millions,' the Governor told him.

'Millions?' Tomakkin did not know the word.

'A thousand times a thousand,' Rolfe explained.

Tomakkin stared in disbelief and then, realizing it could only be a joke, he grinned widely in appreciation. He was better than the actor in the playhouse who came out dressed as a Savage and proclaimed himself Messire Tabac and argued with dull English Sir Toby Ale as to their merits. The laughter no longer seemed impolite, for like Messire Tabac Tomakkin was delighted to find a cheerful company.

Lady Rebecca strode ahead, not heeding Tomakkin's words nor his exclamations of marvel as they entered the city gates and the maze of buildings and narrow, overhung streets emerged on them out of the fog; though she missed nothing. Only when they came to the citadel did she pause as her gaze traveled up and up the gray stones of the castle to where the turrets were lost in mist.

'Is all England walled and gray?' she asked.

They hastened to assure her.

'The meads!'

'The lakes!'

'The downs!'

'The New Forest!'

Each bespoke that part of England which was home.

'It would take ten nations a hundred years to cut and pile those stones,' Tomakkin gasped. 'It is like the work of the mighty tribes to the south. . . .'

'It is my residency,' the Governor said modestly.

'It is too great a punishment for whatever you have done,' Lady Rebecca replied.

'Sir Ferdinando has not done anything, Rebecca,' Rolfe murmured, embarrassed. 'Not anything to be punished for.'

The Governor laughed in some relief when he saw that her eyes were amused.

'James's Court will relish Your Ladyship, for Jamie dearly loves a wit. The pity of it is, he thinks he *is* one.'

They crossed the yard, in the center of which stood incongruously the modern house of the Governor. Inside, the dark gallery was lit by the flames of a roaring fire. They were received by Lady Gorges, the Governor's wife, her curiosity controlled only by her breeding.

The Savages, though, were not restrained; they shuffled the rushes under their feet, they felt the ancient armor, peered into the Venetian mirror, and fingered the crystal drops of the candelabra. Tomakkin was the first to discover the pictures on the tapestries.

'Who?' he demanded, pointing to a dark-faced lady descending from a barge.

'It is the Queen of Sheba,' Lady Gorges explained, 'being received by King Solomon. He had a thousand wives,' she added as a point of information.

Tomakkin was unimpressed. 'Where? Why did she come to see him?'

'Across the sea – no, in the other direction – another sea . . .' She turned away. 'You must be exhausted, my Lady.'

'It is only this corset. Do you wear one?' Lady Rebecca prodded Lady Gorges' waist. 'You do. It is unbearable.'

'It is, sometimes,' Lady Gorges agreed.

'*Why* did she come?' Tomakkin pulled at her sleeve.

'Why? Oh – she – Why *did* she come?' Lady Gorges appealed to her husband.

'She came to pay homage to Solomon's wisdom. He was the wisest man in the world,' the Governor explained, amused both at the Savage and at his wife's distress.

'It is you,' Tomakkin said to Lady Rebecca, negating the ridiculous explanation. 'You have come from across the sea to pay homage to the wise King James.'

Lady Gorges glanced at her husband, who stroked his beard. 'It is – quite appropriate,' he agreed doubtfully. 'You must tell it to Jamie. He will appreciate the resemblance.'

CHAPTER TWO

Rebecca stood in the center of the large chamber and let her mantle drop to the floor. She watched her maids, who chattered like parrots while they examined the dark bedcurtains, the carved furniture, the great paintings framed in dulled gold whose colors, obscured by the gloom, were lit by a single candelabrum and the flames from the enormous fireplace. She felt as though they had reached the land between the living and the dead, a land where longing ceased at last, and hope. . . .

Tommy cried, and she stirred sharply, then strode across the room to take him from Manda's arms. He reached for her, and she held him to her face, the contact of flesh to flesh creating a surge of life within her.

'Unfasten me and loose my corset,' she commanded.

Manda obeyed, and the child burrowed his way to her breast. His lips hurt the tender nipple, but the pain was ecstatically sweet to her, like the sear of a hot coal to one who has been paralyzed.

'I thought Manda was to nurse the child – that you had given up this pagan custom. . . . '

She turned to face him. 'He is my son, not Manda's.'

His eyes glowed in appreciation as he saw the child against her full, bared breast. She looked down, but not from modesty. She reacted to Argall's love strangely. She knew the metal of his passion and could temper it, but the warmth he sometimes exhibited left her uncertain and reluctantly stirred.

'Give Manda the child and send the maids away. I would talk with you alone, Rebecca.'

She spoke to her maids and they withdrew, but she shook her head when Manda reached for Tommy. Manda went, closing the door.

Argall watched Rebecca, his smile quizzical.

'And now it is the child you would hold between us?'

She gazed at him cryptically, then down at Tommy who slept,

his lips still clinging to her nipple. She moved carefully to the carved cradle that had been prepared for him and knelt to place him between the covers.

'Is John Rolfe's child a greater barrier than John Rolfe?'

'You know he is. If it had not been for the child . . . '

When she looked up, her eyes were alight with a flame which so fired him that his smile faded and his lips whitened. 'You would have stolen me from my second husband as you stole me from my first. . . . '

He strode to her and caught her up into his arms.

'Rolfe stole you from *me*, didn't he? But you need not have given yourself to him, Rebecca. They would not have forced you.'

'I was a captive. I married John Rolfe to bring peace to my people and yours.'

'But why not me?' he demanded, between anger and pleading. 'You did not love Rolfe and – you could have loved me.'

'Who betrayed me and my father! Who stole me from my Lord by trickery!'

'Kokoum was not your Lord – nor is Rolfe. I did not take you as I could have that night aboard the *Treasurer*. I was willing to wait until you loved me. It could be I was wrong and you would have loved me then if I had used you forcefully.'

She looked at him, her eyes veiled, her lips just parted.

'God's wounds!' he breathed and reached to bind her to him, so tightly that she could feel the throbbing tension which possessed him. He kissed her fiercely, her mouth, her throat and uncovered breast.

She did not stir, nor seem to breathe, her body pliant.

He mastered himself and stood away, his face contorted.

'Damnation! If I did not know, I would think you were not worth this wooing.'

'I am not,' she said calmly, 'for you.'

'When we return,' he said, white-lipped, 'it will be to me you come, and not to Rolfe. . . . '

'Your laws bar that – even were I willing.'

'I have broken laws before this. I will be the law.'

'You hope to go back as Governor?'

'Will you help me, Rebecca?'

Unconsciously she lifted her breast into its covering and went to the window. She drew the arras and looked out on the murky yellow fog which obscured the gardens and the sea.

'Rebecca!'

She shook her head, without turning. She was obsessed with

187

the bleakness of the land and of her own spirit. She had shown nothing to the white men, no amazement at the wonders she had seen in this short time. She had held to her pride and her birthright. But she had known at once her race was doomed. Tomakkin and his stick! ' . . . in twenties, and in fifties, and in hundreds!' Opechancano had said. They had conquered the vastness of the sea, and now it was her land – Powhatan's land! And there was no truth in them. Only in Johnsmith . . .

She heard the door close as Argall went out. She opened the window and let the fog swirl around her and crowd into the room. The garden below was filled with vague and disfigured shapes; it was like opening your eyes under water. The long voyage had been the purgatory they had told her of, and this land the nether world of her atonement.

CHAPTER THREE

Lady Gorges, dressed save for her gown, waited for her husband. She tapped her fingers in staccato rhythm on her dressing table, frowning with impatience. Then she noticed her corset in the mirror, and she broke into a laugh.

'I thought I'd burst myself,' she said to her maid, Annie. 'She poked me in the belly and said, "You *do* wear one. It's unbearable." And it is, too, especially after dinner.'

'But what would you look like without one?' Annie asked grumpily. She had heard the tale, and she was still resentful that she had not been allowed downstairs when the Savages arrived.

Lady Gorges was in too high fettle to take offense. 'Falling out of myself, I suppose. But *she*'d look good enough, slim and straight.' She thought a moment of the strange Princess. Suddenly she sat upright. ''Od's blood, Annie! Do you know they've all seen her naked!'

Annie stared. 'All, my Lady?'

'Before she was civilized. She used to run around with nothing on like the pagan Greeks.'

'My Lord?'

'Not him, noddy. He's never been to Virginia. But Sir Thomas and that Master Rolfe before he was her husband, and Argall, and Captain Smith. He's the one told me about it; I wasn't shocked then; it sounded so pretty and so innocent; but now I know her it gives me goose warts.'

'And what, my love, could affect you like that?'

'La, Ferdie, sneaking up on me like a Savage!'

'*What* gives you goose warts?' the Governor persisted humorously.

'The thought of her all naked in front of those men.'

'You're right,' he agreed. 'It gives *me* goose warts, too.'

Lady Gorges laughed affectionately. 'I only wish it could, my love. But tell me, Ferdie, what am I to do with 'em? I can't have

189

that – that Savage on my right, prince or no prince.'

'I think he would consider it no honor to be placed next a' – Sir Ferdinando pulled his beard to keep his lips in line –, 'a squaw.'

'My Lord!'

'You can put him at my left and divide the other three as you see fit.'

'But how?'

'Sir Thomas has been confiding in me, and while perhaps the lady's husband maintains the least rank, Captain Argall would not be loath to be overlooked so long as he is next to his Princess.'

Lady Gorges turned to him excitedly. 'You mean – is there – is he . . .'

'I gather from the Marshal that Rolfe married her for the sake of her immortal soul, and to rescue her from Argall's desperate designs.'

'Which were?'

'To marry her himself, apparently. If he'd wanted anything else he would certainly never have yielded her to Dale's protection.'

'Ohhh!' Lady Gorges said. 'She's like Helen of Troy!'

'Nonsense, my love. She's a charming creature, but . . .'

Lady Gorges swept up from her dressing table and almost bowled her husband over with the force of her whalebone farthingale.

'Charming! She will be a sensation. The Queen! The Prince! Even the King!'

'Now, Margaret, you're not going to tell me Jamie will trade Villiers for Prince Tomakkin.'

She giggled. 'No, but if Lady Rebecca were a Prince – I tell you she'll be the rage. What a pity her husband is a commoner. Already I've had word from my Lady de la Warr telling me how to receive her – as if I needed to be taught! Can't you see her at the masques at Whitehall, hunting at Theobalds – London will go mad! *La belle sauvage!* And we will be the first . . .'

'The first what?' her husband asked.

'Her first friends, of course. I will go with her myself to London. She will always be grateful to us.'

Sir Ferdinando regarded his wife, and she paused before the gravity of his expression. 'God knows, she will need friends.'

'What do you mean, Ferdie?'

He opened the door of his garderobe, where his familiar awaited him. He started to untie his points.

'She's had little friendship from the English.'

'Captain Smith?'

'Smith, yes. But after he came home – She married some chieftain, you know. Up the Potomac. And Argall learned where she was. It's a story of treachery. Ralph Hamor, the Secretary of the Colony has told it: how she was taken a prisoner to Jamestown and used against her father to bring him to Marshal Dale's terms. He's brought her here, the first Christian, so that the Virginia Company will see what a great colonizer he is. I've just been talking to him. He'll use her to promote the Virginia Company, to attract money and adventurers.'

Lady Gorges waved away her maid. She stared at him. 'What about her husband?'

'Oh, Dale persuaded her to marry Rolfe in order to bring peace between the Savages and the English, but it was really to keep Argall from making himself too great; and I gather, now that he has filed Argall's horns, he has no objection to him putting horns on Rolfe. And Rolfe, too, has interests. He has invented a means for curing the tobacco so it is good as, or better than, the Spanish imports, and a beautiful Savage Princess will do much to spur his merchandise.'

Lady Gorges looked at him, aghast. 'She is a child. . . . '

Sir Ferdinando, his points tied, came to smile at his Lady in the mirror. 'She is like a heron, coveted by three falcons. Each would tear her apart rather than let another have her.'

'But my Lady de la Warr . . . '

' . . . is the wife of the Lord Governor and Captain General of Virginia. His interests are those of the Virginia Company. If the Princess can serve any purpose to increase the revenues of the Company . . . '

Lady Gorges turned slowly and fumbled with the ornaments on her dressing table. She was thinking of Smith's glowing eyes and words he had described the little Savage Princess – some outlandish name he had called her, not Lady Rebecca then. What he had said had brought up a vision of innocence that had lingered – her shyness and her boldness – how she alone had trusted the Englishmen and used to come to Jamestown with gifts and, to the delight of all, would call the boys into the marketplace and make them wheel, falling on their hands, turning their heels upwards, while she would follow and wheel so herself, naked as she was, all the fort over.

'But Sir Thomas Dale makes such a point of being her godfather – her being baptized. He must cherish her.'

Sir Ferdinando turned her to him, his eyes deriding the pleasantness of his smile.

'As Deputy Governor of Virginia, Sir Thomas Dale has built

191

his reputation with harshness and opportunity. And what he thinks of a small Savage Princess, let me tell you: the Lady Rebecca has a younger sister, lovelier they say than she. After Rolfe married the Princess, Dale sent Hamor to Powhatan to ask for this sister to be his dearest companion, wife, and bedfellow. . . . '

'His wife! How could he? Lady Dale is here – waiting for him.'

Sir Ferdinando kissed his wife's brow. 'Lady Dale was half a world away. . . . '

'What did the Emperor say?'

'That one daughter was enough to sacrifice to the English.'

They were startled by Annie, who pushed in the crane which held her mistress's gown. Lady Gorges stood while Annie fitted the wide skirts over the farthingale, adjusted the overdress and fastened on the *tête de mouton* sleeves to match. When she was finished, Lady Gorges inspected herself, touched her hair to see that it was not disarranged. Finally she turned on her husband.

'Men!' she said. 'I hate you all!' She swept past him, pivoting her farthingale so that she could pass through the door. 'Don't dast be late, Milord,' she said menacingly as she went out.

Sir Thomas Dale was down before her. He was a grim man, a soldier, who had had some favor from the Prince of Wales, Prince Hal. God rest the bonny lad! He would have saved their Court from pimps and sodomites if he had lived. But he was gone now, and she felt no added warmth toward this, his one-time tutor – a carnal face and greedy hands that would not gentle a woman to submission.

'You have been long in those heathen parts, Sir Thomas, but I have seen your Lady occasionally, and she has given me news of you.'

'Your Ladyship is kind, both to me and to my poor Lady.'

'It is a charming pagan you've brought home, Sir Thomas.'

'Lady Rebecca is no pagan, my Lady. I would have been proud to have come home with many converted heathens. However, were it but for the gaining of this one soul, I would think my time, toil, and bitter losses well expended.'

'Humph!' said Lady Gorges, thinking of the younger sister. She turned to greet the Lady Rebecca, who wore the same dark, salt-stained velvet she had come ashore in. The flame that had lit her was subsided, her eyes opaque. Oh dear, Lady Gorges thought, do you suppose she is a moody creature? Then, remembering her husband's simile, she thought of the blue-white curtain that dims the eye of the captive fowl.

She felt warm and protective toward the Savage, still so young – she could not be more than twenty. 'I am glad your first home in England is our own. Sir Ferdinando has just given me the delightful news that I must go to London, too, and I welcome the thought that we will travel together. Then you will not be so alone. . . . '

'That is very kind of you, Lady Gorges,' Master Rolfe said.

She glared at him. He had been a scrivener before he left England for the Colony. She drew Lady Rebecca away toward the fire.

'Our London house must be your second home, and I will take you to the shops!' Lady Rebecca's eyes rewarded her suddenly with a gaze direct and warm. She *can* be devastating, the English-woman thought.

'My Lady is generous,' Sam Argall slouched against the mantel looking down at them, 'but my Lady de la Warr has undertaken to assist Her Highness.'

She looked at him resentfully, trying to remember what she knew about him – God's blood, but he was a beautiful rakehell! With a devil in his eye and in his breeks – sea captain and privateer under the patronage of – of course, the Lord de la Warr! The pattern began to take shape. But from the picture she had formed of these men, these hawks – you could not call them falcons – Lady Gorges was by no means prepared to emulate the frightened flight of a dove. She had known of the Princess before ever Dale or Rolfe or even my Lord de la Warr had thought of Virginia.

'I feel as if I knew you well, Milady – so much have I heard, from a friend who knew you long ago, when you were still a poppet. . . . '

Her eyes were on Lady Rebecca's, and swiftly as *they* turned, she looked, too, at Argall. He was so pale his eyes shone light as diamonds, and the skin was sucked back away from his mouth. He gathered himself from his slouched position and forced a smile.

'There will be time to talk about – other times. Sir Ferdinando . . . ' He indicated their host, who Lady Gorges noted *was* late.

Lady Rebecca held out her hand as if to hold Argall off, though he was some distance from her. 'What friend?' she demanded.

As so often when there was a crowd, Lady Gorges' mind had slipped the subject, and she was startled at the tension between the two.

'Friend?' she asked.

'The friend who told you . . . '

'Rebecca'!

Lady Gorges looked from Lady Rebecca's face to Argall's, and, though she did not know in what way, she realized she had an advantage and could hurt him. The others, her Lord, Sir Thomas, Master Rolfe the scrivener, and the weird Prince Tomakkin, moved in upon her, and for a moment she would have been glad to loosen the tension, to change the unpleasant conversation. Argall felt her willingness, but took too quick advantage of it.

'Lady Gorges has undoubtedly met many Virginians, and any of them would carry stories about you if they had known you or not, Rebecca.'

Lady Gorges resented everything about the man, his arrogance, his quickness, the fact that her whom he pressumed to refer to as Her Highness, he *dared* to speak to as Rebecca.

'I have *not* met many Virginians,' she said with dignity. 'Captain John Smith stayed here several times and told me much of your service to the English.'

Lady Rebecca's eyes went quickly from Argall to Dale, then slewed past him as she moved away.

'Is Smith alive?' Rolfe gasped.

'Alive?' Lady Gorges was surprised. She gazed at Argall. 'But you were here with him before you sailed the last time. You two discussed his plans for New England.'

Sir Ferdinando said, 'It was but an hour ago I told you and Sir Thomas: he is still waiting in London for his commission to sail.'

'Yes!' Sir Thomas coughed heavily. 'I did learn he was alive. I had – I had meant to discuss the matter with you, my dear.'

Argall was making a great effort to maintain his poise. 'God's life! We both knew he was alive, Sir Thomas. We realized someday you would have to know, Rebecca, but had hoped to tell you privately.'

She was not listening to him. She went quietly to Tomakkin, and her hand touched his softly. He looked from her to Argall to Dale to Lady Gorges in wonder. Lady Rebecca showed nothing, her face immobile, but her very quiet held them.

'Rebecca!' Argall said fiercely. 'In over six years he hasn't tried to – Please, Rebecca!' She did not turn her head or answer him. Suddenly he pivoted and dashed out of the room. They could hear him as he pounded up the stairs.

'What the devil?' Sir Ferdinando said, but no one answered him. 'Margaret, for God's sake – let's go in to dinner.'

CHAPTER FOUR

He flung open the door to his room and stopped as he saw his man warming a nightrobe before the fire.

'Get out!' Argall ordered tautly.

Jason turned to stare at him, his suet face and currant eyes startled.

'Captain!'

Argall grabbed a pitcher and threw it. Jason scuttled around the edge of the room and out. In a second he returned to close the door.

Argall did not hear him. 'Goddamn it!' he howled, his head raised as though the words were a prayer of lament. Then, if it *was* a prayer, he told God what he thought of Lady Gorges.

'Fat, cackling beldame!'

He hated her. He hated Rebecca. He hated the hypocrite, Thomas Dale. He even, briefly, hated himself. But most of all he hated John Smith.

'I saved his life! I saved his fucking life!' And then, with a brief chuckle, 'I saved his *fucking* life.'

He turned and poured aqua vitae from a decanter and sank onto a settle in front of the fire.

Was all that he had planned for, hoped for, spoiled? He couldn't let it be. He had expected Smith to have sailed – for New England. *Then* he would have told her. Then she need not have known of the letters Smith had written and he not delivered. Nor Smith have known. They would both say it was treachery, but . . .

That maggot Dale had not wanted her to know, either. *There* was betrayal. He had known Argall's lust, love, need, and let him go to England, sure that when he returned . . . He had come back to find her married, already pregnant by that pious, pusillanimous Rolfe. Married, for Christ's sweet sake! He'd never thought of the word. *He'd* have married her. 'She is now a Christian,' Dale had told him. *That* she was not, whatever instruction, whatever

195

vows . . . She was a witch, a Morgan le Fay or Merlin's Niniane, a being as old as time and newborn with every spring. He thought of her as he first saw her, naked and alive – afire. What had President Smith done to spark that glow – old worrywart with the sorry handful of colonists he must teach to feed themselves? King of Virginia! It was fool Percy who had accused Smith of wanting to be that, not seeing at all the bitter concentration of the provider, the shepherd, the colonizer. It was he, Argall, who had dreamed of it . . . with her, to build a kingdom. In spite of tonight, in spite of everything – he clutched himself as he knew what she thought of him, then turned and filled his glass.

But he could not dismiss Smith so simply. He knew, too, what Smith would think. There had been moments when they could have been friends, two men whose lives had been too pressed for friendship. Argall had admired Smith in Jamestown, his drive, his mastery over crazed and whining laggards, as strong as Argall's own over his ship and crew. There had been sympathy between them, unlike as they were, Smith strong because of his belief and responsibility, Argall because of his will. Had it not been for the maid – Pocahontas then . . . Yet Smith had shown no jealousy. And when the time had come, when Smith lay wounded in the Captain's cabin and Argall had tacked with every wind in his swiftest crossing to save Smith's life, *then* Argall had not hated him. But he had carried his rival Smith away, and Argall could return to his Princess.

He thought of Smith in London, changed now, no longer master. An author, waiting after these years to sail again, he had seemed a parody of the President. Did a man forgive a friend who saved his life and then betrayed him?

He filled his glass again and stared into the flames, carried back past hate and violence. So he had deceived her about Smith. But didn't she know his passion? Didn't she know that of them all it was he who loved her? Certain, he had not carried Smith's letters! Certain, he had told her Smith was dead! But Smith did not love her. When he had told Smith of her marriage to Kokoum, Werowance of the Potomacs, Smith had only nodded – said nothing. Why had Smith's love been so easy and hers so binding?

In the years after Smith left, the English had seen no more of her. When Powhatan had retreated up the rivers none knew where, Argall had lost hope. But then, when he learned she had been wedded to Kokoum, he had sailed up the Potomac, seeking. And her uncle, wily, greedy Japasaws, had brought her to him. She had come for news of Smith. And once aboard the frigate he had held her prisoner.

If he had possessed her then – not let her passiveness turn him away . . . *What a fool!* he mourned. He stretched out his fingers close to the fire, believing he was singeing them on her nipples. If he had plunged his steel into her flame – then she would have wanted him.

But instead he had bated his passion, delivered her to Jamestown, trusted her to Dale – who had used her to bargain with Powhatan and, sending him, Argall, on another voyage to England, had concocted with Rolfe this wretched marriage as a peace treaty with Powhatan.

'With *him?*' he had yelled when he returned. 'Why not with *me?* You knew I . . .'

'I knew you lusted after her,' Dale had said sanctimoniously. 'Rolfe assured me it was with him no carnal thing – that he would save her soul.'

'No carnal thing! Was it God that twisted his balls?'

'Blasphemy, Master Argall!'

'And it was no carnal thing when you sent Ralph Hamor to ask Powhatan for her sister?'

'It would have been another soul to save. And Master Hamor had no right to tell. . . .'

Argall had laughed derisively. 'He's *publishing* it in England. What will your wife say to your saving of souls?'

He had had the satisfaction of seeing Dale's shock and fright, but that was all. Pocahontas was Rolfe's till he could win her from him. And now?

'But I will!' he told himself. '*I* will go back as Governor, and these dizzards pay. I'll have her if it be a rape. She'll feel my steel.'

CHAPTER FIVE

Rolfe followed his wife up the stairway. Pride in her and a desire to protect and comfort her moved him. These feelings, he knew, would evaporate when they were in the room alone, for with her he was always inadequate, though it had been she to whom he had meant to give so much. He had wanted to be generous, to share with this newly baptized lamb his own salvation. *But had she ever let him?* he asked himself angrily, and quelled his anger immediately. *Tonight,* he thought, *I could help her. But she won't let me.*

He closed the door. She stood beside the great bed. Suddenly she started to shake.

'Are you ill?'

'No.' But she could not control her trembling. She sat on the bed.

'Rebecca – I didn't know – I didn't know that Smith was still alive.'

'Dale and Argall knew – and Smith,' she said, and hid her head.

Should he put his arms around her? They had some will of their own, for they stretched out.

'Shall I go away?' he asked. Her head, burdened by its weight of braids, nodded. 'Shall I send Manda?'

'Tomakkin!' she said. He left.

Her eyes closed, she swayed from side to side.

'I will come back,' he had said. And she had known that he was dead. No one had had to tell her. Was it a fault in herself that she had not *felt* his aliveness?

And now, was she not glad that he was alive? Or was it worse that he had lived and not come back – or sent word?

Liars! Liars! Liars! A race of liars!

She was at the fire warming her hands when Tomakkin entered.

'Pocahontas?'

She went to him and laid her head against his shoulder. She spoke in Powhatan's language.

'Tomakkin Brother, take me home.'

He stroked her hair, which had fallen loose and hung to her knees.

'Were you at peace at home?'

She shook her head against him, then suddenly raised her face and stared, not seeing him.

'I was at peace with Powhatan.'

'Before the English came?'

'Yes.'

'And if they had not come, would you have been at peace with Kokoum, to whom Powhatan gave you?'

'I am Powhatan's daughter.'

He shook his head. 'You would never have been content to be squaw to any brave your father named.'

She stared at him, knowing how wisely he spoke.

'The white man's love is different from ours, Pocahontas. We take a maid to tend our wigwam, to cook and carry, a soft body, a vessel for our seed. While they – they speak to you of love.'

She turned from him, unable to endure the burden of her grief.

'They are a friendly people and great builders,' he said, as though he had memorized the words for Powhatan. 'But Powhatan was wrong to judge them at forty-eight hundred – they must be at least ten thousand.'

She looked at him wearily. 'They are many times ten thousand. They will sweep our country and destroy our people, and I have helped them – I have blinded Powhatan's eyes. . . .'

He frowned at her, aghast. 'You are Powhatan's peace offering, and they love you.'

'They have used me to make a great lie.'

'Argall? Dale?' She shook her head. 'Smith?'

'Don't speak to me of Smith. It is for him I have done so much. He was to me – Powhatan! And I did not know until tonight that he still lived. . . .'

She started away, but he caught her shoulders so that she stood quietly, her back toward him.

'There have been Queens in our land, but they were squaws who listened when a Werowance spoke – there have been wives who were favorites as Matatiske was to Powhatan – and maids like you, for whom even Powhatan would shake the earth; but from them we do not draw our strength or goodness – our kings come from the mothers, not the wives of kings. Woman is the

199

vessel, man the source – you should remember that, Pocahontas.'

'Oh, go away!' Rebecca said. He moved toward the door. 'And tell John Rolfe to come to bed,' she added crossly, but in much better spirit.

Rolfe parted the bed curtains and stared down at her in the flickering light. She was still and naked and of such a rosiness as to make him blink. Her eyes were closed, and he knew it would not be he she would receive. Tonight the passive flesh would not stay passive. She would push his chest and cry out against him even while her legs would knot around him, tying him to her, desiring with frightening, insatiate urgency – but not him, her husband – him she received submissive and unstirred.

He trampled his hose into his shoes and pulled himself out of both. He bent to her and at his touch her body arched to meet him; her mouth opened and her teeth clamped her wrung lips. He whipped himself into the passion of a man he had never seen, but whom he knew as he had thought you could not know another man.

CHAPTER SIX

He had lodgings in Holborn Street, close to his publishers in Chancery Lane. He had only to walk across Lincoln's Inn Fields to watch the pages ground out, to see the words that he had struggled with take form irrevocably. He had made friends with the young advocates in Lincoln's Inn, and, of course, in the Fields he had many friends – peg-legged sailors, soldiers who had fought with him in the Lowlands or in Tartary. They greeted him, and he stopped, and if he did not remember them, he talked all the same till they called up the battle or carouse, and then he saw them again and wondered at their grizzled wigs and withered phizzes. Because they were old he felt old, though he was only thirty-six, with his Admiralty before him; and he left them thinking that writing was a sluggard's work, that there was not time to pause, but only time to do. Then he sought them again, because they recalled the moments of swift action and decision, and he thought: *If I was so, I can be so again.*

His publisher loved him, for his books sold well. His publisher admired writers because they dealt in intangible wares and not even a publisher could judge of their worth, but he admired them most when they were able to write what caught the popular fancy.

The books *he* wrote, he told himself, were True Relations, nothing fantastical, but sometimes when he thought of them and of his experiences, the whole seemed fantastical in the extreme. He liked to say to himself, 'I have conquered Kings,' or 'I have loved Princesses and they have loved me,' but it did not seem believable even to him. Why should those who read his books believe him? And yet, he assured himself humorously, it was all true; he had and he had – yes, he had!

It was only when his words were spewed forth on the printed page, definite black on negative white, that it was credible; and then, in spite of his *True Relations*, he was someone else. You

201

hadn't meant to make yourself a hero, but there you were, a hero all the same.

It was twilight, and he crossed the Fields on guard, his hand on his sword hilt, conscious of the weight of his pistols in his belt, for as well as cronies, every manner of cutthroat lingered here, though they would not be apt to notice one whose slops were patched, whose hair was ragged. Tonight, he thought, the printing will be finished, and Clerke must offer me an advance. Then I will be shorn and dressed like a gentleman and next time must take the long way round.

He was aware of a man who had risen from the grass and was following him. He turned, hands on the butts of his pistols.

'Captain!'

'Who is it?' he asked, hating his own startled suspicion. The man must know him or he would not have called his rank.

'Partridge.'

'Partridge!' His arms wide, he went to embrace his comrade. 'How are you?'

'Well enough. Waiting for the day when we shall sail. . . .'

'And so we shall!' Smith said with fervor. 'As soon as my tract is out the Company has promised ships – and then we will see again New England.'

'It will not be like Virginia?'

'It will not be like Virginia. We will take only men who know and love the land.'

'You have heard from Plymouth or from Portsmouth?'

'Have heard what?'

'That she has come.'

'That she. . . ?'

'The Princess.'

'Pocahontas?'

'Aye, the Princess!'

'Has come here?' He shook his head, sensing all it meant. 'With her husband?'

'Aye, and Dale and Argall.'

'To England – not yet to London, thank you.' He gripped his comrade and turned swiftly on.

Clerke handed him a book. It was a thing complete.

A Description of New England, it said, *or the Observations and Discoveries of Captain John Smith.*

It was an excitement that never failed, to hold in his hands the completion of his labors, but now he seemed unaware.

George Wither, the young advocate and poet whose satires had landed him in Newgate gaol, only to be rescued by Princess Elizabeth herself, perched on a table.

'Do you like it?'

'Like it?'

'The poem?'

'The poem?'

'I wrote!'

He remembered then that he had asked Wither to write a complimentary verse, and here it was, black on white, like his own life. He read it, uncomprehending.

'It's an excellent poem,' he said.

'I thought it was lousy but it was meant well.'

Smith took the book – it was a pleasant thing, mainly because it said *the Observations and Discoveries of Captain John Smith* – and buried it in his greatcoat.

'Shall we drink to it?' Wither asked.

'Not tonight.'

Clerke said, 'You have to have a drink.'

'Not tonight.'

Wither uncurled his long legs and bounced onto the floor. 'God's beard, I didn't come tonight for compliments to my poetastery. Monsoor Clerke has a fat packet in his breeks for you, and it's your bounden duty to wet our whistles. It's not every day a doughty Captain publishes his relations.'

Clerke brought forth a sack of shillings, jingled it pleasantly and stretched it toward Smith. Wither grasped it.

'Let the noble Admiral pay first!' Smith had been named Admiral of New England by the Plymouth Company, though as yet they had not supplied the ships for his Admiralty.

'Truth,' Smith said, recollecting himself. 'I owe you both a drink, and more!'

CHAPTER SEVEN

The Mermaid glowed like a coalfire in a darkened room. The light of candles shown as cold stars against the red blaze on the hearth. Guests stirred and hulloaed as Smith entered with Wither and the publisher. Among them were some actors and many poets, for there were more poets in London than bakers.

'Johnnie's printed his book,' Wither announced loudly, as though all the world cared, 'and he's a sack full of shillings.'

The room cheered – those Smith knew and those he did not know. The great poet, Ben Jonson, and several others came forward to press his hand.

'It's a good book,' Wither said. 'I wrote a poem about it.'

'That should finish it,' Jonson said. He had a sarcastic tongue for rivals. Even those who fawned in youthful adoration he scowled at and prodded scornfully with his branded thumb – until they ordered him canary.

'Fill the tankards, host.' Wither said, already proprietor of Smith's pocketbook.

All hulloaed again, and Smith grinned. It was a company he loved to frequent, men of a different mark from all the world, but tonight they might really have been visitors from the habitat of a mermaid, for they swam before his eyes, assuming weird shapes and distortions. He could think only of the maid, his Princess, live and lithe, her skin and hair as vibrant as her limbs and eyes . . . spirit itself, and his, *his*, *His!* What is *she* thinking? What is *she* wondering? Does she think him . . . ? Of course, she thinks him false. And has he not been?

He tasted the sweet, strong malmsey; then as the talk became close around him, emptied his draught.

'Our Admiral celebrates,' Wither said. 'Have you ever seen him tipple before this?'

'*Tonight* I celebrate,' Smith said and held out his tankard once again.

Jonson raised his cup six inches from the table. 'To Will!' he said glumly, squinting with his misfit eyes.

And all drank to the actor-poet who had died three months ago at Stratford, a rival Ben had scorned but loved to bait and bicker with across these very boards.

There were more toasts: for Jonson's sweet Oriana, England's Queen – for Wither's Princess Elizabeth – and for fair mistresses of many would-be gallants – for Smith's Lady Tragabigzanda and the Princess Pocahontas!

'*Quel homme!*' murmured Wither fondly.

Smith tiredly drained his cup. *What was it like for her?* he wondered. This savage England? With an English husband? With an English marshal and an English sea captain to sponsor her? How did she find it, who had thought so much on this land because it was his own? *He*'d heard her story, of course, from Ralph Hamor, who'd come back a year ago: how she'd been married to the Werowance of Potomac; how Argall had sailed up the river and taken her by trickery, then delivered her to Marshal Dale at Jamestown. That was what he could not credit – that Argall, who had wanted her so hot-bloodedly, would give her up to someone else. Then she had been baptized and married to a Master Rolfe. They loved each other, or so Hamor said, and she was happy. Now they had brought her here to use her again. How, he did not know. To advantage themselves . . . Virginia . . . as they had used her to force peace on Powhatan. And he, to whom her mind would turn, could not protect her. . . . He thought of those who might help her: Sir Thomas Smythe, Treasurer of the Virginia Company – he was an honest man, though he thought of profit; Prince Charles, who had been John Smith's patron; Queen Anne . . .

They talked, and he dozed, and when he awoke he was alone with Wither save for the party of actors from the Swan.

'I stayed with you, old friend,' Wither said, 'and I saved your shillings, for I made old Clerke pay for the drinks. It was a profitable sleep.'

'I thank you,' Smith said. He rose, felt of his pistols and his sword. 'It's to bed for now.'

'We'll walk each other home. 'Two strongarms are safer i' the night.'

They were up Friday Street to Westcheap, wide and deserted, the shadow of the cross wavering in the light of a bracketed torch. They passed Newgate prison, where Wither muttered a little prayer – which would have seemed a Popish thing had Smith not remembered his friend's imprisonment there – and crossed the bridge over the conduit to climb Holborn hill.

The city was asleep, blanked out by the darkness and the silence, and they trudged quietly. Smith stopped and savored the night, the starlight and the loneliness, then closed his eyes, for suddenly he felt her presence – the fay child!

'You think much tonight,' Wither said, drawing him from his dream.

'I have forgot much – and tonight has freshened my remembrance.'

They walked on and reached his dwelling. He turned to Wither, his hand outstretched.

'Good night.'

Wither whirled his cape and produced a flagon of malmsey.

'Not good night, till we have finished this, which I filched from our good host. I'll come up with you.'

The hardest words for man: 'I weary of your company!' 'I am tired and would go to bed.' 'Go away and come again tomorrow.' Smith looked at him, at the bottle, tried to refuse, and then silently shrugged and waved the way so that Wither preceded him into the house.

On the stairs they crossed, and Smith led Wither into his dark chambers. He lit the candle and set it on his writing table. He found two mugs.

Wither measured out the wine and, lifting his own cup, asked in that manner of his which probed with a surgeon's scalpel: 'What have you remembered that before you had forgot?'

Smith glared, and pondered, throwing the puppy from the window.

'It would not be,' Wither pursued relentlessly, 'that today the Princess Pocahontas is in England?' Smith sat cold and anxious not to reveal the verity of the thrust. 'Tell me the story again.'

It was not an impertinent request, since indeed Smith had written the tale and told it, too, many times, as he had all his adventures. It was only that once again it was vivid and real as the wound he had closed his mind against.

'You've heard it, 'he said gruffly. 'Let it suffice.'

'But you never told you were in love.'

Smith sat stolidly. He had not told nor thought it. He had known that she loved him, as a child might love a seducer. *Had* he been her seducer? He had known overmastering passion and burning regret. He had known shame and degradation, deep pity and waves of longing for her warmth and youth and sweetness – but he had not known he was in love. Now he knew it! Now!

'My great Captain, tell me the rest of the story,' the poet said.

What rest? He had told how she had saved his life, how she had come those many times to Jamestown, how often she had saved the colonists with gifts of corn and stood between her father and themselves. What had he not told? The taking of a child who threw herself on him in a passion of play, the love she had forced on him, demanding, nay commanding, his reciprocation. If he had told that, the ribald sentences of his peers would smear her innocence. If he told that, there would be no difficulty colonizing Virginia.

The fumes of the malmsey were nearly as strong as a quick draught. He sat, the cup far from him, letting his mind clear.

'What is she like? Is she slim or fat, tall or short?'

'She is straight and slim – not tall. She was a child,' Smith said and wiped his brow.

'Too much a child?' Wither asked meaningly.

Smith arose and threw his tankard to the floor. 'Take your malmsey and go home.'

' 'Od's wounds, *mon capitaine*, I would not raise your wrath nor speak the lady false. It's only that with a poet's nose I smell a love both true and pure.'

How pure no man would ever know, for carnality was purified and purity magnified in the innocence of her body offering. How true, not he could say, nor even she. . . . But she had married – twice – and come with her son to England, her son by Rolfe.

'It was no love for poets. She was a child and I her father. She called me father. . . . ' He flinched at the truth and at the lie. 'If I had stayed . . . '

Wither picked up Smith's cup and filled it. 'If you had stayed, it would have been a romance for Avon's bard.'

True, Smith thought, and rubbed his swimming head.

'No one has ever seen you drink like this,' Wither said un-tactfully. Smith said nothing, and Wither went on. 'She came out of the forest to care for you when you were wounded of the gunpowder and said good-by . . . '

Oh, sad good-by!

'Why did you *not* go back?'

'I was finished by the time I left,' Smith said against his will. 'My good was negated by enemies who envied what I had done – could do. My power to do was taken from me. . . . Here, it was a fight. The Company had charges against me, and I against them.'

'But you are not a man to stop for charges. Did you not tell her you would come back?'

Smith, tormented, got to his feet and deliberately untied the

207

points that bound his breeks. He pushed them down, revealing a vast and awful scar, powder-grimed and still raw-looking after six years.

'Would you go back with that?' he demanded hoarsely.

Wither took the candle, and the darkness closed in upon him and the wounded privates of Smith.

'Did it geld you?' Wither asked in awe.

'I feared it did,' Smith said, pulling up his breeks and fastening them.

'And did it?' Wither insisted.

'I'm well enough for the stews,' Smith said shortly. He moved pointedly toward the bed and started to undress.

Wither arose and moved to shake his hand.

'*Mon capitaine*, you are a hero of our time, and what you have told me here shall not be repeated.'

Smith shook his hand and sat, doublet untied, till Wither's footsteps had echoed down the stairs. Then he buried his head in his hands, thinking of the maid arriving alone, even though surrounded, in England. What she had done for him! And what could he do for her?

At length he arose and replaced the candle on the table. He sat and picking up a quill, carefully dipped it in ink.

He began:

To the most high and virtuous
Princess, Queen Anne of
Great Britain

Most Admired Queen,
The love I bear my God, my King and Country, hath so oft emboldened me in the worst of extreme dangers that now honesty doth constrain me presume thus far beyond myself, to present your Majesty this short discourse: if ingratitude be a deadly poison to all honest virtues, I must be guilty of that crime if I should omit any means to be thankful.
So it is,
That some ten years ago being in Virginia, and taken prisoner by the power of Powhatan their chief King, I received from this great Savage exceeding great courtesy, especially from his son Nantequos, the most manliest, comeliest, boldest spirit, I ever saw in a Savage, and his

sister Pocahontas, the King's most dear and well-beloved daughter, being but a child of twelve or thirteen years of age, whose compassionate pitiful heart, of my desperate estate, gave me much cause to respect her: I being the first Christian this proud King and his grim attendants ever saw: and thus enthralled in their barbarous power, I cannot say I felt the least occasion of want that was in the power of those my mortal foes to prevent notwithstanding all their threats. After some six weeks fatting amongst those Savages Court-iers, at the minute of my execution, she hazarded the beating out of her own brains to save mine; and not only that, but so prevailed with her father, that I was safely conducted to Jamestown: where I found eight and thirty miserable poor and sick creatures, to keep possession of all those large terri-tories of Virginia; such was the weakness of this poor Commonwealth, as had the Savages not fed us, we directly had starved. And this relief, most gracious Queen, was commonly brought us by this Lady Pocahontas.

Notwithstanding all these passages, when inconstant Fortune turned our peace to war, this tender virgin would still not spare to dare to visit us, and by her our jars have been oft appeased, and our wants still supplied; were it the policy of her father thus to employ her, or the ordinance of God thus to make her his instrument, or her extraordinary affection to our Nation, I know not: but of this I am sure: when her father with the utmost of his policy and power sought to surprise me, having but eighteen with me, the dark night could not affright her from coming through the irksome woods, and with watered eyes gave me intelligence, with her best advice to escape his fury; which had he known, he had surely slain her.

Jamestown with her wild train she as freely frequented, as her fathers habitation; and during the time of two or three years, she next under God, was still the instrument to preserve this Colony from death, famine and utter con-fusion; which if in those times, had once been dissolved, Virginia might have lain as it was at our first arrival to this day.

Since then, this business having been turned and varied by many accidents from that I left it at: it is most certain, after a long and troublesome war after my departure, betwixt her father and our Colony; all which time she was not heard of. About two years-after she herself was taken prisoner, being so detained near two years longer, the Colony by that means was relieved, peace concluded; and at last rejecting her barbarous condition, was married to an English Gentleman, with whom at this present she is in England; the first Christian ever of that Nation, the first Virginian ever spake English, or had a child in marriage by an Englishman; a a matter surely, if my meaning be truly considered and well understood, worthy a Princes understanding.

Thus, most gracious Lady, I have related to your Majesty, what at your best leisure our approved Histories will account you at large, and done in the time of your Majestys life; and however this might be presented you from a more worthy pen, it cannot from a more honest heart, as yet I never begged any thing of the state, or any: and it is my want of ability and her exceeding desert; your birth, means and authority; her birth, virtue, want and simplicity, doth make me thus bold, humbly to beseech your Majesty to take this knowledge of her, though it be from one so unworthy to be the reporter, as myself, her husbands estate not being able to make her fit to attend your Majesty. The most and least I can do, is to tell you this, because none so oft hath tried it as myself, and the rather being of so great a spirit, however her stature: if she should not be well received, seeing this Kingdom may rightly have a Kingdom by her means, her present love to us and Christianity might turn to such scorn and fury, as to divert all this good to the worst of evil: where finding so great a Queen should do her some honor more than she can imagine, for being so kind to your servants and subjects, would so ravish her with content, as endear her dearest blood to effect that, your Majesty and all the Kings honest subjects most earnestly desire.

And so I humbly kiss your gracious hands.

John Smith.

June 1616

CHAPTER EIGHT

Fat Anna, rustling the pages of a letter, walked along the gallery leading to the King's apartment. As she approached the Royal Chamber the steps of the Queen of Great Britain quickened so that she entered almost at a run. Her enormously wide farthingale jittered violently, making her appear to have set sail in a tub on a very rough sea.

Gallants diced or played at cards on the benches or the floor. Pages watched, their ruffs hanging loose, doublets untrussed. She was dimly aware of one who made water against the wall. All looked up as she passed.

'How lustily does Oriana charge to seek her Lord's embraces!'

'He'll not charge *her*, I warrant you.'

'No, though he charges much, it's Villiers who receives.'

Fat Anna nickered nervously and plunged through the arras into the Privy Chamber. Here were assembled the Gentlemen of the Bedchamber waiting to be summoned to attend the King's levee. Breathlessly she demanded of the First Gentleman that he announce her to His Majesty.

'Bellana!'

'Fair Oriana!'

'The day holds promise from your coming.'

The color receded from the Queen's cheeks, leaving them pink and white. She smiled and greeted the handsome nobles gracefully, her eyes coquetting as she acknowledged each. When the First Gentleman returned to bow her in, it was a moment before she could recall her previous indignation. She entered in a rush.

James the First of England, Sixth of Scotland, sat on the edge of his bed, dangling his spindleshanks which protruded from a grayed nightdress. A tasseled velvet cap gave him a rakish look. He regarded her curiously.

''Od's my life! But it's a foulmart's den I pass to greet 'ee, Jamie,' she complained.

'Have yon rascals been misbehavin' wi' you, Nanny?'

'Misbehaving!' She told him the puns.

He laughed appreciatively. 'It was Carleton and Danvers, I could guess. Both bonny lads and ready wits.'

She had seated herself, and he came to stand over her, his head cocked. His tongue was too large for his mouth, which hung open, framed by his thin beard. He would have appeared an idiot save for his intelligent eyes.

'Since to board ye would pleasure neither of us, Nanny, what *have* you come for?'

She remembered the letter. 'They've written me a petition. And she sounds a lovely lass. I think I'll see her.'

'A lass?' He frowned.

'Come now, there's that sex, too, you know!'

'No cause to scold me, Nanny. We've agreed we share the same tastes.'

She stared at him a second, seeking his point.

'You mean for comely lads?'

He laughed, and she with him. Thus had they drawn the curtain on the past bitter years of jarring and heartbreak.

'Well, who's your lass and what's the petition?' he asked at last, impatiently, for she always sustained her laughter longer than he when he had made a joke.

'A Savage Princess – from Virginia! Her name . . . '

He had taken the letter and was skimming through it.

'Her name is Pocahontas, and I've heard of her before. She's the Emperor's child.' He looked at the signature. 'This Smith I've heard of, too.'

'He knows Baby Charlie, who's named some places on his map. She sounds a gay and picturesque thing. Will you command her here, Jamie? And I'll have Ben think out a masque, and Inigo will make a forest scene. And we will *end* this tedium!'

'Aye,' James said, still staring at the letter. 'I like not their bringing a Royal Princess to my land, and I not told. And married to a commoner. It would seem – this simple Captain is the only one appreciates her dignity.'

The usher opened the door and announced Sir George Villiers, Master of the Horse. James and Anne both looked up with pleasure. It was plain the Knight had no doubt of His Majesty's welcome, for he followed almost on the heels of the usher. He crossed the room and kissed the King on the mouth. He paused before turning to the Queen to delicately wipe his lips where James had slobbered. Then Villiers kissed her on both cheeks.

'How's my Dog Steenie?' James demanded.

'But barely awake. It's not yet midday. How fares Your Sowship?'

James scratched himself. 'Thank 'ee! Thank 'ee, Steenie,' He gazed fondly on his favorite.

'And you, Sweet Majesty?'

'I'm happy, Steenie. We are going to have a Savage Princess, and there will be a masque about Virginia. The actors will be naked heathens.'

'And I will be a redskin!'

James leaned on Villiers, his head practically on the brocaded shoulders.

'The Court will love to see our Steenie naked. Aye, Nanny, we'll command your Princess. Now, run along. Run along.'

CHAPTER NINE

On the flood the *Treasurer* sailed between the marshy banks of the Thames, distant at first like the wide-spreading arms of the Chesapeake, then narrower where on either side the sea meadows stretched.

Rebecca stood on the high poop deck, watching with interest the shores as watered as her own. Only at home it would be all sparkling blue and gold, and the greens would vie, dark against light, sunlit and shadowed, so that you longed to plunge into their depths. In spite of what they told her, she could not believe that there were forests here.

Groups of houses dotted the shore now, and wharves; and ships were hove to, waiting for the ebb. As the habitations increased, so did the traffic, shallops and pinnaces, all traveling toward London. Rolfe pointed out landmarks. She barely heeded. She quickened to the sight of a city, thinking it London, but he told her it was Gravesend. She absorbed its strange sound, trying to give it meaning in the language she had so carefully learned. Graves end! Was it the burial ground? She did not ask. *The grave is the end of life*, she thought. *Does the grave, too, have an end?*

At Greenwich he showed her the castle where was born the virgin Queen for whom the Englishmen had named her land. It was the same mighty pile of cold gray stone that she had seen before, but her attention fastened to it. She was interested in all things which concerned the woman who had ruled this nation, but more than Queen Elizabeth's castle, Rebecca wanted to see her city.

'That's Drake's ship, the *Golden Hind*,' Rolfe said, pointing to a vessel which was moored near the castle.

She thought of the Admiral who had conquered the Spaniards and sailed around the world. The tale came to her warmed by Johnsmith's ardor – she could see so clearly the light and shadow

214

cross his face – but she was shut off from it as if there were a wall of glass.

'Sir Francis and Sir Walter!' Johnsmith had said, and she, hero-worshiping, had sensed *his* hero-worship. 'Sir John,' she had wanted to say, but she had not, for there was only one with whom she would have compared him.

Rolfe caught her arm, and she looked. The river was alive with boats, many as the sturgeon in the spawning season, sailing vessels like their own, small barges poled or drawn by animals from the banks, wherries gaily bedecked. Who could believe? Powhatan would not believe!

'The Tower of London!'

Her eyes widened to absorb its girth and shot up the length of the great towers, for surely it was not one but a city of towers.

'Sir Walter Raleigh is there?'

'*Was* there. It's told he's been released.

Johnsmith loved Sir Walter. He would have been so glad – *was* so glad.

'London Bridge!'

She tore her eyes from the Tower, from the busyness of the river scenes. Indeed, the bridge must be without compare in all the world – with countless arches, overhung with houses; the water swirling under it in mad haste; the small boats catching the current as they rode the rapids. On top a gate were pales from which rotting heads stared sightlessly down at them.

'Spaniards?' she asked, wondering at the Englishmen's shock when they had first seen drying scalps and learned what they were.

'Traitors!'

She blinked. 'So many of them?' But she had known in Virginia the number who would have betrayed Johnsmith.

'It signifies no great crime in England in these times to be condemned a trator,' Rolfe said lightly.

The craft around their vessel, the screaming from the shore, brought her back suddenly, frighteningly aware of the terrible life of London; and coincident with the thought and sudden sense of haste, the sound of bells dinned out from all directions as though the air were beset by spirits who sought to drive the mortals mad.

Rolfe pulled her hands from her ears. 'It is high noon, and every church in London tolls the hour.'

She stared at him and turned to grip the rail. When the bells ceased she sensed an instant of silence, then the cacophony of sounds seemed an extension of the brazen nightmare; quarreling voices, singsong voices of vendors tootling into shells, the cries of watermen soliciting fares, the clatter of metal-tired wains on cobbled streets, the barking of dogs, the braying of asses. *Does one* live *here?* she thought.

'It's Billingsgate!' Rolfe told her, amused, yet sensing her shocked nerves. 'The noisiest quay in London!'

She thought of the silent forests, of the braves who, frozen with wonder, had first viewed the great winged canoe of the English, and of their swift flight through the woods to tell what they had seen and ask Powhatan if it betokened friend or enemy. She regarded the line of masts and rigging alongside the shore. Their arrival was but one of many to this raucous people.

Tomakkin came to her side. With a wide gesture he hurled his thoroughly notched stick into the river.

'You were right,' he said in Powhatan's language. 'No man can number them. If Powhatan counts the stars in the sky, the leaves on the trees, or the grains of sand upon the shore, then he will know how many are the English.'

For the first time she felt friendly and at home with herself. She touched his hand fleetingly and smiled.

'These things Powhatan has not seen.'

Sir Thomas Dale sent to ask her to come to the captain's cabin. She went below, Rolfe with her.

Dale and Argall arose as she entered. Dale took both her hands and led her to a seat.

'My child, we are at the end of our long journey.' She did not speak, but gazed at him steadfastly. 'You will meet folk far greater than you have ever known.' He waited for her, but still she was silent. 'It is in your power to do much for that land we all love. You know our constant need for funds to aid us in our building and our colonizing. Here, the Church is of great importance in forwarding such projects, and by your behavior they shall know the first fruits of my labor – our labor. In you they shall see the first heathen to be converted and baptized a Christian.'

They all looked at her anxiously, but she said nothing, nor altered her gaze.

'Can you not answer your White Father?' Dale asked.

'I no longer call you Father.'

Dale cried out. 'You have been born anew. . . . All that I have done for you!'

'How do you mean to act, Rebecca?' Argall asked. He was strained, for her smile had not touched him since the night at Plymouth; but always between them was a recognition of strength and a sort of sympathy.

216

'It is not for you to ask,' Rolfe said furiously. 'She is my wife, and I shall answer for her.' She regarded his assertiveness with some surprise.

'She is still my ward,' Dale said indignantly.

Rolfe quickly fell into line under the touch of the baton. 'I don't deny it, Sir Thomas. She will be docile for her husband's sake. Won't you, my sweet?'

'I shall behave as Powhatan's daughter,' Rebecca said.

Dale began to lecture her.

'What are you doing to my pretty?' Lady Gorges stood at the door, her eyes flashing. 'Spoiling her pleasure with your dreary words.' She entered and drew Rebecca up. 'Come, my darling! London is a town of marts and goldsmiths, and these traffickers in maids are prepared to deck you handsomely.' She threw a haughty glance over her shoulder as she herded Rebecca out.

On deck, she appraised Rebecca's gown and hair. 'I have been long at my toilet, else I wouldn't have let 'em get you in their talons. But *you!* La, never mind! You'll be a rare sight when we're done.'

Rebecca smiled at her. She was a Wironausqua in this land, a worthy one, but full of chatter.

A barge nosed the *Treasurer* in to dock. From the shore were wafted malodors of all descriptions, though rotting fish predominated.

'It's Butolph's Wharf!' Lady Gorges held her handkerchief to her nose. 'I *do* love London and miss it sorely. Ah! There's Sir Thomas Smythe! Oy, Sir Thomas!' She waved madly. 'Treasurer of the Virginia Company,' she told Rebecca. 'A merchant with ships that gird the world. Jamie knights such men these days. But you can depend on Sir Thomas.'

Rebecca agreed with Lady Gorges instantly he came aboard and was brought to her by Sir Ferdinando. Sir Thomas regarded her, took her hand and bowed, kissing the back of his own hand as Lady Gorges had told her gentlemen did at Court. He stood upright and looked her in the eyes.

'I have loved Virginia and believed in her. I have received cargoes of fool's gold and every specious product. But now I have something real – and precious!'

He was tall and straight and nearly of an age with Powhatan. His gown was finely textured and bordered with fur; it was longer and different from any she had seen. Around his neck he wore a heavy gold chain. His mouth and eyes were large and generous like his words. She knew him for a wise Cockarouse.

'I have sailed up a river of dreams,' she said, not to be outdone,

217

'but when you take my hand, I, too, find that which is real.'

He smiled at her warmly from his heart, and all the coldness vanished, the coldness she felt toward Argall and Dale and Rolfe, who were around her now to greet Sir Thomas Smythe.

'She is our treasure from Virginia,' Dale said, and Rebecca was surprised at the indifferent glance Sir Thomas Smythe turned toward him. She judged by that how a great Werowance he was, for Dale had been all-powerful, greater than any Englishman, in Virginia.

'You will dine in my house,' Sir Thomas said to Rebecca, while his eyes included the company.

CHAPTER TEN

Once again the land rocked under her feet. In London, Lady Gorges had explained, she must have her face covered as well as the rest of her, and her eyes were bright and excited through the slits of her vizard. Sir Thomas's steward went before, waving his wand of office, to halt the carts and barrows so that the gentry would not be splashed. Lackeys shooed the pigs, which were allowed loose since they cleaned the streets of garbage and sewage. Ashore the smells were even more noisome and penetrating, and Lady Gorges gave her a pomander, a fruit called an orange, stuck through with spices, to hold her nose.

Sir Thomas's house was in Philpot Lane. It was cool and dark in contrast to the narrow, closed-in streets, and sweet smelling, for the floors were strewed with lavender and rosemary.

With great courtesy, Sir Thomas questioned her about Powhatan and his alliance with the English; and she, as Powhatan's daughter, answered him and was unaware of the raptured gaze of the Three who had wanted her to exert her charm.

They feasted, and she used the implements to eat with as she had been taught, though even this great man and Lady Gorges used their fingers and teeth to part a particularly tasteful morsel from its bone. As in Powhatan's land there was little talking while they ate, though there was no dancing or music to entertain the guests. Also, the meats were boiled and savorless compared to those they served at home, which came juicy from the barbecue and flavored with hickory ash.

Still, it was a pleasant meal with such a gracious host, and the low-paneled room reminded her of the feast aboard Argall's first frigate. She looked to him, remembering, and found his eyes fixed on her, fiercely imploring. Imploring what? That she forgive him? That she love him? Or that she aid him now in becoming Governor? She did not know, and, she thought wearily, she did not care. What she longed to ask, she could not bring herself to say. Where is *he?* Is *he* in London, too?

Rolfe broke the silence. 'We must seek lodgings. Will you recommend a tavern, Sir Thomas? In these long years abroad we don't know which is respectable and which is not.'

Sir Thomas Smythe paused, put down his fork and wiped his fingers daintily.

'No doubt the Company has prepared . . . ' Dale said with a chiding look at Rolfe for having spoken out of turn.

'Aye, we had,' Sir Thomas Smythe said. 'But all is different.' They watched him expectantly: Dale, Argall, Rolfe; Lady Gorges with quick interest; Sir Ferdinando like Rebecca, with faint and desultory surprise; and Tomakkin mildly, for here he moved as bidden, sometimes amused, but often bored.

'I have received a sudden and positive communication from my Lord de la Warr. His Majesty commands the Lady Rebecca's presence at Hampton Court speedily. I know not how the news of Your Highness's arrival reached His Majesty, but from my Lord's message, it would seem best to go at once – even this afternoon. Her Ladyship will find quarters in the palace of the Bishop of London at Brentford, who is His Majesty's chaplain and one of our Council for Virginia.'

Rebecca watched him, feeling no surprise, till she sensed the instant shock and amazement of the three who held her captive.

'The properest lodgings for such of you gentlemen as choose to attend her Ladyship is *The Three Pigeons*, a clean and wholesome hostel,' Sir Thomas Smythe finished.

They absorbed his statement slowly.

'I am the Lady Rebecca's husband,' Rolfe said at last. 'She should lodge with me, or I with her.'

'His Majesty has appointed a commission from the Privy Council to deliberate as to your right to marry a Royal Princess without the Crown's consent.'

She did not know what the words implied, save for their effect. Rolfe's hand, which was raised, started to shake so that he hid it in his lap; he turned deathly white. Argall's hands clapped the table, and when she looked at him he held her eyes – in his she read a mad hope. Dale regarded her consideringly, as though this thing which he possessed might be of more worth than he had dreamed.

'As the guardian of the Princess Pocahontas – the Lady Rebecca, whose great love and happy conversion will testify . . . '

Sir Thomas Smythe cut him short. 'Henceforth, the Lady Rebecca is the King's ward.' Dale flushed. 'It is not believed,' Sir

Thomas went on smoothly, 'that any treason should be imputed, as was the case with Lady Arabella Stuart's marriage, when her husband and his abettors were imprisoned. . . . '

Dale's mouth fell slack. The color drained from him so that his ruddy cheeks were like yellow apples. Only Lady Gorges maintained her composure.

'Jamie, for once, speaks like the Solomon he claims to be. But you are mad, Sir Thomas, to expect this child to journey to Brentford at once. For her sake – for your sake – all our sakes – I must have her in Cheapside and the Royal Change, where we can expand ourselves to buy all the things'll make this treasure the jewel His Majesty wants to see. Give me not one purse but sixteen, 'nd I'll buy her sarcenets and fabrics that'll set her off as never Princess was. We will find a tailor and a tailoress in Brentford, but I must have the stuffs!'

All, including her husband, looked at her with anxiety, but Sir Thomas threw back his head and laughed heartily.

'And that you must and shall! For never lass came to these isles – no foreigner but English born, as Virginia is England's sweet extension – so fair!' he eyed Rebecca's gown ' . . . so lacking! . . . nor so deserving love!'

Leaving three anxious men, Rebecca went with Lady Gorges to Cheapside. What mad pleasure! It was no narrow alley, but a wide clearing that stretched from here to there! And all along its fringes the traffickers bared what they came to trade, even as Newport had laid down his all before Powhatan.

They passed the spice shops, rich with their mingled odors, the fumivendulus's shops, decorated with green tobacco leaves, where was sold the Virginia tobacco Rebecca's husband had perfected. Was he her husband? she wondered. Or was she to be plucked from him by his King, as Powhatan could have canceled out a marriage if he chose? She felt nothing – only a vague regret at John Rolfe's sorrow, for he loved her and had used her gently.

But that regret was lost at once in her incredulous delight as they came to the stands which were covered with stuffs of gorgeous colors. Here Lady Gorges bargained, and for a few, a very few, insignificant disks of metal, long lengths of cloth of silver and gold were handed out, bright silks and shiny satins and grasslike velvets, some cut in intricate designs.

Through the noisy Poultry they progressed, and Rebecca noted that she and her dark-skinned maids did not create the stir or wonder among these busy folk that the white skins had aroused in Virginia.

In the Royal Exchange was more to marvel at. It was a two-storied building with a handsome tower. On the lower floor was a row of open galleries where merchants cried their wares.

'What do ye lack, gentles? What will you buy?'

The walk inside was thronged with customers searching through the loaded stalls. The floor was polished stone cut into small pieces and laid so as to make a pattern.

What riches! Rebecca thought. And she remembered the starving men at Jamestown.

Lady Gorges moved surely, matching threads and ribbons, pricing laces and fine ornaments. Dandified bucks stood idly, prinking, and ogling the pretty countergirls. These gallants were not indifferent to Rebecca and her train and turned to stare and occasionally make remarks, which words Lady Gorges returned with tart humor.

'Now, Goldsmith Row,' she said at last. 'For we have not spent it all.' She looked at Rebecca. *What a darling she is!* she thought. *Let my Lady de la Warr have the joy of presenting her.* I *have had* this!

Here was the richest street in London: the splendor of the golden tower and fountain on the corner, the steep-roofed houses with gilded and painted façades, the proud signs of the jewelers.

The sparkling cut gems dazzled Rebecca. She paused over a chain of red jewels far too costly for their purse, but still shown to tempt them. She turned the ring, which she always wore with its stone inside her palm, to compare the color.

'For this many hearts must have been drained,' she said, awed. They stared at her. 'For only heart's blood makes this jewel.'

'The red stones are called rubies,' the goldsmith explained. 'I'll show you emeralds. They are green as grass.'

She shook her head. 'It is heart's blood!'

'It is from the earth.'

'It is from a man!'

'My love! Don't be so stupid! It's a precious thing' – Lady Gorges looked at the ring – 'though finer will be given you. But's from the earth – a stone. Who told you it was heart's blood?' Rebecca did not answer. 'It was some rake, I'll warrant you!'

Rebecca turned away. Had *all* he told been lies?

CHAPTER ELEVEN

The offices of *The Treasurer and Company of Adventurers and Planters of the City of London for the First Colony of Virginia* were housed in Sir Thomas Smythe's house in Philpot Lane. Its shutters were open onto a walled garden where roses and gilly-flowers sweetened the June air.

Sir Thomas Smythe, Sir Ferdinando Gorges, Sir Thomas Dale, Captain Argall, and Master Rolfe smoked their fine Virginia tobacco and sipped appreciatively of their Spanish sack. The three Virginians glanced from time to time at the ordered disorder of an English garden and savored the remembered pleasure of an English lawn. Primroses and pansies made a patchwork along the flagstoned walk, while hollyhocks, peonies, foxgloves, and daisies massed in profusion.

'If we had listened to Captain Smith . . . ' Sir Thomas Smythe said, 'but all we cared about was the Westward Passage and a cargo of gold.'

'You mean what Smith advised – that they make the colony self-sufficient and work toward sending their own products to England?' Argall asked, remembering that evening when he had brought Smith word of the Great Supply.

'Which we *are* doing now,' Sir Thomas agreed, 'though' – he smiled at Rolfe – 'the emphasis is perhaps too great on your fine tobacco. It increases the revenues of the Company, but still Virginia is dependent on our ships for most of its provender. They are a hungry people, the Virginians, with the forests and the Bay teeming with food, and acres that should be planted to corn turned only to tobacco. We will be wiser when Smith founds his colony in New England.'

Rolfe was listening to this praise of his predecessor with indignation; he had heard little to Smith's credit; and he himself had received too many rebuffs in the last days, including these

223

remarks of Sir Thomas Smythe's, however urbanely spoken, to be generous.

'But Smith would have made himself King,' he protested, 'in Virginia. Why do you think that now . . . '

'You have been listening to old calumnies, and you have not known the man. If he would have, do you not think he could have? During the first year there were but thirty-eight Englishmen alive, and if Smith had not nurtured them they would have starved rather than work, as they did after he left. But now *that* time has passed, and tobacco has become the first asset of the Company, – in large part due to you, Master Rolfe. Which brings us to the present and to the little Princess, who is perhaps our greatest treasure. As Sir Thomas has pointed out' – he indicated Dale – 'her having been converted will weigh heavily with the Church, and be sure the Bishop of London, who is a member of our Council, will make the most of it. She can also do much for the Virginia tobacco trade to wean it from the Spaniards – as did your perfection of its flavor – for I have been assured that as she is seen and known she will make all things Virginian the fashion.'

'As my wife . . . ' Rolfe said.

'Ah, that is what we had hoped, that she would be tied to you and your import. We have, in fact, issued letters, broadsides, and pamphlets, and Captain Smith's latest tome is already released. However, these plans must alter with the King's whimsy. We had expected to present a pious Savage maid to Their Majesties. But he has chosen to consider her royalty, and who, having known her, could imagine *her* complaisant?'

They sat, remembering the scene in the captain's cabin before their landing. Who, indeed?

'But this idea of *lèse majesté* . . . ' Dale broke out.

Smythe smiled. 'Don't let that trouble you, Sir Thomas. I am sure there will be no accusation of treason. Much will depend on Lady Rebecca, of course. If she says she married Master Rolfe of her own free will and that Powhatan's consent was not coerced . . . '

'She should be convinced, Kinsman.' Argall was a distant cousin of Sir Thomas Smythe. 'There *was* some persuasion.'

'But who captured her?' Dale cried out. 'Who connived this use of her?'

'We all did, Sir Thomas.'

Smythe held out his hands. 'Gentlemen, do not lose your case by accusing one another. I have heard there was some trickery, if not treachery. In fact, I would not commend our own attitude here in London. But the Lady Rebecca seems to be amenable and friendly. Let us concentrate on showing her that we in England cherish her and country, since I greatly fear for her innocence when she meets the wickedness of the Court. I am more grateful than I can say, Sir Ferdinando, for the offices of your good lady. It was God-inspired you brought her with you.'

Gorges bowed gravely. 'Lady Rebecca is dear to her as her own daughter, Sir Thomas.'

There was a pause as a servant refilled the wineglasses and the pipes. Each inhaled deeply, and as they exhaled, curls of smoke spiraled between them.

'Tell me,' Smythe said to Argall, 'when I think of John Smith, I always wonder. . . . Was there any idea that she loved him?'

Sir Ferdinando's eyes scanned the three Virginians. For an instant they accepted the shock of the question. Then Argall carefully placed his glass on the table.

'No, Kinsman, other than as a child.'

Rolfe and Dale sat stolidly, not looking at each other. *This is my wife they speak of*, Rolfe thought bitterly. *Or is Smythe already taking it for granted that she is not?*

'He never indicated it to me,' Sir Ferdinando said softly.

'Nor to me. Yet I have seen his eyes when he spoke of her kindnesses, which seem in many cases to have been personal, rather than for love of Englishmen. And both he and Percy have told how she ran through the night at her own peril to give warning of her father's plan to surprise and kill Smith's band when they lay at his capital city. And in the beginning, when she first knew him, she saved his life, remember, at the risk of her own.'

Argall paused before speaking. If Percy had talked to Smythe about Pocahontas, had he not also told of those nights he had watched through Smith's window the lovemaking in the firelit room? But perhaps with belated apprehension he had not wanted to admit his spying. Argall smiled faintly.

'It's a romantic thought, Cousin, I could expect to hear it from Ben Jonson's tongue sooner than yours. But the lady saved other lives as well – Tom Savage's and Dick Wiffin's, to name but two.'

Smythe nodded. 'Many have reason to be grateful, though few seem so. Yet I recall in Smith's glossary of the Savages' language, where in the midst he wrote: "Let Pocahontas bring me her baskets and I will fill them with beads." It was a tender thought.'

'Written about a child. She was but thirteen years old.'

'You may be right. As you say, I am romantical, but I like to think of it. And I wonder if John Smith is not the one to present her case to Their Majesties.'

At once all three Virginians were vociferous. Smith was discredited in Virginia, with Powhatan as well as with the English. Why bring up the past when she was now in loving hands?

Smythe stood up. 'We will see how she fares. She has not always been treated gently by those whom she has helped so much.' Argall and Dale flushed, but did not speak. 'Yet surely you must know that they will meet. Whatever else, they were friends with much between them.'

Sir Ferdinando without embarrassment studied one troubled face and then another, and wished fleetingly that his tactless Lady were present to drop the truth like a smashed tureen.

'It should be an interesting encounter,' he said. 'In Plymouth she seemed much disturbed to learn he lived, since she had been told that he was dead.' Seeing the effect of his words, he thought that Lady Gorges would be proud of him.

'Had she so?' Sir Thomas Smythe looked at the flushed faces of the others. 'I am sorry that she should see our people as liars as well as conquerors.'

As they rose and filed out of the room, Argall lingered and half closed the door.

'I had no part in this.'

'I hope not, Sam.'

'You know I have other interests, that I have high hopes of going back as Deputy Governor.'

'I have thought about your prospects.'

'Will you support me then?'

'Sam, you have a habit of recklessness. Behave yourself.'

The ladies arrived back at the house in Philpot Lane to find that, under instructions from Sir Thomas Smythe, all their baggage had been transferred from the *Treasurer* to wherries, which waited above the Bridge to carry them to Brentford.

'If you have not everything,' Sir Thomas said to Lady Gorges, 'you could remain behind and rejoin Lady Rebecca tomorrow.'

'Oh, but we have! Everything!' and she dangled the empty purses toward the piles borne by tradesmen's assistants and their own servitors.

'It is almost biblical to look at her maids so dark, bearing these rich burdens,' Sir Thomas said, amused.

'From the first it was,' she said and told him of Tomakkin and how he had compared the Princess to the Queen of Sheba.

He stroked his beard, his eyes glowing with pleasure.

'By God, be sure she says that to His Majesty.'

Lady Gorges asked herself if she would – *she* was not anxious to further the interests of the Virginia Company. But Lady Gorges liked Sir Thomas, and she, too, wanted this winning Savage to be a success at Court.

'*I* am not presenting her,' she said pointedly.

'Would to God you were!' she exclaimed, and Lady Gorges assured him with her smile.

The three Virginians were desperate to have a private word with Rebecca. She stood like a reed, supple but straight in the crossed winds of their desires.

It was Argall, of course, who seized the first opportunity. As she went to her room, he followed her, and from habit, her maids dropped back.

'Rebecca!' he said, and then, 'Pocahontas!' She was stirred at the sound of her own name, and, turning to him, she saw his

227

beauty and the beauty of Nantequos, and she was strangely drawn. 'If they annul this marriage . . . '

'If he takes me from John Rolfe, would he give you to you?' she asked gently.

'The *Treasurer* waits! I would take you to Virginia, or *any* shores! Only love me!'

For the moment there was no passion, no ardor, only weakness and longing, and she thought: *How consuming is the love of these men! They waste themselves for a squaw till they seem men no longer.*

'Sam Argall,' she said, '*you* know . . . '

'When you see him now, Rebecca — will you look at him with new eyes, the eyes of six years later, and think of me?'

'Will I see him?' she asked weakly.

'If you don't will that not prove . . . '

She did not answer, but turned and went into her chamber.

She stood, cloaked, hatted, and visored, when Rolfe burst in. He was pale and more intense that she had ever seen him. He pushed back the door, closing it.

'You made your vows to me. You are my wife!'

She pulled the mask from her face to gaze at him with surprise. 'I have not unmade those vows. I am your wife.'

He sagged with relief. 'What devilish machinery is here, I don't know. I thought it was Argall. I know he wants you. Do you love him, Rebecca?' Silently she shook her head. The words he longed to utter were so apparent that she felt a sharp pang: Do you love *me*? But he could not bring himself to say them. He wiped his face. 'This talk of treason!'

And, knowing him, she could not help but wonder if his agitation came not solely from this danger. He was a brave who would act as a squaw bade him. And he cared much for the flesh that covered his handsome frame. She thought suddenly of his head with its golden curls impaled on the Bridge Gate.

'When you meet the King, will you tell him . . . ' He did not know what he should tell the King, so he stopped and gazed at her.

She considered. 'I will tell your King that I am Powhatan's daughter, and it is Powhatan who disposes of me.'

He made a movement toward her, but she had already raised her vizard. She thought: How often — how often! — has he moved, and I have drawn the curtain before me which he does not know how to tear aside.

Dale waited till she came to the foot of the stairs. Then he moved forward, blocking her.

'My child! You hold much bitterness toward me because of this Smith – because I did not tell you.' She looked him in the eyes, only slightly stirred at the name which had so long moved her with its heart-wringing sound. But in her palm the red stone burned, and she wondered: *How can it* not *be heart's blood?*

'If you would tell His Majesty how sweet it is to be a Christian – how ardently I exhorted you!'

Why, she wondered, *was she kind to Argall, who had stolen her, and unkind to this man, who had merely used her?*

'I will ask him,' she said, 'why Christians lie!'

She moved past him down the stairs to Sir Thomas Smythe, who took her hand ceremoniously and escorted her into the street.

The wherries waited, cushioned and luxurious. Sir Thomas kissed the back of his hand, then drew her to her to him and kissed her cheeks.

'My joy is great in knowing you. If you were *my* child I would not let you embark on this perilous journey.'

She gazed at him, surprised, since she had been told only that she was to travel up a river.

'My dear,' he said with sudden impulse, 'if you need a friend – send to me, or come to me!'

Rebecca drew the mantle of her dignity about her.

'I am honored to have such a friend, and I have no fear.'

She and Tomakkin rode with Sir Ferdinando and Lady Gorges in the wherry ahead, followed by a boat bearing her maids and Manda with Tommy. The Virginians traveled in the last wherry. It was a strange sensation to her to be away from them, for each had hardly allowed her from his sight, jealously guarding lest another steal her favor.

She found herself wonderfully relaxed with Sir Ferdinando and Lady Gorges. Even the Wironausqua's chattering seemed welcome as Rebecca sank back on the cushions and watched a pale new moon sink toward a western land. Gracefully the King's swans floated to their resting places, their cygnets paddling to keep close. It was the slow and melancholy hour of twilight, and all sounds and sights came to her blurred, but at the same time amazingily clear, so that though she hardly heard or saw, she would remember always . . . the cries of 'Eastward Ho!' 'Westward Ho!' from the watermen . . . Lady Gorges pointing out palaces of the great on the Strand. ...

'It's Denmark House! The Queen's residence. And here's Durham House which Sir Walter Raleigh forfeited with his disgrace.'

Even as Rebecca turned to stare, it grayed into the whole, for they traveled swiftly with the tide.

'He is not imprisoned now?' she asked.

'No, he has been released on his foolish promise to find a gold mine in Guiana. If he does not, he says he'll come back and be beheaded, which is the sentence he has remained under for thirteen years. All England hopes he'll find the gold or not come back,' Lady Gorges added with a deep sigh.

'You are cruelest to those who serve you best,' Rebecca said, thinking of Johnsmith.

'No! No, my dear!'

'Yes, yes, my dear!' Sir Ferdinando said.

'Well, anyway . . . There's Whitehall, that's the King's residence. They've lived apart for years. And over here's Westminster.'

The sky had darkened, and the sounds passed away until they no longer assailed her ears. Even Lady Gorges' voice faded from her consciousness as she saw the forests – at last the forests! – and heard the soft ripple of the oars in the water.

With eyes wide open she lay and let *his* words sweep her. So grievously hurt, so close to death, and she, with nothing but her will to hold him there. He had not let her tend him or look – only Nantequos – but she had looked!

The wherries stopped first at the tavern to allow the Virginians to disembark with their trunks and budgets. They came to her to say good-by.

'I will wait on you,' Argall said, with double meaning.

'I will see you tomorrow, love!' Rolfe shoved him out of the way.

'My child, remember . . .'

The wherry moved upstream before Dale could tell her what to remember. Lady Gorges giggled.

'What now?' Sir Ferdinando asked.

'Jamie has become a magician.'

'What foolish fancy have you, Margaret?'

She pointed back to the hanging sign on which three birds were painted.

'It was three falcons we brought here. And see, already they have been transformed into three pigeons.'

In spite of himself, Sir Ferdinando laughed.

CHAPTER THIRTEEN

The new moon had slipped into the dark blue emptiness when they reached the water gate of the Bishop's palace, and night birds opened up their throats. One, whose song was inexpressibly poignant, she searched for in the tall trees; but shadows cloaked them both, her and the bird.

John King, Bishop of London, received them. He was a happy man, he head as round and polished as Johnsmith's magic jewel. 'Delighted! Delighted! Delighted!' he said and looked it. Indeed, he looked as if he had come from birth and would pass to death, delighted. 'And to think we have to persuade these English laggards to journey to your land. When they see *you* . . .'

'Has there been any word from His Majesty as to the presentation?' Lady Gorges interrupted.

'I forwarded Sir Thomas Smythe's request that several days be allowed for Lady Rebecca to rest and to prepare herself. I have not heard, but I am sure it will be complied with.'

'It is all important! She has little but what you see her in. I have brought the wherewithal from London, but clothes must be made here. If the tailors labor night and day . . .'

'Yes-yes! Yes-yes!' the Bishop said, far more interested in Rebecca herself.

'What of my Lady de la Warr?'

'My Lord and Lady lodge at Hampton Court. My Lady leaves all in your good hands. She will call on Lady Rebecca before the presentation.'

'Humph!' Lady Gorges said. But she found herself content.

At her chamber door Rebecca took Tommy from Manda and went in. She looked around in pleasure at the empty room, then sat on the floor and placed Tommy before her. He chortled at the unaccustomed intimacy.

'They seek to change me, these English. Is it because *they*

231

would be what they are not?' she asked the baby, poking at him with her finger. 'When I am with you, then I am real.'

She swooped him up suddenly and carried him to the window. Outside, the forest stretched, the trees limned against the not yet black sky.

'I will throw off these clothes. I will fling you across my back, and we will run nightlong until we are among our own people.' She looked at Tommy with bright eyes, and he laughed back as though he were more than willing.

She held him to the window, and they looked out. It seemed it must be true that they could do this. Where walls ceased, England too must end.

The two days following were feverish. Rolfe, Argall, Dale, all came, but Lady Gorges would admit none of them. Rebecca was in an agony as the seamsters and tailors fitted and pinned, turning her this way and that; and Lady Gorges drove them all to frenzy with her orders and her ever changing mind. What time Rebecca was free from these ministrations, Lady Gorges taught her etiquette.

At last Lord and Lady de la Warr were announced, and they were too important for Lady Gorges to refuse. Hastily she had Rebecca readied so she could meet them with some semblance of decency.

Rebecca knew at once how mighty were these two compared to any she had met. Both seemed of a great height from the way they held their heads and the angles of their noses. Lady de la Warr was blonde and very beautiful, but cold. Her Lord was proud as Opechancano, though he possessed immense charm and condescension. His beard fringed his long face, which added to his aloofness. Rebecca received them with dignity. Lady de la Warr and Lady Gorges kissed, but Rebecca sensed that the caress was perfunctory on both sides.

'Tomorrow, His Majesty has said he will see her. Is she ready?'
'She will be.'
'May I see her gown?'

The two ladies went out, and Lord de la Warr seemed immediately less stiff. He sat on a table edge dangling his amazing boot of soft leather laid in folds and pleats like cloth. He eyed her with the appraising eyes of a Werowance who scans a group of maids to choose a wife.

'Captain Argall's told me about you,' he said with an air of withheld approval.

Argall had spoken much to her of his influence with this Lord who was his patron, though they were surely near of an age.

'I have been myself in Virginia,' he went on in a lazy voice. 'But I did not encounter the Emperor, your father, or Your Highness either.' His mouth quirked, and she thought he was amused to give her such a rank in England.

'No,' she said gravely, remembering what those who came with this noble had found in the door of Johnsmith's house. 'Powhatan lives forever up the rivers now.'

'But you love the English and have become a Christian?'

'I love the words of your God,' she said.

They heard the two ladies returning, and instantly he was on his feet looking as stiff and distant as ever. *Is this another brave who fears a squaw?* Rebecca wondered.

Both women were more animated since they had been speaking of clothes.

'Tomorrow then, at one o'clock. I'll bring my rubies for Your Highness to wear.'

'I do not wish to wear rubies,' Rebecca said.

Lady de la Warr looked at her as though she had not realized the Savage Princess had a mind to will or not.

'Perhaps she will wear your pearls,' Lord de la Warr said, watching Rebecca.

'Yes, I will wear pearls.'

'I do wish you'd let me see the curtsy you've been taught, Lady Rebecca.'

'Before your King I will curtsy.'

CHAPTER FOURTEEN

From early in the morning she was in the hands of the dressers. Her hair they worked longest over, coiling it now high, now low, in small braids which snaked over her forehead and about her ears, in poufs and other monstrosities; but finally they gave up and bound it in a simple chignon with a golden net. Her gown was of tawny rose and gold taffeta, changing from the one to the other as she moved, catching the rose of her skin and the gold in her eyes.

'A pity we can't pluck her brows and raise her hairline,' one said, and Rebecca looked from the maid to the mirror, not knowing who might have forbidden it. At home the Wironausqua of Appromattox had shaved her hair now from this side, now from that, achieving always new effects.

'My Lady finds her naturalness alluring and thinks the King will also.' At this remark all giggled, and again she was left to wonder.

They used a dust to take the shine from her face. They rubbed ruby salve on her lips, and she took the box and dipped her finger, bringing her mouth to shape and a bright color. In Powhatan's wigwam, she would have been painted red all over and not hidden her body in this mass of stiff material. They gave her to drink a pinkish liquid which made her tongue as red as her lips and perfumed her breath.

Lady Gorges entered. 'Let me see, my love.' Rebecca rose and stood before her. '*Una rara avis!* as His Majesty will undoubtedly say, for he loves the Latin. Kohl her eyes to accentuate the slant.'

When this was done, she pushed Rebecca in front of a mirror.

'Now, look! An't you exquisite?'

Her neck was encompassed by a ruff of stiff white lawn in two scalloped layers. Below it her sleeves, large at the shoulders, bulged, and a deep circle exposed her breasts. She thought, I
234

appear very strange and grand, for in Powhatan's nations it was the same.

'My Lady de la Warr will put her pearls on you at the palace,' Lady Gorges said.

Below they met Tomakkin, who looked outrageous in a suit of jade green with one blue and one yellow stocking. Rebecca gasped, suddenly aware of incongruity, wondering if this were all a terrible humiliation – if she, too, looked ridiculous.

'He cannot go like that!'

'Why ever not? He is the heart of fashion.'

'No!'

'It's far too late.'

But she would not move. They searched the house for other clothes which would fit and at last came to her with a suit of black velvet. Rebecca nodded.

'But he's such a pretty thing. And these are winter wear,' Lady Gorges protested.

Rebecca did not reply but stood till they had taken Tomakkin out and changed him.

'And I?' she asked in Powhatan's language when he returned. 'Have they made me look like a silly parrot?'

He stared at her. 'You are like the warm light the sun casts on the wave by which the hunter knows that the fire is kindled and his welcome awaits him.'

She smiled at him with great sweetness and turned to follow Lady Gorges, no longer fearful.

They rode up the river in the painted barge of Lady de la Warr. It was lined with blue velvet, and the cushions were silk and ermine. They passed through the park that belonged to George Percy's brother, saw the Castle of Richmond where lodged the Prince of Wales, Baby Charlie as Lady Gorges called him, and on along the winding river through forest lands that were richly gratifying to eyes which had scanned endless stretches of water and scaled towering piles of stone.

But Hampton Court – the King's wigwam! She and Tomakkin blinked back their marvel at the long stretch of rosy brick rising from the greensward. They progressed on foot through the wildwood to the wonder of the gardens laid out in exquisite proportion, terraces banked with flowers seeded so that their colors formed a pattern, held in check by hedges cut in realistic designs. Why had these English found it so difficulat to plant in Virginia when here they could mold growing things to their wills?

Each man they met, rigid in red and gold, or blue and silver, or green and gray, Tomakkin regarded with awe and asked: 'Is that King James?' But Rebecca explained that the King was mightier than all these English; he sat on a throne as Powhatan, and many braves attended him.

They crossed a bridge carved with the animals of the white men, and passed through a gate into a hall decorated all in green, with vast and intriguing paintings on the walls. Tomakkin was agape at the magnificence, and Rebecca's eyes, too, were wide as she looked from the jeweled tables to the wonderful chandeliers.

There was life around them, but they moved like figures in a dream, for none paid them any notice. Ladies with protruding breasts, the rouged nipples stark against their whiteness, screamed at one another. And almost outshining them, the curled and whiskered lords strutted in all the colors of the rainbow and in fabrics even Lady Gorges dared not afford, though she had paid from the Company's treasury.

At the entrance of the Great Hall, Lady de la Warr met them. She was dressed in pale silvered blue, slashed with cloth of silver, her skirt stretching over a wide farthingale. Rubies glittered in astonishing profusion in her hair and on her gown. But one could notice nothing except her head, which sat atop her flat ruff as though it had been severed and was here offered on a platter – and her large breasts, which looked like unborn twins bulging from her bodice.

'Here,' she said, taking a casket from her page, 'are my pearls. What a pity you don't like the rubies. They would complement your skin.' Rebecca felt to make sure the stone of Johnsmith's ring was turned from sight.

They wrapped pearls around her neck. 'This pendant we'll hide in here. It will show only when you sigh. But you *will* remember to sigh?' Lady de la Warr's voice was rushed, excited. They fitted pearls to her ears and in her hair and on her fingers, the nails of which the maids had buffed with a rosy salve.

Her Ladyship stood off to appraise her. 'For those that like exotic fruits – and plenty do! Come, Your Highness!' She, as her Lord, seemed not to relish using the title. She drew up short before the closed doors. '*Do* you remember everything? Let us *try* the curtsy!'

'There is no need,' Rebecca said with dignity.

Lady Gorges kissed her. 'I will await you in the Queen's Chamber. Now, don't forget what to say to His Majesty.'

She started out as Lord de la Warr entered. He stopped, taking Rebecca in with eyes which paused overlong at her breasts, making her feel for the first time exposed; but surely hers, which were so nearly the color of her gown, were not startling as those of the pale-fleshed squaws.

'He is coming,' he told his wife.

She drew a deep breath. 'Jesu help us! She is very stubborn,' she said as though Rebecca knew no English.

He smiled. 'Your Highness is lovely. If I were Jamie . . .'

'Thank God, you're not!' His Lady said fervently, and then with tight nervousness, 'Let's end this!'

De la Warr nodded to the footman and the door was opened. They passed out into the Great Hall. Here the excitement was more clamorous than it had been in the Green Court, the press greater. Magnificently jeweled and dressed nobles vied with each other and fought for places like unruly squaws when their lord is absent. Ushers shook their white staffs furiously to keep order and sometimes even rapped a noble lord or lady. At sight of de la Warr they crowded lesser knights aside to make a path for eminence.

At the far end of the hall rows of splendid guards stood immobile on either side of high double doors on which the eyes of all were fixed, as though some talisman were contained in their carved panels. Rebecca was caught in the contagion of expectancy. She was at last to see this Majesty whose barest word ruled this vast and haughty people, whose wisdom was like that King in the Bible. She thought again of the words Lady Gorges had urged her to say. A glance at Tomakkin showed her that he was absorbed in fascinated waiting.

De la Warr placed his party to the right of the doors and then turned to Rebecca with a smile of assurance.

'When my Lady curtsies you must curtsy.'

The doors were suddenly flung wide. The crowd in the hall stiffened and fell into a hushed silence. Only in the room which had been opened was there noisy and boisterous sound.

An old man with a gray-yellow straggle of beard came out, leaning on a youth of startling beauty. Some joke passed between them, for the one who inclined laughed and reached up to pinch the young man's cheek. Rebecca noted that Lady de la Warr had swept into a deep curtsy, and she did the same.

'La Warr!' a thick voice said. Rebecca looked up to see the old one.

'Your Majesty!'

'And your Lady!' He raised and kissed her, fingering her bodice. 'We love you, Cecily. You're a' marble, the way women should be.'

The laughter started like a small, uncertain breeze, but it reached a gust when it came to the end of the hall. Lady de la Warr's breasts as well as her face were no longer white but red as Rebecca's own.

'Your Majesty!' she said, flustered – and who would have believed that *she* could have been flustered? 'It is my honor to present to you – my Lady Rebecca.'

The King had paused, not listening, to accept a thimbleful of wine from a gentleman who followed him, prepared. He drank it, his overlarge tongue dribbling as he lapped like a dog. Rebecca gazed at him. He lolled against the shoulder of the youth. His protuberant stomach was accentuated by padded clothes which emphasized, too, his weak, thin legs.

'Who?' he asked. And then as his eyes found Rebecca, he bent forward and raised her.

'A gem from Virginia, Dad,' the gorgeous young man whispered.

The King studied her. His hand reached to his codpiece, and he scratched himself pleasurably, his head thrust forward. He was like one she had known whose mind the Evil Ones had stolen from birth and whom all had pitied. Not *this*, she thought, was Johnsmith's father! The King over all the air, the waters, and the land!

'You're the Emperor's daughter.' He mumbled the words, and it was hard to say whether he spoke thus because of his drink or his thick tongue. He turned to peer up into the face of his handsome prop. 'Wha' think you, Steenie?'

But there was no need to ask. Quite apparently he was one who liked exotic fruits.

'A princess true, sweet Dad. And so you must welcome her.'

The King drew her toward him. 'In England you will be a Highness as in your father's land.' He leaned to her and planted his wet mouth on hers. She felt suddenly weak and feared she would drop to the ground.

'Speak to His Majesty!' She heard Lady de la Warr's urgent whisper, but she could utter no sound.

De la Warr sought to ease the situation. 'And this is Her Highness's brother-in-law, Prince Tomakkin, Your Majesty!'

Tomakkin had not lost *his* voice. 'This is no King! What trickery is this?'

All turned at the stunning sound. Tomakkin stood his ground, indignation consuming him. It was a second before Pocahontas realized with relief that he had spoken in Powhatan's language.

'It is the King!'

'King? It is no man! Look at him!'

She turned. James was peering from under his straggling locks, trying to understand why this Savage balked at meeting him. They stared as though each were viewing a freak impossible to believe.

'He is too much in awe of Your Majesty,' de la Warr said diplomatically.

James laughed, hugging Steenie. 'Nae doot our magnificence bemazes him. It's said his Emperor refused to kneel to receive the crown we sent. Let him be at his ease.'

He drew Rebecca into his embrace so that she shared his weight. 'Come, my chiel, we will present you to our Nanny.' He started down the hall, ignoring those who waited hopefully, their eyes lowered. 'We must have a nickname for her, Dog Steenie.'

'Your Sowship shall not fail to find the perfect one,' Villiers said easily.

CHAPTER FIFTEEN

The Queen's Presence Chamber was hung with rich brocades, as gracefully draped as the Queen's ladies, who sank low to receive His Majesty. The doors were open to an adjoining court where dancers had halted their sport, awaiting the King's word to resume it. In high humor, he bade them to continue.

'We've ta'en a fancy to your toy. Nanny love,' he said, kissing the Queen.

She was enormous, both from her own girth and the immensity of her skirts. Her breasts were two great melons, white as cloud. From head to toe she was bediamonded, her yellow hair caught high and ornamented with jeweled stars and butterflies. As she moved, which she did constantly, these dazzled.

The King pulled Rebecca forward. 'Here's your Princess. Only she's to be our playmate, too. It's the Lady Rebecca till Steenie and I think of a better name for her.'

Rebecca did not curtsy, but the Queen overlooked the omission. She drew her forward and kissed her on the cheeks.

'Steenie calls her a gem from Virginia,' James said, looking at Rebecca as though he sought to find what it was so attracted his favorite.

'So she is!' Anne exclaimed. 'And we will have a masque. And *end* this tedium! How comely you are, sweet child!'

Suddenly Rebecca breathed again, for here was warmth and decency at last, a Wironausqua silly for her foibles, but kind and welcoming. She regarded the King, and all the badness that was in his face her mind blanked out; his eyes were lonely and brilliantly seeking.

'I greet Your Majesties from Powhatan,' she said, the first words in English she had uttered since she left the antechamber. She could not say the rest, not bring King James the love that Powhatan had bade her pledge.

'Did she make her speech to His Majesty?' Lady Gorges whispered to Lady de la Warr.

'She said *nothing*! But stood like a ninny when His Majesty kissed her.'

'Poor child!' Lady Gorges moved forward to dip low before Their Majesties.

The Queen was taking a ring with a large stone from her own finger. This she gave Rebecca, who turned imperiously to Lady de la Warr. That great lady hurried to summon the pages who bore Powhatan's gifts to the wise King James and his favorite wife.

The King recognized Lady Gorges. 'Speak, Madam.'

'It's a pretty story may amuse Your Majesty. When she came to us in Plymouth, Her Highness saw some tapestries which show the visit of the Queen of Sheba to Solomon, and she asked the meaning. And when I told her, she said: "It is *I*! I am that dark Queen who crossed the seas to honor a mighty king of great wisdom."'

Rebecca wondered why this good woman lied, then turned, amazed at the King's reaction.

'By God's wounds, she dinna come to beg my gold but drink my wisdom! Do you hear that, Steenie? It's an Hypatia!'

'Let her rather be what she says she is, Sheba!'

'And there's our nickname!' James clapped Villiers' shoulder.

'We'll put it in the masque,' Queen Anne cried. 'Sheba come to drink the milk of Solomon. I love symbology!'

'Be careful how ye twist it then,' James said.

The Queen's Steward ushered in the pages, who knelt before the King and Queen, proffering satin cushions on which, wrapped in silks, were Powhatan's gifts. At the King's bidding the Steward opened out two puttawuses, mantles of intricately wrought turkey feathers, soft and supple, one crimson and one green. The Queen exclaimed in joy, and the King, too, was pleased, fingering the fine texture.

Since there was none to make her oration, Rebecca stood very straight.

'I thank Your Majesty for this rare jewel which you have given me, and which I will treasure. And I bring you here the gifts of Powhatan, who rules all the nations of the land you call Virginia, whose Werowances are more terrible and fierce than the northern cat, whose people are more numerous than the fishes that swim the rivers' – she spurned with her eyes and lips the insignificant numbers of the English – 'who is mightier and more awesome in himself than all his armies and all his Werowances. These gifts Powhatan sends to you with his love, and he vows he will

16

241

remain always the ally of King James and the English.' Her voice was clear and unfaltering, but her heart quailed within her as she delivered these empty words and this great promise. How deluded was Powhatan! And she – in her willfulness and blindness – had helped to delude him. She was glad Tomakkin had not followed her to the Queen's Presence Chamber.

King James pulled at his chin, his head cocked. He answered her at length in a language she understood not at all. Everyone maintained respectful silence, but she sensed their impatience, as did he, for his eyes sought for a face that showed discontent. When he was done, James smiled at Rebecca and cupped her chin in his hand. For a terrible moment she thought he was going to kiss her again.

'Understood ye what we said, Sheba?'

'No, Your Majesty!'

'You must ha' Steenie interpret it for you later, for he's progressing with his Latin so he can converse with his dear Dad and gossip in that noble tongue. Ben't ye, my pretty Dog?'

'Aye, Dad!'

'But since it is marvel enough you ha' learnt English, we answered your fine words and assured you and Powhatan of our love. We will send back our gifts to Powhatan, but you we will requite while you are with us.'

Leaning heavily on Villiers, King James turned to enter the court and watch the dancers.

The Queen, too, rose. She extended her hand to Rebecca.

'You are a great success, Sheba, and we will make much gaiety while you are with us. It is not often Jamie admires a lass.'

After the Queen left the room the ladies who remained clustered about Rebecca. Even Lady de la Warr unbent to praise this one who had charmed both King and Queen. But Rebecca had never cared for the chattering of squaws. She sought Lady Gorges and, taking her hand, walked rapidly away from them.

Lady Gorges, immensely pleased at this selection, let the words gush from her mouth. Rebecca silenced her.

'Where is Tomakkin?'

'Somewhere – with the gentlemen – perhaps, with my Lord de la Warr.'

'I would find him.'

'We will try the ballroom first.'

The dancers moved in stately grace to music which Rebecca knew from Jamestown could be played to a faster, gayer beat. Men and women, they came together, drew apart, rejoined and

242

circled, then passed and marched, meeting at last for a fleeting kiss.

She found herself watching them with enjoyment. There was an insouciance and lightheartedness in their play which was lacking in their graver moments; and when they danced they were less frenzied than her own people. To her surprise she saw Tomakkin in their midst, breaking in the middle as he bent forward, his neck outstretched to receive a lady's kiss. He looked thoroughly at home. Rebecca smiled and leaned against the wall to watch.

A youth came and stood over her. 'I'm Charlie, Prince of Wales,' he said. 'Will you dance? I mean, *do* you? I mean, do you dance our dances?'

His hair was dark and curled about his shoulders. He had a heartshaped face with eyes deep and ardent, a thin, straight mouth softened by the light down which fringed the upper lip. She smiled at him.

'I've learned the *Antic Hay* and *Tom Bedlo.*'

'The lively ones!' He gave an order to a steward who went toward the musicians. The very handsome man the King had called Steenie came and leaned on Prince Charlie's shoulder.

'In this Court I play a second fiddle,' he said lightly, 'but my strings will strum a sweeter tune when Royalty has served its turn.'

She did not know what his words meant, but these two were like the eager braves at home, importunate, their ardor amusingly titillating. She threw back her head and laughed.

They had not expected that – they must have though she could not laugh. All around her, even the King and Queen, paused to stare, their glances probing this new manifestation of humanness. At Powhatan's feasts she would not have dared to laugh, she thought but neither would his braves have come a-seeking.

The music started again to a fast beat. 'It's my pleasure,' Prince Charlie said, taking her hand. She felt all eyes on her. He strove to be masterful, and she thought of Nantequos at his age, and with the thought she was consumed.

He led her to her place among the dancers, who formed in patterns. He faced her, and the dance began. Prince Charlie talked whenever they were together.

'I've a petitioner who's spent many years in Virginia. He's discovered New England, too, His name is Smith.'

They moved apart, joined other partners, twirled and met again.

'Did you never hear of him?' She tried, but could not answer.

'Perhaps, he does not speak the truth about Virginia.'

She turned and was passed from brave to brave, then once more found him opposite her.

'I'd like to come to your land and hunt naked in the woods – I mean, I'd like to see Virginia and meet your father, the Emperor, who sounds wonderful.'

They glided past each other, circled, and rejoined.

'I'll teach you golfing and to ride.'

They marched away, came together, joining hands. They kissed, the sweet kiss of youth.

'Where is Johnsmith?' she asked, frightening herself by the suddenness of her tone.

'Zounds! I don't know.' The Prince would have repeated the kiss. 'He said it was all joy to frolic with the Savage maids.'

'Did he?' she asked dismally, and wanted to know no further.

CHAPTER SIXTEEN

He dreaded the meeting with the same intensity that he longed for it. How had she changed? But more – how would she find him changed? Those nineteen months that he had known her seemed like the bright jewel in the long, tarnished chain of his remembrance. And for that time he had been a different Smith, a better Smith, whatever they had said in England. He had tried, and tried again, to be that same, whose purpose was unfaltering. He had striven to return to the new land, and finally had, exploring New England; and now once more his ships waited, for at last his Admiralty had a fleet, three vessels, tiny though they were, and he hoped to colonize that sweet shore whose bluffs overlooked Cape Cod, and there to find again – 'Johnsmith' – he heard her say it. But first he had to see her.

With the open road the horses broke into a gallop. He was deeply grateful for his companion, England's last hero, the proudest man in the realm, who, too, would soon set sail to seek once more *himself.*

'God's love, but it is glorious!' Sir Walter Raleigh threw back his head to partake to the full the freshening breeze.

What they have done to him! Smith thought. *The noblest bird was ever caged!*

Sir Walt, who loved Virginia and all that was Virginian, would stop to meet the Savage Princess before he went on to Hampton Court to face his King regarding his voyage to Guiana.

With him beside me, I dare to meet her, Smith thought.

The hall of the Bishop of London was hardly less crowded than the King's. All ranks of courtiers attended the Lady Rebecca. Even the Prince had ridden over from Richmond and had emptied the drawing room while he talked to her. Her husband – if he was to be allowed to remain her husband – had scurried out with the rest. And idle talk had it, as idle talk will always

245

have it, that the King had recognized her as a Royal Princess in order to marry her to his son, which marriage would scotch for once and all the Papist and the Protestant parties both, who each maneuvered for an alliance with princess of their faith.

When the Prince had gone, the courtiers flocked back, even more anxious to pay homage to the beauty and the wit of this royal Savage. The Bishop canted with happiness at the popularity of his house and sought to appease all those whose countenances were cast down when greater lords claimed her favor. Her husband, Master Rolfe, was, perhaps, the most difficult of these, since he feared to lose not only his wife but his head.

'Nonsense,' the Bishop said. 'The King will not go to extremes,' and then giggled when he thought how extreme an extreme a head is. He started to tell this merry jest to Master Rolfe, but stopped, realizing the worried young man might not appreciate it.

Sir Thomas Dale had been only slightly less anxious, though he was much cheered since his interview with the Queen. He had been the tutor to her older son, the first Prince of Wales, now dead, alas! Her Majesty had received Dale graciously and assured him there was no question of his complicity in the crime, if crime it was to be considered.

Master Argall was the one the Bishop wondered at. He had not head nor wife to lose, yet he was in a ferment at the attentions to my Lady. *Had she horned her husband with this young rake?* the Bishop wondered. He would not have blamed her, for Rolfe was a dull sort beyond a doubt. If she had ever granted Argall her favors she was quit of him now, for she treated him coolly, and when he was by, her charms were greatest for those others who surrounded her.

An exciting, exciting time! The Bishop smiled to himself. *Everybody* in a tizzy!

His joy was made complete when Sir Walter Raleigh was announced. He went quickly to greet him.

'My *dearest* friend!' They embraced. 'And Captain Johnnie!' He pumped Smith's hand. 'What an auspicious coming!'

'We have come to view your Princess,' Sir Walter said.

Alas, he's aged! The Bishop thought. *Thirteen years! Why, I was old as he is now*, he realized with amazement.

'Of course, you have I know you'd not come so far for a dreary prelate.'

'Oh, but we would!' they both said quickly, for they loved the Bishop.

'You will lodge with me?' Bishop King mentally calculated the number of rooms now occupied.

'I go to the Palace,' Sir Walter said, 'but Johnnie . . . '

'I will lodge at the inn,' Smith said. 'I see that you entertain many guests.'

The Bishop clapped his hands joyfully. 'I will announce you. Your coming will be the dessert, after all the rest.'

They followed him to the drawing room, which was noisy and crowded. The Bishop went to Lady Rebecca and exchanged some words. Her face broke into a happy smile and she cried out in surprise,

'Sir Walter Raleigh!'

She looked toward them. For an instant her face was frozen in its gladness, then it crumpled and she raised her hands to hide it, though she did not cover her eyes, which still stared.

Smith felt choked, and unaccountably his arms ached. Even in her gown of fern-green damask and her herons' feathers reaching toward the ceiling, *she* had not changed.

She gathered her skirts and brushed past them all, out of the room.

'What?' the Bishop asked, looking from where she had gone to the two who had entered.

'Is my visage grown so terrible?' Sir Walter demanded, but even as he spoke he looked over his shoulder, following the Bishop's eyes. Smith stood white as a man newly bled.

'It is I,' he said. 'I will leave.' He turned.

'Johnsmith!'

The cry was paralyzing, like the war whoop of a hundred braves. Tomakkin shoved his way through the mass to confront Smith with widespread arms, to embrace him, pound his back, then pull himself away to rock Smith's hand up and down in the English sign of friendship.

'I have found you! I have found you! Powhatan bade me seek for word of you, but none could tell me. Or would! Liars that these English are!'

He talked in Powhatan, and Smith found himself laughing, with tears running down his cheeks. *Sweet heaven! What will they think of me?* he wondered, but he could not stop.

'Come, Johnsmith. Let us go into the forest. Let us be alone to talk.'

'She does not want me here, Tomakkin,' Smith said in Powhatan. 'It is best I go away.'

'Does not want you?' Tomakkin demanded incredulously. 'She has thought of nothing elese for six cohonks. Come!' He tugged at Smith's arm.

'Sir Walt!' Smith was laughing and shaking his head, because it all seemed too mad, the laughter and the tears, the realities so suddenly called up by the once familiar language. 'This is Tomakkin, husband of the Princess's sister. And he would talk to me alone.'

'Go!' Sir Walter said. 'For heaven's sake, go! I am more moved by your love than by my own undoing.'

Smith did not even flush. It was no secret now – from any man, nor from his own heart.

Without more ado, he took Tomakkin's arm and went toward the gardens and the park.

Tomakkin talked with urgency. 'Powhatan bade me seek you out – if you still lived – and you shall show me your God and King and Queen and Prince which you have told us of.'

'Our God, Tomakkin, you cannot see, for we make no images. But he is here and all around us. I feel him closely in your love.' Tomakkin waited, searching his face. 'I had heard that you have seen the King.'

'They tricked me, Johnsmith. It was not your King. It was . . . ' He stopped in disgust.

Smith colored. 'It was the King,' he said in an even voice. Tomakkin peered into his face unbelievingly. 'It is not the man, but the office which is royal,' Smith finished with difficulty.

Tomakkin pondered this. 'You gave Powhatan a white dog which Powhatan fed as himself. But your King gave me nothing, and I am better than your white dog.'

Smith could not reply. They had reached the forest. It was a wildwood of elms and oaks and birch trees, ferns and moss. If one looked deep, not back, it was the forest of Virginia. Only Tomakkin's velvet breeches, doublet, and starched ruff made the incongruity an absolute.

Tomakkin said: 'If we wander here, on the edge, she can see us and will send for you.'

'Does she hate me so much, because I did not go back?'

'She believed you dead!'

'Why would she think me dead? I sent her word – by many ships! Word, too, for Nantequos and Powhatan!'

'After he carried you to England, Argall returned – with your great Governor, Lord Delawarr. Argall sailed up the river to Machot. He told us you were dead, had died at sea of your wound. He sought her for himself, as his Wironausqua. He would have forsaken the English and joined with Powhatan to have her. But she did not want him, nor trust him. For her safety, Powhatan married her to the Werowance of Potomac, who took

her far up that great river. It was after the slaying of Nantequos . . . '

'NANTEQUOS!'

'Aye!' Tomakkin said sadly. 'He was found at the door of your
wigwam in Jamestown – shot with a musket, but he was scalped,
too.'

Smith turned into the trunk of a tree. Tomakkin did not
attempt to solace him, while through his blinding sorrow Smith
saw the scene: Nantequos coming to his friend's deserted house
– to be set upon – to be shot down . . .

'Oh, God! Who did it? Not – *Not* – the English!'

'It is not known. But Powhatan does not believe it was the
English, who do not scalp.'

'But who?'

The law of silence which had lasted six years still bound
Tomakkin. 'We do not know!'

'Oh!' Smith groaned. 'For her – for Powhatan – what grief!
Tomakkin, my friend, they told me nothing of this!'

Tomakkin shook his head with great sadness. There was in him
such wisdom and understanding; this joking, merry man had
never seemed all this.

'For Powhatan,' Tomakkin said, 'it was the end! For her, she
was convinced you died before Argall told her. I do not think she
knows which was the greater grief.'

'I love her, Tomakkin!'

'And she loves you!'

They walked silently, unable to speak, on the fringes of the
green forest.

A Savage maid came to them, curtsying in the quick dip she had
been taught.

'Pocahontas asks her Lord to come if he is willing. She is in
her chamber.'

Smith quickened to the Powhatan words and their significance:
asks, when he had come to beg; and *Lord*, when Rolfe was her
husband.

He turned to Tomakkin, embraced him, started to speak, could
not. He followed Lady Rebecca's maiden.

CHAPTER SEVENTEEN

She stood at the leaded window, her back to him. He heard the door close quietly behind him, and since she did not turn he was overcome with shyness. She looked so regal, and he knew that here, as there, she was a Princess, too grand for Rolfe, how much too grand for him! He had not – anything! His hopes lay once more in a virgin land. Poor Johnnie Smith building colonies, for he *had* built Jamestown – it had almost perished after he left, but still had not – and now it was His Majesty's Fifth Kingdom.

She seemed a great lady in her gown and coronet with a feather in it, and she did not even notice him. He sighed, and the sound made himself start.

'Your Highness!'

She turned, and her eyes searched his, probed so deep it seemed they must read his soul – if they only could! He went to her and caught her hand, started to drop to his knee. She brought him up to her with unbelievable strength, then suddenly went into his arms, her head against his coat.

'Father! Lord!' she said, and he was swept back to that night when she had come all trembling to his arms.

'Not here, my Princess!'

She looked up at him to see how he had used the pronoun.

'Not here? There, and not here? You promised Powhatan what was yours should be his, and he the same to you. You called *him* Father, being in his land a stranger, and by the same reason so must I do you.'

'King James himself has called you Princess,' he said awkwardly.

She grimaced when he mentioned the King's name, but when she spoke her voice was animated by her strength.

'You were not afraid to come into my father's country and cause fear in him and all his people – but me! And fear you here I should call you Father? I tell you that I will, and you shall call me child, and so I will be forever and ever your countryman.'

His arms tightened. He bent to kiss her hair, but she lifted up her face so that he met her lips. *Home!* he thought. And longed to carry her to a bosky glade and lie so still – so lovingly – beside her, feeling the release her arms betokened.

She started to tremble, then pulled away from him. She looked once more toward the window as she spoke, though she saw nothing.

'They told us always you were dead, and I knew no other till I came to Plymouth. . . . ' Her voice was clogged with bitterness. 'Yet Powhatan commanded Tomakkin to seek you and know the truth, because your countrymen will lie much.'

He drew her to the window seat and made her sit beside him, caressing her hand. He turned his ring upon her finger.

'You wear my heart's blood.'

'It is not heart's blood,' she said in a voice like a little girl's. 'It is only a ruby.'

He laid his face against her head and rocked her gently. 'Did you think I lied, Pocahontas, about my heart's blood? *Now*, you have heard many words turned to make fair symbols. It was a fantasy. . . . But, no!' He turned her body so that he could look into her face. 'It was truth, Pocahontas. It *is* my heart's blood!'

Her eyes raised to his. Could his magic make a lie the truth? And more – all the hateful truth she knew, a lie?

'You know truth then! Yet you know nothing of this world as it is here. Is this then the true world – the better world? For we declare that truth is good. You showed me truths I had not dreamed. And when you believed the heart's blood real – then it was truth!'

She started to cry. 'Why did you *not* come back?'

'Shall I tell you why?'

She nodded, wrenched, her face contorted.

There was silence, and at last Smith spoke. 'I was no man!' he said, feeling how stark his words. She moved only slightly, but her arms about him tightened. 'You did not see my wound. I thought it left me nothing – for any woman!'

She moaned against him. 'Johnsmith! Johnsmith!'

'Now, if the darkness cover me – I sense that I am fit again.'

She threw back her head to stare at him. 'Did you not know, my love?' She hid her face once more. 'Did you not know, Lord, my greatest joy was in your arms – not taken by you, only held? Then you were greater than any brave – for you lifted me high,

high into the sky. And I was bound to you and you to me! Did you not know how mighty is your love?'

He was overwhelmed. 'Pocahontas, I am lost. I do not know! I did not know!'

'What strangeness is there in this land makes *them* so great and you so small? It is something that you understand and accept, but I – I cannot believe this King, these lords, are masters over you. I have seen you mightier than Powhatan! How can it be? Surely this is the land where the upside-down people stand on their heads!'

'And I had hoped to find *Johnsmith* by going again to the New World. I could not find him without you. For you made Johnsmith.'

'I think I did,' she said.

'Tell me of Nantequos.'

'Oh, *no!*'

'Was it the English?'

'No! No, it was not the English.'

'You cannot tell me?'

'No.'

He longed to ask so many things: about Kokoum, how Argall had captured her, of her marriage to Rolfe. . . . But these things he could not speak of unless she opened the doors; and she was absorbed in her private woe.

'I made many lies, as I made *Johnsmith*,' she said, and his belly cringed, knowing that to her *Johnsmith* was ranked with the lies which she had believed and made real to Powhatan.

'Argall came up the Potomac. I know now he sought me out. I should have known it then. He talked to Japasaws and made a bargain for a copper kettle that I would be tricked to board his ship. But I wanted to go – I wanted news of you. Japasaws' wife begged to go aboard and see the winged canoe of the white men, and Japasaws forbade it, scolding her and striking her, and she kept weeping. Finally he said, 'Pocahontas knows these people – if *she* goes, too . . . ' So I went, not caring. We sat at dinner, and Japasaws kicked Argall's foot. I thought it was treachery, but I did not know toward whom. Finally it was time to go ashore, and Argall told us I was to go with him, his prisoner to Jamestown. Japasaws and his wife wept traitorous tears, but I knew then I was betrayed. Argall would have taken me that night, but I had learned the white men, as some beasts, do not touch the form which appears dead. So I was dead to him. He wanted me alive.' Her words carried her back. 'He had no thought of God or King or Country – only of me! I believe he truly loves me.'

'Pocahontas, do you not think I love you?' Smith asked in agony.

'I know! I know how much.' She smiled at him with infinite sweetness. 'But I would not love a brave who loves God and King and Country less – though if I were a brave I would choose, with each of these, where I would love.'

The words he had said to Nantequos seemed spurious. Her God – whatever god she worshiped – how fine! Her King – Powhatan or James? Her country – the wildwoods against this!

'I cannot think, you move me to such grief.' She looked at him distantly, appraisingly. 'Do not look at me like that!' he begged.

'I would not grieve you. I love you! And you are all that I believed you were. But your England is false. Your King?' She held herself, shivering. 'Your God? He sounds a lovely god, but it is hard to believe the English worship him. And I . . . ' She sighed with great poignance. 'I have been the Judas – not for silver or for copper, but for my heart's own longing!'

'Never believe it!'

'Aye! Sam Argall brought me to Sir Thomas Dale, and many boats of corn were demanded from Powhatan, which were sent, and all the stolen weapons, of which Powhatan gathered what he could, and those white men who had fled the English were to be returned – Powhatan returned these, though it hurt him sorely, for the punishments of the English are fearful. But when all was done, Sir Thomas said it was not enough, and I stayed prisoner. And Powhatan said' – her face grew somber – 'that not even for his daughter would he sell his empire.

'In Jamestown Sir Thomas grew afraid of Argall's love for me – as I said, he would do anything if I would love him. Dale sent him away on a mission, and they took me up the Pamaunkey in a pinnace, plundering and pillaging on the way, saying they had brought Powhatan his daughter – but all the things that he must do to claim me!'

She fell silent, and he sensed what was in her mind: the scene of self-torment and desolation . . . in the dark cabin of the pinnace, the vaunted cause of these miseries to her people.

'At Machot Powhatan's braves stood against them and would have done them battle.' Her head lifted with pride. 'Dale demanded word with Powhatan, who had retreated far into his forest fastnesses. He would not come, but my brothers came. While we waited, John Rolfe had written a letter. It was a fancy thing. . . . '

She smiled through her heartache, rocking herself back and forth. 'He would marry me, though in England he would make

253

a fairer match. He had no carnal affection for me; I was of a generation accursed, and he would make a Christian of me. His desire was told me, and I said yes.'

'I don't understand. Why did you marry him, Pocahontas?'

'Could I see Powhatan's city destroyed, or deserted as Werowocomoco? Could I stay on that ship while the English and Powhatan's braves joined in desperate combat, I the cause of all?' She shook her head tragically. Then she resumed in her monotonous voice. 'I went to my brothers, and I told them that I would be the symbol of friendship of the English for Powhatan and Powhatan for the English. And that my marriage would be the pledge of their alliance against our enemy. . . .'

'Against whom?'

'Against the Chickahomanies – oh, Johnsmith, against Opechancano! Only I know certainly!' she mourned. 'It was Opechancano struck down Nantequos!' Her face sank into her hands, and he caught her, holding her against him.

His mind rocketed from the sweet cessations he had known with Pocahontas, to the beauty of his friendship with Nantequos, to the greatness and the sorrow of Powhatan, to the bitter Opechancano. . . . *Sweet God!* he thought. *That was real! This world is false! And she, the fragile bridge between them both!*

CHAPTER EIGHTEEN

The *Masque of the Search for Wisdom* was to be *al fresco*. For it Inigo Jones had had a canal excavated from the river to cross one corner of the silk-hung canopy he had designed to cover the audience. He superintended now the building of Solomon's temple on a giant revolving stage. He looked up to see Ben Jonson approach, tapping his palm with his rolled-up script.

'Hoity toity!' Inigo said to his assistant. 'It's trouble now.'

He awaited Jonson's coming silently. His smirked lips and half-lidded eyes dared the poet. Inigo was tall and thin and blond, loose-jointed, while Jonson was small, bullheaded, and of swarthy complexion; his slanted eyes gave him the look of a sneer, and he felt he might as well let the rest of his face go with it. He surveyed the work, saying nothing, blew out his breath consideringly, then stepped over to examine the plans.

'Well?' Inigo demanded at long last.

'You can't have Venus and her maidens rise out of the water in front of Jerusalem. It's not decorous.'

'*I* know that! But *you* wrote it.'

'I had her talk to Sheba in the middle of the sea.'

'There will be a *curtain* of *fish-netting*, strung with shells and corals and oddments.'

'And you pull them back and there's the temple?'

'Look!' Inigo said with exaggerated patience. He pointed to the plan. 'I've made a circle for the canal *outside* the canopy. Sheba's barge passes *off* scene and re-enters again stage *right*. In the meantime we draw the curtains and display *Jerusalem* with Solomon spouting all those silly words about a thousand wives, not *one* appreciating his wisdom.'

Jonson ignored this. 'What does she wear?'

'She has a blue feather robe – a gorgeous thing!'

'I thought Oriana was going to wear a feather robe – the one Sheba brought here.'

255

'She can't come out of the waves in *feathers!* That's for the Virginia part. As Venus the Queen'll have her breasts bare and wear a skirt of seaweed lace over a wide farthingale.'

Jonson chuckled. 'The water'll pull that right off her.'

'She'll come up over *there* – from that pit. It will only *look* as if she rises from the wave. You don't think she's going to get her *hair* wet!'

Jonson pointed to the other set. 'You'll have plenty of trees?'

'Sheba comes out of the real forest, down a long alley onto the stage. Who's going to play Powhatan? I haven't designed his costume.'

'Who but Villiers, with nothing on except the King's red feather robe.'

'*Nothing!*' Inigo screeched.

'Nothing but a codpiece. It's what *they* wear, and that's the way he'll have it. He'll be painted red if that'll help.'

'Since Sheba's come there's been no talk among these rakes but shedding clothes and sporting in the woods,' Inigo said disapprovingly. 'They even go hunting with bows and arrows.'

Jonson smiled glumly. Inigo was of Queen Anne's household and hence privy to the Court, while the poet resided at the tavern.

'Did they catch anything?' he asked.

'Lord Buckhurst caught an *ague*. And it's *said* Prince Charlie caught the *Princess*.'

Jonson looked up. 'He still pursues her?'

Inigo laughed gaily, happy to have captured Ben's interest. 'Hotter than ever since the story of her love for this Captain Smith. You should write a masque how she saved his life. It's the rapture of the Court and it will be the *rage* of London. Do you think it's true?'

'Aye. Johnnie spins great yarns, but it seems they mostly happened. He'd not've dared write of it to the Queen if it was false.'

'You know him?'

'I know him well. He's at The Three Pigeons. So's her husband.'

'Did they agree?' Inigo asked avidly. 'It must have been hard on Master Rolfe when she showed her love so openly the other day.'

'It was not *they* who disagreed. It was the two Captains, Argall and Smith. Whenever they spoke they were at each other's throats. It was always Master Rolfe or Sir Thomas Dale who came betwixt 'em.'

'To quiet scandal?'

'I construe, though it would seem the lady's soared above 'em all, leaving them cold and far away.' He looked again at the plan and the set. 'It ain't so bad, Inigo.'

'And the masque is not the *worst* you've writ, Ben,' Inigo said generously.

CHAPTER NINETEEN

In an easy slouch, George Wither, poet, leaned against the lintel of the ale-room door till his eyes found John Smith and Ben Jonson in their corner. He sauntered toward them. Jonson's glance raked him and then turned to the bottle of canary. He waited till he was sure Wither was within earshot.

'What drives the curse from London's kennels so soon this season?'

Smith was on his feet. 'George!'

Wither grinned at him and sank into a chair. He picked up the bottle.

'Sweet Ben!' he said softly. 'Since Will's song is launched on Avon's stream, there is but you!'

Jonson, who had reached to retrieve the bottle, jerked back indignantly. In his own way he had loved Shakespeare, but he brooked no comparison.

'The last insult,' he rasped as Wither filled a cup. 'I paid for that bottle, Sir.'

'Wonders!' Wither studied the wine. 'I never thought I'd taste such rarity.'

Smith signaled the waiter and another bottle was placed on the table. 'Drink up, gentlemen,' he said heartily. 'To amity!'

Jonson clasped his branded thumb and shoved it toward them. 'I got that for killing a man – in a drinking brawl.'

Wither laughed. 'Ben, I'm not that good a poet. Who sings so sweet as you and has the world to listen?'

Jonson picked up his glass and regarded the others with his mismatched eyes.

'Now Will is dead?' he demanded belligerently.

'Of course,' Wither said innocently. 'You have no rival.'

Jonson, more than half-drunk, considered the words suspiciously. Then his attention was diverted.

'Look who comes here.'

Sir Thomas Dale, Sam Argall, and John Rolfe paused as they saw who occupied the corner and turned to search for a further table. They found one and settled, self-consciously avoiding Smith and the two poets. They called for clay pipes and made ado of filling them and having them lit.

'Pharisees!' Jonson said and spat out of crooked teeth.

'Ben,' Smith said evenly, 'if you are going to quarrel, I shall leave.'

'Who wants to quarrel, Johnnie? I'd only have you go on with what you were telling before yon – before our friendly George joined us. He wants to hear about the Princess, too.'

'I've come from London to hear just that,' Wither said. 'The rumors grow and make her the most prized subject in the realm.'

'I hope it's so,' Smith said. 'That she should be made great. . . .'

Jonson was on his feet, his voice drunken and loud. 'It's Johnnie wrote the letter brought her to this Court. He told her *worth*. . . .'

Smith forcibly dragged Ben back to his chair, but Argall first, then Rolfe, then Sir Thomas rose. Rolfe, followed by the others, came to their table.

'You wrote the letter sponsoring my wife?'

'I sponsored no one,' Smith said. 'I asked the Queen to sponsor her.'

'What right . . . ?' Sir Thomas Dale pushed to the front.

Wither and Jonson were both on their feet. There was a pleasure in them, Smith sensed, that here was the battle. And both of them would delight in troublemaking. Smith from his seat spoke mildly.

'It is I, who above any else, must be grateful – to whom she was the most generous.'

'Generous?' Argall taunted. 'You took what you cozened from her.'

Smith shot up, his hands clenched.

Wither, suddenly a diplomat, said, 'Gentlemen, sit down. This is not a quarrel. Captain Smith wrote a letter. He meant only to honor the lady. You are all servants of the Company.'

Reluctantly they drew up chairs. Wither waved to the waiter for cups, while the others glowered across the table.

'Why should the Captain's letter have bothered you? Surely, not even you, Master Rolfe, would deny that he was her – first friend.'

Sir Thomas, who had sucked dry his pipe, scowled at the interlocutor. 'He did not bring her a baptized Christian to England.

What did *he* do, except use her to his advantage?'

'Ah, Sir Marshal' – Ben Jonson, from a seeming stupor, blew his nose into the hearth and came to life – 'the Captain, as you say, took his opportunities and used 'em. But what about yon rakehell – and yon . . . ' He pointed to Argall and then to Rolfe. 'And you, Sir?' His finger was in Dale's chest.

'I?'

'Didn't you take her as Argall's prisoner and use her against her father?'

'Ridiculous! Did Smith tell you that? She wanted to marry Master Rolfe.'.

'*Did* she? But tell me, good Sir Thomas' – Jonson's tilted eyes were amost shut with drunken malevolence – 'did you reward her for her generosity? Is it you or Captain Smith who has made her the heroine she is?'

'Heroine, Sir? She saved the Captain's life, it's true, but *I* have not known her generosity. Rather she has cause to reverence me who opened to her the gates of her salvation.'

Wither erupted with a laugh that caused both Dale and Rolfe to scrape back their chairs. 'The noble Marshal, saver of souls. I've heard how you'd saved her sister, too – if you could've got her into your bed.'

Dale choked apoplectically. Argall blew a cloud of smoke.

'Tell us our reasons to be grateful to – the Princess.'

Jonson prodded Smith. 'Tell them, Johnnie – how they'd not've had Virginia, save for her. What you were telling me.'

As the heads pivoted toward him, Smith grinned.

'It's a pretty surmise, and likely, too. For it was not just my life she saved – not once but twice – and the lives of other Englishmen as well; but she saved our nation – she and her brother.' His face clouded at the thought of Nantequos. 'If Powhatan had come against us that first year when we were but thirty-eight sad and sorry souls, or again during the Starving Time, it would have been the end of our Colony – those who came later would have left, even as they did after Roanoke.'

'You were not the last adventurers,' Argall said.

'But it is not adventurers alone that make a colony. It was sixteen years after Roanoke before an expedition was tried again. And our King, you admit, is not an enthusiast.'

'Not with the Spanish Ambassador, wily Gondomar, whispering in his ear,' Jonson leered, enjoying himself.

'The Spanish King is anxious indeed that Virginia should have failed. And by now do you not think that Spain would have extended her colony of Florida? It could be we would not even succeed in New England, where I seek to go, since the new colony must depend on Virginia's success. And the Dutch are established at New Amsterdam, thanks to our nation's backward policy; in 1609 I wrote to Henry Hudson of the river that now bears his name, and he could find no support in England – he had to go to Holland. How much less enterprising would our King have been had the Virginia Colony failed? And with the French in New France, hostile neighbors on every side, it could be that England would have been barred forever from that fair country had – the Princess – not loved the English.'

Jonson's hooded gaze swept the faces of the three Virginians. 'The English – or an Englishman?'

Argall's fist slammed the table and he stood up.

Smith, too, rose. 'Gentlemen, you should be grateful – our country should be grateful – for it is by this maiden's aid, England holds her Fifth Dominion. History,' said John Smith, 'may prove my surmise.'

He turned to face Argall, who blocked his path.

'Master Argall . . . '

'There'll come a time, Captain!'

Smith smiled. 'Oh, yes, I promise you that. I promise myself!'

CHAPTER TWENTY

It was summer, and, as in Powhatan's land, the earth was vivid with color and ripe with fruit. It lay before them, dappled with gold and shadow through leafy corridors. The hedges were bright with hornbeam and myrtle, the meadows pied with yellow and pink and blue and purple flowers. It was an England Pocahontas had not seen, as she accompanied the King's Court on its summer progress.

Unused to horseback, she sat trussed in her saddle, following behind with the elderly and less energetic while the bold gentlemen and ladies in their silks and jewels and gaudy plumage reached for a mile ahead. Alongside jogged the footmen in bright livery, and behind lagged the sumpter mules and the vast caravan of two-wheeled carts drawn by six-horse teams carrying their furniture and baggage, even tents, for what house could welcome the thousand or more who formed this company?

But soon the gents found her, Villiers first, of course, and she was coaxed into a faster gait, pleased and laughing to be so coddled. The Queen, corseted to an extremity, rode elegantly in the fore, her farthingale almost engulfing the exquisite housings of her jennet, who proudly sported bouquets of plumes on head and tail to match those which adorned its mistress. King James was belted in his saddle as Rebecca was, but he led the rollicking pace, pausing every few minutes to sip from his stirrupcup.

From Hampton to Nonsuch. Nonsuch! A wave of remembrance carried her back . . . the fair city on the bluff overlooking Powhatan's river . . . the city Johnsmith had named Nonsuch for Queen Elizabeth's incomparable palace. . . . It was there he had refused all that Nantequos offered. . . .

They were six nights at Nonsuch; at Oatlands, five; at Windsor, twenty: palaces of such grandeur her eye could not span, her mind compass. And around them each, unlike the London she had seen, there stretched the forests, or the parks, as the English called them, welcoming and fair.

It was the King's pleasure to hunt from dawn till late, and Rebecca accompanied the *chasseurs* to the verges to watch as they crashed through thickets, knocked at fences, blew horns, and urged on their baying dogs, while men afoot beat through the brush with kettledrums to drive the quarry toward the gentlefolk. And she remembered the silent forests of Powhatan and wondered no longer why the Virginians had failed to subsist from their hunting. Here it was their dogs who leaped ahead and brought the deer to earth so that the mighty lords could kill it with their knives.

She marveled, too, to see them ride abreast through fields of grain, the horses' hooves crushing the green stalks which had been planted so tenderly. The careless huntsmen seemed unaware.

It was on the fourth day that the King's favorite hound, white Jowler, did not return from the hunt, nor could the grooms find any trace of him, which vexed His Majesty greatly; though he was equally happy when, two days later at the time the Court was in the fields, Jowler appeared to join the rest of the pack. But when the King embraced him he found a paper tied about his neck with the words: 'Good Master Jowler, we pray you speak to the King (for he hears you every day, and so does he not us) that it will please His Majesty to go back to London, for else the country will be undone; all our provision is spent already and we are not able to entertain him longer.' James declared it a merry jest and laughed heartily, saying he would lie another fortnight and then be gone; but Rebecca puzzled, knowing that a Weroames did not take, but provided, and brought always more than he received.

They left Windsor to travel the twenty miles to London where they would break the progress for a night, so that the King could meet with the Privy Council. *Would he bring up the nullity of her marriage?* she wondered.

She saw Archy Armstrong, the King's jester, riding back along the cavalcade toward her. Her first night at Hampton Court, when she had been brought there to rehearse for the masque, she had seen him, of course, standing out in his belled red and yellow motley with his hood from which sprouted asses' ears and which was topped with a cockscomb, and his baton with its replica of his own head, its bells, and its inflated bladder. She had thought him a Priest or Conjuror, for at home these dressed strangely and carried rattles with secret devices. He had been pleased when later she told him this.

'Oftentimes in England the fool and Priest are one, Milady,' he said with his twisted smile. 'It's fact there's more fools at Court than poor Archy, who is a sheep-stealer, turned fool for profit.'

She had not understood him, knowing nothing of fools or sheep-stealers either, but now she thought she did, though she vowed to question him about the sheep-stealer.

That same evening, at the end of a dinner notable for the extreme drunkenness of lords and ladies and the uncomfortable flitting of lice and fleas from the filthy floor rushes, the Master of Ceremonies had sounded a tone on a silver bell, and as the musicians struck up, she had been startled to see the King's Jester hurtle onto the floor in great backward leaps. Instantly, Sir George Villiers joined him, leaping as high, twirling as he jumped, each trying to outdo the other till the gentlemen waiters, and even Prince Charlie, entered in, and they formed in groups making patterns of great intricacy. They ended, building a cone the height of four men with the Prince atop them all.

When they broke they went each to a lady, Charlie to her, the Prince thrusting Villiers aside, and led them onto the floor in a wild romp. When the music slackened and Charlie at last allowed Villiers to claim her, the King cried out:

'No, no! You lazy callants. Deil take you a'! I came to see you dance, and dance ye shall.'

Before the musicians could change the rhythm, Villiers had leaped into the air, touched his toes with his fingers, and then caught her up to swing around the room till she was limp and dizzy in his arms, while the King called encouragement.

When at last in pity Villiers slowed and finally stopped, the nobles shouted. Charlie came to her then.

'Sheba, you must show us your dances, the ones you dance for Powhatan.'

She was breathless and laughing, her farthingale still quivering. She stretched out her arms to still it.

'In this?' she gasped. 'Milord, it is not possible.'

'Wear what you do in the forests.'

'Tomorrow,' she had promised; and, though Villiers was by far the most accomplished dancer in the Court, she had not wanted his importunacies; so she had come to Archy Armstrong.

'Sir Fool,' she said, 'will you dance with me tomorrow for the King's pleasure?'

'By'r Rood, Milady, I will dance with you for *my* pleasure.'

And she told him of the dance of the deer and the hunter.

That night she had worn her white doeskin aprons and a vest embroidered in beads and shells, and her hair was bound with copper and with peak; and Archy had pursued her, bow in hand, leaping, not as Nantequos but high enough, among the tables of the Great Hall where ladies as well as gentlemen lolled in pleasure. And when, at last, she had received his arrow and lay crumpled on the rushes they were greeted by the applause of King and Queen and all who saw it.

From that time the King's Jester had been her friend.

Archy Armstrong had many enemies – for a cruel wit, for arrogance exceeded only by Villiers', and for his wicked tongue which flicked more readily the great than the humble; but, most valuable of his possessions, he had the King's love, since he had served Jamie when he was James VI of Scotland, and Jamie dearly treasured the *mot juste*, the *riposte vite*, and enjoyed a laugh at himself; so that even Villiers, who hated Archy, dared not scourge him as he deserved. But behind Archy's bitter grin and love of gold, there was an unsuspected softness for the lorn, the bereft, the unprotected; and the gallant Savage Princess had touched that softness.

Poor wee lassie, he thought as he rode down the line toward her, *in her high-crowned hat and feather and her red gown and gold lace that sets off the dusky glow of her complexion. How much more truly she was royal in her buckskin aprons and her pretty shells. Aye, she hasna idea of the madness of this Court.*

As he passed the band of Villiers' men, suddenly there were catcalls and rude gestures; and one reached out with his halberd and tripped the Jester's piebald horse, who lurched and reared, tossing Archy from his saddle. Nimbly, he turned in the air and landed lightly on his feet, and all in a second had regained his saddle.

A shout had gone up when he was thrown, 'There falls the Fool!' but now the band were silent, abashed by his agility. He gave the halberdiers his thumb.

'The King's Fool falls each day; the King's Dog falls but once,' he taunted and dug in his heels, followed by a roar of outrage from Villiers' men at this use of Jamie's nickname for their master. It meant Archy'd be tossed in the blanket tonight unless he stayed plastered to Jamie's side, but it was worth it. He doffed his cap to the Lady Rebecca and kissed the back of his hand.

'Sweet Sheba, are you bemused and bemazed by our royal progress?'

'Surely, it is a thing of wonder, Sir Fool. But no, so does my father, the Powhatan, progress, and in each of his principal cities there is his own great house which awaits him.'

265

'And his lords' – he indicated the milelong procession – 'are they so grand?'

'They are different.'

'And his ladies dinna lie on the King's table, sodden wi' drink, I'll warrant ye. What do you think of our noble bawds?'

'It is sad for them, but sadder still to see their drunken lords, who rule these nations of England.'

'Whist, Milady! Whist! What you say could well be treason if it's whispered to other than asses' ears.'

'Treason seems a light thing here,' she said reflectively. 'It is said my husband may be accused of it for marrying me.'

'Would that make Your Highness unhappy?'

'But yes. I hold nothing against him.'

'Do you want to be free of him, Milady?'

'I do not know, Sir Fool. It seems that I am caught in a tide that moves not forward nor back. If I am freed then I am caught once more in the forward movement.' They pressed on for awhile in silence. At last: 'Tell me of the Privy Council. It is they, is it not, who will decide if I be married or no?'

Archy's sharp eyes studied her, his head aslant. 'That august body are thirty fools come to judgment, the wisest fools in the kingdom.'

'Like the Cockarouses of Powhatan.'

He gave a sudden laugh. 'The Cocka*louses*!'

'Powhatan's wise men.'

'If he includes one fool, then the Emperor is wise indeed. But nae thirty of 'em.'

She gave a sidelong glance, and her cheeks dimpled. 'Here, perhaps, they would call Tomakkin a fool, for he is always strutting. But he is a cockarouse, too.'

'What has become of this wise fool, Prince Tomakkin?'

'Some of the English lords have carried him to London.'

'And are teaching him a merry dance, nae doot.'

She laughed. 'Tomakkin will like that. But tell me of the Privy Council.'

His mien became at once grave; his brows knit; his voice deepened. 'Assembled here are thirty wizards come to decide the fate of the realm. They may say what they please, so long as it dinna displease the King; but in the end the thirty minds must meet in the decision of one. And if they nae agree they are sent hame or to the Tower to think better on't. Is it so with Powhatan's Cocka*louses*?'

'No,' she said, then added honestly, 'though it is Powhatan who finally decides.'

'A divorce now – it isna all that popular in this country, though in Scotland it'sna so difficult. Since the scandal of the Countess of Essex's suit for nullity and her marriage to Jamie's onetime minnion who preceded yon wee Doggie up afore' – he indicated the front of the procession where Villiers rode beside his King – 'Jamie's nae apt to push anither divorce so handily. His Commission meets now to decide if *lèse majesté* was intended when a commoner presumed to marry a princess royal, yoursel'.'

Her puzzlement was apparent and drew a wry laugh. 'Faith, Milady, dinna fash yourself'. It will go as the King says, but he's nae a hard man, our Jamie. Tell Fat Anna if you want it or no, 'nd she'll be your friend. Jamie fears her as he does the flames.'

But what it was she wanted she did not know.

They rounded a hill and her eyes were pleasured by the crumpled, sunlit velvet of the placid slopes, protected by the noble majesty of ancient oaks underneath which sheep munched ceaselessly. The animals reminded her of her question.

'Master Armstrong – what is a sheep-stealer?'

'Why, one who steals sheep.'

'And you – did that?'

'Aye – right thankfully.'

'But why?'

His mouth quirked. 'So m' Mither 'nd m' Da' could eat. 'Nd poor Archy, 'Nd a' the bairns.'

'But is there not game in Scotland? And fish?' Her mind flashed to the surfeit that had been killed and consumed on the King's Progress.

His grin was sardonic. 'More than here, Milady. And better. But for poaching on the King's preserves' – he put his hands around his neck and stretched it – 'while for stealing a crofter's sheep it's only a hand you'll lose – and maybe your ears.'

She stared at him. 'You cannot shoot from the forest – or fish from the rivers?'

'Nae if ye're poor, Milady. It's sure hanging.'

'I don't believe . . . The animals are free in the woods, and they are every man's. . . . '

In Virginia Powhatan had withheld his corn, but he had not told the English they could not hunt – or fish!

Archy's eyes were warm at her consternation. 'The beasties are sacred, sweet Princess, for they cause the great lords pleasure.'

'Do you mean,' she demanded, 'that those folk we've seen who planted those fields our horses trampled – that they cannot seek food in the trees or in the streams?' The plentitude of game had

267

been her only consolation as she had seen the grain crushed so ruthlessly.

'Nae one wee bunny, Milady. Nae one sma' minnow.'

She was stricken, then saw the compassion on Archy's face.

'But you? What happened when you stole the sheep?'

'I was brought to the King's judgment. Jamie liked to play Solomon to the poorer folk in Scotland.' His bitter grin redesigned his face. 'And I was a bonny carle. But not like yon catamite.' He flashed a look toward the head of the column. 'Jamie wasna so particular then, 'nd he would hae me. "I'll nae be boogered," I said and thought on't. "Though I'd rather have my arse cleft than lose m' hand." 'Nd Jamie laughed and made poor Archy's fortune.'

She understood not one word of it, only that it was a *Court* of Fools, and sanity was nowhere.

CHAPTER TWENTY-ONE

London is a bowl where, when stirred, can be found all the naughtinesses that make the eyes of young boys gleam, though they dare not commit them, for fear of father, Priest, Werowance – or Powhatan. But here, if one be noble – as *they* use the word – there is no fear of birch or club or even burning stake – which last was the penalty at home for wanton rape.

Tomakkin was a youth again in London, with none to say him nay, but many to goad him on to carouse with the Young Eagles. And was it not his duty to see all, so that he could bring back word to Powhatan?

He, as much as Pocahontas, was the rage with these fine lords and rakish gentlemen. They caught him up and swept him on, seeking greater deviltries to make him exclaim with wonder or with pleasure.

There was Tom Bushell with his charmed tongue and gorgeous clothes, who served Lord Francis Bacon; and the handsome preacher, Dick Corbet, a merry wag; and dark Sir Ed Herbert with his stepfather, Sir John Danvers, five years younger than himself, Wat Raleigh, Sir Walter's son, full of rude jokes and quick to take affront, but withal a *bonhomme* as his comrades called him; and tall Jack Selden, getting rich soliciting, though more successfully on the bed than on the Bench it was told, which fact Jack would be the last to refute. These were the gentlemen!

For the lords, there were the two great Herberts, Earls of Pembroke and Montgomery, one loved by the King, the other by the Queen; the two Sackvilles, the first, the spledid Earl of Dorset, by his dress and manner the finest gent in England – not to except Villiers. These last, favorites of the Court, Tomakkin did not love, despite their plunging gaiety.

Upstairs at Friar Bacon's the Young Eagles sat out on the leads and mingled hippocras with canary, till Tomakkin in exuberance proved his might by leaping to the sign which bore a hooded head, swinging back and forth before he dropped to the street to the applause of all. They visited tavern after tavern, calling ribald jests and singing till the night guards sought them and they dispersed down the dark alleys to join and begin again at waterside. Here, on a challenge, he and Wat Raleigh took off their clothes and plunged into the river, racing to the steps. Tomakkin won handily to Wat's disgust.

He learned the aching head, inflamed eyeballs, and dry tongue and mouth were not a sign of coming death, but could be cured with a long draught of that which had made him ill. He learned other things. They taught him new words, which, when he used them, brought forth explosive laughter and, if there were ladies present, blushes, though they giggled, too. He learned the haunts of London till he knew them as he knew the nations of the Pamaunkey and the Powhatan. And for this while he was not homesick.

Across the Thames were the stews, and here for pence, he and his hosts drank what they could hold and still enjoy the buxom wenches.

Or at the theatres they met the fairest of the *bona robas*. These were all courted by the Earl of Dorset, and if he was of the company their smiles and glances were for him only. But if he stayed at Court or with his Lady, the beauties were soft and utterly beguiling.

Girlish Venetia, tall and lissome, of an incredible sweetness, was the newest and most favored and sought after. It was on her lodging that they wrote one night:

> Pray come not neer
> For Dame Venetia Stanley lodgeth here.

There was Bess Broughton of the lovely form – she would look after Dorset with wistful glance as he took Venetia in his carriage, knowing well the pleasures of his extravagance and caresses, then turn with smiling readiness to those who would only too gladly fit the glove that he had cast aside – and pay a handsome price to do so.

Or the Bishop's lady, fair Mistress Overall – admired for her wondrous eyes and tender heart, for she could not deny any. And Tomakkin heard – if he believed – the aged Bishop knew and minded not, sweetly loving all mankind, as did his Lady.

Then there was the other world, the Countesses – Wironausquas they would be in the land of Powhatan. Their Lords were great, living in wigwams whose stones piled to the smoky sky.

270

These dames, too, received him generously, or, if they were occupied, he practised with their she-blackamores, intrigued to see his coppery skin contrasted against their shiny blackness.

He found, from low to high, that London ladies, despite their formidable armor, were more accessible than squaws.

He learned to gamble, to play at Hazard, Gleek, Primero, in public houses where he was received with such elegance and courtesy he felt himself as at home as in the wigwam of a friendly Werowance. They fed and wined him, and only then did they lead him to the tables. The players staked sums and won and lost, and so did he, till he had lost his all. But then a Lord, Dorset or Montgomery, threw a purse upon the table, and the play went on till Tomakkin had won, and he loved mightily this sport.

They took him to the cockfights, fiercer truly than mangy lions who were baited by the mastiffs at the Tower, and here again he lost, then won.

He saw the death of a traitor at Charing Cross. It was a fine punishment for a traitor, though he could not fully comprehend the man's crime. He had put words on paper, as Johnsmith did, but this man's words condemned His Majesty. All men, Tomakkin had found, condemned His Majesty – even those whose fortunes the King made – but this man had made no secret of his abhorrence of the King's Vice. They stripped him, cut off his genitals, and then, finger and toe, his limbs, till he was a screaming trunk with knees and elbows only. These they bound and secured to four magnificent horses, who reared and were a sight to see, red-eyed, manes waving, as they sought to bolt. They were restrained till all was sure, and then whips sent them off, east wind, west wind, north wind, south!

'He has been drawn and quartered,' someone explained to Tomakkin, who blinked, wondering why Johnsmith had spoken against the disjointing and casing of the skin done by Powhatan's people.

They took him to Piccadilla House, far in the country, nearly to Hyde Park. It was a great mansion offering entertainment, gambling, and bowling on two fine greens. He was expert with the ball they handed him, knocking down all the pins at one sweep, which made them cheer and bet on him, though the odds soon became not worthwhile.

They are very rich and luxurious, he thought, *these English who live on an isle and know no fear because they own the seas! Why do they seek other shores where they suffer and starve? If*

271

Powhatan could trade here! But is was unthinkable. These nobles would laugh at baskets of corn.

They took him to a Conjuror who possessed great magic: powders, stones, the horn of an animal called a unicorn. He greeted the Young Eagles in a black robe and high peaked hat on which were painted stars and moons. He told Tomakkin's future by the stars: that he would know great loneliness and would die when he was thirty in a battle against a lord of his own race. Tomakkin accepted this, knowing that the great god Mahomny would receive him lovingly, but he vowed Opechancano would fall with him.

After he heard what was to pass, he sported yet more feverishly.

Johnsmith took him to his own lodgings from the Mitre, having found him drunkenly asleep. When Tomakkin awoke, Johnsmith handed him a towel wet with cold water for his head.

'A draught of sherry-sack is a speedier cure.'

'I have none,' Johnsmith said tersely in Powhatan. 'Dress and we'll talk. It is that you need.'

'It was taught me by my friends a draught of what has made you drunk is what will cure the morning's head.' Tomakkin spoke in English, hoping Johnsmith would do the same, for the sound of his own tongue made him as uncomfortable as Johnsmith's condemning eyes.

Johnsmith threw back the cover and poked Tomakkin's belly, which was bloated.

'What Werowance are you?' He tossed a mirror on the bed. 'Look at yourself!' Tomakkin did not want to look. He felt hurt and misused.

'I only do as other braves,' he said defensively in Powhatan.

'Braves! Do you think your companions are the braves of England? They are boys who have not been huskanawed, despite their years. Come, get up!'

Shamefacedly, Tomakkin dressed.

They walked along the Strand to Charing Cross and through St James's Park. Johnsmith's words were gruffly affectionate, but they were devastating. Tomakkin grew gloomier and gloomier.

At last Johnsmith caught Tomakkin's shoulders. 'Now, don't think how desperately you have sinned, but leave your lodgings and come and live with me, and you will meet English braves who are both true and wise, and shall find that all London is not depraved.'

Tomakkin felt a grain of comfort. If Johnsmith loved him still . . .

'This very night you shall meet such. I will take you to dinner with me to Dr Gulstone's where will be Sir Walter Raleigh and his like.'

Tomakkin's eyes glowed. Powhatan himself had liked to hear of Sir Walter.

'Wat Raleigh is my great friend,' he said, hoping to alleviate his sins.

'I don't know him, but if he is like his father . . .'

Tomakkin doubted that he was.

Dr Gulstone was an aged Cockarouse with a squared beard and twinkling eyes. He received Tommakin warmly, making much of his coming.

'Those gathered tonight all love your land – Virginia. Here's Master Purchas, who's written much of the explorations, and Master Hariot who went as geographer on Sir Walt's second expedition to the New World. Sir Walt himself will come.'

Sir Thomas Smythe arrived and Sir Edwin Sandys, both great Werowances. And then Sir Walter came with Wat's bulk towering behind him. Sir Walter greeted Tomakkin, so that he felt very glad and knew, that Johnsmith had spoken truly about these and also the Young Eagles.

Wat embraced him. 'At least I shall not be alone with the ancients. My Dad would not have had me come, saying I am like a bear in good society, forever quarreling when I drink. But I promised to behave mannerly, and since we are to talk of Guiana he let me come. It is well that you are here, for if I be lewd, at least I will have company.'

Tomakkin did not reply, feeling ashamed.

The gentlemen asked him many things about his land and his religion, and he expanded before their kindliness and interest, telling them of Mahomny who is a great hare living beyond the sun and who receives the dead if they have been good and not like the wolves, unchaste. He sends them to a pleasant, fertile land where is a great plenty of game and fruits, but if they have been evil, to a barren plain where they must root and starve. Tomakkin's voice broke when he spoke of the unchaste wolves, and he avoided Johnsmith's eyes though he felt their gaze, which was both amused and accusing.

They brought him a drum, and he beat out the rhythms that were used at home, then gave the drum to Johnsmith and himself stripped to the waist and showed them the dances of war and love and for the gods. These the gentlemen admired, and they commended him with affection and interest.

273

At dinner they talked more, though now Sir Walter spoke of Guiana, and what he hoped to gain.

'Hopes to *lose*, rather,' Wat muttered. 'Namely his head.'

Sir Walter, who sat next Wat, looked at his son sharply. Wat had partaken heavily of the wine, and his face was flushed, his body slumped.

'Drink no more!' his father commanded in a low voice, which Tomakkin, who was on Wat's left, overheard.

Wat laughed loudly and rudely. He pulled himself up and spoke out as though he would relate a merry jest.

'This morning, not having the fear of God before my eyes, but by the instigation of the devil, I went to a whore. I was very eager of her, kissed and embraced her, and would have boarded her, but she thrust me from her and vowed I should not. "For" says she, "your father lay with me but an hour ago." '

Sir Walter's face was white even to the lips. With a great blow he struck his son across the mouth.

Wat paled and sneered. 'I cannot strike my sire. . . . ' Suddenly he buffeted Tomakkin on the face. 'Box about, it will come to my father anon.'

Tomakkin had Wat by the throat. Johnsmith pulled him off, holding him.

Large as Wat was, Sir Walter hauled him from his seat by his doublet.

'Go – to your home where you'll be flogged for the knave you are.'

Wat looked at his father, started to speak, then his eyes fell and he left.

Sir Walter bowed to the company. 'I apologize that I have bred an oaf and brought him here. Gentlemen!' He nodded and went out.

Tomakkin could not speak, nor could the others. Sir Edwin Sandys wrung his host's hands and left; the rest followed his example.

Outside Tomakkin was glad for the darkness and Johnsmith's silence. They called themselves the Young Eagles, but they were carrion birds, defiled by putrescence.

It seemed that nothing would be resolved. Smith delayed the departure he had longed for. Not Dale nor Rolfe nor Argall sought their homes despite the years that they had been away. All were like disembodied spirits in a limbo of anxious waiting. Rebecca saw them seldom, though they haunted her anteroom at Denmark House on the Strand where she had gone to attend the Queen after the summer months in the country.

For himself, she was content – as content as her aching bitterness would allow her to be. She moved, a listener intent, seeking an elusive meaning.

The Queen's Court was not as the Court of James, which was at Whitehall, neither boisterous nor debauched. She had Tommy, and she pleasured in him more without the Three to tell her what she ought to do. Her freedom here in the Queen's palace was greater than it had been since Argall stole her. Most·of all, she was free to be alone!

The Privy Council Commission had reached no decision regarding her marriage, nor had she – nor did she care to see any from Virginia, not even Johnsmith. For, though she loved him sadly and understandingly, he was too closely aligned with the deep grief she must bury so that she could live.

Legends had sprung up about her all over London. Alehouses, wineshops, and taverns suddenly brought forth fresh painted signs with her likeness and names honoring her: *La Belle Sauvage*, *Pocahontas*, *The Indian Princess*. The people cried out and pressed close now when she went to the bull-, bear-, or otter-baiting at Paris Garden, to the theatre, when she appeared in the streets in a gilded caroche, or ahorseback with Prince Charlie and assorted nobles.

Charlie had taught her how to ride. He was her charmed and charming swain, making love to her boyishly, amusingly, without real intent. He taught her also to play golf, that new Scottish

275

game, taught her the dance steps that were now popular, to play tennis and shuttlecock and mall, and to gamble at dice and cards, for she had money of her own now the King had given her a pension.

Villiers had dallied to more purpose. On the summer progress he had cornered her many times and practised the gamut of his wiles, even force, upon her. But he had been repelled by the pliant, unresponsive being in his arms – repelled and shocked.

'It's not Charlie!' he had said. 'You're not like this because of a younker! Is it that – *Smith*?'

She had not answered, only waited. He had turned on his heel, and from that time he had not sought her alone, though he continued to show rivalry to Charlie at the dances.

Did she love Smith? All asked the question, for now the story of his rescue was subject for songs and poems.

Charlie asked it! It was the only time he tried to break through the comradeship that bound them. They had ridden off from their party in Hyde Park and dismounted at a stream. They drank, and she threw herself on the grass under a great oak. Suddenly he was on top of her, kissing her in a way he had not tried to do before. From him she did not freeze. He was very dear and, she knew, innocent, for his lovemaking was experimental. She turned her face from him.

'It's not how you behave in Virginia?' he asked, interested.

'No,' she said. 'It is not like your father's Court.'

Instantly he was abashed. He rose and pulled her to her feet.

'I don't want to be like that either. I am sorry, Sheba.'

She drew him forward and kissed him lightly as in the dance.

'Couldn't you love me a little?'

'I love you a great deal.'

'Then?'

'When you are the King, you may take what wives you will, or, as the English call them, concubines. But not other men's wives, Charlie.'

'It may be you are not a wife.'

'It may be.'

'You love *him*, don't you? John Smith.'

She had not answered Villiers, but with her friend she must be true.'

'Yes.'

'It's a most romantic story!' he said with some enthusiasm.

She kissed him again and went to her horse.

Smith asked it!

He had taken her to Blackfriars Theatre, and she had seen a play called *The Tempest.* It had been the most enthralling evening in her life. For three hours she had been transported into a world, not like her own, not like this England. She had lived in other people: the maiden Miranda, so fair and loving; the magical father whose power made her think piercingly of Powhatan; the monster Caliban, half-fish, half-man, whom she had pitied; and the sprite Ariel, who wondrously flew through the air and set her heart singing as it reminded her of the sweet woods of Virginia . . . and more and more and more: Ferdinand and the bawdy sailors, like Johnsmith and the ragged Englishmen; and a fool, not wise like Archy Armstrong, but a clown. Never had she dreamed such magic could be wrought.

She sat still spellbound after Prospero asked the audience:

> 'But release me from my bands
> With the help of your good hands.'

until she realized that she was supposed to applaud or he would not be freed. Then she was on her feet, clapping; her heels caught the rhythm, and they slapped the boards. He must be freed!

Master Jonson watched her.

'Johnnie, bring her to the Mermaid.'

'She can't go to the Mermaid. She's a princess.'

'She's a rare kind of princess, Johnnie.'

She had turned to look at them, and it must have been her eyes which convinced Johnsmith, for she desperately did not want this day to end.

'I'll bring Her Highness. Be prepared for her.'

He had guided her from the theatre to avoid the crush, and with her linkboys had found their waiting wherry. As they went down the Thames she had but dimly heard the calls of the boatmen or the gibes of the theatregoers, so lost was she in the spell of words she had sometimes only partly understood. She hardly listened even to Johnsmith's voice till he said, 'I told Will Shakespeare of the wreck, and from it he wove this romance.'

'Say it again. I was not listening carefully, as you know I must.'

'It was the *Sea Venture* – you remember the flagship of the Great Supply – how Somers, Gates, and Newport would none take second place, so all rode her, and she was wrecked on that island in the Bermudas. Shakespeare speaks of "the still-vexed Bermoothes" – did you notice it?'

'He wrote this play from – what *we* have known?' she asked, breathlessly.

'Not only that; I accused him of stealing what I told of Rawhunt when he portrayed Caliban.'

She thought of Rawhunt and the monster Caliban. They were not the same, yet there was something. . . . It had seemed another world, hardly to be believed in, yet believeable. And now to have her own world tied to such a history. She had been half-convinced that what Shakespeare wrote was true, but her mind soared as she thought of what imagination could achieve.

'Will was a terrible thief,' Johnsmith finished his thought.

The fire and the candlelight were welcoming as in Powhatan's wigwam when Johnsmith, his arm under hers, led her into the smoky Mermaid. They stood a second to accustom themselves to the focussed light and the deep shadows.

'It's Johnnie and his Princess!'

Ben Jonson stood, his tankard raised, and then the whole room of braves stood and cheered. Not once, in King James's Court, had she lost her dignity, but here she pressed against Johnsmith, not knowing what to do.

'They love you, sweetheart. Smile at them.'

She lowered her jeweled vizard and smiled. Sir Walter Raleigh came and took her hand and kissed it, then led her into the midst of those many and seated her so that he was at her left hand, Johnsmith at her right.

They stood and toasted her again and again, and she thought: *why?*

'You've stirred our hearts, Milady. The Captain's written of you, but I think we scarce believed him.'

Johnsmith, his head close to hers, whispered, 'That's George Wither, a middling poet, but a friend. . . .'

They were charmed by her, though she felt she had little she could offer them, for they were not as those in the Court whose ardor she could teasingly temper – they were men of mind, and though her spirit quickened to what they said, she was overcome, since in Powhatan's Councils she would be mute.

Ben Jonson broke the train of compliments. 'We have here a princess in a tavern, gentlemen. Think of that. It's such curiosity, I shall put it in my play.'

'Spare us the plot, sweet Ben,' George Wither said, and then with a burst come an avalanche of new customers into the Mermaid.

She sat, astonished, as Johnsmith brought them to her: 'Dick Burbage, the world's greatest mime, tonight's Prospero.' He had been full of majesty, and he was an aging man, short where on the stage he had seemed tall, portly, smiling, and half apologetic.

'And this is Will Sowers, our Caliban.' Her mouth fell open. That monster! And he was young and personable.

He laughed at her surprise. 'I left my scales at Blackfriars, Madam. But I'd not betray you. I've secrets would make even such as you an ogre.' She turned from him quickly, hoping he would go away.

She was delighted with Ariel, Jim Petit. He was one she would have frolicked with in Jamestown, a freckled boy she took to instantly.

'How did you learn to fly?' she asked innocently.

He gave a whoop of laughter, and other joined, embarrassing her.

'He's strung on wires,' Sir Walter came to her rescue. 'Jim Petit's the sweetest lark in London. Did you like his songs?'

'They were beautiful,' she said shyly.

His grin apologized for his laughter. 'I'll sing one just for you, Milady,' and sitting crosslegged at her feet, he gazed up at her and sang in a low sweet soprano:

> 'Take, O, take those lips away,
> That so sweetly were forsworn:
> And those eyes, the break of day,
> Lights that do mislead the morn:
> But my kisses . . .'

He was interrupted by new arrivals, the very young man she recognized as Ferdinand and a sullen-faced boy with red eyes.

Ben Jonson presented them: 'Nat Field and son, my Lady.' She could not believe the man was old enough to be the boy's father, but she was more amazed when Jonson said: 'Nat Junior was tonight's Miranda." This bumbling, beam-lipped oaf the lissome, radiant maiden!

'Why would a youth play a girl?' she asked Johnsmith.

'It would not be seemly for a female on the boards. The boy sopranos are in much demand – this one the most.'

Nat Field had made a handsome leg and was dragging his offspring forward. 'Bow to her Ladyship,' he commanded, and as the boy stood stubbornly, he said in an audible aside, 'or I'll give you another drubbing.' Reluctantly, the boy bobbed.

'What's with your scion?' George Wither asked.

'Didn't you hear him when Miranda first sees me in the forest. She says: "I might call him a thing divine, for nothing natural I ever saw so noble," and the cub says: "for nothing natural I even saw so *feeble*." Tomorrow he'll play all his lines standing.'

Everyone laughed. 'What had he against you, Nat?' Ben Jonson asked.

'He was wagging his tail at Jack Allen, who's had an eye for it, too, I tell you. I boxed his ears and sent him into the wings.'

'Best watch it, Nat – boys for the women are rare, and he's the most sought.'

'Don't I know! And doesn't he! His heads' blown up like the moon. But unless he spends his life a quean, he'd best learn to be manly, for in another year they'll pelt him off the stage when his voice breaks and the fuzz sprouts. Too many of these boy-women never get over their mincing and end up catamites.'

'Best not look my way, Nat Field,' Jim Petit said, his fists doubled. They laughed and drank to him, till his grin returned.

'And you didn't do so bad, Nat,' George Wither said. 'You planted him' – pointing to the still pouting boy – 'when you were barely out of petticoats.'

'I was fifteen,' Nat Field said with a smirk, 'and if I have my way he'll make me a grandfather before I'm thirty.'

'I'll not forget your Juliet,' Sir Walter put in. 'You were so amorous, I'd have taken to buggery if you'd' have had me.'

The actor grinned. ' "O, Romeo, Romeo, wherefore art thou Romeo?" God, I can remember how romantical I felt. And now I find myself making love to my own son, who is a clod.'

She could see that Johnsmith was not pleased with conversation, but most of it she did not understand, and she liked their good humor and their revelry.

'I was telling Pocahontas that Shakespeare got the story of the wreck from me, and perhaps Caliban.'

'More than that. More than that,' Ben Jonson said. 'He calls Miranda "a nonpareil", and is his dance of the Nymphs not like Lady Rebecca and her maidens?'

George Wither plunged into the fabrication. 'Surely, he based Ferdinand and Miranda on you and the Princess. She saved his life as her Ladyship saved yours.'

'If he followed my description it was Ariel she served as model for.'

She was happy that she should be Ariel, winging through the woods – that that was how he thought of her. She leaned back and let the talk surround her, like music dimly listened to. She moved her eyes from face to vivid face and lingered longest on Johnsmith's – the quick gleam, the waiting to speak, the bright smile. Oh, *here* was Johnsmith's England! *Here* were the good folk!

They rose and cheered her again when she left, their arms and glasses raised.

She and Johnsmith and her attendants returned to Denmark House by water. The moonlight was reflected in the river, the city quieted at last. She lay back listening to the melancholy chants of the rowers, suspensefully happy. It did not matter whether she was Miranda or Ariel – she was both. That he had told her Will Shakespeare had written about her was enough. . . . She sensed his arm before it crept around her.

'Pocahontas, I wait only to know.'

'To know what?' She had been content to be so with him, to have no thoughts between them, only the stillness.

'If you love me!'

'I love you!' she said, suprised. She felt him quicken beside her. 'You are the only one.'

He bent his head to her shoulder. 'You have forgiven me?'

'Yes, if I ever blamed you.'

'There was no place to go – nothing to say – after our words at Brentford,' he said desolately.

'No, we said it all.'

'Yet we have not!' he said more strongly. 'If you love me. I'll not let you go!'

I let you *go!* she thought. She was grateful that he made no move toward her – did not try to kiss her – but she was fearful of the exultation, the new life she sensed in him. *Has the time for a decision come?* She asked herself. *Can one not float like this unendingly?*

'May I see you tomorrow, Pocahontas? Can we talk of this?'

'Yes,' she said, thankful that he had postponed the moment. 'Tomorrow evening.'

Did she love Smith? Rolfe asked it!

He came to her before her morning levee. Queen Anne was not jealous of her maids as had been Elizabeth – nor wanting to know all and share in their antics as did King James with his gentlemen, invading the privacy of any lady whom he thought received a gallant, even to a bride her groom, to relish vicariously the buck's pleasure. The Queen did not question who entered her ladies' chambers, so long as they did not ask who entered hers.

Rebecca swept on a robe and met him.

'You've avoided me!' Rolfe said accusingly.

'I?' she asked, amazed.

'Rebecca! You've forgot I am your husband!'

She stared at him. Truth! She had. She knew well his fair hair, his pleasant face, his comely body under the ungainly clothes, his willingness to placate her. These deserved more than she had given him. But, in this instant, she knew that he was not her husband.

'Why do you look at me like that? Can't you be a wife? Aren't you afraid for me? I'm the father of your child!'

'Afraid of what?'

'The Privy Council sits tomorrow. They will send to question you.'

'They will?'

'How I married you? If you were forced? If you love me?' He moved toward her. 'Rebecca, say you love me!'

He grabbed her in his arms and bent his head to kiss her breasts, fumbling them. He was not one who recognized withdrawal; he had always taken her submission for consent. She pulled away from him, rearranging her robe.

'What have you to fear?'

'My head! If they decide *lèse majesté*!' he said desperately. She spread her hands, not understanding him. 'If they think you were forced – by me and Dale!'

'I was not,' she said, 'so do not worry!'

'Not worry! God Rebecca!'

'I will tell them I was not forced. I married you of my own will as Powhatan's pledge.'

He closed his eyes. 'That should answer it. And you love me, don't you, Rebecca? You love me *enough*?'

'I don't love you at all,' she said, startled at her own words.

He looked at her, the muscles of his face tightening and drawing upward. She thought with revulsion that he might cry.

'I am sorry, John Rolfe. I have not loved you. In Powhatan's land – that is all one needs to end a marriage,' she said with amazement, utterly relieved of this great weight.

'*You* are no Christian! You're *still* a heathen!'

'I am very unsure about your religion,' she agreed.

'They *burn* heretics in this country!'

'Do they?' she asked. She was sorry to see him thus. In his belligerence he was like a child. To threaten burning when he had cared so much for a head – *it was a head that she had stroked,* she thought.

He collapsed before her indifference. 'What'll you tell 'em, Rebecca?'

'That I was not forced. That I consented to the marriage. That Powhatan knew and approved. That it was done as an alliance. Will that save your head?'

'Aye, but not my heart!'

She wanted to laugh. Trust the English for a quick turn of speech.

'I will not live with you as your wife if I go back to Virginia or stay here. But I would not harm you, John Rolfe, in your own country.'

'You *never* loved me!'

'No.'

'You're lost!' he said sadly. She turned away from him. 'It is Argall, isn't it? You think of him.'

Her eyes widened. 'He is the one man I know would have turned the earth and changed the skies to make me love him.'

'Then it is Smith! He had you first. He had the bloom of you and went away.'

She could not look at him. She made an impatient movement with her hand.

'Is it Smith?' he asked in a quieter voice.

'I love Johnsmith,' she said, 'but it is not why I do not love you.'

She walked to the door and opened it, waiting, but he did not move. She herself went out.

The Queen asked it! She led Rebecca to a corner, sat, pulling her down, their skirts spreading in billowy folds, one green, one gold.

'Sweet Sheba, I have word from Jamie. The Council meets tomorrow and requires your presence. Tell me, sweeting, do you love your Lord, or rather this master who calls himself your husband?'

'I was not married by force. I had my choice. And Powhatan consented since it meant an alliance with the English and peace between our nations.'

'You save his head, methinks!' *But not his heart!* Rebecca thought, remembering Rolfe's turn of phrase.

'If you're unmarried, you may stay here – and we'll have such gaiety,' Queen Anne said.

'I would be very sure I saved his head,' Rebecca said thoughtfully.

' 'Od's my life, child! It was a manner of speech only. Jamie doesn't hack off heads so easily. Sir Thomas Dale's as bad as you – came *streaming* tears. These masters lose their heads before they *lose* 'em!'

Rebecca reached back and laughed. 'It's true, Your Majesty! I've been worried about heads since I came to London. If His Majesty will be as Powhatan, and kindly say I am not married,

283

and let Johnrolfe be free to find a fairer match in England' – she paused – 'I will be so grateful.'

The Queen looked at her anxiously. 'It isn't Charlie, is it? He's such a rogue, and he's told me of his passion. But he's the Prince of Wales, you know.'

Rebecca studied the Queen, a half-smile of incredulity on her face.

'You mean – do I love him?'

'You aren't ambitious?'

Rebecca laughed merrily, and presently the Queen joined her. 'I wish we were all Savages!' Anne said.

'I beg Your Majesty does not tell Charlie that I laughed, for I *do* love him and would keep him for my friend.'

'Then who?' the Queen demanded. 'You must love someone!'

Rebecca paused as though she caught and held a moment.

'Is it that romantic feller – the one you rescued – who wrote me – *Smith*?'

'I love a mighty lord,' Rebecca said, 'and I find I miss him sorely.'

'Of your own race?' Queen Anne asked, delighted at this confidence.

'Yes!'

'Is he tall?'

'He is tall and comely, great and wise. He is Powhatan,' Rebecca said, and suddenly her heart felt smitten, so that she screwed her eyes to keep the tears from showing.

CHAPTER TWENTY-THREE

She found that she waited for him. How strange to have hesitated, when for these years she had suspended self and heard his step, his laugh, had physically reacted to his touch, though he was not, she had believed, anywhere upon this earth.

Even before he was announced, she whirled, glad cry on her lips.

And there he stood! So trim and handsome – she had not noticed this before – his suit of tawny, cut in the latest fashion, his hair and whiskers brushed and shining, a hopeful smile upon his face. She went quickly to him.

'Johnsmith! Lord!'

He held her very close and tenderly. 'Have you seen through the clouds?' he whispered against her. She did not stir. 'Do you know now I love you?'

She trembled, and suddenly he picked her up like a child and carried her to the window seat. He sat and cradled her, and now he was as Powhatan, security in his arms and his soothing tones. No longer less than nothing in this less-than-nothing Court. He was her Lord and Father! Her arms crept up around him, and she cried like the small Matoaka.

'My love! My love!' he crooned.

'I know not what to say,' she said in English.

He answered her in Powhatan. 'Then do not say it. But love me and be comforted.'

And so she lay, and her weeping ceased, but still she did not speak, and she thought: *How great is my Lord whose breast is this sweet pillow of comfort! Who is mightier than he who will not be defied, yet dares to cherish?*

'I am spent. I love you so!'

'Spend yourself no further. For I love you. And my greatest joy, too, is to hold you thus, without passion, in my arms.'

He bent and kissed her brow. How strange and magical were

285

his kisses, for her flesh received, her heart opened, and she was uplifted!

'To me you were always a child – and I feared my lust for you greatly. I loved most when I received your innocence and was blest by it.'

She was not the only one – she knew it now. The love that she had felt – the ecstasy of love – he had received from her before she knew of it.

He spoke slowly, powerfully.

'Tell me how it is that I, who was never willing to have a home, who have never known a tie, not even with the home of my youth, should know this homesickness. Not when I was away from you did I feel it, but *now* when I am with you . . . What am I homesick for, Pocahontas? You are my love and you are here!'

'Your love is there – with my love. We are lost shadows. Oh, Johnsmith, take me back! Let us find our loves!'

He sat for a long time, rocking her. 'Argall goes back as de la Warr's Deputy Governor,' he said at length.

She would have stirred within his arms. *Does he?* She thought. *He has won half of what he wants.*

'I cannot go back under him.'

'No!' Her repudiation was absolute.

'I cannot travel up the rivers and become one of Powhatan's Werowances. You realize that now, Pocahontas?'

'Yes.'

'I go to New England, north of your country. And I will make a colony.' *So he would!* She though. 'And I will come and claim you, Pocahontas, when you are back.'

Secure in his arms, she pondered all the impossible things he was asking of her – that she get back to Virginia – that she fore-sake her English husband and find refuge among Powhatan's people. . . .

'I will wait for you. I will wait for you as I did not wait before!'

She raised her face for his kiss. 'Lord, you are the sun's warmth and the moon's shadow, and I am swept into your arms!'

She felt his body quicken. 'No!' she breathed. 'No! You have given me great joy! All the joy there is. I beg you – go!'

Then, when he was leaving, she went after him. 'Come to me at Denmark House after the Privy Council.'

The Privy Council was at the King's palace of Whitehall, almost to Westminster. Dressed in black velvet and silver, with a hooded cape lined in sable around her shoulders, she left her chambers.

Prince Charlie awaited her. He kissed her on the mouth.

'Sheba, I had thought – if you needed a gallant, would I do?'

Her eyes sparkled. 'Who else has such a champion?'

'Are you calm, Sheba? Are you frightened?'

'When my arm lies on yours, how can I be frightened?'

A light snow was blowing when she reached the courtyard. Charlie handed her into a gilt caroche, a footman closed the door, and the Prince swung himself onto a prancing gelding. He gave the signal, and they moved out into the Strand where traffic had been halted by two score guards in royal red and purple who lined the road.

She raised a jeweled pomander to her nose. As always, when the land gates of Denmark House closed behind her, she was aware of the poverty – not like the starving men of Jamestown, but degraded by filth and disease. In spite of the cold, a shivering crowd stood, awed by the panoply. Amid the staring eyes and the children running from the horses' feet, carrion birds, common in the cities and sacrosanct because they devoured the offal from the streets, made black smudges against the snow, undisturbed till the procession was upon them when they flew in cawing protest. A kite, gray and ruddy brown, swooped and grasped a morsel from a raggedy boy's hand. He stared at the sudden emptiness, then broke into a stream of curses, ending in tears. Prince Charlie's valet threw him a silver coin, and at once there were cries from all sides, begging alms.

At the ancient monument of Charing Cross where the road split north and south they passed St Martin's in the Fields and followed the river. When they reached the walls of the palace they turned right and crossed a field to the Tiltyard. Charlie dismounted and came forward to assist her as a footman opened the door of the caroche. The Prince led her up the wooden stairs to a gallery where a Yeoman of the Guard stood at attention. Looking down, inside the palace yard, she could see the tennis court where Charlie had taught her, and the bowling alley. She crossed the bridge by the Holbein Gate and watched the stream of traffic below, passing from London to Westminster, for Whitehall was divided by this street. Then she was in the Privy Gallery, and at the Anteroom to the Council Chamber Charlie kissed her again.

'It will not be long,' he whispered. 'I will await you and happy results. Be sure my Dad will rule as you desire. He has been well instructed.'

She laughed lightly and on the laugh turned to see John Rolfe

287

and Sir Thomas Dale staring at her in stupefaction. She paused at their look, then thought what they had seen: the worldly lady, jeweled and furred, kissed and whispered to by the Prince of Wales, this the pagan maid they had saved from the Savage forests and from perdition, had corseted and seen baptized and bound in holy wedlock. The Prince of Wales! She thought of what Lady Gorges had told her, of Sir Ferdinando's likening her to a heron in the clutches of three falcons, and involuntarily she laughed again, shortly. They turned stonily to face the two guards who stood before the doors to the Council Chamber.

'Please!' she said, for she had not meant to hurt them. They did not turn, and with a shrug she relinquished her damp cloak to her lady.

'We have heard all facts pertaining to this union, so unsuited, between the Lady Rebecca and Master Rolfe, and have examined the witnesses who were party to it, and made our decision.'

Rebecca stood immobile before the long table, her eyes on the King, who looked for once regal and wise. Flanking him were the noble lords and bishops of the Privy Council, robed and chained in gold. She had met most of them at Hampton Court or on the progress, but only her friend and former host, John King, Bishop of London, had greeted her with a smile, nor had she expected anything else, for they were grave and stern as the Cockarouses of Powhatan. She thought of Archy Armstrong's 'the wisest fools in the kingdom' and contained her smile.

Behind her she was aware of John Rolfe and Sir Thomas on their knees, their heads lowered.

'There is no apparent treason here, since this great Lady freely and of her own will bestowed herself upon this commoner, and the consent of her father, the Emperor, was obtained. It is her statement, as well as that of Sir Thomas Dale and Master Rolfe, that this marriage was to forge an alliance between her father's people and our own. This has been the immemorial precedent for marriages of State – though I ken not,' James said in a humorous aside, 'where one party commenced life as a scrivener! It is our judgment that it is unfitting for a princess to call such a one her master.

'Howsoever, since this marriage was performed under the laws of our chiurch by an ordained minister, it is not within the power of this Commission to dissolve it nor to illegitimatize the off-spring.

'But we decree – and it is with the concurrence of this lady whom we love – that while still married, shall she be considered unmarried – that Master Rolfe shall not seek to have carnal knowledge of her nor any claim over her person – and that, as our wards, she and her son can be under the royal protection.

'Master Rolfe!'

Rolfe looked up. 'Your Majesty!' He was deathly pale, and his voice trembled. *Did he care*, she wondered, *that much?*

'It is our understanding that Master Argall sails in a fortnight for Virginia and that you go with him as Secretary to the Colony. It is our will that the Lady Rebecca remain here with Her Majesty.'

'I thank Your Majesty!' Rolfe bowed his head again.

In the gallery, courtiers and ladies clustered around her, and in the gallants' eyes she saw a quickened interest. Prince Charlie kissed her exuberently as though she had been fully freed. John Rolfe passed her. She turned and spoke to him, but he went on, not pausing.

Sir Thomas Dale, however, came and kissed the back of his hand.

'You spoke well and bravely, Your Highness, and I thank you for what you said on my behalf.'

She wanted to laugh at his formality. How often he had kissed her mouth. But he would not care to be reminded of that now. And it was he, for his own aggrandizement, had willed that she be considered a Highness. This fabrication he had wrought had suddenly turned real, and he was lost in his own meshes.

Looking after him, she was suddenly aware of Archy Armstrong at her side.

'How sma' the mighty when the season changes an' they ha' cause to grovel,' he said with his jeering grin.

'Oh, Sir Fool! I cannot believe that I am a princess here. I know those in Virginia who were so great and are now so low. It seems, if things be constant, in England I should be a serving wench.'

'Milady,' Archy said, 'what could you ever be – but yoursel'? Right Royal!'

CHAPTER TWENTY-FOUR

Argall waited for her at Denmark House. He felt tense, pushed. He must sail, and unless he do now in weeks what in all these years he had not been able to do, she was lost to him forever. The decision of the Privy Council regarding her marriage had been meaningless. Rolfe had never been the obstacle. Between the two of them he knew she would have chosen him. But the King's decree that she remain as part of the Queen's household was absolute unless she, herself, besought His Majesty to let her go. True, Smith sailed, too, to New England, the rival in body and spirit gone – but there were these many others, great lords; and if the bishops nullified the marriage while Argall was in Virginia . . . As Deputy Governor he could not sail back and forth as he was wont to do.

He paced and then stopped before a mirror, arranging a lock of hair. He had grown a mustache and slight beard, which became him, and he looked handsome even to the bright feather in his hat. He knew it was a comely face, a face that women loved. But not she *Why?* he asked himself.

Damn Smith! Damn and confound him! What did he have that had held her rigidly faithful, though she had believed him dead? To come on her as he had so casually after six and a half years! Yet her love had been manifest. Or had it? Had her emotion not been the same as at Plymouth? A sense of betrayal! In London she had avoided Smith as she avoided them all, he thought with sudden hope.

Still he hated Smith. The great contempt with which Smith had ignored him in Brentford! No word of reproach for the undelivered letters – for the lies! In spite of the consequences, Argall had done all he could to bait Smith – to bring him to a quarrel.

'You shall have your reckoning at a proper time, Master Argall.'

So I shall! Argall thought.

He heard her step, and quickly he erased his bitter thoughts. He went to her eagerly, not kneeling, not supplicating.

'Will you send your attendants away, Rebecca? I would talk with you.'

She was surprised. It was Smith that she expected. She regarded him a moment, then bidding her maids remain she passed with him into her chamber.

'I have heard the decision of the Privy Council.'

'I am sad for John Rolfe.'

He brushed this aside. 'Rebecca, you can't stay here! You don't want to stay here! This is not your home!'

She laughed shortly. 'It was you told me it was – when you brought me here.'

'Rebecca, you must persuade the King. He will listen to you. Or the Queen will intercede for you.'

'It is better I do not go on the same voyage as Johnrolfe. . . . '

'I'll refuse to carry him.'

'I would not ruin him. I want only to be free of him – free of you *all*!' she finished.

'And Smith?'

'Not Smith.'

'God's life!' he stormed. 'Smith will be away as well. Nor can he leave his colony any more than I.'

'I have not said I would wait here for Smith. Powhatan is in Virginia, and he is old.' Her voice repudiated the word. 'I will come on a later voyage.'

'Rebecca!' He held out his arms to her. 'Can't you be kind?'

'To be kind is to be everything. I do not love you!'

He pulled her into his arms, then laughed as he felt her relax, become pliant.

'That will not put me off this time. You are quit of Rolfe, Rebecca. And I am all there is in Virginia. I will be to you . . . '

She whirled herself away, eluding his grasp.

'Can't you see? I want nothing of you!'

He felt a surge of triumph. It was the first time she had resisted him. At last he had broken the glass of her protection? He moved toward her.

'Don't!'

'If I had taken you – you would have loved me.'

He lifted her in his arms. She made no outcry. Did she fear the scandal, or, knowing the consequences of his act, did she fear

291

for him? Her nails dug at his eyes. His head shot away from them, but he was fired with passion. He dropped her on the bed and pinned her with his body.

'This I should have done,' he said and ripped her gown from the bodice to the waist.

She fought up and away from him, toward the wall. 'I hate you, Sam Argall!'

'You won't!' He had untied his points, and he came toward her across the bed.

The door crashed open. They both turned. Smith crossed the room. He jerked Argall from the bed and struck him on the jaw. A fierce exultancy possessed him.

'At last!'

'At last!'

Both stripped off their doublets and their shirts.

They came together, circling, like bucks hesitant to intertwine their antlers. Their hands were open, ready to grasp. Though each had worn rapiers, they had not thought of them, but cast them off with their clothes.

Smith charged. His head slammed Argall's chest, while his fists pounded Argall's belly. Argall fell back, gasping. His feet moved in a dancing step. He wheeled inward, weaving so that Smith's heavier movements could not follow him. He darted in suddenly and struck Smith on the chin. Smith's head shot up, his body arched. Argall followed, jabbing, but Smith's back met the the wall, and he propelled himself forward, raining blows.

They locked and twined, like two serpents. Smith's leg pressed around Argall's, while his weight bore Argall back. Argall bent almost double, twisted himself and was free. He came in, flailing, but Smith met him with punches like heavy stones pounding into his belly. They locked again. Argall's thumbs pushed against the eyeballs; he buried his teeth in Smith's stretched throat. Smith brought his knee up, smashing it into Argall's groin. Argall went limp from vertigo and agony and felt himself raised over Smith's head to smash against the fireplace.

He was unconscious. When he opened his eyes, Smith was standing over him, waiting for him to rise. Argall looked up groggily and slowly forced himself to his knees, then weakly onto his feet. Smith's fist crashed into his face. Argall fell back, slumping against the wall.

'He is finished!' Rebecca cried.

His hands touched metal. Even as Smith turned to her, Argall rose drunkenly and brought the poker down on Smith's head, laying it open. Smith staggered and caught himself against the table. He found his enemy through glazed eyes, bellowed, and bore down. He caught Argall midriffs, raised him high over his head, spun about, and flung him against the wall.

The blood was warm and sticky in Argall's mouth. He choked from it and spat, ejecting a tooth. Another hung raggedly from its gum. He tried to rise and could not. At last he forced himself to his elbow.

'Kill me now!' he demanded.

Smith swayed on his feet, his eyes glaring and unfocused. Blood matted his hair and beard. Rebecca went to him and took him in her arms.

Argall fell back and lost consciousness.

CHAPTER TWENTY-FIVE

His groans awoke him. He was in his own lodging. He lay still, fearing to move. Tenderly he touched his taut, stubbled chin. His mouth hung open, and he did not try to close it. Slowly he let his memory delineate his enemy. *If he had only killed me!* Argall thought and wept into his pillow.

His familiar fetched a barber-surgeon who examined Argall. 'No bones broke save your nose, and I doubt bleeding will mend that.'

Argall cursed him and sent the servant for a tub and hot water.

He looked at himself. His belly was blue and so sore he could hardly bend. His chest was marked with purple veins. His cods were swollen. He peered into a glass. His face was a ruin, one eye closed and brilliantly discolored, his nose smashed, his mouth swollen like an open sore, revealing the gap where three teeth had been.

'It was a pleasant face!' he murmured regretfully.

The barber was wringing out towels. He bound them around Argall's cheeks. Argall yelled in agony, then let himself be lowered into the tub. Slowly he relaxed. The water soothed his lacerated body. They poured water over his shoulders. 'God!' he muttered. He tried to hate and could not.

The pain in his groin made him think of Smith on that swift voyage home when Argall had tacked to catch any gust, the sooner to get help for the demented man in Argall's cabin. *I saved his life – and all of him, I construe,* Argall thought bitterly. Smith had not wanted to live – had cried out to die in his delirium. Argall handled himself gingerly to reassure himself. *That would be worse than death,* he thought with a spasm of sympathy.

They dried him with soft cloths and laid him out on the bed, propping the bedclothes so that they did not touch his body.

She did this for him, he thought, picturing it. He stifled a sob. 'It's all over now!' he said aloud.

The next day he could sit up and take some gruel which his servant spooned out to him. He sent for his shipmaster to see how the ships progressed.

Bennet entered briskly, but he stopped aghast as he saw his Captain.

'They told me you'd been in a fight, but with *what*?'

Argall tried to grin, but it made his lips crack. 'A former President of Jamestown.'

'Jesu, Sam! He must be great as Goliath.'

'No, but tall enough to reach to here – and here.' He indicated his nose and eye. He threw back the covers, disclosing his battered body.

' 'S wounds! Are you goin' to live?'

'That and sail, I intend. What's the word, Ben?'

'The late colonists are promised to be boarded in a sennight,' Bennet said and stretched out a pouch. 'The *Maria* arrived from Jamestown with letters for you from Captain Yeardley.'

'I'll study them. Is this all?'

'What's to help *you*?'

'Only time. And that will not restore my pretty phiz.'

'It was not your only stake with the ladies,' Bennet said consolingly.

'No, but it was a mighty convenient approach.'

He saved the reports till night when he could not sleep. And then, in the candlelight, his eyes skimmed through them. He made notes as he read. Suddenly he stopped and returned to a paragraph he had passed hurriedly.

Powhatan has resigned his sceptre to his brother, Opitchapan, who is lame and a weak leader. None understands the *why* of this, least of all the Savages themselves. But he says that he is tired and cares no more to struggle, that the farther we push with our hordes, the farther will he retreat up the rivers with his people, rather than fight us. This is strange, for there has been no clash with Powhatan since the marriage of his daughter with Master Rolfe. Powhatan has removed himself from Machot, which is once again Opechancano's principal city, and has retired where none may find him. Opitchapan dwells at Orapaks, but it is not thought he will long continue as The

Powhatan, for Opechancano is a much more wily and clever ruler. One would have expected Powhatan to give Opechancano his crown.

Argall lay back, pondering. At last he removed the papers and blew out the candle. In the darkness his thoughts raced.

More than Smith – more than any – she loved Powhatan. How she would suffer at this picture of a tired and desolate old man who had been great! Would she stay here after she read this? Would she wait for another voyage? He lay, trying to restrain his mounting excitement.

'Tomorrow,' he told his body, 'ache and creak all you please, you shall journey to Denmark House!'

CHAPTER TWENTY-SIX

He opened his eyes and knew where he was. He had awakened before, but now he woke to her presence. He moved his bandaged head and found her face floating in the light of the candle she held. She wore a loose robe, fur-trimmed, her long braids across her shoulders. He smiled.

'How do you feel?' she asked.

'A new man. How long did I sleep?'

'Since supper. Six hours.'

He reached out his hand and took the candle to put it on the headboard. He turned back and drew her toward him.

'Kiss me, Pocahontas.'

She bent and touched her lips to his brow.

'No! Kiss me!'

She brushed his lips, then on his pressure let her mouth fall open to his, but as he tensed, she pulled back.

'You must not!'

'Of course I must. What do you think these months – let alone these years – have done to me?'

'But your head . . .'

He indicated the sheet where it bulged above his crotch.

'It rises to you. It seeks its home.'

She glanced briefly, then met his eyes. 'Let me see.' She moved to take the sheet.

'No!'

'Johnsmith, if it is to be, then – we can no longer hide what is there. It would always be between us.'

'I can't let you!'

'Don't you think I saw – my maids saw – when we undressed you? A wound is not a shame.'

Suddenly he threw back the sheet, shutting his eyes, as his mind, to what was there. When he opened them she had dropped her robe and was removing her nightgown. But he was limp!

He cursed. Calmly, she reached out and grasped his shriveling nothingness, then softly, still holding it, she lay down beside his bandaged body.

'Love me with your lips.'

As he touched her warmth and sweetness, as he tasted the milk from her full breast, he felt himself grow strong and palpitant in her hand, which had not stirred. How long since he had known this luxury of joy! To share with a woman – the only woman – who loved him, a passion of fulfillment. The ardor and vitality of all their past lovemaking swept through him like a wind. He moved to cover her.

'No, love! Let me come to you!'

And so she had taken him, not he her. And he had cried out as she had, for the spasm of ejection was more than he could bear and so was the release.

When she would have left him, he had said, 'No!' and she had stayed. And when he had risen to her again and she would have mounted him, he had said, 'No!' and she had lain passive till he entered her. His ribs had screamed, his legs had nearly buckled, but he had brought her to her climax, along with his, in long searching strokes.

'My love! My love! My love!' she had cried, and he had lain alongside her, his head nestled in her neck, and his mind had cried, 'My love!'

What completion she brought to an act that with another seemed an exercise! How had he borne these years apart? For surely he and she were one, not for now, but since first she saved his life. 'Father! Lord!' she had called him, and he had been both. For who had power to exalt the man she clove to?

She is like a river, spreading abundance over all she touches. How many times? Since she had saved the starving men at Jamestown . . . ? Since she had come to him through the night? A deep tenderness possessed him – the child who had laid her head on his to protect him from the death stones – who had come to see if he was hair all over – who had fled from Nantequos when he wanted to see the heart's blood – who had dropped onto him by the river and yielded up so willingly her maidenhood. . . . What countless times she had brought him surcease, had restored his faith in himself, in Virginia. She was the essence and the being, and he had not known it.

When they awoke, he had taken her again, gently, for his body ached; yet he tested for sensation, and as his loins collapsed, he knew that she had found joy in their union.

298

Later, wrapped in furs, they had gone out onto the balcony to watch the dawn on the river. The rising sun made glittering rainbow colors.

She touched his turbaned head. 'How is it?'

'It's mended. Save when you make me dizzy.'

With this night, the violence, the frustrations were behind them, and he sensed this yearning toward one another was not so fine but of a more durable quality. Certainly now he knew his love.

'You will wait – for the next voyage? And I will come to you at Pamaunkey?'

'Yes.'

'And I will pledge myself to Powhatan and take you to my new land in New England – you and your son?'

'Yes.'

'You are not afraid to return alone?'

'When my feet are on my own soil, what power can stop me? I will cast off these. . . . ' She wiped her hands across her robe as though she wore a farthingale. 'I will sling Tommy across my back, and my feet will know the path!'

'My sweet, brave love!'

'I have been false to many things, Johnsmith, for your sake, but I have never been false to you.'

'Nor any!'

'When I see Powhatan I will know.'

'Pocahontas, I cannot say it has not been – this gulf. But we have found each other again.'

'Oh, yes!' she said and kissed him quickly, so she could not think. Never, till she saw him sail up the river!

'I should thank Argall for this joy.'

'Thank him not. Nor trust him! Sweetheart,' she said in English, 'when you go, I will be here – to watch your lights float down the river.'

'And I will think only of my return – to Virginia – to you, my home!'

CHAPTER TWENTY-SEVEN

Argall awaited her. She stared at him, and her hands went to her cheeks. He was a grotesque, not to be dreamed, having known his beauty. Her mind veered from Nantequos, his face destroyed by the tomahawks.

'I regret that you should see me. Though not my face – nor anything about me – could charm you.'

He would be amazed, she thought, *if he knew how much his comeliness has stirred me*. So like Nantequos! The aliveness of his skin, covering relaxed muscles and well-knit bones – an arrogance of manner which concealed much sweetness.

Without his requesting it she pushed aside the arras and held it so that he could enter her chamber.

'I would not come,' he said, 'after what has passed, to be presumptuous, or to crave your pity.'

'Speak, Sam Argall!' she said entreatingly, He stared at her, absorbing, in spite of what he had said, her pity, knowing and relishing that for this once her spirit reached toward him. 'We are not strangers. If we are enemies, we are not strangers. Speak!'

For a moment it seemed that he could not, nor would she have dared to show so much her feeling, except that when she had had him carried away she had known that all was ended between them.

He echoed her thought. 'I have been trounced and paid as I deserved. I will never repeat – nor try to do . . . You cannot know how sorry sad I am.'

Distrust was born of his very sorriness. She remembered how she had only now warned Johnsmith.

'You come with a purpose?'

'Have I your forgiveness, Rebecca?'

'As you have said, you were paid. . . . '

He held out a paper. 'Here is a letter from Deputy Yeardley, who awaits my coming.'

300

She took it and moved toward the window seat to read. She glanced back once, but he stood where she had left him. She read the letter, at first wonderingly, scanning the details of the Colony's misery. Then: 'Powhatan has resigned his sceptre to his brother. . . .' She read the paragraph once and read it again. She laid the letter down and went through her windows onto the leads. There she leaned against the wall.

What did it mean? How *much* it meant! Did Powhatan feel that his strength was less than Opitchapan's, his lame, indecisive brother? 'He is tired and cares no more to struggle. . . .' She, too, was tired, but she had the strength, could give it back to him from whom she had drained it! 'Powhatan has removed himself from Machot, which is once again Opechancano's principal city. . . .' She – *she* had made Powhatan and Opechancano forever enemies . . . and Nantequos had died . . . and Opechancano came again to Machot. *Her* guilt! None to share it! Nothing to alleviate . . .

She leaned against the wall, too desolate to weep. If she could see him! If she could have the sense of him! But in this letter, in her own heart, he seemed dead. Or was it she? She, caught up into that between-land where one regrets – where one sees one's sins and their results and can no longer alter them!

She found that she was standing with her arms outstretched, willing herself with Powhatan. The love these bucks demanded: Argall, Rolfe, and even Smith! It was Powhatan she longed to comfort – to pull his grayed head down upon her breast and cherish it – to release from *her* arms the sweet security which his had ever offered.

'Too tired to struggle!' she cried out and leaned against the stone.

She did not know how long she stayed. When she returned Argall was waiting as she had left him. He came to her and took her hands.

'Rebecca, *I* know! It is none of us you love! It is Powhatan!'

She regarded him, surprised at his understanding, not softened by it.

'If you return at once, it need not be on *The George*, which I command and where Master Rolfe sails, but on the *Treasurer*, my Vice-Admiral, which carries a new captain.'

'Thank you, Sam Argall.'

'You must persuade the King – perhaps the Queen!'

Charlie! she thought.

'We leave in a sennight, more or less.'

'I will be ready,' she said.

Tomakkin told Argall's news to Johnsmith, who came to her. She had gone to Charlie, and he had promised, reluctantly, to speak to the King. But still she felt caught in crosscurrents where nothing was to be accomplished. To wait was intolerable. She found herself alternately shaking with cold and consumed with heat.

When Smith entered, she was standing alone, her crossed arms clasping her shoulders to still their chill pulsing. At once he drew her to him and embraced her till she felt warmed by his own bloodstream. He did not speak, nor did she. And in the silence, she knew that in her self-condemnation she had wronged him. Once more, so tenderly, he asked of her nothing, but sought to give all of him.

'Sweet love, have you thought that Argall lies? His trickery has cozened you before this.'

She pulled away, not wanting to leave his harborage, but knowing that there she was betrayed, because in his arms it was Johnsmith who filled her heart and mind.

'Oh, yes, I thought it! But he gave me the letter. And I know inside me it is true.'

'May I see it?'

He followed her into her chamber where she took the paper from a casket. While he read she walked out onto the leads, unfeeling of the weather because of the coldness within. The damp murk of the winter day pierced her lungs, and she was wracked with coughing. He came to her quickly.

'Pocahontas, don't stay out here! You are ill.'

She shook her head and pointed down the river. The wet mists swirled and embraced the smokes of all the soft-coal fires in London, smudging the somber skies with an ugly brown.

'Not ill,' she said, 'except for that, which one draws inside till it chokes and corrodes.' She turned in his arm and went back to her bedroom; he closed the windows. 'When I am in my own land . . .'

He returned to reading the letter. 'I don't understand – why Opitchapan? He can never take your father's place. Do you think Powhatan is infirm?'

'There is an infirmity of the spirit,' she said in a low voice, 'when everything is dark.'

'Pocahontas!' They turned as Tomakkin came from the ante-chamber. 'What did the Prince say?'

'He does not want me to go. But he promised he would speak to the King. For it can be no other way. This is the third spring since I have seen him,' she added bleakly. 'Since I went to Potomac with Kokoum.'

Johnsmith extended the letter. 'What do you make of it, Tomakkin? What has struck Powhatan such a blow?'

Tomakkin looked into Johnsmith's eyes, then into hers. When he spoke it was wholly to her.

'It was a blow struck long ago, not mortal then, but so long festering it is mortal now.' She said nothing; but both stared at Tomakkin's sad, keen eyes as though they would find there the truth. 'When Nantequos was slain and the English came again, he saw the end and blamed himself.' A low gasp parted Pocahontas's lips, but that was all. 'With Opechancano his enemy, the land divided and torn by war, he felt himself less than he had been – that Opechancano had been right – and yet he could not submit to the brother who had struck down his son. He would not have you see his weakness, Pocahontas. It was why he married you to Kokoum and sent you up the Potomac. Then when you were taken and he could not rescue you nor ransom you, he retreated far up the rivers, as you know, and said he would go farther till the English should not find him. Because you asked it and because he would save his people who remained on the lower rivers, he agreed that you should marry Rolfe. But without you or Nantequos, what did he have to live for?'

She had not stirred, though now her gaze was no longer fixed but turned inward. Smith longed to take her in his arms, but her stillness forbade it.

'But Opichapan?' he asked. 'Why him?'

'Is there another? It follows the law – his next brother. And Opitchapan is friendly to Opechancano and to the English. Powhatan no longer has will to fight, and so he seeks for peace.'

He stood a second, somberly; then he smiled, and touched Smith's shoulder, and left. It had been a sad secret for this cheerful lord.

Smith took her arms and held her a moment, then kissed her unseeing eyes.

'Now,' he said, 'if he asked me, I would be Powhatan, not English!'

She clasped him, unable to speak, for he had said it all, everything she would have him say.

'Only with him would I have you, and there I will find you.'

After he had left her, she wondered if she had said anything, if she had told him how greatly she was moved, how deeply she

303

loved him. For *his* love, it had been worthwhile. And Powhatan
had known that.

While her body shivered in an ague which none perceived, she
realized that she had created Johnsmith in Powhatan's image to
satisfy her own desire. He had understood this, but had made
himself an entity; so that she felt bound by, and destroyed by, the
two men she loved. Bound by their magnificence! Engulfed in
their destruction!

To have compared him with Argall, she thought starkly.
*Argall would have moved with her ambition. Johnsmith had
showed her her own desire!*

CHAPTER TWENTY-EIGHT

When the command came, she knew that tonight the King would give her the answer she yearned for. It mattered only so far as it would ease her leaving. For she would go! She fingered a note from Argall and crumpled it.

If he refuses, I'll wait for you at Plymouth. Manage to come to me there, and I swear not Monarch nor aught else will keep you from Powhatan.

She thought of Johnsmith's words to her; she had been cozened before this. But what did anything matter so long as she was delivered on Virginia's shores? Those years she had not seen her father had not been due to her lack of courage, but to Powhatan, who had bitterly spurned any contact with the English, had refused to be compromised even by her, his daughter.

But tonight, she thought, if the old King smiled, she might be freed, even from Argall. She regarded herself critically as the overdress of peach-colored satin was lifted over her piled head-dress and her bare shoulders, and fitted onto the wide farthingale. She put on the coral and turquoise earrings and necklace the Queen had given her, and then more bravely added to the color of her lips and nipples, the latter hidden by a wide ruche of Mechlin lace. She dropped a pendant into the hollow of her breast and, thinking of Lady de la Warr, she sighed until the bright thing came to light and sparkled. Ostrich feathers, cream and peach, were fastened in her hair by a jeweled pin. On her right hand she wore the Queen's diamond, an emerald she had won, and a handsome snake of gold with green eyes. On her left, she turned John-smith's heart's blood till it caught the light. It was lone and very dear on her hand.

'It is time,' her maid whispered, and Rebecca took the cloak that was held out to her and hurried to join the Queen at her toilette.

Queen Anne was already gowned when Rebecca entered, and ladies were scurrying to and fro with proffered and rejected jewels.

'My love!' Anne said as Rebecca swept her deepest curtsy. 'You dazzle us!' She stopped a lady who was retreating with a tray of glittering pink sapphires. The Queen herself undid Rebecca's earrings and necklace and replaced them with the jewels which caught the color of her gown. She drew the pendant from between Rebecca's breasts. 'They'll not spoil it, sweet. Only make the gem more bright.'

Rebecca looked up gratefully, and all the kindness she owed this mighty Wironausqua welled in her heart.

'Ah, love,' Queen Anne said, raising her, 'how will we part from you? You've brought such gaiety . . . '

'It is not yet sure, Your Majesty. . . . ' Rebecca said carefully. 'You mean Jamie? Smile at him, sweeting. And show a tear for your poor father — Jamie has a tender heart.'

In the saloon, the minstrels played, Italians sang, and Rebecca tossed her cards without a thought, her attention on the King who drooled his wine with Villiers kneeling beside him. Once an Ace slipped from her fingers, and she felt the sharp slap of the Queen's fan.

'Watch what you play, fool!' Queen Anne commanded.

When they broke to dance, Villiers came toward her.

'May I take you to the King,' he said. Mutely she followed him. Again she sank, her satins crumpling about her.

'Sweet chiel!' James said. 'It's been a joy, ye ha'. We'll nae forget ye.' And suddenly her heart lifted.

His voice was loud enough to draw the Court. She sensed the lords, and then the ladies.

'So ye'd leave us, lass?'

'I would not wish . . . ' she murmured, barely to be heard. She raised her eyelids, and her eyes were luminous with unshed tears. 'It is my father, Sire.'

Jamie drew back as though in amazement. 'Here is a chiel who reverences a parent! Hark ye, all! D'ye love y'r father, Sheba?'

She could not bring herself to answer. 'Your Majesty . . . '

'Aye, it is a virtue to add to others. What it means to M' Majesty to have such a plea before me! I would that Baby Charlie and other English sons and daughters 'd be as mindful of their loving parents.' He patted her cheek, and again she shrank from being kissed. 'We'll not choose t' lose ye, Sheba. But our hearts go wi' ye. And we'll send our presents with our love to the Emperor, your father.'

He noticed Villiers and others of his lads stirring impatiently, waiting to claim the lass when he had finished, and he wondered vaguely why her dark charms so captivated them.

'Steenie,' he said, 'your arm.' He stretched out a hand for his thimble of wine. With a shrug, Villiers left the field to Charlie, who claimed the dance.

She felt freed, and her feet flew.

'You're happy, Sheba?'

'Yes. Oh, yes!'

'Don't be!'

'Not be happy?'

'Not to leave us, Sheba. I – I think I'll not find such joy again.'

She realized: he had won this happiness for her.

'Dear Charlie, my heart will never leave you. No lady ever had such a knight.'

The thought cheered him immeasurably. 'We'll have a fête before you sail. We'll carry you aboard at dawn.'

She threw back her head in pleasure. 'And I will dance night-long in the court dress Her Majesty had made for me, and which you've never seen.'

'Sheba, I shall miss you!'

'And I'll miss you! You are the brother whom I love.'

'Brothers are not fashionable,' he said petulantly.

'Mine is! The most fashionable!'

'When I am King, I'll make you Queen of Virginia.'

The words hurt her. She had wanted that once – a lifetime ago. Queen of Virginia, with Johnsmith and Nantequos Kings! She thought of Powhatan, who had made himself nothing. If she had made Johnsmith, as he had said, she had unmade Powhatan.

'You grow so sad of a sudden, Sheba – these days! I wish that I could comfort you.'

She pleasured in his youth. 'You do!' she said positively.

Suddenly she found herself passed from Charlie's arms to Villiers', and she allowed herself to be tossed into the air, caught and tossed again. She echoed his cries of triumph, until at last all was drowned in the shouts of approval by the Court. She was drunk, and she had not sipped the wine. When they finally stopped, Villiers held her tightly in his arms.

'Stop shaking, Sheba,' he pleaded.

With the knowledge that she was to go, she could not bide the time. All around her were unreal, and she fled from them to will with all her might the day the ship would leave, to collapse the watery gulf till she should be with Powhatan. Only Tommy did she recognize fully, and as the days passed he came to cry out against the burning that fired her flesh.

She drove her maids in a frenzy, so at the end there was nothing for them to do. Then she lost herself in the gaiety of the Court, the gayest and most hectic of them all.

But at last it was the night before the dawn. She gasped when they bound her in her corset for Charlie's fête, feeling it press sharply on the pain that girdled her, the ache for Powhatan.

'You are in a fever,' Manda said. 'You should rest in bed.'

'No! No! It is just my eagerness to be gone.'

CHAPTER TWENTY-NINE

John Smith scattered sand on what he had just written and looked out at the grayed rooftops. The sun was blurred and soiled by the browning river fog, but he had still an hour. He would see her, he thought, and tomorrow she would be gone . . . with the dawn . . . with the tide. . . . He looked at the last items he had put down.

5 ells of coarse Canvas to make a bed at Sea for two men	5s
1 coarse rug at sea for two men	6s

He dipped his pen and continued:

Victual for a whole year for a man, and so after the rate for more

8 bushels of meal	2£
2 bushels of pease	6s
2 bushels of oatmeal	9s
1 gallon of aquavitae	2s 6d
1 gallon of oil	3s 6d
2 gallons of vinegar	2s

He started to add, then tossed his pen, splattering the page, and laughed.

I should have been the director of a commissariat, he thought, rather than Admiral of New England. Inventories should be my livelihood. He remembered the five hundred odd souls he had left in Jamestown and how he had itemed their stores. There had been enough, he told himself. And now there would be but fifteen men who would go with him and remain to be the first colonists of New England. Three ships waited on his Admiralty in Plymouth, and these would freight him and his fifteen stalwarts out, would load their holds with fish and return, leaving him to winter in the New World. It was a miserly command, miserably provided for. But it had been his choice. The Biscayners, the French, the Dutch, had all offered him commissions, and he had no doubt he would fare better with any of them. Henry Hudson had gone to the Dutch, and England had lost the bay that Smith had found and the settlement that was called New Amsterdam. But, in spite of his words to Pocahontas, he was an Englishman; the seeds of Lincolnshire were in his blood. More than anything he wanted to build a colony for England. And with fifteen men, God willing, he would do it!

He picked up his pen to continue the list of what they would need. But thoughts of tomorrow intruded. On the tide, Pocahontas would sail. The captain's cabin of the *Treasurer*, which he knew so well, would be hers. He closed his eyes and counted the planks above the bunk, conned so endlessly on that last desperate trip home. Would Argall's painted scenes be still on the walls, though Argall was gone?

And how, he thought, with all his promises, was he to leave his fifteen men and claim her in Virginia? They sailed away from each other, though they reached the same land. She would be with Powhatan, and he with Savages who knew no empire, who had never heard the great King's name, except from him.

With Powhatan! And all that Tomakkin had said, all that she had mourned, overcame him as he saw that King defeated and destroyed. And who would protect her? Not King James, once they had passed into the Atlantic. Not Argall's promise, for he was outside of truth. But she was not afraid. Like a child she did not regard the danger, aware only that her father needed her.

And she was ill, he thought. Surely, she was ill. He had not accepted it, but her cough, her shivering . . .

He rose and stacked his papers neatly and put them in a drawer. Then he spread his suit of tawny on the bed and brushed it, attacking mudspots with a moistened finger. He rinsed the stockings of his hose in the basin; they would dry on his legs. His boots he brushed and wiped with a damp cloth. He stripped and sponged himself, shivering in the March air, put on clean linen, his damp hose, and his tawny suit. As he adjusted the lace at his collar, he thought of Ben Jonson and the curiosity of his princess in a tavern. How much more curious that poor John Smith should seek a princess in a palace. But his heart knew she waited for him.

The guards at Denmark House knew him, and he was ushered

quickly to her apartment. A maid admitted him to the receiving room. His eyes were on her chamber door, but he could not stifle a gasp as she appeared.

She was in cloth of gold. Her undergown was rustling taffeta, and from shoulder to shoulder a necklace of sapphires spread, only partly concealing her breasts. Her hair and eyelids were sprinkled with gold. Poor John Smith!

She saw his bemazement and came to him quickly. 'Am I more wonderful than in Powhatan's land when I wore my puttawus and crown of peak? Johnsmith, I am your love, and you my lord.'

And it was so, he thought, as she did not hesitate to crush her gown and self against him. Was he different for his tawny suit?

Her lips were hot against his. 'Pocahontas, you are so warm.'

'It is the flush of love. Remember?'

He did, and felt helpless – for her gold and jewels were an invitation to pursue but not to consummate.

'You are happy that you are to leave?'

'Oh, yes!'

'You are not afraid?'

'What should I fear? Argall rides another ship – with Rolfe. And the King has made me royal. I will be escorted to my father.'

'In Virginia, Argall knows no king – or governor.'

She turned from him impatiently. 'Johnsmith, do you think their walls can hold me. I came to you through Powhatan's guards.'

He brought her back into his arms and laid his head against her stiff coiffure.

'I will not forget it!'

'And if they were to hold me,' she said reasonably, 'one whisper, even if it were to Chicahominy or Pamaunkey, and do you not think they would storm the gates for me, for even to Opechancano I am precious.'

He knew that she was: all England treasured her – and Virginia! It comforted him in this moment of good-by.

'Johnsmith, you grieve! Think of our love and all that is to be!'

He looked at her, erasing the gold dust and the paint, striving to find the maid that he had not been wise enough to understand and make his own.

She sensed his reluctance, that she had made herself too grand. Her arms raised and crept around his neck.

'Lord, love me with your lips.'

He kissed her gold-flecked lids, her carmined mouth; he bent and kissed her breasts, brushing aside the jewels.

'Pocahontas, I cannot say good-by.'

'It is not good-by. I wait for you. No one will touch me again.'

'And I will come for you to Powhatan and call him father.'

Her breath caught, and he knew that what he had said was what she wanted. Her maid came with her sable cloak. They looked at each other, not accepting that it was the last good-by.

She took the wrap and held out her hand. 'They will carry us to St James's. Walk beside me.'

He went with her to the courtyard where the Queen was being lifted into a chair, her farthingale an engineering problem. Nobles of the Court lifted the shafts, and behind an escort of guards she started the procession across the Strand and into St James's Park. When Pocahontas's chair arrived, he helped her in and walked beside her into the pleasant trees. They faced the sun which had burned through the smokes and fog of London and lay heavily brazen against the treetops. Then it disappeared, and there were rays of crimson, gold, and palest pink, a green one could barely decipher, and overhead a gilded blue that was like a baby's laugh.

Bleakly he trudged beside her chair, knowing this was an end, whatever – wherever – the renewal. He knew her grandeur. What could he offer? Yet she loved him – loved *him*! Not Argall, Rolfe, or any lord at James's Court! But deeply as his love possessed him, he saw no hope of claiming her.

The sun's setting was like a last incomparable promise. He had never seen its like in England. 'God!' he prayed.

Her hand reached toward him through the window of the chair, a small hand, exquisitely tended, the nails buffed to jewels – a hand, he thought, which had pounded corn, boned fish, ground arrowheads – a hand which had caressed him brow to toe, had stolen his fears and tribulations, had brought him to the passion which had been relief and ecstasy.

He took and raised it to his lips, then saw that his heart's blood ring was turned so the jewel could be seen by all. He knew that she believed in him.

They were nearing the palace gates. She leaned out of the window. 'I will be watching. In the Corn's Ripening Time you will come.'

He stumbled, but held to her hand, cherishing it. He realized it was hot and pulsing.

'Pocahontas, you are fevered!'

'It is the excitement.'

'Don't go!'

'I must.'

He released her and stood as the caravan went on, then turned toward the shadows and the darkness.

CHAPTER THIRTY

St James's, Prince Charlie's palace, was aglow with a thousand tapers, and all the Court turned out to bid her good-by. She moved among them nervously, her body possessed with tension. She laughed much and danced and danced, holding the rhythm of her whirling to the music's beat.

Many approached her, hoping that this last night she would dally with them amorously, but she glided out of arms as easily as they sought her. Their faces spun before her: Charlie, Villiers, Dorset. But she saw others, too: Dale, Argall, Rolfe, the constant Three, and Smith – and Nantequos – and Rawhunt. Not Powhatan! Was she drunk from their wine? She had hardly tasted it.

Love! she thought, being passed from arm to arm. *How merrily these English dance! How merrily these English love!* All of them loved her. And she? She loved her father. That was safe. In his arms she was safe. In her arms . . . Oh, to feel him there!

The candles dimmed. The scene within grew gray. Older lords and dowagers snored against the settles.

'It is time to go,' Charlie said.

It is time to go, she thought.

'My wherry awaits you.'

She took his hand and let him lead her out. How cool the night! How welcome to her brow!

'Your hands are like fire!'

'I am like fire,' she said. 'Aflame for Powhatan!'

They rowed leisurely down the river, and the slowness made it seem they held her back. She wanted to tear off her gown of heavy gold brocade and leap into the river, letting the tide and her strong arms speed her on, letting the water lave her heated body.

She cried to them – it seemed to her with frantic urgency – to hurry on, but her voice was lost in the laughter and the calling

314

back and forth from the wherries which accompanied them, filled with the still frolicsome courtiers.

She felt stifled, unable to breathe. She tore herself from Charlie's arm and leaned out, far over the stern.

'To see the London she will sorely miss!' someone said near her.

'It is not so!' she gasped, not knowing she spoke in Powhatan.

They were wraiths around her, who haunted this waiting place to the Land of Death. They did not heed her words. She must escape – escape into the pure air where she could breathe – escape and flee to Powhatan!

The *George* lay at Greenwich, but not the *Treasurer*.

'Ahoy, the *George*!' Prince Charlie called.

'Ahoy, Your Highness!' Captain Argall answered.

'Her Highness's ship *Treasurer*? Where lies it?'

'It was necessary to send it ahead to Plymouth for her cargo, Your Highness, so she'll not delay us on the voyage.'

She knew Argall's treachery. She denounced him.

'Sweet! Speak English!' Charlie begged.

Her mind spun. She tried to grasp the words. They appeared and hovered to tantalize her, but she could not hold them.

In the pristine light Charlie looked at her. 'Sheba, you are ill! You shall not go!'

The ship's ladder swung close on the rise. She caught it, hung a moment as the wherry fell, while all cried out. One foot found a rung through her encumbering skirt.

'Haul it up!' Argall shouted.

They pulled her aboard.

'Sheba!' Charlie called. '*Au 'voir!* God bless you!'

She stood a moment watching the wherries below like phantom boats. Here, where she had climbed was life. She felt a resurgence. Argall, Rolfe, Tomakkin, all watched her anxiously. She started toward Tomakkin and fell in a heap of gold brocade at his feet.

They took her ashore at Gravesend. Couriers were sent on their fastest horses to inform His Majesty and beg the royal surgeons come. A mariner who loved Captain Smith sped, too, along the road.

Smith answered the pounding on his door. He flung it back.

'The Princess!'

'*What?*'

'Is ill – at Gravesend! Catarrhal fever!'

315

Smith's eyes widened with shock. Then he rushed past the man and pounded down the stairs.

While his horse clattered along the road, Smith prayed.

'She is but twenty-one years old!' he reminded God.

Over the stretching Dover Road he raced. *As she came to me, I go to her*, he thought, and then suspended thought to vanquish time.

The flames that leaped before her eyes were scarlet red, even as the flames which had showed her Nantequos. So now she saw the weary Powhatan.

He looked out over the land he loved, then turned with utter sadness and wept into his arm. She cried out to him:

'Weep not for Pocahontas who betrayed you! You did not weep for Nantequos!'

With his name she heard the wailing. She cringed in agony and despair. Not once again could she look on Nantequos borne so. But this was no youth's body that they held. It was a brave whose skin had leathered, his muscles sagged. They laid him down, and she bent to look. A voiceless cry of grief wrung her throat. From him the spirit had departed. His face was no longer tired, but deep in peace.

'Let me know your peace! I come to you, Powhatan!'

The flames mounted, and from their heart glowered the bitter, brooding face of Opechancano, and from the fire filed his braves, painted in burning colors. They swept the forests of the upper rivers, and then stood still and proud as Opitchapan knelt to Opechancano who wore the robe and crown King James had sent to Powhatan.

'We will not rest! We will not rest till we have driven the white men from our land!' Opechancano said.

The fire was a molten river now. Tongues of flame licked out at her, searing her. And down the river rode the war canoes of Opechancano. They landed stealthily, and then with piercing shrieks his braves leaped on the English settlers, tomahawking and scalping.

Opechancano stood over the carnage, a grim smile on his face.

The river turned, and on its tide other winged ships sailed into the Bay, unloading Englishmen, some few at first, but more and more, till it seemed the isle they called their home must be emptied and its millions sweep the forests. She saw their forts — not Jamestown only, but on the Point and up the rivers ◦ ◦ ▪

316

spreading . . . growing. . . . And their guns sought the depth of
forest, the reach of river.

'You cannot stop them, Opechancano!' she cried.

'She has never come out of her delirium,' they told Smith.

He went to the bed where they held her down. He leaned across
and took her in his arms. She quieted instantly. He bent and
kissed her brow, praying wordlessly.

The flames receded, and she felt a blessed coolness. She was up-
lifted, in an ecstasy like that she had felt in the forest with John-
smith, but greater – infinitely more sweet.

She turned to see if he was with her, sharing this. But he was
there on his ship, his face set and lonely. He grasped the helm and
drove toward the storm that lay ahead.

THE CUNNING
OF THE DOVE

by Alfred Duggan

'THE CUNNING OF THE DOVE is the story of St Edward
the Confessor . . . unwrapped from the shroud of
ignorance, and even contempt, that has enveloped him
and presented as a credible human being; a saint, indeed
but one whose unworldliness gave him political foresight . . .
He did more than make the splendid foundation of
Westminster; he realised that what the English needed
was a Norman ruler who would unify the country.'

—The Observer

'Before Duggan wrote this novel Edward the Confessor
was probably the dimmest of English kings. But Duggan
is a master . . . Brings to life a whole remote age which
we accept, miracles and all.' **—Evening Standard**

THE NEW ENGLISH LIBRARY

NEL BESTSELLERS

Crime

T013 332	CLOUDS OF WITNESS	Dorothy L. Sayers	40p
T016 307	THE UNPLEASANTNESS AT THE BELLONA CLUB	Dorothy L. Sayers	40p
T021 548	GAUDY NIGHT	Dorothy L. Sayers	40p
T026 698	THE NINE TAILORS	Dorothy L. Sayers	40p
T026 671	FIVE RED HERRINGS	Dorothy L. Sayers	50p
T015 556	MURDER MUST ADVERTISE	Dorothy L. Sayers	40p

Fiction

T018 520	HATTER'S CASTLE	A. J. Cronin	75p
T013 944	CRUSADER'S TOMB	A. J. Cronin	60p
T013 936	THE JUDAS TREE	A. J. Cronin	50p
T015 386	THE NORTHERN LIGHT	A. J. Cronin	50p
T026 213	THE CITADEL	A. J. Cronin	80p
T027 112	BEYOND THIS PLACE	A. J. Cronin	60p
T016 609	KEYS OF THE KINGDOM	A. J. Cronin	50p
T027 201	THE STARS LOOK DOWN	A. J. Cronin	90p
T018 539	A SONG OF SIXPENCE	A. J. Cronin	50p
T001 288	THE TROUBLE WITH LAZY ETHEL	Ernest K. Gann	30p
T003 922	IN THE COMPANY OF EAGLES	Ernest K. Gann	30p
T023 001	WILDERNESS BOY	Stephen Harper	30p
T017 524	MAGGIE D	Adam Kennedy	60p
T022 390	A HERO OF OUR TIME	Mikhail Lermontov	45p
T025 691	SIR, YOU BASTARD	G. F. Newman	10p
T022 536	THE HARRAD EXPERIMENT	Robert H. Rimmer	50p
T022 994	THE DREAM MERCHANTS	Harold Robbins	95p
T023 303	THE PIRATE	Harold Robbins	95p
T022 968	THE CARPETBAGGERS	Harold Robbins	£1.00
T016 560	WHERE LOVE HAS GONE	Harold Robbins	75p
T023 958	THE ADVENTURERS	Harold Robbins	£1.00
T025 241	THE INHERITORS	Harold Robbins	90p
T025 276	STILETTO	Harold Robbins	50p
T025 268	NEVER LEAVE ME	Harold Robbins	50p
T025 292	NEVER LOVE A STRANGER	Harold Robbins	90p
T022 226	A STONE FOR DANNY FISHER	Harold Robbins	80p
T025 284	79 PARK AVENUE	Harold Robbins	75p
T025 187	THE BETSY	Harold Robbins	80p
T020 894	RICH MAN, POOR MAN	Irwin Shaw	90p

Historical

T022 196	KNIGHT WITH ARMOUR	Alfred Duggan	50p
T022 250	THE LADY FOR RANSOM	Alfred Duggan	50p
T015 297	COUNT BOHEMOND	Alfred Duggan	50p
T017 958	FOUNDING FATHERS	Alfred Duggan	50p
T017 753	WINTER QUARTERS	Alfred Duggan	50p
T021 297	FAMILY FAVOURITES	Alfred Duggan	50p
T022 625	LEOPARDS AND LILIES	Alfred Duggan	60p
T019 624	THE LITTLE EMPERORS	Alfred Duggan	50p
T020 126	THREE'S COMPANY	Alfred Duggan	50p
T021 300	FOX 10: BOARDERS AWAY	Adam Hardy	35p

Science Fiction

T016 900	STRANGER IN A STRANGE LAND	Robert Heinlein	75p
T020 797	STAR BEAST	Robert Heinlein	35p
T017 451	I WILL FEAR NO EVIL	Robert Heinlein	80p
T026 817	THE HEAVEN MAKERS	Frank Herbert	35p
T027 279	DUNE	Frank Herbert	90p
T022 854	DUNE MESSIAH	Frank Herbert	60p
T023 974	THE GREEN BRAIN	Frank Herbert	35p
T012 859	QUEST FOR THE FUTURE	A. E. Van Vogt	35p

T015 270	THE WEAPON MAKERS		*A. E. Van Vogt*	30p
T023 265	EMPIRE OF THE ATOM		*A. E. Van Vogt*	40p
T017 354	THE FAR-OUT WORLDS OF			
	A. E. VAN VOGT		*A. E. Van Vogt*	40p

War

T027 066	COLDITZ: THE GERMAN STORY		*Reinhold Eggers*	50p
T009 890	THE K BOATS		*Don Everett*	30p
T020 854	THE GOOD SHEPHERD		*C. S. Forester*	35p
T012 999	P.Q. 17 – CONVOY TO HELL		*Lund & Ludlam*	30p
T026 299	TRAWLERS GO TO WAR		*Lund & Ludlam*	50p
T010 872	BLACK SATURDAY		*Alexander McKee*	30p
T020 495	ILLUSTRIOUS		*Kenneth Poolman*	40p
T018 032	ARK ROYAL		*Kenneth Poolman*	40p
T027 198	THE GREEN BERET		*Hilary St George Saunders*	50p
T027 171	THE RED BERET		*Hilary St George Saunders*	50p

Western

T016 994	EDGE No 1: THE LONER		*George Gilman*	30p
T024 040	EDGE No 2: TEN THOUSAND DOLLARS			
	AMERICAN		*George Gilman*	35p
T024 075	EDGE No 3: APACHE DEATH		*George Gilman*	35p
T024 032	EDGE No 4: KILLER'S BREED		*George Gilman*	35p
T023 990	EDGE No 5: BLOOD ON SILVER		*George Gilman*	35p
T020 002	EDGE No 14: THE BIG GOLD		*George Gilman*	30p

General

T017 400	CHOPPER		*Peter Cave*	30p
T022 838	MAMA		*Peter Cave*	35p
T021 009	SEX MANNERS FOR MEN		*Robert Chartham*	35p
T019 403	SEX MANNERS FOR ADVANCED LOVERS		*Robert Chartham*	30p
T023 206	THE BOOK OF LOVE		*Dr David Delvin*	90p
P002 368	AN ABZ OF LOVE		*Inge & Stan Hegeler*	75p
P011 402	A HAPPIER SEX LIFE		*Dr Sha Kokken*	70p
W24 79	AN ODOUR OF SANCTITY		*Frank Yerby*	50p
W28 24	THE FOXES OF HARROW		*Frank Yerby*	50p

Mad

S006 086	MADVERTISING		40p
S006 292	MORE SNAPPY ANSWERS TO STUPID QUESTIONS		40p
S006 425	VOODOO MAD		40p
S006 293	MAD POWER		40p
S006 291	HOPPING MAD		40p
